I0563932

CHILDREN OF THE FALLEN

By Corey McCullough

Rust on the Allegheny: A Novel

THE FALLEN ODYSSEY SERIES

The Fallen Odyssey
The Fallen Aeneid
Shadows of the Fallen
Children of the Fallen
The Cycle of Aurym

ROGUES' GALAXY SERIES

A Knife in the Dark
A Knife in the Dark: Alloyheart

CHILDREN OF THE FALLEN

COREY MCCULLOUGH

CHILDREN OF THE FALLEN

1st Paperback Edition

Copyright © 2024 by Corey McCullough

All rights reserved. No part of this book may be reproduced in any
form.

ISBN: 978-1-964478-11-1

First printed in the United States of America in 2024

9 8 7 6 5 4 3 2 1

For "Ebo" Stewart,
Who had the patience to read Book One of a strange fantasy story written by her great-grandson, and the kindness to encourage him to keep going.

THE OIKOUMENE

YTHIA

Raedittean Sea

Mythaean Territory

Castydocia

DARSIDA

Eeth

Endenholm

ATHACEA

Darvelle

Nolia

Athacean Sea

Lundholm

Zorothin

OTUNMER

Raeqlund Empire

Dvuuk-land

Altirin Sea

Ecbatan Empire

ERUM

or'qan

Rohghost

Aznocht

Ellenean Ocean

Thubestine Hegemony

ATHACEA

Rædittean Sea

Skyre

Lyphix

Ephixes

Winhold

Castydociana

Orlia Flats

Thucymoroi Mountains

Borderwoods

Irth

ENDENHOLM

Cervice

Ronice

NOLIA

Graveland

Panum

Lundholm

OTUNMER

MYTHAEAN TERRITORY

Eppex

Arillion

Syleaux

Hartla

Gaius

Matellus

onn

Greenspring

Drekwood

DARVELLE

Deen

Isabelle

DARSIDA

NORTHERN RAEDITTEAN

Raedittean Sea

MYTHAEAN TERRITORY

YTHIA

Esthean

DARSIDA

THE STORY SO FAR

One year after a life-changing car accident, seventeen-year-old JUSTIN HOLMES was inexplicably transported from Earth to an alternate world called the OIKOUMENE, the home of a mystical power known as AURYM.

After joining forces with LEAH ANAVION, the exiled heir to an empty throne, Justin embarked on a journey that led to the discovery of his identity as an ETHOUL: a powerful inter-world traveler known to some as a "fallen angel." He was soon pursued by AVAGAD, a dark lord devoted to DAEMYN, the deadly antithesis of the life force of aurym.

Throughout Justin's journey, he met allies like the immortal scholar and scribe ZECHARIAH, the fire-wielding mercenary AHLUND SIMS, a one-eyed ship captain named GUNNAR ERIX NIMBUS, the silent soldier HOOK BARD, the hot-headed lieutenant OLORUS ANTONY, the powerful warrior KALLORN RHODOS, the spirit warrior teacher CYAXARES, and the stalwart soldiers LYCON BELESYS and ADONICA LOR, among others. He also uncovered a startling revelation: BENJAMIN HOLMES, Justin's own father, had once been a spirit warrior of the Oikoumene like his son.

After a trip back to Earth to speak with his father, Justin discovered a new power through a stone given to him by Benjamin: the ability to temporarily call back the spirits of the fallen. And he learned that Avagad served a far more powerful master, the god-king of the demons known as the NAMELESS ONE, the wellspring of all daemyn.

Leah, now the queen of Nolia and commander of an ARMY OF LIGHT, has decided to mobilize her forces and invade Avagad's seat of power in ERUM, half a world away. But still lurking in the shadows is an old foe: INNOCEN, a rogue aurym warrior who was turned into a CYTHWRAITH, a thrall of the Nameless One.

In a commandeered demon ship, Justin set sail into the unknown east, prepared to go to any length to finally face Avagad and the Nameless One. Little does he know that his journey has just begun. . . .

PROLOGUE

The houses on Main Street Extension all looked the same. Or at least, they did today. Anytime western Pennsylvania got a fresh, heavy batch of lake-effect snow dumped on it, the cookie-cutter homes on this street became difficult to tell apart.

Jeff Emerson tossed a shovel loaded with snow over his shoulder. He paused to readjust the velcro straps on the wrists of his winter coat. The sun was hardly up, and not one of his neighbors had so much as touched the snow that had fallen on them overnight. It was a point of pride for Jeff that, so long as he could help it, he had his driveway cleared first. And, further, that he did it the old-fashioned way; he was still young enough to get the job done with nothing but a shovel and some elbow grease.

That disaster of a driveway next door, however, was going to need a snowblower. Or a plow.

It was getting to be a sorry-looking state of affairs over at the Holmes house. Between last night's snow and what they'd gotten the day before, it was nearly a foot and a half deep. And the freezing rain forecasted for the evening wasn't going to help matters. Any snow not cleared by then would be encrusted in a layer of ice, and getting through *that* would require an approach more like mining with a pickaxe than shoveling.

Jeff supposed that if nobody did anything about it by tomorrow morning, he would do the neighborly thing and clear it himself. Ben couldn't do it, of course. And Justin was a good kid, but teenagers were still teenagers.

Still, it wasn't like the boy to let it get so bad.

Of course, thought Jeff, *the last time I saw that kid, he was dressed in a* toga *or something. Hope he isn't getting into any weird party-lifestyle sort of crap.*

He felt for that kid, losing his mother so tragically and all.

A toga, thought Jeff. *Jeez.*

People coped in funny ways sometimes.

Jeff was leaning on the haft of his shovel to take a breather when he saw the moving truck pull up.

The Holmes driveway was so packed with snow that the big truck only managed to pull in a few feet before the tires started spinning. Then, the driver thought better of it and reversed to park on the street with its four-way lights flashing.

"Well, I'll be darned if *this* isn't a new development," Jeff thought aloud, scratching at his dark beard.

Jeff was expecting two Holmes men to get out of the truck, and he was correct. But he was wrong about which two Holmes men they were. Instead of Ben and Justin, Jeff recognized the driver and the passenger as Paul and Harry Holmes.

Paul was Ben's brother and Justin's uncle, whom Jeff had met and shot the breeze with a few times in passing. Harry was Ben's father and Justin's grandfather. Jeff had never spoken with the man before, but he had seen him plenty of times from over the side-yard fence. From what Ben told him, a bad stroke had recently robbed poor Harry of much of his ability to speak.

Paul Holmes cut a rather comical figure as he stepped knee-deep into the snow of the Holmes driveway and trudged step by miserable step toward the front door of the house.

"Them tennis shoes'll be soaked clean through," Jeff mumbled under his breath with a laugh. Then he raised his voice and called out, "*Hey,* Paul!"

Paul jumped. "Oh, hi," Paul said. "Emerson, right?"

"You got it," said Jeff. "Jeff Emerson." He threw a thumb toward the box truck. "Don't tell me Ben and Justin are *movin'*?"

Jeff came by his thick western Pennsylvania "Pittsburghese" accent naturally, but that wasn't to say that he didn't give it a little extra oomph from time to time. People liked characters, and Jeff liked being one.

"Actually, this is *our* stuff in the truck," said Paul. "Dad and I are moving in."

"No kiddin'?" said Jeff. "Well, the more Holmeses, the better, far as I'm concerned. Long as you ain't *Cleveland* fans! I'll warn you now, if I see a *Brahns* flag, I'm runnin' you out!"

Paul made a face. A strange face. He trudged closer to the fence and lowered his voice.

"Well, Jeff," Paul said, "about that. . . ."

"About what? Cleveland?" said Jeff.

"No, no," said Paul. "About Ben and Justin."

"Oh," said Jeff. "Something the matter?"

"To tell you the truth," said Paul. "I'm not really sure. A week ago, Ben sent me a text that said he and Justin were having trouble living in the house without Claire. He said the mortgage was paid off, and he had talked to a notary and was signing the deed over to me."

"That," said Jeff, "is one helluva text."

"I know," said Paul. "I tried to call him about a hundred times after that, and he never picked up. He didn't return any of my messages. That's the last I heard from him. I couldn't get ahold of Justin either."

"Well, I haven't seen either of them around for a few days, but. . . ." Jeff craned his neck to look toward the Holmeses' place, at the windows in the side of the garage. "Truck's still in there."

"I know," said Paul. "I was here last week. The truck's still parked in the garage, but both of them are gone. And all their stuff is still in the house. It doesn't make sense. It's like they just disappeared."

Jeff scratched at his beard again. This was starting to get a little in-depth for the kind of casual, over-the-fence conversation he was used to. There was being neighborly, and then there was getting *too* familiar. Meanwhile, the old man, Harry Holmes, was still just standing at the end of the driveway, alone in the snow.

Jeff had never held Benjamin Holmes in anything but high regard. But there were rumors about that man. Rumors about the car wreck that had taken Claire's life. Jeff's friends had told him that Ben hadn't been at the scene of the accident when first responders arrived. He had been missing for something like six hours. The story was that he had turned up later that night, claiming to have been thrown from the vehicle over an embankment, saying he had woken up, then crawled up the hill himself.

Jeff couldn't deny that the whole scenario sounded suspect. Parts of it didn't quite add up. And now, with this sort of behavior to top it off. . . .

"Disappeared, huh," said Jeff. "I don't much like the sound of that. I almost think you ought to call the police."

"If I don't hear from one of them before Justin's Christmas break is over and school starts back up, I'm going to," said Paul. He glanced toward Harry, standing at the end of the snowy driveway beside the truck. "This house is going to be a huge help. It's getting to be too much trying to take care of Dad in my third-floor walk-up apartment. He's worried about their disappearance." Paul paused, then added in a low voice. "To tell you the truth, it's actually not the first time this sort of thing has happened to our family. My biological mother, she. . . ."

Paul trailed off. He cleared his throat.

"Sorry," said Paul. "Didn't mean to unload all that on you. It's been a strange couple of weeks, and I was just hoping somebody in the neighborhood might have some answers."

Jeff took a closer look at Justin's grandpa. The old man was still just standing there, alone in the snow. But he now appeared to be looking at something in his hand.

For a moment, Jeff considered telling Paul about seeing Justin wearing a toga. Then, he thought better of it.

"Ah, I'm sure they'll turn up!" said Jeff, waving a gloved hand dismissively. "With this weather, they probably couldn't get outta here fast enough. I bet we'll hear from 'em any day now."

"I hope you're right," said Paul.

"At any rate, welcome to the street, neighbor," said Jeff. "Need to borrow a shovel?"

Paul made a pained face as he looked down at his covered feet. "I might."

"Well, you know where I live," said Jeff. "Just knock."

Paul started back toward the truck, taking weird, unnatural steps to try to match the footprints he'd left in the snow, so as not to get those tennis shoes any wetter than they already were. It made him look like a real sissy.

And Harry Holmes was still just standing there by the truck, looking at whatever he held in his hand.

Jeff squinted. It looked like the old man was holding . . . a rock?

"Jeez," Jeff Emerson muttered under his breath as he went back to the shoveling. "Just what we need. *More* weirdos in this *tahn*."

PART I

HEMISPHERES

CHAPTER 1

"I AM HERE," said a voice like a nightmarish, off-key choir.

Justin looked around, searching for the source of the words. All around him was darkness, extending for great distances, and yet, there was somehow still a sense of containment, as if he were deep within a large, enclosed space. He couldn't remember where he was, where he'd come from, or how he'd gotten here.

"Hello?" said Justin.

His tiny voice echoed on for what felt like ages. But there was no answer from the darkness. An ethereal light source provided enough illumination for him to see the ground he stood on—enough for him to see that he was just one step away from a great, open pit extending down to unknowable, inky black depths.

"MY ARRIVAL DRAWS NEAR," said the choir, roaring and wailing and growling all at once.

A pulse of cold, violet light crackled up along the interior walls of the pit. Justin attempted to take a step back from the edge. Instead, he felt himself tilt forward involuntarily.

He tried to stop himself, but his body kept going, leaning ever farther over the precipice of the yawning chasm. It felt like losing one's balance, but the more he tried to fight to regain it, the more he lost control.

He was on his toes now, the blackened depths beckoning him like inexorable gravity.

"MY ARRIVAL DRAWS NEAR," the choir said again. "I HUNGER FOR THIS WORLD."

Justin's feet lost contact with the ground, and he fell. His body tumbled over itself. He felt air rushing past him, gentle as the passing breeze on a swingset as a child at first, then as rough as sticking your hand out the car window, and then as hard as a seaside gale, ripping at his hair, making his eyes water. The violet pulse flashed again, all around him now as he fell.

"FINALLY," said the voice, consuming the entirety of his experience. "YOU ARE *MINE*."

Justin's whole body jerked as he recoiled, jolting himself from the nightmare. Overcompensating for the sensation of plummeting through the blackness, he would have thrown himself to the ground if his hands hadn't been gripping something.

For a moment, he could only stand and blink in confusion, his heart pounding. He had fallen asleep on his feet, standing at the helm of a demon ship, and the object his hands gripped was the ship's wheel. Looking around, he saw nothing but the empty deck beneath a dark night sky.

Justin let out a long, jittery breath and placed a hand over his pounding heart. Falling dreams. He hated falling dreams. They reminded him of being a kid, tucked beneath a colorful, cartoon-character comforter in his bedroom, hearing the indistinct up-and-down cadence of voices and canned studio audience laughter from the TV downstairs.

Just a dream, born on the thin cusp between consciousness and sleep. That's what he wanted to believe. But he had spent too long in this world, had seen too much of the darkness this place had to offer, had heard that nightmarish, off-key choir of voices too many times to dismiss it as a dream.

The Nameless One, thought Justin.

It was the dead of night, and with cloud cover obscuring the stars and moons, the ocean became a flat expanse of darkness upon darkness. At the helm of a blackwood demon ship, on that black expanse of water, a world away from his childhood bedroom, Justin tightened his grip on the wheel. He shut his eyes tight, trying to push back the weariness, but it was the third or fourth time he'd fallen asleep on his feet tonight.

Try as he might, he was fading, and he knew it.

He let go of the wheel with one hand and massaged his aching shoulder. Almost three days ago, he had set sail on this ship, embarking alone from an island in the Raedittean Sea. So far, he had gone two and a half nights without rest, other than accidentally drifting off a few times.

Sleep was not an option for a one-man crew. His course followed the northerly current, which simplified things, but he still had to adjust for variations in the wind and waves. You couldn't just lock the ship's wheel in position to maintain a steady course. The winds and seas were too unpredictable. It was a process that required constant attention, constant adjustments, and constant strain on the body. And Justin was starting to feel the effects.

The sea was unchanging. Daunting in scale, mesmerizing in its endless monotony. When he stared too long and listened too intently to the white noise of the wind and the crash of the waters against the hull, he found himself slipping into a sort of hypnosis. And the clouds that had rolled in just before sundown tonight weren't helping matters. Back at Esthean, the hidden city of the Guardians, his teacher Kallorn Rhodos had taught him how to navigate by the stars. But with the heavens blotted out by cloud cover as they were tonight, all he could do was hold a steady course until the stars appeared again and hope he didn't drift too far off course in the meantime.

The sun was brutal during the day. But at night, the darkness became oppressive. Darkness ahead. Darkness above. Darkness below. And the caress of the sea breeze. And the rocking of the vessel against the rolling waves. . . .

Justin's head lolled forward. He jerked backward hard enough in response that it hurt his neck. He hadn't even realized he'd closed his eyes.

"Come on, hold it together," he scolded himself in a whisper. "You've got this. Everything will be fine."

Everything would be fine. . . . He hated it when he had to tell himself that.

Justin squinted at the horizon. There appeared to be a break in the clouds ahead. With any luck, it would give him a chance to spot a familiar constellation and confirm his course. Or fix it, if necessary. All he needed was to determine his position relative to the connecting point between the constellations of Yaress and the Wolf's Paw, and it would tell him if he had managed to maintain his intended direction.

Focus on that break in the clouds, he told himself. *Keep watching until you can see through it. You can stay awake that long.*

Justin's wardrobe had been supplied by his father. Upon his recent return to Earth, Benjamin had given him a linen tunic, trousers, and boots. Over it all, he wore a toga-like cloak. And beneath that, he wore a set of dark wrappings, wound about his left arm to give it the width it no longer had. His left arm, his demon arm, had been changed from human flesh into a narrow, rock-hard appendage by the transforming touch of a cythraul, a high demon.

The armor, shield, and long sword that his father had given him were stored in a cabin below deck. He had no need of any of that at the moment. But hanging from a baldric slung over his shoulder was a short sheath. It was meant to hold a dagger. Instead, it contained the remaining half of the broken sword of the Guardian Ahlund Sims. The rest of the blade had been lost in their battle with the enemy, Avagad.

When all hope had seemed lost, as Avagad had held the injured body of Ahlund in place, Ahlund had run the sword through his own body to strike the dark lord, giving Justin the chance he needed to escape, and sacrificing himself in the process.

To distract himself, Justin took a few folded sheets of parchment out of his trouser pocket. He had decided to forego lanterns or any other light sources that could possibly be spotted from afar by night. So he pulled out his gauge stone, the normally unremarkable-looking pebble capable of lighting up when exposed to aurym, the power of the spirit.

Justin called on aurym, feeding a tiny sliver of power into the stone. It took on a gentle, emerald-green glow in his hand. Beneath its light, he examined the sheets of parchment. On them were copies he had made of several maps. One was a depiction of Erum, the easternmost continent of the Oikoumene. On it was a strange dab that looked like dried blood.

Avagad's center of command, thought Justin.

That was where he had to go. To find the dark lord and end all this.

He flipped to the final map in his hands. This one showed a landmass that Justin had never seen on any map of the Oikoumene. It had not even been present on the globe in Avagad's tower when Justin had snuck in and copied these maps. But for some reason, it bore the same dab of dried blood.

Justin tucked the maps and the gauge stone away. His mind was wandering, his vision was blurry, and he knew he would fall asleep again if he didn't do something. Finally, he reached into his pocket and pulled out another aurstone, the one his father had gifted to him before his departure from Earth. It was about the size of a chicken egg, pitted and uneven like common limestone but with a ruby-colored surface.

This time, as Justin called on aurym and fed it through the stone, a bluish vapor coalesced in the air in front of him. For a moment, it only hung there like a bright patch of inexplicable fog.

But as he continued to feed more aurym through the stone, the effect increased. The indistinct shape of the fog condensed into a pillar of transparent blue light taller than Justin. And soon, the pillar assumed the shape of a human body.

Like an image sharpening beneath a lens, the details of hair, facial features, and clothing gradually gained substance. And finally, the fully formed image of a seven-foot-tall man stood before Justin, looking down on him stoically with his arms crossed.

"You look tired," said Ahlund.

"Give the man a prize," said Justin.

Ahlund Sims had the physique of an oak tree. In life, he'd had shoulder-length auburn hair and a hard jaw lined with small hairless scars. In death, nothing had changed about his physical appearance except that the scars were gone. That, and the way he stood. It was as if a great weight that he had carried in life had been lifted from him, making those muscle-knotted shoulders rest easier and the creases in his brow seem not so deep or troubled.

Ahlund was dead. There could be no mistaking that fact. But the human spirit was *made* of aurym. And this stone could cause aurym energy that, in life, had formed a departed person's being to recoalesce and take physical form again.

The phantasmal, semitransparent blue form of Ahlund's head looked one way and then the other, surveying the ship and the dark ocean surrounding them.

"How far have you gone?" asked Ahlund.

"It's been three days," said Justin. "I don't know how to tell how many miles that means. Or if I'm even still on the right course."

Ahlund nodded. "There is a reason that a sailing ship requires a full crew," said Ahlund. "A single sailor can't do it alone."

Justin rubbed his eyes. "Now he tells me."

Ahlund stared at him. It was disquieting, the way Justin could, at once, see Ahlund's eyes *and* see through them to the empty air behind his spirit form, but he was getting used to it.

"Ahlund," said Justin, shaking his head. "I can't keep this up all day and night. Are there any islands we can stop at so I can rest?"

"Landing anywhere other than your final destination is not an option," said Ahlund.

"What?" said Justin. "Why?"

"You were lucky the demons only tied this ship to the rocks. If they had put down the anchor, it is unlikely that even two of us working together would have had the strength to haul it up."

"So I can't put the anchor down," said Justin, "because I wouldn't be able to get it back up again?"

"Correct," said Ahlund. "Nor can you hope to put this vessel ashore anywhere without the risk of running aground and never getting it unstuck again."

Idly, Ahlund reached out and took hold of his old, broken sword in the baldric hanging over Justin's shoulder. His blue, vapor-like hand drew the solid weapon from the scabbard, and Justin felt its weight lifted from him.

Ahlund held up his old blade and studied it. A satisfied smile crossed his face, as if he had missed the feel of it in his hand. It was the sort of face he never would have made in life. But this version of him, this new form, no longer bound within a corporeal shell, did not seem to be weighed down by the same inhibitions or mental burdens that had troubled him in the flesh.

"In short," Ahlund continued, "you can't stop."

Justin blinked at him. "At all?"

Ahlund's ghostly visage shifted back and forth with a slow shake of his head.

"But how long will it take to reach Erum?" asked Justin.

"Weeks," said Ahlund.

Justin made a noise in his throat. An Earth-teenager sort of noise— the kind of agonized groan he and his classmates made whenever Jeff

Emerson or one of their other teachers assigned homework on a Friday, or when he received a particularly cringe-inducing text from his dad.

He opened his mouth, intending to tell Ahlund that sailing like this for weeks was impossible. That although there were buckets of drinkable water below deck, the only food he had was a small supply of dried meat that Cyaxares and the Guardians had thoughtfully left behind for him beneath the cover of an overturned canoe, and he was already running low on that. And, if all that wasn't enough, he could be going *backward* right now for all he knew, with the clouds covering the sky and blotting out his only method of navigating.

But he forgot everything he was about to say when he noticed the look on Ahlund's face.

Justin was used to seeing looks of annoyance, anger, and disapproval from this man, his mentor and long-time traveling companion. But this expression was something else.

Ahlund looked . . . tired. As tired as Justin had ever seen him. So tired, in fact, that even as Justin watched, he swayed on his feet a bit. The bluish glow of his figure faded slightly, then returned to full power. He shook his head and blinked rapidly, as if trying to clear a haze from his eyes.

Justin looked down at the aurstone in his hand.

"This is getting to be too much," said Justin. "Isn't it?"

Ahlund hesitated. "The first time you called me back," he said, "it was a matter beyond my control. The aurym that formed the spirit whom you knew in life as Ahlund was compelled to take this shape again. But each time since then, it has become increasingly difficult for me—or the aurym that makes up what once *was* me—to take this form."

"The first time, we were near the place where you died," said Justin. "But maybe, the farther we get from where you were separated from your body—"

One of Ahlund's knees gave way, and he had to reach out and grip Justin's shoulder to prevent himself from falling.

Justin nearly fell, too, beneath the big man's full weight. Despite the transparent, airy appearance of the hand that steadied itself against him, this was no illusion, no vision, no metaphysical manifestation.

Like any form of spirit energy channeled through an aurstone, the aurym that was produced had physical properties and substance.

Justin tried to help Ahlund stand, but the man didn't seem to have the strength to do so. So Justin guided him into a seated position on the ship's deck. There, Ahlund let go of Justin and sat with his shoulders slumped, his broken sword cradled in his lap.

Justin looked out to sea. The break in the clouds was getting closer. He would be able to see through it soon. But he was no longer thinking about navigating by the stars.

He pushed more aurym power through the spirit-calling stone, hoping that it might lend Ahlund more strength. But nothing changed. This didn't seem to be a matter of power but proximity.

"As I get farther away," said Justin, "will I not be able to call you back anymore?"

Ahlund said nothing, which told Justin everything he needed to know.

Justin closed his eyes tightly, suddenly fighting tears. It had been hard enough to lose Ahlund once.

This time, Justin really would be alone. Truly, entirely on his own in this strange, hostile world.

"I guess I thought," said Justin, "I don't know, that you would be able to come with me the whole way."

Ahlund closed his eyes. "That does not seem to be the case," he said. He took a deep breath before speaking again, as if doing so cost him great effort. "When the winds are calm, lash the wheel in place and rest. You will drift off-course and will have to adjust, but it can't be helped. Accept the setbacks and do what you can to compensate for them. Only take short rests. Never a full night's sleep. The current will take you to Ythia. Travel north, staying within view of the coast. At that point, there will be no major landmasses between you and Erum. With any luck, you'll. . . ."

Ahlund trailed off. He held one hand up in front of his face, palm forward, and waved it in front of his eyes like a man in total darkness, testing to see whether he could see the movement. His eyes seemed to have lost focus. They showed no sign of recognition.

"I never should have gotten aboard this ship," said Justin. "What was I thinking? That I could just point myself in the general direction I wanted to go, start sailing, and eventually, I'd get there somehow?"

Ahlund made an amused sound from deep in his throat. "That," he said, "is the only way anyone gets anywhere."

"But if I miss the mark," said Justin, "or if I don't see the coast in a few weeks like I'm supposed to, what do I do? Turn around?"

"You are a solitary man on a sailing ship," said Ahlund. His voice cracked a bit, and he had to clear his throat. "Turning around would be even more impossible than stopping."

Justin swallowed hard.

"Is that *fear* I sense in you?" asked Ahlund. "Don't let it in, Justin. Emotions are nothing but unrefined instincts, no more sophisticated than an animal's drive for self-preservation. Rise above those base feelings."

Ahlund winced a bit, set his jaw, then continued.

"Remember, following aurym means denying the self. The more committed you are to aurym, and the less committed you are to preserving the self, the more aurym will preserve you. It is. . . ."

"A great paradox," Justin finished for him.

Ahlund grinned. "So," he said, "you *were* paying attention."

"You taught me so much," Justin said, struggling to get the words out. "You were there all the way back at the beginning, when I was so annoying and so helpless and so . . . dumb. I mean, *man*, was I stupid. After you died, what I wished most of all was that I had said thank you for teaching me and for saving my life so many times."

Justin was so accustomed to seeing dour sneers and nasty scowls on Ahlund's scraggly, bearded face that a kindly look from this man should have been unnatural. Yet it somehow didn't seem so out of place now as he smiled and said, "No, Justin. It was you who saved my life."

Justin closed his eyes and took a deep breath, trying to steady his nerves in the face of all that lay ahead of him. Weariness overcame him, and he drifted off again.

CHAPTER 2

A dull *thump* startled Justin awake. Opening his eyes, he found that Ahlund's broken sword, previously sitting in Ahlund's lap, had fallen to hit the ship's deck. Ahlund's body was no longer there.

"Ahlund?" said Justin.

He pushed aurym through the spirit-calling stone in his hand, but the ship's deck before him remained empty. He called on more aurym, so much that he strained with the effort. He pulled out his gauge stone and set it burning green to get a better view of the ship's deck around him. But there was nothing.

Justin retracted his aurym from the spirit-calling stone and slipped it back into his pocket. Using his gauge as a lantern, he picked up Ahlund's sword from where it had fallen. The hilt was still warm from where Ahlund's hand had held it.

"Thank you," Justin whispered, hoping that Ahlund could still hear him somehow.

A light from above caught Justin's eye. He looked up to see that the break in the clouds he had noticed earlier was now directly above him and widening. Like a parting curtain, the dark clouds were being pushed aside by the wind to reveal the stars above.

Maybe it was some difference in the composition of the atmosphere, but never, even on the clearest night on Earth, had he been able to see the stars as clearly as he could see them on any ordinary evening here in the Oikoumene. Rather than intermittent dots of individual stars, the celestial bodies appeared as bands and clouds of tens of thousands of pricks of light, varying in color from white to blue to amber, like a glowing pointillist painting.

These alien heavens had played a complicated role in Justin's experience in the Oikoumene. The two moons—a large bronze one called Cnidus and a small bluish one called Nun—had been some of the first things he'd seen after waking up in a strange old man's hut on the Gravelands. That had been before Justin was recruited to help rescue a kidnapped princess, a seemingly straightforward quest that quickly fell apart, turning into something far more complicated.

Normally, the two moons were set apart from one another in the night sky. But as the clouds parted, Justin saw that Nun had slipped in front of Cnidus, creating a partial eclipse.

But something was wrong.

Justin's brow furrowed. He squinted up at the moons. Was it just a trick of the light, or was he so delirious that he was seeing things?

Nun wasn't blue anymore. It had become a dark shade of purple.

Before Justin could speculate on the implications of this, something in his peripheral vision caught his eye.

Previously shadowed by the overcast night, now illuminated by the eerie, unnatural glow of the purple moon, were the black sails of ships on the horizon ahead of him. Dozens of them. Maybe more.

Realizing too late that he was still holding his brightly glowing gauge stone in the air, Justin hastily withdrew his power and doused it.

"*Stupid. . . !*" he hissed at himself.

All this time, he had been so cautious, only to mess up now. Even a keen-eyed lookout might not have seen a solitary black ship with nothing but moonlight to illuminate the sea. But a glowing emerald beacon out here on this flat expanse of otherwise black ocean?

"I haven't changed a bit," he said, running a hand through his sweat-dampened hair. "Still the same old colossal idiot."

A few quiet moments passed. Enough time for several pieces of information to become clear to Justin. The ships were getting closer, not farther away. They flew black flags, and their hulls were made of the same sort of strange black wood as this ship. Demon ships.

Justin set his jaw and tightened his grip on Ahlund's broken sword. A pulse of daemyn, demonic energy, ran through him, bone-deep. To most of his body, it felt uncomfortable. But his transformed demon arm was different. It grew energized by those effervescent daemyn energies, drifting through him as if borne on a cosmic breeze.

His arm hungered for daemyn. It wanted more of it.

Beneath the light of the purple moon, the fleet of black ships was getting closer. Out here, there was nowhere to flee, even if he *had* known enough about sailing to try.

"If this is it," said Justin, "I go down swinging. For Ahlund. For Leah. For everybody."

Justin tightened his fingers around the hilt of Ahlund's sword. Smoke rose as the blade came alight, glowing as red hot as if fresh from the smithy's fires.

He pushed more power through the aurstones in the blade, and a beam of blue flame bloomed outward from the stump, extending long enough that it became a pillar of azure fire as long as the weapon's previous length.

"Mind, body, spirit," said Justin. "Aurym, give me strength."

CHAPTER 3

Six months later.

Leah hadn't been planning to put up a fight. But it didn't matter. These people weren't about to even give her a chance.

They grabbed her by the arms and forced her hands behind her back so hard that she felt a stab of pain as her right shoulder was almost hyperextended. She managed not to cry out but couldn't bite back a sharp intake of breath.

For a moment, she thought they would force her to the ground. Instead, multiple sets of unfriendly hands held her upright as a sack was pulled roughly over her head, plunging her vision into total blackness. Then came a shock of cold metal as a pair of shackles closed over her wrists, and she heard the snaps of their locks engaging.

They worked in silence. She felt her belt buckle ratcheted open, none too gently. Her sword belt was pulled free of her trousers, along with her sheathed Nolian saber, the only weapon she carried. The brooch beneath her chin was undone, and her red cloak was torn from her back. They even took the satchel that contained her healer's supplies.

And still, they said nothing, made no attempt to speak to her, not that it would have mattered. She didn't speak any of the languages of Central Erum, this land so far from her home, this place she had traveled so long and hard to reach.

All for this, she thought bitterly.

The hands let go of her, and something sharp touched the small of her back. The tip of a spear, she surmised. There was a nudge, and she didn't need to speak these people's language to guess the meaning.

She walked forward blindly. The chains of her shackles rattled behind her back as she went. She could smell her own breath trapped in the sack tied over her head.

Leah listened closely as she walked, trying to count the sets of footfalls around her, which was quite difficult within the echoing confines of this tunnel. There had been just two guards present when she'd approached the fortress gates. Three more had rushed to join them. But now, it sounded like at least five sets of feet were escorting her down the corridor. She wondered which of them held the key to her shackles and which one had her saber.

The echoes changed suddenly. The tunnel was opening up around her, and she felt a breeze from somewhere up ahead, carrying with it the humidity of the misty forests of this region.

An open-air courtyard of some kind, she realized.

She sensed many eyes on her and wondered what kind of people they belonged to. The first thing she'd noticed about the guards at the entrance had been the color of their skin. Not a dark shade like her own. Not deep brown like the Cru or the Raeqlu people. Not lightly tanned like a Mythaean. Not white like an Enden, a Rorrdvuuk, or most of the people of Darsida. Instead, their skin tones had an almost copper hue.

Leah knew that the two major cultures of Erum were the Ecbatans and the Aznochti, but she wasn't knowledgable enough about this part of the world yet to distinguish between them. Still, she was willing to bet that these people were Aznochti, if only because they smelled so amazing. The Aznochti people were said to be the Oikoumene's most skilled perfumers. And, having spent most of the past six months in remarkably close proximity to soldiers and sailors, a pleasing odor was something Leah could appreciate even under her current, less-than-ideal circumstances. Presently, she caught a whiff of—

Whether it was one of the guards' fists, the butt end of a spear, or something else, Leah didn't know, but the strike that hit her across the back of the head was so hard that she stumbled and almost dropped to her knees. Colors bloomed and swirled before her eyes in the darkness of the sack over her head.

Make yourself look vulnerable, Leah reminded herself, and she allowed her head to droop forward a bit as if she were close to blacking out.

She was given no time to recover. A set of hands grabbed her from behind and pushed her forward, and with her arms bound behind her back, there was no chance for her to catch herself. She had the presence of mind to turn in mid-fall and land on her shoulder instead of her face and chest, but the blow to the head had affected her equilibrium, and she misjudged the distance. She hit the ground much harder than she expected, but she still did not allow herself to cry out. There was a limit to how pathetic she was willing to appear.

A harsh voice from behind her rattled off a series of impatient words as its source drew nearer, causing Leah to brace herself for another attack. But before the next blow could land, a shout erupted from somewhere ahead of her, a female voice, buttery smooth but exceedingly deep.

Leah sensed the guards around her freeze in place. There was a pregnant pause, and the deep female voice spoke again in a string of syllables. One did not need to know the language to recognize the tone of unquestioned command; whoever this was, she was in charge.

Multiple sets of hands grabbed Leah and pulled her to her feet, and she made a show of shrinking from their touch.

Another string of syllables from the deep female voice. This time, Leah surmised that they were directed at her. She pegged the source to be roughly twenty feet away. There was a moment of silence as they waited for an answer.

"I do not speak your language," Leah said loudly, then spoke the same sentiment in Zorothi and Thubestine.

"The western tongue," said the deep female voice, using Leah's native language of Waelik. "You are every bit as far from home as you look."

The unseen speaker said something else, something that Leah didn't understand, and in response, the sack was pulled from her head.

Leah had to squint against the light that flooded in. It was an open-air courtyard, as she had surmised, and she had been correct about its size. If anything, she had underestimated it. What she had not expected was how many occupants were present within it. There were the guards who had escorted her—six of them, she could now see—plus at least fifty onlookers assembled along the edges of the courtyard.

The onlookers were not uniform in appearance. Leah noted a strong mix of cultures present here. Only a few of them were outfitted in armor and weaponry like the guards. The walls of the courtyard stood twenty feet high, surrounded on all sides by jagged mountain peaks.

Despite the heights of the surrounding peaks, this was the clearest view of the sky that Leah had seen in weeks. Central Erum was a rocky, mountainous region of dark, ancient hemlock forests whose thickly needled boughs trapped an ever-present haze of mist and often blocked out the sun even at midday.

With so much to take in, it took Leah a moment to notice the throne.

It was not a throne of any kind she had seen before, but undoubtedly a throne all the same. In the exact center of the courtyard stood a stone pillar ten feet high, and atop its summit sat a chair constructed of carved ivory. Its seatback was a pair of scapulae from some great beast. The armrests were jagged, curved tusks.

And upon the ivory throne sat the largest woman Leah had ever seen.

This woman was not just big. She was *improbably* big. From a distance, it was difficult to guess her exact size. Leah's Rorrdvuuk friend Megara, who was six and a half feet tall and as broad at the shoulders as the most musclebound men Leah had ever known, came in a distant second to the person on the throne before her.

The improbably big woman leaned forward. One hand rested balled in a fist in her lap. The other hand clutched the haft of a voulge: a cleaver-bladed polearm as tall as herself. Her shoulders were rounded masses of muscle. Her arms and legs were like tree trunks. Her jaw was thick, her brow was wide, and her black hair was bound in a tight knot at the top of her head. At first glance, she appeared to be clothed in a simple white toga, but Leah could see the edges of a breastplate beneath it, gauntlets on her arms, and armored greaves. None of it matched, which wasn't surprising. It must have been murder trying to find *anything* that fit her, let alone a matching set.

"I am told that you came to my gates, alone, and surrendered to my guards," said the big woman, the rumble of her voice carrying through the courtyard like distant thunder. "Have you come to pledge fealty and plea for mercy? Or was it some other, *equally misguided* ambition that brought you here?"

Leah drew herself to *her* full height—one inch and a half over five feet—and spoke loudly.

"I am Leah of House Anavion, Queen of Nolia, the Heartland of Athacea, and High Commander of the Army of Light out of the West. I have come seeking an audience with the one they call the Warlord of the Deep."

The woman pursed her lips and nodded. "I am she," she said.

But before Leah could say another word, the Warlord said something directed to the guards around Leah. The guards looked questioningly at each other. Then, one of them stepped forward and checked Leah's hands. He removed the ring from her finger, the one that held her healer's aurstone. The other guards then examined her neck and arms, looking for any other pieces of jewelry she might be wearing.

Wise, thought Leah.

It was said that spirit warriors were a rarity in Erum, not because the people of this region lacked the ability, but because so few aurstones were found naturally in this part of the Oikoumene. As such, it didn't surprise Leah that the guards had not thought to take away her ring. But this Warlord of the Deep, as she was called, was not so ignorant.

Of all the items that had been taken from her, Leah felt the removal of that ring, which contained her healer's aurstone, the most keenly. She had worn it since she was eleven years old. Her late father had given it to her the day she'd enrolled in the Cervice Academy.

And in a land where aurstones are such a commodity, thought Leah, *I don't suppose these people will be willing to give it back.*

The Warlord stared down at Leah as if sizing her up for a reaction to her ring being stolen. The woman's head was so big that her eyes looked strangely tiny in their sockets.

At length, the woman grinned knowingly at Leah, showing teeth that seemed too small for her mouth.

"You remind me of someone," said Leah.

Leah's words had the intended effect. The Warlord tilted her head in curiosity.

"He was not a warlord, but he was a warrior," said Leah. "I believe he claimed to be from the jungles of Ythia. A man called Lisaac. He carried a weapon like yours. And he was of . . . comparable proportions."

The Warlord of the Deep thoughtfully stroked her oversized jaw. "Was he as big as me?"

"I'm not sure," said Leah. "A friend of mine had to kill him. There wasn't much left of him to go by after that."

The Warlord gave Leah a look of cautious appraisal. "One in one thousand Ythians is born this way," she said, gesturing toward her great physique. "Of those, only the strongest survive the condition to reach adulthood."

Leah had suspected that it was something like that, the side effect of a physical disorder, hereditary in nature.

"Your friend must have been a mighty warrior to have killed someone like me," said the Warlord.

"He is," said Leah.

"I see," said the Warlord. "High commander of an army out of the west, you say? If such an army exists, it is intruding on my lands. I will have the details of its location, its size, and its purpose. Fortunately, we have ways to loosen even the stubbornest of tongues."

"Skipping straight to torture?" Leah said flatly. "You could try asking nicely."

The Warlord feigned an apologetic expression. "I don't like it any more than you do, but I'm the nervous sort, you see. I don't like taking action unless I am certain of the accuracy of the information I have to work with. And I am aware of no more effective motivator than strategically applied discomfort. I hope you understand."

"I came here," Leah announced, raising her voice to its highest volume yet, addressing not the Warlord but the onlookers in the room around them, "for the ethoul. I came here for Justin."

The resulting murmurs from the assembled crowd told Leah that more than one of them, even if they didn't speak her language, recognized a few of her words.

"The ethoul?" said the Warlord, speaking up hastily to try to quell the court's whispers. "The fallen angel? A myth and no more, many would say. What makes you think he is here?"

"The ethoul has been missing for half a year," said Leah. "Since before I set out from my homeland in the west. Since before I crossed the entirety of the Oikoumene, making war when and where I needed, leaving a trail of blood in my wake. Now, I learn that he is being held prisoner in your dungeons."

She narrowed her eyes on the Warlord, and the Warlord narrowed her eyes right back.

" I have come for Justin," said Leah. "And I will have him, one way or another."

A quiver ran up the polearm in the Warlord's hand as her grip on the weapon tightened. "You dare to threaten me with your foreign army?"

"Do you think I would come here alone if I required an army?" said Leah. "One in one thousand is born like you, Warlord? There is not one in ten million born like me. You will free him from your dungeons, or I promise you, you will die."

The Warlord's face had gone red with rage. The muscles in her jaw twitched. She barked a few quick words in Aznochti, and the guards grabbed Leah and began to drag her away.

Leah maintained eye contact with the Warlord for as long as possible. Long enough to see the Warlord's lips peel back in a satisfied sneer, revealing rows of tiny-looking teeth, like pebbles sunken in her gums. Then the sack went back over Leah's head, a fist struck her in the stomach, and she folded in on herself as she was dragged away.

C H A P T E R   4

Sharp escarpments of rock rose on all sides, hundreds of yards thick at their bases yet as jagged and thin as skims of frosting at their summits. Thick stands of hemlocks blanketed the bottoms while thin pines clung to their steeper surfaces. In a mist-shrouded cranny between two such peaks, deep in a high-altitude hemlock forest as old as time, Hook Bard lay crouched beneath the root mass of a fallen tree, ready to kill.

As usual, Hook's hair and clothing were damp. Truly, he could hardly remember the last time they hadn't been. The hanging mists of this place coated every surface and seemed to sap body heat out through every pore. And once you were damp, getting dry again was no easy trick, thanks to the lack of sunlight; the thick canopies of the old hemlock boughs shadowed the forest floor so thoroughly that even at midday, it gave the look and feel of perpetual twilight. For good reason were the rocky cliffs and chasms of Central Erum called the Mistlands.

Hook had never seen anything quite like this strange region. In the oldest sections of the wood, the shadows were so oppressive that almost nothing could grow on the forest floor, leaving a rutted surface of old needles, constantly dampened by the rains and mists, never sunned enough to be dried through, carpeting the hard bumps of raised, gnarled roots. Wildlife did not thrive in such places. You rarely saw a deer, rarely even heard a bird. It gave the misty forests a haunted, abandoned sort of feeling.

But here, at the base of this giant fallen tree, enough sunlight was able to break through that some bushes had taken root and grown enough to provide potential nourishment for passing wildlife. And so it was here that Hook hid.

And if there was one thing Hook Bard was good at, it was hiding.

He wore no armor, only a simple tunic and light boots. He carried no shield or sword, just his long, golden lance—a weapon plundered from the tomb of an Ancient Ellenean king. He had taken to wearing a black bandana to hold back his long, dark hair and to hide the scar that ringed his forehead like a halo. It was a serviceable replacement for the strip of cloth he had once worn, even if it did not carry the same sentimental value.

Careful not to move his body and give away his position, he shifted his gaze. His dark eyes darted back and forth to take in the forest surroundings. There was nothing that Hook particularly *enjoyed* about hiding. It just came naturally to him. There was something about him that shadows seemed to cling to. Even as a boy growing up back in the Mythaean city-state of Ephixes, he'd always been able to blend into a crowd when he wanted to, to pick a pocket without being noticed and then quickly disappear down a back alley. Later, as a man, hiding in plain sight became more difficult. But even then, he'd had a knack for moving quietly and a level of intuition that bordered on prescience—a sort of sixth sense to tell him when someone's head was likely to turn in his direction, and when was the best time to transition from one shadow to the next.

A rustling up ahead. A scratching sound, followed by the pitter-patter of tiny bits of bark being sprinkled upon the dark, moist needles of the forest floor.

Still not moving, Hook looked toward the sound. He saw the pieces of bark on the ground, then shifted his gaze slowly upward and found its source: a small, reddish mammal with pointed ears and a long, bushy tail, scaling its way skyward between hemlock boughs. Hook made a mental note of the animal's location, knowing he could dismiss any minor sounds that came from that direction, and turned his attention back to the surrounding forest floor.

He didn't know what that little creature was. He had never even seen a forest like this one until a couple of weeks ago. There were times, if he was being honest, when he wondered what they were doing in a place like this, on the opposite side of the Oikoumene, so far from anything and everything he'd ever known. Leah's Army of Light had grown to nearly one hundred thousand strong, and they had all come here on Leah's orders, marching toward. . . .

Toward what, exactly? Their collective doom, most likely.

Your job is not to question, Hook reminded himself. *Your job is to fight. Hide and fight.*

Even before it was his job, that's all he'd ever done anyway.

This continent, it was said, was home to Avagad and his demon hordes. The Army of Light's ships had set ashore on it with the objective to invade demon territory and topple Avagad's empire from within. But so far, in the time they had spent navigating the rocky peaks and chasms of the Mistlands, they had not encountered a single enemy.

Granted, avoiding the enemy had been precisely the point of braving this inhospitable region, proceeding inland via what would have otherwise been considered a thoroughly inadvisable route. But the Army of Light was a force of one hundred thousand, and Hook couldn't help but wonder. Had they really gone unnoticed by the enemy? Or had they been *allowed* to come this far?

Did the dark lord, Avagad, already know they were here? And were they marching into a trap?

Hook broke his motionlessness only long enough to wipe a handful of moisture from his face, not sweat but accumulated humidity from the mists.

Hiding and fighting. Hiding and fighting. He was good at both. But even he had to admit, it was all starting to lose some of its appeal.

Maybe, he thought, *you will live long enough to one day put your weapons down.*

There came a rustle from up ahead. Not the kind made by a small mammal. The kind made by something big and heavy.

Hook tightened his grip on his lance. A peaceful end to this life of hiding and fighting did not feel like a likely future.

The rustling grew louder. Hook heard a deep snort. Then a roar.

What followed was a sudden, thunderous pounding of great, padded feet. Hook heard Olorus Antony shout from somewhere in the woods ahead, *"Here he comes!"*

CHAPTER 5

"He's a big one!" Olorus added in his bellowing voice. "Coming straight toward you! *Don't miss!*"

A big one? The sound of damp earth, old needles, and rotted branches being tossed up and crushed beneath the heavy trample of giant feet made that clear. And coming straight for him? The rapidly increasing volume of all that racket, nearing the fallen tree and the dislodged root mass where Hook was crouched, told him everything he needed to know.

Hook's view of his surroundings was badly limited from here. But it also made it less likely that the charging beast would see him—until it was too late.

Hook cupped his hand behind the butt end of his lance and set it against his thigh, preparing to put his full body weight behind the weapon. Its blade was forged of pure a'thri'ik aurstone, and Hook wondered what this weapon's former wielder—an Ancient Ellenean king—would have thought to know that this elegant weapon was being put to such use.

And then, the beast burst forth right in front of Hook, and there was no time left for thinking.

Olorus was right. He was a big one. But, to be fair, all elasmoths were big. The body of a bull but three times the size. A face like a steed without the prehensile trunk. And a single horn at the front of its head, nearer to its snout than its cranium—a mass of bare bone as thick around as the base of Hook's waist and tapered to a conical point at the end.

The animal's eyes found Hook in the path of its charge, and in the instant it had to decide whether to flee or attack, it chose the latter.

Another man might have thought about diving out of the way. Another man might have feared for his life, realizing that putting himself in such danger had been a mistake. Another man might have thought about the potential irony of having survived so many dangers and hardships and battles and woes just to be gored or trampled down by a big, dumb animal that was just trying to defend itself.

But Hook Bard had not survived this long by *thinking*.

The elasmoth thrashed its head toward Hook, leading with its giant horn. But staying low and unseen in this undergrowth had had the intended effect; the narrow distance left between Hook and the creature prevented it from lowering its head to strike at him. It gave Hook enough of an opening to leap forward, leading with the lance braced against him, and drive the tip into the creature's body, hard.

The elasmoth's own forward momentum did much of the work. Angled inward, the a'thri'ik tip sank into the tender spot between the creature's shoulder and chest. There was a great deal of initial resistance. Then Hook felt something give inside, and the spear punched deep, all the way up to his hands.

The animal recoiled, taking the lance with it. Hook knew better than to try to hang on. He would have been flung through the forest like the payload of a catapult, so he let go and dove for cover.

The elasmoth went thrashing through the trees, snapping brittle, old hemlock boughs that were low to the ground and flipping over large, mossy stones as it went.

Once the animal had fled far enough that Hook felt relatively certain he wouldn't be trampled or gored, he stood. The elasmoth's instinct was to flee in a serpentine pattern, weaving back and forth between the tree trunks. It worked so effectively that Hook already could see no sign of the animal whatsoever. He could only hear the crashing and thudding of its footfalls somewhere ahead. It never ceased to amaze him that creatures so big could avoid being seen so well when they wanted to.

Hook heard one final rustle and a thump, followed by a deep wheezing sound.

Then, nothing.

Hook let out a long breath as he stepped out from behind the root mass of the fallen tree where he'd been hiding. It took him only a moment to find the trail: a fine red mist sprayed out at steady intervals. It meant he had gotten the lung, as he'd intended. And, also as intended, he'd managed to do it without getting *himself* killed in the process.

I am sorry, he thought. And in the manner of his long-dead Islander mother, he closed his eyes and thanked the departing spirit of the animal for its sacrifice.

"Hey!" came a gruff call from the trees behind him. "Are ya dead?"

Hook closed his hand into a fist and rapped his knuckles against the nearest tree trunk in a playful, musical rhythm.

"That's either a no," Olorus replied, "or a very talented woodpecker."

Moments later, Olorus Antony came pushing his way through the forest, leading with his Nolian kite shield, making nearly as much racket himself as a full-grown elasmoth. He paused to brush fallen hemlock needles from his beard. Once, that beard had been a lustrous, auburn mane with only a bit of wiry gray infiltrating here and there. Now, the wiry gray had overtaken the auburn almost entirely.

Olorus was twenty years Hook's senior, and although Hook often teased him about his age, his vitality had always made those twenty years seem like a negligible disparity. But Hook couldn't help but notice that his longtime partner was starting to look and act his age.

Using his kite shield like a walking stick, Olorus propped it atop one of the region's characteristically obtrusive rocks jutting out of the ground and made a sound in his throat as he climbed over it—a distinctly old man sort of sound. He placed the flat of his hand against a hemlock trunk to steady himself.

"I hope you didn't miss him," Olorus said.

Hook cocked an eyebrow.

"Ha!" Olorus barked. "Forgot who I was talking to for a moment!"

Once he'd caught his breath, Olorus resumed walking. A single-edged short sword hung at his belt. Like Hook, he also carried a polearm, but it was the modern, standard-issue variety of spear used by the Nolian High Guard, not an exotic and ancient lance like the one presently in the side of the elasmoth.

Olorus stepped up beside Hook and gave him an amiable slap on the shoulder. "Lead on, mighty hunter."

"This way," Hook said in the language of hand-signs.

He stepped forward to follow after the elasmoth. But not before drawing his belt knife. Based on the feel of the strike and the look of the blood trail, he guessed that his spear-thrust had been a killing blow. But there was nothing more dangerous than an animal with nothing left to lose.

Or a human, for that matter, Hook thought unpleasantly, and he proceeded to follow the trail.

He had never been much of a hunter in his previous life. But hunting expeditions had become a welcome reprieve from the drudgery of extended marches, not to mention increasingly necessary. A mobile population as large as the Army of Light required *a lot* of food. Keeping everyone fed would have been impossible if not for the aurym powers of those who could use *y'dur'a*, the "godsbreath" aurstone that grew plant life to full bloom in a matter of seconds. Hook's introduction to the godsbreath stone had been in the form of Gunnar's plant-growing powers, which Gunnar tended to put to more creative, and often far more aggressive, uses. But the same aurym abilities could be used to feed entire populations by growing crops from seeds to fully mature foodstuffs every night as needed.

If the use of the godsbreath stone had been a more common talent, the work of crop-growers across the Oikoumene would have been made redundant. But even among the entire Army of Light, only a few individuals had the gift. And with a limited selection of plant-based foods available, there were only so many sources of protein and fat.

Hunting expeditions like this supplemented the Army's diet with much-needed animal protein and fat. And so, across Darsida, Erum, and a few of the intervening islands, Hook had brought down creatures he had never even seen before. Some of the results tasted better than others. But beggars couldn't be choosers. For bigger game, he preferred to use a spear or lance instead of a bow. Olorus sometimes hunted with a crossbow, but Hook had an aversion to that weapon ever since what happened to Jocasta.

Hook slowed to a halt and closed his eyes, wincing as he tried to shut out the image of Jocasta staring at him, her lips parted ever so slightly, with the bloodied head of a crossbow bolt that had shot her in the back protruding from the front of her chest. He would never forget that look on her face of disbelief and grim understanding just before she tumbled overboard and sank into the churning waters of the Raedittean Sea.

It was Hook's fault that they'd been there that day. It was his fault she was gone.

"Something the matter, lad?" said Olorus from a few steps behind him.

Lad, thought Hook.

Even now, with Hook in his early middle-age, he still called him that.

"*I am fine,*" Hook signed over his shoulder without looking back, and he kept going.

If he had only listened to Jocasta. If he had only chosen to put aside his vendetta gainst the Mythaeans and his vow for revenge, he and his beloved might have lived a life of peace together. But he had chosen the way of war. And it was she who had paid the price.

He'd had his chance to stop fighting, and he'd missed it. Now, there was nothing left to do *but* fight. If nothing else, he was going to fight well.

Hook paused at a tree with a great gouge in its trunk, then followed the trail ahead of it with his eyes. About fifty yards away, a furry bulk lay on the ground, with a thick, conical horn pointed skyward. There appeared to be no movement.

"There! You see it?" said Olorus, pointing out through the trees at the body.

Hook let Olorus think he'd seen it first. He pretended to follow his gesture, pretended to spot it. Then, he favored his hunting partner with a satisfied smile.

"We shall feast *tonight*!" Olorus roared, adding a belly laugh that echoed through the forest.

They had proceeded toward the elasmoth's body and were less than twenty-five yards away from it when Hook froze in mid-step, coming up short at the sight of a human figure, which had been out of sight until now, standing beside the elasmoth's body, examining the fallen creature.

Hook let out a low, single-note whistle. Megara looked up from the elasmoth and turned in their direction. She had already pulled Hook's lance out of the animal's shoulder and was rubbing it against the creature's furry hide to clean off the congealed blood.

Megara, like Hook and Olorus, was one of Leah's most trusted generals in the Army of Light. Formerly a warrior of the Rorrdvuuk barbarians, she was a big woman with muscle-packed arms that rivaled most of the men Hook had ever known. Like Hook, she had been a galley slave at the oars of a Mythaean ship in a former life. They both had the same halo-like scars across their foreheads. Slave's brands. And they both communicated exclusively nonverbally, in the form of hand signs, thanks to their brutal treatment while enslaved by the Mythaean Thalassocracy.

Even from a distance, Hook could see the tenseness of Megara's shoulders and the unusual expression on her face. He had come to know this woman quite well during their time spent serving together, and one thing was clear.

"Something's wrong," whispered Olorus, reading her body language.

"Yes, it is," Hook signed.

When they were a stone's throw from Hook's kill, Megara tossed him his lance, and he snatched it out of the air. She was a woman often given to good humor, but there was no trace of it on her tattooed face now.

"We have a problem," Megara signed.

"What is it?" said Olorus.

"It is Leah," signed Megara. *"She is gone."*

CHAPTER 6

Hemlock forests blanketing sharp hillsides. Rocky bluffs wreathed in mist. Great moss-covered boulders jutting from the landscape as if scattered haphazardly, some bearing the signs of having been worked by prehistoric human hands in some long-ago, forgotten era. The Mistlands of Erum were mysterious, almost otherworldly in their untamed, savage beauty.

And Gunnar Erix Nimbus was bored to tears with all of it.

What the hell are we doing in this blasted place? he wondered for what must have been the nine-hundredth time.

It didn't matter how many times he asked; he hadn't arrived at a satisfactory answer yet.

Crouched beside him, Pool and Borris breathed heavily.

"Don't much like the feel of this place, Cap'n," said Pool, adjusting his ample frame.

Despite the fact that Gunnar's proper rank was admiral, and Pool and Borris were *themselves*, in fact, captains, old habits died hard. They still often referred to Gunnar by the title they had called him back on the Greenspring River, when they had been his fishing crew and he, their captain.

"Neither do I," admitted Gunnar.

"Gives me the collywobbles, it does," said Borris, speaking in his signature lisp, caused by a badly healed scar at the side of his mouth. "Major Lycon ought never to have gone into that accursed place."

"He was following orders," said Gunnar. "*Bad* orders, but orders nonetheless. And Lycon's not one to say no to orders."

For weeks, their army had been wandering—and if *wandering* wasn't the proper term for what they were doing, he didn't know what was— through the puzzle-piece-like, geomorphic formations of Central Erum, through valleys and along narrow canyons snug between high peaks. The landscape had the tendency to jump straight up from level ground to sheer cliff faces one moment, then plummet straight down into a yawning abyss the next. And all of it was forested so thick that you could barely tell that the path you were on was leading to the dead-end of a sheer drop-off until you were practically on top of it, meaning you'd have to turn around and march back the way you'd come.

The whole ordeal actually had him missing the open ocean, which was saying something, given that his experiences on the water always tended to end just about as poorly as experiences on the water could end. But at least on the ocean, you could see where you were going and what was coming. The sea may have been pitiless, but at least it was honest.

But this place, thought Gunnar. *It's like these lands are trying to trick you.*

And it appeared that he was about to face the region's most interesting twist yet.

Ahead, the hemlock forest ended at a rock wall. But this rock wall was unlike anything the Army of Light had encountered during their time in Erum.

This rock wall was a city.

Like everywhere else in this damnable region, there were great boulders sticking up everywhere. Some looked like the ground around them had been furrowed away to reveal them buried beneath; others looked as if they were transplants from elsewhere, having fallen from higher portions of the mountainside and landed there to form new mountains of their own.

Gunnar sat on the most chair-like rock he'd been able to find, with Borris and Pool crouched beside him. All three of them wore full sets of a'thri'ik plate armor—except, in Gunnar's case, for the helmet. Gunnar could not abide helmets. Sure, they were practical, and perhaps his refusal to wear one would be the death of him someday. But for a man with one eye, the prospect of *further* reducing his field of vision to what could be viewed through a thin visor was an unappealing one. If it came down to a question of protection versus awareness, he much preferred his odds if he could see an attack coming and had a chance to get out of the way.

Overtop of the armor was a long, hooded cloak. This was not an option but an essential piece of covering for armor that, if one wore it in the absence of sunlight, glowed a brilliant shade of green.

Overall, the a'thri'ik armor wouldn't have been Gunnar's first choice of outfit, but there was no better defense against demons. Leah and her people had discovered several hundred sets of a'thri'ik armor and a'thri'ik-forged weapons in the Treasury of the Ancients within Cymorikka beneath the Shifting Mountains, and with the Cru's permission, they had hauled off as much of it as they could carry. It was a shame they hadn't been able to take more. Out of the entire Army of Light, only about three hundred soldiers could be outfitted in a'thri'ik armor at any given time. Gunnar counted himself fortunate to be one of the high-ranking few who got his own set. Except for the helmet, which he'd been happy to give away.

It isn't too late to turn around, thought Gunnar, studying the city on the wall. *You know you're walking into a death trap. You* know *that.*

Nothing new, Gunnar replied to himself. *I've been in plenty of death traps and managed to slip out of them all so far.*

And you think this makes your odds more *favorable?* the first part of him said in response. *If anything, you're due.*

I suppose a cynic could argue that.

Or a realist.

Seated on the mossy stone beside Borris and Pool, Gunnar removed his Mythaean Royal Admiral's hat, his substitute for a helmet. His long, black locks spilled out from beneath, and he scratched at the back of his head in thought.

Why not just send somebody else in? he thought.

Maybe I will, he answered.

Maybe you will? Maybe?

Yes, maybe, he replied. *And I. . . .*

But suddenly, Gunnar couldn't think.

In an instant, it was like his whole world had gone sideways. He could only sit there, frozen in place.

His heart began racing. The pores on his head opened up. He couldn't move, couldn't think, couldn't do anything.

This wasn't the first time such a thing had happened to him. The first time had been in the crypt of the Ancient Ellenean king back in Athacea. His vision had tilted wildly like a ship swaying on rough seas. His body and mind had inexplicably stopped working, and he'd been convinced that he was dying.

He didn't think Hook or Adonica had even noticed his freeze-up at the time. It had lasted only a few seconds, and then everything had returned to normal. At the core of it, the only way he could describe the experience was a disconnect between mind and body, during which he was wracked with sudden, abject terror.

And that had been *after* killing a five-headed sea monster.

Since then, it had happened to him a few dozen other times. It sometimes occurred in moments of duress. But there were other times when it seemed entirely random, with no discernible pattern to explain what triggered it. One moment, everything was normal. The next, it was like his mind fell down a hole, leaving his body standing at the top, trying to recover. In addition to the confusion and terror, it always gave him an uncanny certainty that he had been in the same place and time before.

Presently, a few seconds passed, and the world righted itself. Gunnar sat, blinking rapidly to try to clear the remaining haze. He glanced sidelong at Pool and Borris. They didn't seem to have noticed.

Ahead of them, Adonica Lor suddenly appeared from behind a boulder the size of a large house. He did his best to look normal as she approached.

Hold it together, he told himself.

You hold it together, came the response.

Adonica held none of Gunnar's qualms regarding headgear. Even before finding the cat's eye armor, she had always worn a helmet of the Hartlan City Guard into battle. Now, she wore an a'thri'ik great helm, which fit over the head like a barrel, with the only opening being a pair of narrow visor slits at the eye line.

Following along behind Adonica were Sif and Tel of the Cru. And behind them was a team of ten soldiers. All wore a'thri'ik armor and the standard-issue long cloaks over it. The weaponry they carried was as varied as their backgrounds.

Gunnar knew only one of those ten soldiers by name. She was a woman from Darvelle who'd joined up with Leah's forces shortly after her country had made peace with Nolia, formerly a longstanding enemy. Her name was Estoq, and Gunnar had been surprised, to put it lightly, the first time he'd spotted her among the Army of Light's forces. The two of them had something of... a history. So far, however, neither one of them had addressed this or even acknowledged the other's existence.

When Adonica reached Gunnar's rock-chair, she pulled the great helm from her head, revealing a sharp-featured face and icy-blue eyes. Her skin, like most of the coastal dwelling people of Hartla, had been deeply tanned when Gunnar had first met her but had paled a bit over the course of the long, bleak winter spent traveling through Darsida. These first few weeks of spring had been equally sunless thanks to Erum's shaded, mist-shrouded forests and high cliffs.

"The scouts undersold this damn place if you ask me," said Adonica.

"How so?" asked Gunnar.

Trying to look casual, he took a handkerchief from one of his pockets and mopped at his brow, where his freeze-up had caused beads of sweat to accumulate.

"Well, for a start," said Adonica, "it's bloody huge."

"Who ever heard of people building into the side of a cliff?" asked Borris. "What were they, pigeons?"

Adonica took a moment to tighten her blond ponytail, then cocked a head toward Sif and Tel. "Your people live in the mountains, don't they? Is your home anything like this?"

Sif shook his head. "This city dwarfs even our Home beneath the Thucymoroi."

Sif and Tel carried their helmets cradled in their arms, revealing their long, dark beards and smooth, hairless heads. Skin tones among the Cru people varied from dark brown to almost black. In the tradition of all male Cru warriors, they kept their heads clean-shaven and never cut their beards.

Cru fighters made up a comparatively small percentage of the Army of Light. Their male and female warriors alike were some of the most level-headed and dependable soldiers that Gunnar had ever served alongside. Sif's beard was long enough that he braided it when he went into battle. And Tel's *would* have been longer had he not accidentally singed off a good six inches not so long ago while literally playing with fire; it had been discovered that Tel could use *a'thri'jha*, the fire aurstone, like Ahlund. But there was a steep learning curve involved, and one paid heavily for mistakes.

As the team of ten soldiers took up positions behind Adonica and the others, Tel stroked his shortened beard and looked up at the city. "I have never seen anything like this place," he mused.

Gunnar would have been forced to agree. There were some pretty big cities in the Mythaean Thalassocracy. He had seen a few impressive urban centers during the Army of Light's journey through the Oikoumene's central continent of Darsida, too. But this place was on another level, literally.

The cliff city ahead of them started at ground level like any normal settlement but then extended upward almost vertically, with levels of the city built on terraces in the rock wall. There were at least a dozen of these terraces, stacked on top of one another, climbing upward several hundred feet and stretching, side to side, a mile long. It gave the city the look of a staggered shelf. The cliff was so high and the mists so thick that Gunnar couldn't even see the top from where he sat.

It was an impressive feat of architecture. But it lacked one key element that Gunnar tended to associate with cities.

People.

"Is that place as lifeless as it looks from here?" asked Gunnar.

"It certainly appears that way," said Sif. "But looks can be deceiving."

"We didn't see anyone," said Adonica. "But *something* prevented Lycon and his team from returning."

"I don't like this place," said Borris. "Don't like it at all."

Gunnar absently twisted his long mustache as he watched a small flock of birds alight from the mossy ground and sail, silently, over the lowest portion of the empty-looking city and disappear within.

Lycon Belesys had entered this city with a team of scouts to search for a route leading through it. The hope had been that the Army of Light would be able to bypass some of the rough territory ahead by traveling through this city and up and over the cliff instead. After all, whatever civilization had built this place, they'd clearly had the engineering capabilities to navigate vertically within the city. It stood to reason that there would be a road that led up to the top of the cliff as well.

If there was such a way, and if the path was safe and unwatched by demon eyes, the Army of Light could potentially shave weeks off their travel time.

But Lycon and his team had entered the city three days ago, and no one had heard from any of them since.

"Who's to say they didn't make it through without any problem at all?" offered Pool.

Gunnar shrugged. "Fair point. I mean, hell, it's a long way up there. You can't even see the top from here. They could be on their way back down right now, and it's just taking 'em a while, you know?"

"You *know* how by-the-book Lycon is," said Adonica. "If it was going to take longer than expected, he'd have sent a messenger to inform us. The fact that he hasn't means he's either dead or needs help."

"Just trying to look on the bright side..." grumbled Pool, dejectedly.

"Aurym training has taught me to sense things that cannot be seen," said Tel. Perhaps unconsciously, he adjusted the armored glove he wore, where an aurstone was embedded that allowed him to call forth fire from the palm of his hand. His deep, dark eyes scanned the vertical cityscape with intensity, and he seemed almost to shiver. "I sense something very wrong here."

Tel was on point today, because Gunnar would have once again had to agree with that particular statement.

Although Gunnar had never *technically* finished his aurym training under his spirit-tutor back in his home city of Eppex, he was still in tune with the sensations of aurym and daemyn in the world around him, and he couldn't deny that the city ahead was about as unfriendly a place as you could expect to find. It was not quite as bad as the Drekwood back in Athacea, but it had a nasty feel to it nonetheless. And, of course, Adonica was right; Lycon would never have missed a check-in. That guy would jump into deep water wearing full armor if a commanding officer gave him the order.

"Well?" said Adonica, turning to face Gunnar. "You're the ranking officer. We going in, or not?"

"*I'm* the ranking officer?" said Gunnar.

Adonica made a face at him. "Who else would be?"

"*Admiral* Gunnar Erix Nimbus," said Gunnar, thumbing himself in his chest. "It's right there in the name. I'm in charge of *boats*. Sif, aren't you a general or something? That's gotta be higher than admiral—on land, anyway. Right?"

Sif said nothing. The man was too wise to get pulled into the middle of something like this.

"Our titles mean squat," said Adonica. "Otherwise, I'm due for a big promotion. Last I heard, I'm still a *captain*. Which means, in theory, I'm of equal rank with your two fishing buddies here who can barely button their pants right."

"Hey!" said Pool, as Borris checked his pants.

"You watch your tongue—Borris and Pool are saints," said Gunnar.

"Like it or not, it's your call, Gunnar," said Adonica. She leveled a significant look at him. "Do the right thing."

Again, Gunnar took off his Royal Admiral's hat and scratched his head in thought.

"I agree that Lycon's been gone too long," he said. "Let's send someone in to search for him."

Adonica made a gesture toward the group—herself, Sif, Tel, the team of ten soldiers assembled behind her, and finally, Gunnar.

"We're here," she said. "Send *us* in."

Gunnar examined the group of heavily armed soldiers. "I was thinking something a little less conspicuous. A few scouts, maybe."

"And if *they* don't come back, then what?" said Adonica. "*Then* we would go in, right? So, let's just skip ahead one step and take action now."

"You know how Zechariah feels about this sort of thing," said Gunnar. "He keeps scolding us for taking too many risks personally, for not delegating enough."

"You're really letting that old man get to you?" Adonica said.

"Just because he's a stuffy old killjoy doesn't mean he's wrong about *everything*," said Gunnar. "He does have a point; we've got an entire army at our command, but we still seem to do an awful lot of the heavy lifting ourselves. It doesn't make sense for us to keep risking our own lives over stuff like this when we could be sending people out who are more—"

"Replaceable?" said Adonica, sneering at Gunnar.

The change in the body language of the ten soldiers assembled behind her was palpable.

"That's, er, not what I was going to say . . ." said Gunnar.

Backpedaling was not a good look for a commanding officer, but sometimes, you didn't have much of a choice. Even Borris and Pool squirmed.

"Now, come on," said Gunnar. "What I meant was—"

"I think we *know* what you meant, Gunnar of House Nimbus, Son of Erix, of the royal bloodline of the Mythaean Sovereign King, Unifier of the Raedittean Archipelago," said Adonica. "Yes, Your Highness, I can see how, to you, ordinary people must seem quite expendable."

Gunnar started to reply but bit his tongue, literally, to stop himself. Even when he was right—which was most of the time, in his humble opinion—his mouth often had a way of making things worse. Sometimes, it was better to just take the loss and move on.

"In spite of his flawed delivery, I do see the wisdom in Gunnar's words," said Sif. The man shifted his weight uncomfortably. His entire left side had been burned in an aurym-powered battle, leaving raised scars on his face, neck, and head, and he had a bad leg from it that sometimes gave him trouble. "I am an Elder of the Cru. Tel has also become a leader in his own right. At a point, it becomes unwise to put ourselves at risk when another would do."

Adonica's jaw twitched. "We can talk about this all day, or we can take action. What's your decision, Admiral?"

Gunnar sucked on his teeth. He found himself trying not to look at the ten soldiers assembled behind Adonica. Some of them were Mythaeans. Some were from Athacean nations like Nolia and Darvelle. Others were from some of the populations who had joined up with the Army of Light in Darsida. One was even a Hartlan, like Adonica.

Like Lycon, too.

"We should return to camp and report the situation to Commander Anavion," said Gunnar. "She may decide to send scouts, or she may order a rescue mission of some kind, in which case maybe one or more of us will be back here to search for Lycon. Either way, *she* decides how we proceed."

"Is that an order, Admiral?" said Adonica flatly.

Gunnar hesitated only briefly. "Yes," he said. "It is."

Adonica nodded, then turned to face the ten soldiers behind her.

"I'm going in after Lycon," she said, "and I'm doing it now, even if I have to go alone."

It was not often that Gunnar found himself at a loss for words, but as Adonica put the great helm over her head, he found himself saying something that sounded a bit like, "Hey, but I just. . . ." and trailing off because he wasn't sure what else to say.

"If any of you are willing to come along with me, I won't soon forget it," said Adonica, ignoring Gunnar's indistinct mumbles. "Lycon would do the same for any of you." She paused to shoot a look over her shoulder at Gunnar, and even though he couldn't see her face beneath that helmet, he could sense the distaste as she added, "Even you, Admiral, *replaceable* though you are."

And with that, Adonica started walking toward the city without looking back.

After a few seconds, the squad of ten soldiers made their choices. Five stayed behind, and five followed Adonica.

A perfect half-and-half split, thought Gunnar. *What are the odds?*

For a few seconds, all Gunnar could bring himself to do was stand there, looking back and forth between Sif, Tel, and the five soldiers who had chosen to obey his orders. He blinked in confusion, then turned to face Adonica and the soldiers departing with her.

"Adonica," called Gunnar. "Captain Lor!"

She did not turn around. None of them did.

Gunnar threw his hands in the air. "What does she want me to be the ranking officer for if she's just going to up and commit treason the first order I give?"

Neither Sif nor Tel nor anyone else had an answer.

"Sif, take everyone back to camp and report to Leah," said Gunnar. "Maybe I can still talk Adonica out of it."

"Best of luck," said Sif.

"Thanks, the seas know I'll need it," mumbled Gunnar.

"We're coming with you, Cap'n," said Borris as he and Pool stepped up.

"I know you would," said Gunnar. "But I'm not going anywhere. Head back with Sif and Tel."

"Is *that* an order?" asked Pool.

"Nah," said Gunnar, slapping the two of them on their shoulders. "Just a friendly request, my boys. I'll be back in two flicks of a trout's fin."

"Well," said Borris hesitantly. "Okay."

Gunnar started jogging after Adonica and the others.

"Captain Lor!" he called. "Adonica! *Hey!*"

And that was how Gunnar entered the vertical city in search of Lycon Belesys against *his own* orders.

CHAPTER 7

The sack wasn't removed from Leah's head until just before she was pushed into the cell.

To her surprise, there were no torches or candles to be seen, and yet the underground world around her was not dark. Instead, her surroundings were bathed in an eerie green glow. It emanated from the very walls, where veins of bright emerald stones shined.

Cat's eye, thought Leah.

A'thri'ik, also known as theynrald, also known as cat's eye, was a type of stone with a unique physical property. In the presence of sunlight or moonlight, it appeared as dull as any ordinary stone. But in darkness, it emitted a steady green luminescence. The Ancients had used this substance, a light source that required no fuel or maintenance, to illuminate their underground cities, including Cymorikka, beneath the Shifting Mountains back in Athacea, the sanctuary where so many of her people were currently in hiding from the demon armies while she was on the warpath. It had been over half a year since she'd last had any contact with them. She prayed that the city remained secure.

Looking around, Leah saw that in the larger chamber outside of her cell, entire stalactites of a'thri'ik hung from the ceiling like luminous natural chandeliers. She had assumed that this fortress had belonged to one of the kingdoms of Erum, perhaps one of the civilizations that had been brought low by demon hordes since Avagad's rise to power. But now she wondered, was it possible that this place was more like Cymorikka? Could this be part of an ancient underground city, perhaps connected to a much larger complex leading deep beneath the earth?

The guards left, closing a door on the other end of the chamber with a thud. She heard the clank of a key turning to engage the door's lock.

With some degree of difficulty, Leah stood to take stock of her situation. The cell was about ten feet wide by ten feet long, but it had a high ceiling. Its rear wall was solid rock, with a few veins of cat's eye to provide some light. But the front wall and the sides were comprised of iron bars mounted by bands of metal and bolts driven straight into the rocky floor and ceiling.

Even with the sack over her head, it hadn't been difficult to keep a mental count of the turns, doors, and number of stairways they had descended to get down here. She estimated that they were at least one hundred feet underground. As she looked around, she recited the list of the turns and stairways she had memorized, over and over again in her mind, to shift the set of instructions from her short-term to her long-term memory. Retracing her steps later, if need be, would be a simple matter of reciting those memorized instructions backward.

Her cell appeared to be one of several built in a row, but the distribution of a'thri'ik light sources was not enough for her to see much of the interior of the other cells.

She walked to the rear of her cell and rested against the wall. They had left her with the shackles still on and her arms still wrenched behind her back, which made it difficult to find a comfortable position.

Leah tried to recall the maps of this region, tried to picture where this fortress was located relative to the Altirin Sea and the canyons of Central Erum. In her downtime, she had studied all the maps of these lands that she could get her hands on, so that by the time they'd reached the eastern continent's shores, she was nothing if not well-educated about this land's geography.

What she hadn't been prepared for was its *topo*graphy.

As it turned out, maps couldn't do justice to the landforms of Erum. Leah was used to her homeland of Athacea, where there were plains, rolling hills, and one major mountain range. Back there, if a map showed that two places were twenty miles apart, you could generally take it for granted that it would take twenty miles' worth of traveling to get from one to the other.

But things were not so simple here. Erum was not a land of plains, rolling hills, and mountains. It was a land of cliff faces, sheer drops, sharp ridges, rising peaks, hidden passageways, and dead ends. Here, two locations that looked twenty miles away on paper might require a hundred miles' worth of rough travel over unforgiving, hostile terrain. And for a force that had grown as large as the Army of Light had, these developments had complicated things.

Leah allowed her body to slip to the floor to sit in the quiet darkness. She closed her eyes and breathed deeply. The silence down here—a penetrating silence that seemed to push against her eardrums with the pressure of a physical entity—was almost soothing.

You could almost forget you were being held prisoner down here, she thought with a bitter grin.

Recently, even her nights had been restless. Yes, she slept. But it'd been a long time since she felt like she'd had a *real* night's rest. How long had it been since she had felt at peace, inside *or* outside? How long since she had just sat quietly, alone, and—?

Leah heard a small, quiet exhale from nearby in the dark.

Not alone after all, she realized.

Not until now had she noticed the motionless, lumpy bundle huddled up in the far corner of the cell next to hers, easy to mistake for an abandoned old blanket or an empty sack. Old leaves clung to the edges of the ragged fabric. But as she watched, she heard the sound of breathing again, and she saw the bundle move.

"Justin?" said Leah.

As her voice echoed through the green-hued underworld, the figure in the cell stiffened with recognition.

Leah's heart beat hard in her chest. The bundle shifted, revealing a pair of shoulders and a cloaked head that raised to make a half-turn in Leah's direction. She saw that fine yellowish hair hung from the head.

Leah's throat had gone dry. With her arms bound behind her back, it was a struggle to crawl across the cell floor, but she scrambled until she was leaning against the iron bars that separated her cell from the next. It was as close to the cloaked figure as she could get.

"Justin!" she repeated in the hiss of a whisper.

The figure shifted to face her. In the green light of a'thri'ik, Leah saw a face wreathed by yellow hair above and yellow facial hair below. The face was grim and haggard, though it was difficult to tell whether this was due to age or rough treatment. There was a haunted, hopeless look in his eyes.

As Leah stared at the poor wretch, her hope withered.

"You're not him," she said.

The man's cracked lips parted in confusion.

"Sorry," said Leah. "I'm looking for someone."

"Did you say Justin?" asked the yellow-haired prisoner.

"Yes," said Leah. "Justin Holmes. I came here to find him."

The prisoner cleared his throat. "They *say* Justin is here, somewhere," he said in such clear Waelik that it surprised Leah. "The truth can be narrowed down to one of only three logical conclusions. The Warlord and her guards are lying, or they are telling the truth, or they are mistaken. So far, I have been unable to discern the answer."

"How long have you been here?" asked Leah.

"Weeks. I think. Maybe longer. One can lose track of such things quite easily down here."

"I don't doubt it," said Leah. "Maybe it was a mistake for me to come here."

"Justin would not think so," said the yellow-haired man.

Leah's head snapped in the prisoner's direction. There was something in his voice, something about the way he phrased that sentence, that gave her pause.

"What do you mean?" she asked. "Who are you—?"

Leah's question was interrupted by the sound of the heavy door across the main chamber being unlocked. It swung open, and a large figure emerged—so large that it had to duck to fit through the doorway. The Warlord of the Deep.

A visit in person, so soon, thought Leah. *My words in the courtyard must have disturbed her even more than she let on.*

The Warlord was alone. She shut the door and strode to the front of Leah's cell to face her. She carried no weapon, but she didn't need one.

Now that Leah was closer to her, she decided that this woman was bigger than Lisaac had been after all. And judging by the look on her face and the way her heavily muscled frame heaved as she stood there, she was not pleased.

Leah ought to have been frightened. Logic told her that if this giant human so wished, she could have opened the metal door that separated them, crossed the cell in a few steps, and crushed Leah's head against the bars.

Perhaps Leah should have remained silent in light of this fact. But, weighing the situation, she decided it was a matter of prudent and sensible strategy for her to speak first.

"I see no instruments of torture," Leah announced in a clear, bold voice. "Do you use your bare hands? That is grim work."

The Warlord's hard expression faltered. "I must admit, I find your indifference to your plight . . . unnerving."

"Thank you," said Leah. "I noticed children in your courtyard above. And elderly people. From several different cultures, by the look of them. You gathered them all here for protection against Avagad and his demons, didn't you?"

The Warlord narrowed her gaze at Leah. "Tell me how you learned of this place," she demanded.

Leah nodded. It seemed a fair enough request.

"My forces and I have only been in Erum for a few weeks," said Leah. "It has been rough traveling, and we have encountered few locals, friend or foe. A few days ago, my scouts met a group of Ecbatans who shared that they were searching for a hidden fortress said to exist among the cliffs. There, they said one called the Warlord of the Deep was accepting refugees, taking people in under her protection. My scouts questioned how this Warlord could hope to protect *anyone* against Avagad and his demons. The response was that this Warlord was rumored to have a bargaining chip. A prisoner whom she hoped to use to make a deal with the dark lord and keep her people safe. A prisoner called Justin. The fallen angel from beyond the Oikoumene, whom Avagad is said to seek."

Out of the corner of her eye, Leah did not miss the way the haggard-looking prisoner in the adjoining cell shifted beneath his blankets at the mention of Justin's name. Nor did she miss how the Warlord's frown deepened as she spoke.

Leah and her Army of Light had traveled across almost the entire Oikoumene to reach Erum, and her scouts' encounter with the Ecbatans was not the first time they'd heard rumors about the fallen angel. Even far into inner Darsida, there had been talk of the fallen angel who had come from beyond this world to fight for humankind. A man with such aurym power that he could defeat entire hordes of demons with a single swing of his sword.

Some said Justin the ethoul was a strapping, hulking man of giant proportions, possessing otherworldly strength. Some said he had one arm. Others said that one of his arms had been lost in battle and replaced with a glowing green blade.

Justin had been missing for a very long time. The last time Leah had seen him was in the palace of Hartla. Gunnar had seen him most recently when he had taken him and Ahlund to an island in the Raedittean Sea to search for the hidden sanctuary of the Ru'Onorath. But even that had been long ago now. And other than a few echoes of aurym power that Leah had sensed, which may or may not have signaled Justin's return to or departure from this world, the wild rumors of his existence were all that was left of him, as far as she knew.

But what had struck her about *this* more recent rumor was that it was the first time she'd heard a story of the fallen angel being defeated.

Getting captured, imprisoned by a warlord, and held as leverage against Avagad and the demons didn't sound like the sort of thing that would happen to a legendary hero. It sounded more like the sort of thing that would happen to a real person.

The sort of thing that could have happened to Justin, thought Leah.

She had told herself, long ago, that she had given up on the hope of Justin's return. Not because she didn't believe in it but because she couldn't afford to. She was High Commander of the Army of Light, a force of one hundred thousand souls whom *she* had led all this way. She had to assume no one was coming to save them. The Army of Light had to act as if only *they* could save themselves.

And yet, after hearing a rumor like this, what sort of friend would she have been if she hadn't come running?

Zechariah must be furious at me, she thought.

"Where is this 'Army of Light out of the West' that you claim to command?" said the Warlord.

"Three days' travel east of here," said Leah. "I can provide directions for your people to scout the area to confirm my claim if you wish."

The Warlord scowled at her. "Then why would you come here alone?"

Leah, who had been on the ground up until now, struggled to get to her feet, but after a few moments, she managed it. It was a calculated action, giving her time to stall and, hopefully, making her subsequent deflection less obvious.

"The reason I noted the children and elderly among your people," said Leah, "is because I can relate. When my forces departed from the west, we were fortunate enough to be able to leave our children, infants, nursing mothers, and elderly in a safe place." She looked around at the cavernous underworld, lit with green. "A place not so different from this, in fact. Our travels took us through many lands where people have been enslaved by demons. Others, in the resulting instability, were enslaved by their fellow man. Each time, my forces freed as many as we could and took them under our care. The result is that there are now many children, infants, mothers, and elderly among our numbers again. There is not a day that goes by that I don't worry over their fates." Leah bowed her head slightly. "I sympathize, Warlord, with the heavy burden that is upon your shoulders."

"I would be more receptive to your sympathies," said the Warlord, "had you not publicly promised to kill me just a few minutes ago."

"In both sentiments," said Leah, "I am equally sincere."

Only now did Leah notice the fine chain necklace around the Warlord's neck. At the end of it hung Leah's healer's ring.

"If this western army of yours is real," said the Warlord, her sunken eyes gleaming, "then Avagad will be pleased to learn of its whereabouts."

"So," Leah said sadly, "you really are an ally of the dark lord."

"Not yet," said the Warlord. "So far, this fortress has kept my people safe against the demons, but that will not last. It's becoming clear that our only option is to broker a truce."

"There is no truce with demons," said Leah. "None that will last, anyway. If you hope to protect your people, your fight is *against* Avagad. Not alongside him."

For a moment, just for a moment, there was a flicker of softness on the Warlord's face. Was that uncertainty that Leah was seeing? Or regret?

The Warlord tilted her great head to one side, examining Leah's face. "Whether or not you truly command an army as you claim, it is clear that you have seen some fighting and lived to tell about it."

The scar that ran down Leah's forehead and face was a nasty keepsake from a wound that had chopped loose a flap of her scalp, severed off part of her ear, and nearly taken an eye. The trauma and blood loss might have killed her had it not been for the quick aurym-healing of her ally Lycon Belesys. But even his skills hadn't been enough to save her ear, of which only the cartilage of the top half remained.

"We are warriors, you and I," said the Warlord. "But that is not true of everyone. Nor should it have to be."

"So it is preferable to join with the darkness? To attempt to pacify an insatiable enemy?" said Leah. "Even if you give them Justin, how long do you think Avagad and his demons will remain satisfied? How long until they demand offerings of a different sort?"

The Warlord sighed. "You do not understand what you are saying."

"Do not presume to know what I understand," said Leah. "You do not know who I am, *what* I am. What my people have been through."

"I want to show you something," the Warlord said. "Come closer."

Leah hesitated. The man with the yellow hair in the adjoining cell shifted, perhaps trying to silently communicate something to Leah. But finally, and perhaps against her better judgment, she walked forward, closing the distance between her and the front of the cell.

As soon as Leah was within reach, the Warlord extended her great hand through the bars of the cell. Leah started to step back, but the Warlord's hand closed around her shoulder—

There was a pulse of power, and Leah's vision went black.

PART II

THE ENDLESS

ENIGMA

CHAPTER 8

No sooner had the Warlord's grip closed around Leah's shoulder than Leah was alone, in another place, in another time.

The sensation was disorienting, like being spun about by a violent wave beneath deep water, and it took several moments before she could tell up from down. Gray shadows lined the edges of her vision like a ring of smoke, but when she finally steadied herself, she found that she was inside a great chamber. Not an underground dungeon beneath a fortress lit by glowing a'thri'ik, but somewhere else entirely.

All around the chamber, torches burned. The ceiling came to a point in its center high above her, so high that it extended almost beyond her vision. She turned, and the sight of what lay before her caused an icy hand to close into a fist around her heart.

The center of the chamber had no bottom. Where there ought to have been a floor, there was only a yawning circle of darkness. A hole descending to black, fathomless depths, with sheer walls like sleek, spiraling obsidian.

And upon those obsidian walls, climbing like insects up from the unseeable bottom, were demons.

There were coblyns and cythraul alike. Endless numbers of them. The cythraul used brute strength to push handholds and footholds into the walls, their fleshless, skull-like heads cracking open with hellish roars as they climbed. The coblyns followed along behind, leaping gracefully from one newly gouged lip in the wall to the next. Their high-pitched, cackling howls sounded like the laughter of children heard at half-speed.

Suddenly, Leah's perspective shifted again, and she was farther back in the chamber, watching from a distance. The demons were pulling themselves up out of the hole and onto solid ground, marching outward across the floor. No sooner had one wave left the pit than the next followed it: more hellish creatures rising from the shadowed chasm. Demons beyond count. An endless horde, birthed out of the depths, marching toward her—

Leah's return to the Warlord's dungeon cell was just as jarring as her departure. The fresh wave of dizziness that assaulted her reminded her of rolling down grassy hills as a little girl. She would have toppled sidelong, with no way to catch herself thanks to her shackled arms, had a large hand not been there to grip her shoulder and keep her steady until she could get her bearings.

When her vision stopped swaying, Leah looked up. The Warlord was holding her, preventing her from falling. When Leah could stand on her own, the Warlord let go and withdrew her hand.

There were still gray shadows on the edges of Leah's vision, and it took great effort to clear them. From the adjoining cell, the yellow-haired man clothed in the bundle of rags and dried leaves let out a long sigh as if he had been nervously holding his breath.

"What was that?" Leah breathed. "What did you do to me?"

"You wear the ring of a spirit healer," said the Warlord, "so you must have some understanding of aurym power. My true name is Nefari. And I have an aurym ability of my own. One of farseeing."

Nefari the Warlord backed away from the bars of Leah's cell. Leah noted that she was breathing rapidly, and she crossed her arms over her chest as if trying to suppress a shiver of her own. It was odd to see someone so big look so frail.

"You have much to say about fighting Avagad and his demons," said Nefari, "and much judgment against me for neglecting to do so. What you don't know, Little Queen Anavion out of the West, is that I *did* fight. I did not give up on this war. I lost it."

"Lost it?" said Leah.

"In the early days of Avagad's reign," said Nefari, "I led a force of many thousands against his demon armies. Hence my title. The battles were long and bloody. There were times when it seemed that all was lost. But there were also times when it felt like we might win. Finally, the idea came to me, a stratagem the enemy would least expect. Instead of continuing to wage a defensive war, we would take the fight to the enemy. We would invade *his* lands and conquer *him*. I was on the front lines, leading our final assault, when we invaded Avagad's capital city of Rohghost in the east."

"Rohghost?" said Leah. It was not a name she recalled from any of the maps she had studied.

"We fought," said the Warlord. "And we lost. My people died. Everyone I called a friend . . . or a lover . . . was lost to me."

Leah shifted uncomfortably in the cell.

The plan she's describing, thought Leah, *sounds an awful lot like the plan my army is executing right now.*

"I'm sorry for what you lost," said Leah.

"I managed to escape from that defeat with my life," said Nefari. "I retreated into the wilderness and found this fortress. And with the help of a few benefactors, I built this place into a sanctuary for other survivors. Despite everything, I *still* intended, one day, to fight again. But then, I began to see visions like the one I just showed you. Images of that Pit. Is it any wonder my assault failed? Even if, at full strength, my army had stood at the top of that Pit and killed and killed and killed—slaughtered every demon that poked its head up out of the fathoms—we would have all died of exhaustion before we reached the end of them. I realized that there would be no fighting this enemy. So, here in this hidden fortress, watching over these people, knowing that one day the demons could find us, I could only pray for a miracle."

Nefari locked eyes with Leah. "And then, a miracle did happen. Who should appear at our gates but the fallen angel? The one whom Avagad is said to be seeking above all else."

"So, he really is here?" said Leah. "You really do have Justin?"

"You will not find him," said Nefari. "But yes. He is here. . . . I have no quarrel with you, Little Queen, or with the fallen angel. This is how my people survive."

"You plan to deliver him to Avagad," said Leah. "To use him as a bargaining chip to gain the dark lord's favor."

"It is our only chance of surviving against the demons."

Leah shook her head. "You're wrong. There can be no bargaining. The only way any of us can survive against these things is to defeat them."

"Fool!" the Warlord snarled, spittle flying from her mouth in a sudden rage. "You act as if it is so simple! You saw the same thing I saw.

How would you fight an enemy of such numbers, climbing up out of the depths without end?"

Leah sneered at her. "I would sooner stand at the top of that pit and do the cutting myself, for eternity if need be, before I resorted to sacrificing humans to the enemy out of some misguided hope for mercy from monsters. War is our only option."

Tensions were growing high. Had Leah not been half this woman's height, the two of them might have been nose-to-nose with one another through the bars.

"Avagad is a deceiver," snapped Leah. "Do not delude yourself—any deal you strike with him will not be binding!" For a moment, her voice echoed through the dungeon. Then she took a deep breath and added in a low tone, "Do not do this. Do not give them Justin."

Beneath Leah's icy gaze, the Warlord's expression softened a bit.

"I'm sorry," said Nefari. "I can tell you care about this person. But it must be done. I only seek to do what is best for my people."

"As do I," said Leah.

The Warlord shook her head, incredulous. "How can you say that? How can you say war is the only option when you just told me everything you have to lose? You have infants and children with you, like us! Would you march *them* to battle?"

"If that is what it takes, then so be it!" shouted Leah.

Nefari the Warlord recoiled from Leah's outburst. In the stunned silence that followed, she looked like a scared child. It was as if Leah were seeing through the charred exterior of well-done meat to a still-tender center. Leah had no such tenderness. Not anymore. It had been burned out of her.

Finally, Nefari turned away. She crossed the chamber and unlocked the door to leave, but not before turning to face Leah one last time. There was a look of disgust on her face as she said, "Truly, it is you, not I, Little Queen, who is the warlord."

Leah watched Nefari go. The slam of the heavy door and the key turning in the lock reverberated through the cavernous dungeon.

CHAPTER 9

For a few moments after the Warlord's departure, all was silent. In the wake of the Warlord's vision and her convicting words, Leah found being alone with her thoughts in the quiet darkness to be a thoroughly disagreeable experience.

A raspy voice broke the silence.

"I was worried she had done something to hurt you," said the prisoner in the next cell over. "When she grabbed you like that."

Leah shook her head. "It was just a vision," she said. "Nothing more. But I should have been more careful."

The prisoner started to say something else, but a fit of hard coughing overtook him, and he spoke no more for the moment.

Leah looked around. The two of them were alone down here. And although the Warlord hadn't delivered on her promise of torture during her visit this time, it didn't mean she didn't still intend to do so. Perhaps it would come sooner rather than later.

She went back to her seated position against the rear wall of her cell, leaning back until her head rested against the cool stone.

That vision of the Pit with demons pouring out of it. . . . Leah was quite sure that image would never again be far from her mind.

"Did you really come here because you were looking for Justin?" said the yellow-haired man after he recovered from the coughing fit.

"I did," said Leah.

The prisoner took a look around at the dungeon. "You didn't happen to have an escape plan for once you got inside, did you?"

"I was hoping diplomacy would work," said Leah.

"I see." The prisoner managed to hide any disappointment from his voice.

After a few moments, he cleared his throat and spoke in a level-headed, appraising sort of way.

"In the case of Justin, let us consider the *facts*," he said. "It has been the better part of a year since the last substantiated sighting of the ethoul. Long enough, perhaps, that one could be forgiven for thinking that he left us for good this time."

Leah furrowed her brow. Again, there was something about the way he spoke that struck her, but she couldn't put her finger on it.

"One would think," the man went on, still not looking at Leah, "that if the enemy had destroyed or captured Justin, we would have heard about it by now. I think it is more likely that he is dead, indisposed somewhere, or has left this world forever.

"I was brought to this fortress after I was injured in a demon attack. The Warlord and her people rescued me and healed me. But then, I heard the rumor that Justin the ethoul was imprisoned in this place. The Warlord, despite her outward altruism, grew blunt and unreceptive when I requested to see him. So I took matters into my own hands. Perhaps my zeal blinded me to my age. Growing old, Dear Leah, is almost as difficult to track as the passage of days in a dark dungeon. I went in search of Justin down here myself, intending to free him if needed. But in my weakened state, I was caught, and I have been paying the price for it ever since."

Leah blinked in surprise as she considered the man's words.

He called me Leah, she realized.

The Warlord had only referred to her as Queen Anavion in their conversation just now. Not by her given name.

"How do you know who I am?" she asked.

"Because he spoke of you," said the prisoner.

Leah crawled across the cell floor until she was pressed up against the bars. She found herself having to moisten her lips before she could speak.

"Who?" she said.

"Justin, of course," said the man.

Leah felt her breath catch in her throat.

Only now did the man turn to face her fully. He remained seated in a crumpled sort of posture, but he no longer looked quite so defeated and weak. The jaw beneath his yellow beard was strong. The cloth wrapped around him, which she had at first taken as a blanket with dried leaves clinging to it, she could now see was a fine cloak with faux leaves sewn into the fabric, perhaps as a means of camouflage. It was only because the cloak was so dirtied that she hadn't recognized its finery.

"Who are you?" Leah asked.

The man did not smile, yet there was something in his eyes that communicated amusement at her question.

"My name is Kallorn Rhodos," he said, "of the Ru'Onorath."

"The Ru'Onorath?" gasped Leah. "You're one of the Guardians of the Oikoumene like Ahlund."

"Oh, nothing like Ahlund," the man said with a small shake of his head. "But not for lack of trying."

"But where is Ahlund? And Justin?" said Leah. The questions spilled out of her so quickly she could hardly speak fast enough to keep up with them. "You've really spoken to Justin? Where? And what happened to him. . . ?"

These mounting questions erased any trace of humor from the face of Kallorn Rhodos, replacing it with a deep, distant sorrow.

"How I wish I did not have to be the one to answer those questions for you, My Lady," said Kallorn Rhodos.

And then, he began to tell Leah everything.

CHAPTER 10

It was just as Megara had said. Leah was gone. The only trace of her was a brief note, currently in Olorus's hand.

The process of tearing down camp almost always felt more labor-intensive than setting up. But with any luck, the Army of Light would be on the move within the hour, embarking on the next leg of their journey eastward across Central Erum. Most of Leah's makeshift quarters had already been taken down. Hook leaned against one of the remaining tent posts. Megara stood with her great arms crossed. Olorus leaned over Leah's table. And Zechariah paced back and forth in front of them.

Hook could hardly remember a time when he had seen Zechariah so worked up. The old man's long beard was damp with the mist of the hemlock forest, and his bushy white eyebrows were sharply downturned in agitation.

Out of everyone, Zechariah had changed the least since Hook first met him. He wore the same plain gray robes and had the same unassuming look, making it easy to mistake him for the simple "scholar and scribe" he claimed to be. The biggest difference was the metal hook at the end of his right arm, where a hand had once been.

"I trusted her," grumbled Zechariah. "When those messengers arrived with claims of a fallen angel being held prisoner, I knew where her head would go, but I trusted her. I warned her that acting on unsubstantiated rumors would put herself, our mission, and the entire Army of Light in jeopardy, and she said she *agreed* with me—that she would never do anything so foolish! And I *trusted* her! More fool me for believing that she had started using some of the brains in her head!"

Hook decided to let the comment go. Megara, however, visibly bristled. She raised her hands and signed, *"She is doing her best."*

"She is chasing after distractions," snapped Zechariah.

"I remember you also called it a distraction," said Olorus, clearing his throat, "when she wanted to help those Zorothins stranded on that frozen lake, besieged on all sides by coblyns with nothing but fissures in the ice preventing them from all being killed. You wanted to bypass them. Leah decided to intervene. We took minimal casualties, and if she hadn't insisted against your advice, several hundred people would have either been killed by coblyns or starved to death."

Zechariah opened his mouth to say something, but Olorus wasn't finished.

"And then there were the slaves we freed in Merosys," Olorus continued. "You, Zechariah, said that freeing them from those oligarchs wasn't worth our time. If Leah had listened to you, those people would have been left to their torment until, inevitably, the demon armies pushed through and destroyed them along with their captors. Instead, those people are now protected by our army, and we gained several powerful aurym fighters from among them. Need I detail any of the other times Leah has done the hard thing when it was right, *in spite* of her advisor?"

"Every one of those incidences," said Zechariah, his voice growing in volume as he spoke, "resulted in days or weeks of our time. Time that has accumulated into months, delaying a mission that, from the very beginning, has been hanging by a thin strand over an inferno. If you will spare me any further tearfully sentimental tales, I will spare you from mention of all the times when I was right. The trap in the swamp. The cythraul at Othraedu. What happened to *our steeds*."

Olorus gave a flat expression and produced a huff of breath but said nothing.

During their travels, it had been noted that the demons went after steeds with great zeal. In one particularly bloody attack, a horde of coblyns had slaughtered several hundred steeds in a single night. Eventually, it had become clear that they were intentionally targeting the animals wherever they could find them, presumably as a long-term strategy to cripple the humans' primary means of transportation on land.

Crossing the Altirin Sea between Darsida and Erum had been a complicated matter, and it had been quite impossible for the Army of Light to bring anything but a fraction of the steeds they still had at that point. They had hoped they would be able to replenish their cavalry in Erum, but here, things seemed to be even worse. As a result, the Army of Light had very few steeds to go around.

"I am not heartless!" Zechariah said. "At one time, you may have had the luxury of pursuing every endeavor you thought was *right*, as you put it, to nobly risk your lives for the sake of others. But you gave up that luxury when you became leaders. Now, your safety, your lives, are not just your own! Leadership must come first. Every time Leah, or any of you, foolishly and needlessly puts our mission in jeopardy to satisfy your own personal sense of morality or justice, it makes me think I need to find *new* leaders!"

Zechariah trailed off. And in the silence that followed, Hook was reminded, despite its size and power, what a fragile and tenuous alliance the Army of Light truly was.

It was nothing short of a miracle what Leah had pulled off to get this force here. He hated to think what would happen if the turmoil brewing within Leah's inner circle spilled over to the common soldiers.

Hook, trying to get things back on track, gestured to get Olorus's attention and asked, *"What does the note say?"*

Olorus cleared his throat, then read, "'Dear Zechariah. I lied. Leah. Postscript: If there is a chance Justin is there, I must try.'"

Olorus set the note aside.

Hearing the words read aloud only further aggravated Zechariah. He raised his hook-hand, twisted the tip of his beard with it, and resumed his pacing.

Olorus and Megara exchanged satisfied smiles, and Hook tried not to let his own amusement show. He was concerned for Leah's safety, of course, but the old man fuming about it wasn't helping anything. And it was rather entertaining to watch.

Ahlund and Zechariah had believed Justin to be the key to defeating the demons. And so Ahlund had taken the boy to be trained by a sect of spirit warriors to help hone his powers for the fight he would face. But that had been half a year ago, and no one had seen Justin or Ahlund since.

That said, there had been rumored sightings of the ethoul, the most recent of which stated that he had been captured and imprisoned by an Aznochti warlord. Hook thought it sounded rather unlikely. Apparently, Leah thought differently.

"And to top it all off, she sneaks away *alone!*" Zechariah said. "This is a disaster."

"Come now," said Olorus. "It's not all that bad."

Despite his growing ire, Zechariah managed to lower his voice before he spoke again so as not to be overheard by any passersby in the camp. "Our high commander has abandoned us. Our route forward is unclear. Sif just returned to camp, along with Tel, Borris, and Pool, to report that Adonica disobeyed Gunnar's direct orders and took a squad of soldiers into the city to try to find Lycon and his missing company— and then Gunnar followed after her! And meanwhile, though you may not realize it, entire sections of this Army of Light are in turmoil. Just the other night, blood was shed between a Raeqlu infantry regiment and some of Gunnar's people."

"A scuffle or two among soldiers deep in their cups is nothing new," Olorus said with a shrug. "The Mythaeans and the Raeqlu are always at each others' throats, anyway."

"Yes, so commonplace it almost isn't worth mentioning," agreed Zechariah in an overly patronizing tone. "Or it would be, if not for the details. If any one of you had stepped away from your *own* ambitions long enough to investigate the matter more closely, you might have realized that the Raeqlu involved in the fracas are now *missing*."

Up until now, Hook had taken Zechariah's complaints as little more than so much hot air. But this got his attention. He straightened up and signed, *"Missing?"*

"Gone," said Zechariah. "A few eyewitnesses claim they loaded up in the night and marched out of camp without a word. Not one of them has been seen since."

"Deserters?" said Olorus.

"Or defectors," suggested Megara.

"Hmm," said Olorus. "I somehow doubt that. Who would march all this way, go through so much fighting, just to then join up with Avagad and his demons?"

"It is possible that there are forces at work that influenced their decision," said Zechariah. "Moving parts that we are unaware of. In any case, *none* of you, the so-called leaders in charge of this army, knew about it, so wrapped up are you in your own affairs. Our ranks are thinning, and now Leah is gone. Have you three any notion of what will become of this army if she does not return?"

"I am sure she will return," signed Megara.

"Where did they say this fortress was supposed to be?" asked Hook.

Zechariah gave him a look as if he wasn't sure he wanted to tell him. Then he sighed and answered, "To the northwest, on a high-altitude plateau. Between the summits of three tall crags."

"Not a very likely place for a *fortress*," said Olorus.

"Prior to the demon invasion," said Zechariah, "it was not uncommon for Aznochti nobles in this region to have summer estates in the higher altitudes, with enough fortifications and infrastructure to serve as a secondary place of rule in the event of a disaster. The roads leading to such places were winding and treacherous, with some dead-end paths constructed as decoys and others guarded and trapped to discourage enemies from searching for them."

"A good place to hide from demons," signed Megara.

"For a time," said Zechariah. "If there is such a place, it must be well hidden and well defended to have survived this long." He sighed. "I warned Leah. I tried to tell her. It's got to be a trap. That's the only explanation. A trap laid for *her*."

"A trap for Leah?" Olorus said. "We haven't encountered any of Avagad's forces since Darsida. They do not even know we are in Erum. How, then, could this be a trap laid for her?"

"Do not be so certain our presence in this region has gone unnoticed. Leah has made a reputation for herself as a bleeding heart. A rumor about Justin in trouble is exactly the sort of bait Avagad would use to lure her into making a mistake."

Hook had to concede that they might have reached eastern Erum months ago if not for Leah's decisions to help local populations. She had saved the lives of many people who may not have survived long enough to be freed when—and if—the Army of Light defeated the demons. But if word of Leah's compassion had reached Avagad, perhaps he would use it to his advantage.

Her sympathy for those in need also had the unintended effect of adding to the Army of Light's numbers. They had numbered in the tens of thousands upon their departure from Athacea six months ago. They were now almost one hundred thousand strong.

And not all those people were soldiers. Many were civilians. What had once been an army was now more like a self-contained, self-governing, mobile nation. There were families. Young children made orphans by the war. Sick people. Elderly. Pregnant mothers. Nursing infants. Even on the warpath, even in the midst of the deepest darkness, life went on.

"But what if it is not a trap or a rumor?" signed Megara. *"What if it is true? I have never seen this angel. I have only heard stories about what he can do. Is one person really powerful enough to make a difference in our war?"*

"The answer to your question is yes," answered Hook. *"But that is not why Leah would go looking for Justin. He is more than that. He is a friend."*

"Aye," agreed Olorus. "Even if he couldn't make a difference in our war, Leah wouldn't abandon him to imprisonment and suffering, no more than she would any of us."

Megara rubbed her chin. *"So, what do we do?"*

"Today must proceed as planned," said Zechariah. "Every moment we tarry, we put ourselves at increased risk. The army must continue on its march and reach its intended milestone, with or without its commander."

Zechariah paused and looked at Hook, Olorus, and Megara.

"I suppose," he said, somewhat disgusted, "the three of you want to go look for her."

"As I said," said Olorus, "she wouldn't abandon any of us if we were in trouble."

"I believe in her," signed Megara, *"but she still might need our help."*

"So might Justin," added Hook.

"I don't suppose I could convince you to delegate this task?" said Zechariah. "To send soldiers? To send scouts? To send *anyone* other than yourselves?"

"No, I do not suppose you could," signed Hook.

Zechariah shook his head in exasperation. "If you leave, do you know who is left to command this army?"

Megara shrugged and signed, *"Itz?"*

Itzacoatl, better known simply as Itz, was a companion who had been with Leah since Cymorikka. Itz was a kindly old fellow and an indispensable member of Leah's forces, but he was not exactly leadership material. He was a native of this region, an Ecbatan, with strong aurym abilities in the a'thri'ik stone. He was also one of the oldest men Hook had ever seen—present company excluded—quite hard of hearing, and woefully short-sighted.

"The honor will fall to you, of course, you old billygoat!" Olorus said cheerfully, gesturing toward Zechariah. "And don't tell me part of you hasn't secretly wanted it that way from the start!"

"I am supposed to be an *advisor*," grumbled Zechariah. "What good is an advisor whose advice is never followed? Go on then, all of you. Get out of here."

As Zechariah marched off to oversee the army's preparations, Hook turned to find Olorus and Megara both watching him expectantly.

He would never get used to people looking at him like that. As a leader. Especially when one of those people, Olorus Antony, was his former commanding officer.

"Let's gather our things," he signed. *"We can ride within the hour."*

CHAPTER 11

Stupid, thought Gunnar. *Stupid, stupid, stupid.*

Surely, that was the only word for it. For no one but Admiral Gunnar Erix Nimbus would have been stupid enough to follow

Adonica on her fool's errand into the abandoned vertical city just moments after telling everyone else not to. No one but him would have been stupid enough to disobey *his own* orders.

There had been chances to turn back. First, at the city. He could have left then, having at least soothed his conscience with the fact that he had at least attempted to make Adonica reconsider. Instead, he kept following her.

Several streets later, he still could have turned back just before they took the first set of switch-backing stairs upward to the second level of the city. He could have left, gone back to camp, and told everyone there that he'd done everything he could, but there had been no talking this soldier out of her mission.

But now, several hours had passed, and not only had he followed Adonica and her group all the way up to the third level of the city, but they had taken so many twists and turns that he already couldn't remember the way back. Now, he couldn't leave even if he *wanted* to try to do so, alone and without any backup—which he didn't.

Sometimes, I think you do these things to yourself on purpose, said that nagging, annoying, insufferably accurate part of himself.

And why would I do that? he thought.

You know why. Because you hate yourself, and you know you deserve everything coming to you.

Would you shut the hell up? he shot back.

Would you? it replied.

Nah, I guess I wouldn't, he had to admit.

As unnerving as it had been to look up at the towering, mist-shrouded vertical city and see it sitting empty, being inside it was far worse. Somehow, this place seemed both more advanced and far more ancient than any human population center that Gunnar had ever encountered before. The architecture was an odd mixture of a variety of styles, an indication that this place had been built, defended, conquered, rebuilt, defended, and re-conquered over the course of many cycles throughout centuries, if not millennia. There were places where porticos appeared to have been carved out of the very stone of the cliff. There were domes and columns. These sorts of elements, Gunnar was familiar with. But most of the city was built in a fashion that he had never, in all his travels, witnessed before: a jagged, terribly abrasive style of steeples and spikes, towers rising like skyward-pointed spears, and sharp, steeply pitched rooftops.

Some of these sharply pointed buildings were larger than common sense told Gunnar should have been possible and were supported not only by wide foundations on the ground but by jagged flying buttresses set upon arches that hung outside of the buildings for support, often seeming to crisscross with other buttresses sticking out from other, adjoining buildings. The result was an intermeshed, scaffold-like, hanging maze of stone.

The architects had carved elaborate designs and decorations into these features, from animal effigies to larger-than-life statues of humans to entire stone trees, but *color* did not seem to have been of equal priority. The prevailing theme was gray upon dark gray upon darker gray. For hundreds of feet, this spine-ridden, multi-leveled city extended upward, so high that even on the third level, Gunnar could still not see its top through the lingering mists.

Like most urban places that Gunnar had experienced in his lifetime, seeing it from the outside led one to certain assumptions about navigating its interior that quickly proved false once you were within it. Landmarks that were prominent from the outside weren't always easy to see when you were down at street level. The jagged building tops and flying buttresses impeded one's sight so much that Gunnar's vision was, at all times, limited to his immediate surroundings. He may as well have been a child in a cornfield.

On the plus side, it was usually obvious which way was forward. They were headed *up*. And so, as long as they could see the place where the vertical city rose before them like a great wave on the sea, they knew which direction to go.

Gunnar found it dizzyingly disorienting. *Cities* were not *supposed* to rise up before you like that.

Adonica led the way, and Gunnar and the five soldiers followed. It was unnerving to be in the midst of such an impressive city and yet to find it so devoid of life. For some reason, the doors of every building they passed were raised four or five feet above street level, meaning that one had to climb a stoop several steps high to reach a building's first floor. And there were so many of them. So many doors for someone, or something, to be hiding behind.

Gunnar had always heard Erum referred to as the heart of civilization. The Ecbatan empire, the neighboring Aznochtis, and the Thubestine Hegemony in the south were some of the oldest and noblest societies in the Oikoumene. These storied cultures were said to make the Mythaeans, the Athaceans, and the other peoples of the West look backward and barbaric by comparison. But traveling through Erum felt like they were wandering through a world that had been laid to waste by an apocalyptic event. Perhaps because that was precisely what had happened.

And the same fate awaits our lands in the west, thought Gunnar. *Unless we can stop it.*

Back on the first level of the city, things had looked relatively normal. In some places, they'd found doors hanging open and people's belongings strewn across the street. The evidence pointed to a mad rush to escape, but there were no real signs of violence.

That changed when they reached the second level of the city. There, they continued to see doors hanging open. But some of those doors hung from their hinges. Personal belongings were still strewn across the streets, but they were sometimes accompanied by dark stains on the cobblestones. Windows were broken in from the outside.

And everywhere, Gunnar saw sets of parallel scratches gouged on doorframes and window shutters: the claw marks of coblyns.

Coblyns, low demons, only stood about as tall as a human child. But what they lacked in size, they made up for in numbers, often traveling in herds of a hundred or more. In the wild, they were animalistic and unruly, just as likely to attack each other as to attack their prey—only a small step above mindless carnivores. But they fought like disciplined soldiers when under the command of a higher form of demon to give them orders.

Coblyns were not difficult to kill. They disliked the sun. And while they did not appear to require rest or water, they did require sustenance, which they gained exclusively from the still-living entrails of other life forms—usually animals, sometimes one another, and, when they could get them, humans.

Presently, Adonica started down a street with several large arches spanning it, one of which appeared to have once been a bridge linking two buildings on opposite sides of the street but had been broken halfway across, leaving a pile of rubble in the center of the road.

Partway down this street, Adonica stopped, reconsidered, then turned to head in a different direction on light feet. The decision felt like it had been made almost arbitrarily. For a moment, Gunnar managed to let this go. But in the end, he simply couldn't keep his mouth shut, which was often his biggest problem.

"Adonica, at the risk of being the one to ask the most obvious question," said Gunnar, "and, believe me, I hate that you are making me that person—do you have some sort of *plan* for finding Lycon in this place? Because if your strategy is to look down every single thoroughfare, it's going to take us the better part of a century."

"Lycon was my commanding officer in Hartla for three years," said Adonica. "One advantage of his penchant for doing *everything* by the book is that I know the protocol he will follow in any given situation. Including what he would do if he found himself in unknown territory, in an urban setting, where there is a high probability of an enemy presence. And fortunately, although I don't always hold the rulebook in high regard, I do know it. As long as we're following standard Hartlan operating procedures, we're following the same path he would have taken. All we have to do is stick to protocol when a variable is introduced." She gestured back down the street toward the fallen archway. "When it comes to damaged structures, for example, the rule is to avoid them. So we swing wide around it, proceed to the nearest safe route, and skip over the obstacle in question."

"You're even starting to sound like him," said Gunnar.

"Three years," Adonica repeated, sounding a bit nauseated.

"Avoiding damaged structures may not be easy in this place," said one of the soldiers. His name was Ptolemec. Like Adonica and Lycon, he hailed from Hartla. And although his face was hidden behind a great helm that matched Adonica's, it wasn't difficult to identify him; he carried a massive battle hammer with a head like a flat mallet on one side and a pickaxe-like spike on the other. "There appear to be more signs of battle up here than there were below."

"I noticed that," said Adonica grimly. "Whatever happened to this city, it didn't begin down at ground level. Perhaps it came from up top and worked its way down."

"Makes you wonder what we're walking into," said Berex, a Mythaean soldier, also in full a'thri'ik armor, who carried a small buckler-style shield and a boarding ax like the kind used by marines on Mythaean galleys.

"This seems as good a time as any," said Gunnar, "to remind you all that it wasn't for no reason that I recommended we *not* enter this place."

Neither Adonica nor any of her five followers offered a reply to that triple-negative statement, although one of them looked Gunnar's way. It was Estoq. As luck would have it, she was one of the five soldiers who had volunteered to join Adonica.

The personal history between Estoq and Gunnar dated back to long before the demon war, but so far, they had both been content not to bring it up, playing a game where they pretended not to know one another any better than the next man or woman. Gunnar wasn't quite sure *why* they were playing this game, but a precedent had been set.

Adonica's "protocol" notwithstanding, navigating this place was going to take ages. This wasn't a mission for an afternoon. They could be here for days.

There were mechanized lifts designed for traversal between the city levels, operated by winch and pulley systems, but Adonica and her team had opted to use the stairs. To say nothing of the potential instability of the lifts if they had been damaged, utilizing them would also be the quickest way to reveal their presence to any watching eyes.

And based on what they had seen so far here on the third level, Gunnar wondered just what sort of eyes might be watching them.

Here, the signs were worse than they had been on the first and second levels. There were fallen structures like that bridge. There were great, rending cracks in the sides of buildings as if weapons larger than any human could hold had been taken to the walls. And there were scorch-marked craters in the street.

Cythraul, thought Gunnar, suppressing a shiver.

Cythraul, high demons, stood between ten and twelve feet tall. Unlike the much smaller, more animalistic coblyns, they were deviously intelligent monsters, almost impossibly strong, and capable of daemyn powers that could level buildings.

Cythraul were indifferent to almost all environmental factors. They did not sleep and seemed to require no sustenance. They were known to occasionally consume their enemies, but this was done in a ritualistic fashion; it did not seem to serve any purpose except as a means of terrorizing their victims. Or perhaps they gained some sort of twisted pleasure from the process.

What made cythraul even more dangerous was that they either possessed some sort of hive mind or were capable of instantaneous, long-distance communication, for what one cythraul knew, *every* cythraul knew.

Suddenly, Estoq grabbed Adonica by the arm, stopping her in mid-stride. Like Adonica, Estoq wore a great helm that covered her face, but it was easy to tell her apart from the rest by the crossbow she carried and the quiver of bolts strapped to her back.

"Captain Lor," said Estoq, in the buttery accent distinctive of eastern Athacea. "I see something. Up there."

Estoq pointed toward the rooftops.

Following her gesture, Gunnar spotted the unmistakable silhouette of a coblyn. It was crouched upon the heights of a parapet on a building not thirty feet from their current location. And it appeared to be looking straight down at them.

CHAPTER 12

The coblyn sat motionless on the heights. Gunnar, Adonica, and the other soldiers froze in place, as motionless as their watcher, staring up at the coblyn's grotesque form.

Or, at least, Gunnar thought it was a coblyn. There was, after all, a third type of demon that was neither coblyn nor cythraul.

Gunnar moved his hand toward his weapon at his belt. Not his cutlass, but a much stronger weapon.

During the Army of Light's escapade through the wilderness of Darsida, they discovered a type of fruit that didn't grow in the west. It was like a melon but much smaller. A culinary revelation, it was not; the fleshy fruit inside tasted like wet stockings and came in such meager portions that it was hardly worth the trouble of cutting through the hard outer rind to get to it. But when the fruit was bored into with a hand drill, its less-than-appetizing contents emptied out and discarded, and its woody rind dried in the sun, the result was an excellent, sturdy spherical container about the size of a child's toy ball.

The sight of soldiers using these dried rinds as highly waterproof carrying cases had given Gunnar an idea. He had taken to collecting the rinds and experimenting with them.

All it took was a handful of his seeds of choice inserted into the rind and a bit of wax to stop up the hole, and he had himself a container of seeds that he could easily and accurately throw wherever he liked. Gunnar's old fishing buddies, Borris and Pool, had begun affectionately referring to his new practice of throwing balls of seeds as "lobbing." And that was how the hollowed-out rinds filled with seeds had gotten the label of "lobber-balls." It was, in Gunnar's opinion, an altogether unsatisfactory name. Terrible, even. But wasn't that always the way it went with nicknames? The one that stuck was never the one you wanted it to be. It was his own fault for not coming up with something better, but he had never been much of a creative type, to his constant detriment.

As Gunnar continued to study the demonic form looking down at their group, he suddenly recognized it for what it really was. His eye scanned the tops of the buildings to either side, where he spotted several more of them.

With a grin, Gunnar stooped to the street and picked up a small fragment of loose cobblestone. He tested its weight in his hand, then hauled back and chucked it up at the coblyn.

Gunnar heard gasps from the others around him as his projectile whizzed through the air. It struck the coblyn in the nose with a *clack* and bounced off.

"What a shot!" said Gunnar.

The coblyn didn't move. None of them did.

Estoq had drawn her crossbow and was frozen in place, with one hand reaching to draw a bolt from her quiver. "What are you doing?" she demanded.

"It's good practice," said Gunnar, patting the improvised bandolier of lobber-balls he wore outside of his armor, beneath his cloak. He looked around at his stunned allies, then shrugged and said, "It's just a gargoyle."

"A what?" said Berex. His grip on his boarding axe was so tight that the knuckles under his glove must have been white.

"A statue," said Gunnar. "For decoration."

Ptolemec propped his battle hammer up on his shoulder and tilted his helmed head curiously to the side. "Why would anyone want to decorate their buildings with something so hideous?"

"Dunno," said Gunnar. "But they won't hurt you. Unless one falls on you."

"All right," said Adonica, letting out a deep breath. "Let's keep moving."

Even after Adonica and the rest resumed their march, Estoq remained in place for a moment longer, staring up at the coblyn statues as if she wasn't quite convinced. She did not move until the final member of their group, Ucydotus, walked up to her.

Ucydotus wasn't a big man. And although he surely could have had a powerful a'thri'ik shield if he'd wanted one, he instead carried a traditional Enden shield, made famous by the tortoiseshell-like phalanxes utilized in battle by Endenholm's infantry.

Ucydotus placed a gentle, reassuring hand on Estoq's shoulder. The familiarity of the gesture caused Gunnar to blink in surprise.

Estoq looked at Ucydotus. The man's great helm bobbed with an encouraging nod, and in response, Estoq's shoulders seemed to relax a bit. The two of them carried on together, marching side by side.

Estoq threw a casual-looking glance toward Gunnar, and Gunnar made a show of pretending not to notice. It was the closest they had come so far to acknowledging one another—or their past.

Adonica hadn't gone more than a few more steps down the street when she came to an abrupt halt. The others took the hint and came up short as well. After a moment, she removed her helmet and craned her neck.

The meaning was clear. She had heard something.

Silently, Adonica gestured toward the nearest building, a three-story house. Like every building in this city, it too had its front entryway raised four to five feet above street level, but the door had been torn from its hinges and lay broken in half beside the steps of the stoop.

Gunnar didn't know what Adonica thought she'd heard, but he knew better than to second-guess her.

It's probably too much to hope that it's Lycon that she's hearing, thought Gunnar.

Yes, it probably is, his other inner voice agreed.

All seven of them ascended the steps of the stoop and tiptoed in through the doorframe, with Gunnar and Adonica being the last to enter.

The building's entryway opened up to a sort of sitting room or parlor. The furniture within it had been toppled and ripped apart. Nearby, a bookcase had been leaned against one of the windows to block it. As he entered the parlor, Gunnar almost stepped on a flat iron bar that would have been thrown across the door to lock it from the inside. A lot of good it had done the occupants; the bar was broken off, snapped right out of the wall.

A sudden noise came from the street outside. Adonica gestured deeper into the domicile, and everyone hurried to find cover behind the wreckage strewn about the parlor.

Gunnar, crouching behind an overturned armoire, peeked out to watch the entryway. From his position, he could see out the door, down the stoop, to street level outside. The sound was growing louder. Loud enough that he soon recognized it for what it was—the clomping and shuffling of feet, getting closer by the second.

Gunnar's pulse quickened as a dark figure suddenly passed by the bottom of the stoop outside, trailing rags of shredded clothing.

A few seconds went by, and another figure came up the street, moving more slowly this time, scanning its surroundings as it walked. It was close enough that Gunnar could see its blackened skin—if you could even rightly call the stuff that covered its body *skin* at all. It was not flesh, in the traditional sense, more like non-flesh.

This creature wasn't child-sized. Nor was it a giant. It was about five and a half feet tall. And it was wearing, of all things, a flowery cotton dress.

Not coblyns, Gunnar realized. *Not cythraul, either. Cythwraiths. The turned.*

Cythwraiths were the third type of demon. They did not mind the sunlight. They did not eat or drink. But they *did* require rest. And, unique to all other types of demons, their origins were understood all too well.

A cythwraith was born by the transforming touch of a cythraul: a daemyn ability that could transform living flesh into the stuff of demons. Every cythwraith had once been a human, turned by a cythraul's demonic touch.

In this case, some poor woman, while she'd been wearing her nicest dress.

Cythwraiths seemed to possess the same hive-mind as cythraul. If one spotted you, every other cythwraith and all cythraul instantly knew your location, making it possible for individuals for miles in every direction to converge on you at once.

Gunnar wasn't sure how many demons might be in this city, but if even one cythwraith spotted them, the rest would instantly know they were here. They couldn't even kill one from stealth, as an untimely end would just as effectively give them away.

The cythwraith in the cotton dress had moved on, but Gunnar heard more shuffling and clomping of feet. The sound was growing in volume. But it was not getting louder due to the proximity; it was the quantity.

Another dark figure walked by, and another, and another, and another.

Gunnar pulled a pouch of seeds from his belt. He called on aurym and set his spirit power dancing within the godsbreath aurstone set in the socket where his left eye had once been.

Not far from his position, Adonica had her sword drawn. Estoq's crossbow was propped against the top of a high-backed upholstered chair, aimed at the doorway. Ucydotus had his Enden spear at the ready. And the others were similarly poised.

Gunnar had been hoping that he was hearing the footfalls of Lycon and his team. Now, he feared that he was. Morbidly, he tried to study the clothing and gear worn by the passersby to see if any of it looked familiar.

How many cythwraiths walked past the door, Gunnar didn't know. They kept on passing for what felt like minutes. And now, coblyns were walking by, too—coblyns that were most certainly *not* gargoyles. A whole herd of them. Fifty, at least. Maybe a hundred.

And finally, one of the coblyns did precisely what Gunnar had been hoping these inhuman passersby would not do.

It stopped, sniffed the air, turned, and climbed the steps of the stoop toward the open doorway like a dog that had scented a scrap.

CHAPTER 13

Leah wasn't certain how long she and her fellow prisoner spoke. But finally, he came to the part Leah had been waiting for.

"After the disaster at Esthean, we escaped to another small island," said Kallorn. "There, we paid our final farewells to Ahlund and the others whom we had lost. In the middle of the night, Justin used his ethoul powers to disappear. That was the last we saw of him."

Leah wiped fresh tears from her cheeks. "All this time," she said, sniffing, "I was worried about Justin. It almost never occurred to me to be concerned for Ahlund. He was my bodyguard for a time, and he always seemed so. . . ." She struggled to find the right word.

"Invincible?" said Kallorn.

Leah nodded.

"He was excommunicated from our order for transgressions against the Ru'Onorath ways," said Kallorn. "But surely, he died a true Guardian of the Oikoumene."

Died, thought Leah. Using the actual word made it seem so brutally final.

She couldn't believe what she was hearing—didn't *want* to believe it. Ahlund Sims, her friend, protector, and mentor, was dead. Avagad had killed him personally.

A few moments later, Kallorn continued.

"Cyaxares and I, plus the remaining Guardians, numbered fewer than forty in total," he said. "We remained another day on that island, clinging to the hope that Justin would return. But the demons knew some of us had escaped. They were surely searching the surrounding waters and were destined to find us in short order if we remained there. In the end, we had no choice but to leave. We gathered together a small cache of supplies and left them in a boat for Justin in case he returned, and we left.

"It wasn't until a week later that we sensed a ripple of aurym power, possibly Justin's return. We attempted to go back to that island to search for him, but we were waylaid by demon ships, forcing us to flee and sail north around the tip of Ythia. By then, Cyaxares was no longer content to remain in hiding. The fall of Esthean had driven all thoughts of isolationism from her mind. There is some connection between her and Avagad, something from a past life. I think part of her still hopes he could be made to see reason if only she could speak to him."

"So, she thinks Avagad still lives?" said Leah. "After your description of what Ahlund did to him with the last of his strength, I was hoping perhaps he was killed."

Kallorn pulled at his unkempt yellow beard, straightening it to a point. "She seems convinced that he yet lives. But whether that is a guess based on intuition or some other knowledge I am not privy to, I cannot say. I am just a soldier."

Leah felt a smirk tug at the side of her mouth. It was the sort of thing Ahlund might have said, once upon a time. And if this man *was* anything like Ahlund, she had a feeling he was a lot more than just a soldier.

Would we even know if Avagad was already dead? wondered Leah. The possibility had never occurred to her.

The name she had given her mobile fighting force, the Army of Light, had taken on almost poetic connotations. Figuratively, they fought the darkness. But there were times when it felt like they were grappling with literal shadows. How could you win that sort of fight?

The ultimate goal was to push east, reach Avagad's seat of power, and defeat the enemy at its source. As far as Leah knew, their passage over the Altirin Sea had gone undetected, and they had scuttled the ships to hide the evidence. They had encountered no demons in Erum thus far, either. If they managed to stay hidden long enough, Avagad and his forces might not even learn of the Holy Army's presence on this continent until they were right at his doorstep. The problem was that Leah, for all her studying of maps, had only a vague notion of *where* in Erum the demon's seat of power was.

Rohghost, thought Leah. *The Warlord said that was the name of Avagad's capital city in the east.*

It was the first true lead she had stumbled across regarding where they might find the head they intended to cut off.

"I already told you the rest of the story of how I got here," said Kallorn. "Injured in a demon attack, I was separated from the rest of the Ru'Onorath and brought here, and my search for Justin was rewarded with imprisonment. I am less clear on how you, My Lady, came to be imprisoned with me. I daresay that if you truly command an army, it might have been prudent to bring a few of them with you."

It was true that outwardly, Leah's plan seemed the height of foolishness. She had come alone. She had left in the night and told no one where she was going or what she intended to do. She hadn't told even her most trusted allies. Not Megara, Hook, Olorus, or Gunnar, her closest friends among the Army of Light. And certainly not Zechariah. Well, unless you counted the note she'd left him.

For one thing, none of her friends would have wanted her to come here alone. But, for another, she couldn't have any of them risking their lives on an errand that might prove fruitless.

"Maybe it *was* a mistake to come here," said Leah. "My father always said I needed to be less impulsive. But he was an impulsive man if ever there was one, so I must come by it naturally. . . ."

But Leah trailed off. On the other side of the bars, Kallorn's body language had changed. He was suddenly sitting much straighter than before, and he appeared to be staring into the distance as if trying to see through the very walls.

"Sir Rhodos?" she said. "Is something wrong?"

"Do you feel that?" Kallorn asked, without breaking eye contact with whatever he seemed to be focused on.

"Feel what?" asked Leah.

Kallorn looked at her with a stern smile. "You are distracted," he said. "Your thoughts are pulled in too many directions. Observe the thoughts but reject the emotions. Focus on your mind, body, and spirit. Listen to the aurym around you. Feel its ripples."

Leah's initial reaction to hearing these instructions was annoyance. She wondered where that came from. Why should she be annoyed at someone who was trying to help her?

She closed her eyes and did her best to cleanse herself of the anxieties, thoughts, and emotions buzzing about in her head. Her hands were still shackled tightly behind her back, but she did her best to ignore the discomfort.

Her thoughts were her own. But the associated emotions were not a part of her; they were uninvited guests, robbing her of peace. She was not her emotions. She was only her mind, her body, and her spirit—

Leah's eyes shot open.

"I feel it," she said.

There had been many times over the past years when she'd *thought* she had felt it. Many times when she'd *hoped* she would feel it. She had even dreamed of it. But now that she did feel it, really and truly, there could be no doubt.

It was a difficult sensation to describe. But once you felt the aurym presence of an individual, there was no mistaking it. Especially that of someone you cared for.

When Leah turned to look at Kallorn, there was a light in his eyes that hadn't been there before. And beneath the scraggles of yellow facial hair, he smiled.

"We were right," said Kallorn.

"Justin is here," said Leah.

No sooner had Leah said the words than she took action: She pulled her hands apart, and the chains binding her shackles snapped.

At the sight of the broken chains dangling from Leah's wrists, severed as if they were no stronger than strands of thread in the hands of a seamstress, Kallorn's smile was replaced by a look of slack-jawed shock.

"Let's go find him," said Leah.

Then she reached out, grabbed two of the iron bars that separated their cells, and ripped them free from the stone with her bare hands.

CHAPTER 14

For a moment, Kallorn only stared at the broken iron bars in Leah's hands. She laid them carefully on the ground beside her, trying her best to make no more sound than was necessary. Then she stepped through the gap and into Kallorn's cell.

Kallorn sat still, staring at her.

"That," he said, "is highly unusual."

"Tell me about it," said Leah.

Wordlessly, she called on aurym and peeled the cuffs off her wrists. The metal squealed in protest as she ripped it apart. She let the pieces fall to the floor in front of her.

"I thought you were an aurym healer," Kallorn said, still not moving from the floor.

"I am," said Leah. "And they took my healer's stone when I entered this place. But that's not my only ability, nor my only aurstone."

Back in Athacea, Zechariah had sent Hook, Gunnar, and Adonica on a quest to retrieve an ancient artifact: the crown of a long-dead Ellenean king with sixteen aurstones set in its antlered headpiece. The idea had been to use those stones to test Leah's people, to see if any of the fighters loyal to her had any latent, unrealized spiritual gifts that could be used in combat against the demons.

Aurstones were a precious commodity. And, under ordinary circumstances, it was unlikely that a person would have the occasion to sit down and test their abilities with many different stones. As a result, aurym powers were normally quite rare. But the gambit with the crown had paid off. By recovering those stones and allowing so many people the chance to put their aurym to the test, hundreds of new spirit warriors had been discovered among the ranks of the Army of Light. And through the talents of the army's most skilled jewelers and metalworkers, the sixteen stones had been cut and distributed to those who could put them to use.

There were those who could manifest their powers in the form of fire, like Ahlund. There were those who could grow plants, like Gunnar. There were healers like Leah and Lycon. Still others could harness the power of sunlight, like Megara. And there were other aurym powers that Leah hadn't even been aware of until she'd seen them with her own eyes.

But no one, not a single soul, had been able to use the stone known as the hydstone.

The hydstone gave its wielder the strength of ten men, speed twice that of a steed at full gallop, and, when the power was focused carefully on individual muscle groups, bodily defenses as effective as chainmail armor. A man called Innocen had once used a hydstone to infiltrate

Leah's forces at Cervice and single-handedly kill many good people, nearly kidnapping Leah in a bid to lure Justin to him.

There had been a hydstone in the Ancient Ellenean crown. But out of the entire Army of Light, not one person had been able to use it.

Except for Leah Anavion.

Leah turned to Kallorn. "You're a Guardian like Ahlund. You must have aurym abilities."

"They took my sword when they captured me," said Kallorn. "We Ru'Onorath forge our aurstones into our blades. It is a tradition meant to signify that our power is only as good as our ability to hold on to it, and anyone who can relieve us of our weapons is worthy of defeating us."

Leah scratched absentmindedly at the place in her shoulder where she had used her skills as a battlefield healer to surgically implant her hydstone into her own shoulder, in the hollow of her collarbone.

"I guess that's one way to do things," she said.

Leah walked to Kallorn's cell door, put one hand on the lock, and squeezed, crushing the metal beneath her fingers. The door swung open with no resistance. She tossed the broken lock to the floor and brushed off her hands.

"I don't know how Justin got himself into this mess," said Leah, "but I'm going to find him."

Kallorn seemed to consider this. Then, he steadied himself and rose up from the floor. It was a labor for him to stand. Once he was up, he stretched his neck back and forth to a chorus of loud pops and cracks. He shook his arms to clear the dirt from his skillfully woven cloak, like a bird ruffling its feathers. Then he grabbed one of the iron bars Leah had ripped out of the ground, held it like a quarterstaff, and made a polite, open-handed gesture toward the broken door.

"I shall follow your lead, Princess Anavion," he said. "Or should I call you Queen?"

"These days, I'm better known as Commander, but I prefer Leah," said Leah, stepping out of the cell and looking around at the dungeon. "The Warlord said he's here. He must be deeper in these dungeons."

"There is a hallway at the rear of this chamber," said Kallorn, stepping out to join her. "It leads to a vast labyrinth. I managed to explore part of it before I was caught. The architecture down there is . . . odd."

"Big? Almost as if it weren't built for humans?" said Leah. "Like an underground city for giants, with sculptures made of a'thri'ik?"

Kallorn looked at her.

Leah shrugged. "Lucky guess."

She paused to rip another iron bar from the cell wall. Then she crossed the dungeon to reach the door through which Nefari the Warlord had previously exited. She braced the end of the iron bar against the keyhole, called on aurym, and sent a burst of power through the hydstone in her shoulder and into the muscles of her arm.

There was a screech and a spark as she shoved the iron bar through the door, causing the keyhole and the lock to become bent and misshapen around it. She pushed it in until she was certain the bar extended all the way through the door. Then she bent the bar sideways and pushed the opposite end into the very wall with a puff of dust and cracked stone shards.

Of the several titles that Leah had shared with the Warlord, there was one she had left out. One that she had neither inherited nor claimed for herself. It was a name the people of the Army of Light had taken to calling her not because of who she was but because of what they had seen her do. Leah Demonsbane.

"I'm not sure if you're trying to prevent us from being followed," said Kallorn, gesturing to her makeshift barricade, "or ensuring that no one we find down here can escape your wrath."

"Followed," said Leah. "Revenge against the Warlord and her people is not what I have in mind. I only want to free Justin. And I've never hurt anyone who gave me the option not to."

Now that he was free, Kallorn seemed invigorated. "You must forgive me if I am not so eager to extend grace to these people." He squeezed his hands tightly around the bar of his cell. What had once been his containment was now his weapon.

"Let's go," said Leah. And they began to move.

CHAPTER 15

"JUSTIN."

Despite the fact that the word issued forth from his own mouth, the sound of that voice never failed to make his skin crawl. Or, it might have, anyway, if Innocen still had his skin.

Innocen felt his own body stand. Not of his accord; he had no control over it and hadn't for quite some time. His body had been beyond his control since the transforming touch of a cythraul had changed him, agonizingly sizzling his human flesh to black demon-chitin, scalding his eyes in their sockets, leaving behind a form of visionless sight that came from the spiritual clairvoyance of sensing aurym and daemyn.

His body was no longer his own. But the soul of the man was still trapped deep within, shackled in the depths, kept in a state of eternal agony and torment. And all the while, Innocen could only watch as the Nameless One, the god-king of the demons, drove the cythwraith body that had once been his.

In his previous life, Innocen had followed the tenets of the Cult of the Hyd, living as a solitary hunter, wielding no weapons except for his bare hands, stalking victims, and feasting on their living human entrails like a coblyn to gain their power. In their final moments, his prey would sometimes curse him, accuse him of being a villain. A beast. A monster. . . .

A demon, thought Innocen.

What devastating irony.

The demon-body stood. Innocen, whose internal screams never ended, who had never for a moment since his transformation been free from the endless pain of the torture of the Nameless One, saw the world around him in the light and dark of aurym and daemyn, with a gray void between. By now, he had learned how to identify certain things. The light of aurym was present in trees and animals, in all forms of life. In humans, its brightness was almost blinding. Was it any wonder the Nameless One and his demons wanted to destroy them? To douse their light fully?

The grayness in his vision signified empty air, dead stone, and lifeless soil. And the blackness was daemyn.

When Innocen was first turned, daemyn had only been visible to him in the silhouettes of demons and in the hearts of some humans, where seeds planted by the Nameless One, through careful manipulation, had taken root and germinated. But now, daemyn was everywhere. It hovered over the ground, floated like a vapor in the air, seeped from the stones. It was a sight both terrible and glorious.

"JUSTIN," the Nameless One said through Innocen's mouth again.

"Yes, Justin! I sense him, too!" Innocen tried to say.

But the words remained inside him, never reaching the mouth of the demon-body in which he remained a captive spectator. And Innocen had no way of knowing if his internalized words were even heard.

The entire time he had been trapped in this form, he had been trying to communicate with the one who had enslaved him, the master of daemyn, the Nameless One. But never once had he received an indication that his pleas were heard, much less gotten a response.

He had watched the Nameless One do dreadful things using his body. Watched him wring the aurym-life out of humans, crush it, tear it apart. But there was a weakness to this form.

Innocen's hydstone was still implanted in his transformed body, but it could not be used fully by the Nameless One, only partially. Why this was, Innocen did not know. But the strength and speed this body possessed were only a shadow of what they had been when he had wielded the power as a man.

"The ethoul!" Innocen cried out between his internal screams. "I know you *want him*! The powers of the Hyd can help! But not while I am trapped like this!"

The body started walking, making its way toward the source of the echoes of power it had felt. And again, a guttural, demonic voice, like the grinding of great wheels, erupted from Innocen's throat.

"JUSTIN," the voice said. "THE BOY HAS FINALLY RETURNED."

"Give me back *control*!" Innocen pleaded. "And I will bring the ethoul to you!"

But there was no reply. There was never any reply.

"*Answer me!*" Innocen screamed inside.

Innocen's body did not slow. He kept walking, moving through trees—hemlock trees, judging by their shape and size.

Innocen's mouth opened and said, "NOW, FALLEN ANGEL, YOU WILL FINALLY BECOME *MINE*."

PART III

HUNTING GIRL

CHAPTER 16

The coblyn was only a few steps away from the door when Gunnar undid the leather strap of the satchel hanging on his belt, withdrew a tiny seed, and tossed it at the doorway.

Gunnar called on aurym. He sent a tiny thread of power through his godsbreath stone, into the seed. It cracked open on the floor and, without taking root, began to grow. A thin vine slithered up the doorframe, like creeping ivy undergoing an entire season's worth of growth in a few seconds, and clung there.

The coblyn's lanky, black body inched forward, crawling up the stoop on all fours. It had no nose to speak of, just a pair of wide nostrils set on a flat face. The lipless mouth, with overlapping, overhanging incisors, parted with a quiet hiss. The nostrils flared all the wider with a sharp sniff, and for a moment, Gunnar could have sworn he saw an expression on its desiccated, corpse-like face: recognition.

With renewed interest, the coblyn crept inward through the doorway.

Gunnar flicked his finger. The vine sprung from its place on the door frame, expanding in size. Its woody end formed a javelin-like point that speared the coblyn's skull just above the right earhole and exited below its jaw.

A death cry would have alerted the entire horde behind it. But Gunnar's aim was true; the skewered brain stem made the coblyn go limp without a sound. Even that would be for naught if it made a racket by crashing to the floor, so, following another gesture from Gunnar's hand, the vine wrapped around the coblyn's neck like a noose and ascended, pulling the body up with it and pinning it to the ceiling of the parlor. There, Gunnar set the vine growing outward in several directions at once until it had formed a spider web pattern, with the coblyn's body suspended at the center.

It was while Gunnar was taking a second seed from his pouch and preparing to toss it just as he had the first, thus resetting his trap, that he felt it coming.

No, he thought. *Not now. No. . . .*

The world flipped sideways.

Gunnar couldn't move, couldn't think. He was frozen.

It was difficult to tell time during these episodes, but after a few seconds of his body standing there, frozen, he became vaguely aware that someone across the room was frantically whispering his name, trying to get his attention. He couldn't even turn his head in their direction, much less respond. He also had a similarly vague awareness that another coblyn from the street had crawled up the building's stoop. But there was nothing he could do.

Gunnar felt the terror seeping into him. There was an acrid smell like burning wood, and he had the sense that he had been here already, had gone through this very scenario before, perhaps in a dream. It was as if he were detached from the part of himself that could take intelligent action. His body was there, but he was not.

Within the limited scope of Gunnar's locked vision, he watched the second coblyn crawl through the doorway and into the room. He watched its slitted nostrils flare as it found their scent. Its head turned, and its tiny, fish-like eyes went wide as it spotted Gunnar standing in full view.

The coblyn opened its mouth, needle-like teeth parting in what Gunnar knew would be the screech of an alarm, a roar of insatiable hunger, or some combination of both.

A sharp *twang* erupted from behind Gunnar, and a crossbow bolt entered the coblyn's open mouth at the speed of a diving falcon. The only sound the creature was able to make was a muffled gagging noise before Adonica leaped forward, grabbed it, and pulled it the rest of the way into the room. She threw the spasming beast down and severed the head from its body with a chop of her sword.

From her place behind the upholstered chair across the room, Estoq hurriedly worked the crank of her crossbow to pull back the weapon's arms and load another bolt.

Elzirda, a spearwoman from Darsida and the fifth of the soldiers who had opted to follow Adonica, watched out the window.

"More coming!" Elzirda warned.

"Block that door!" Adonica whispered, wiping black blood from her blade.

Ptolemec, Berex, and Ucydotus, moving as quietly as they could, lifted the bookshelf from its place leaned against the window and stood it in front of the open doorway. It would have made for a rather second-rate barricade until Berex raised his small, hook-bladed boarding ax and called on aurym. The end of his axe produced a strange shimmer, and a skim of frost began to form along the edges of the bookcase.

As Berex concentrated his power, the frost expanded into a thick layer of ice. He continued the process, working his way around the entire bookcase until the doorway, wide open a few moments before, was not only blocked by the bookcase but tightly sealed, with ice blocking every gap.

Somewhere in the middle of all this, Gunnar's world went upright again. His faculties returned to him, and he was left standing there, blinking dumbly, like a sleepwalker who had suddenly come to his senses. The seed he'd intended to toss at the doorway was still pinched between his fingers.

Gunnar turned toward Adonica and found her staring at him.

"Admiral," she said seriously. "What was that?"

There was no judgment in her voice. It was purely professional. She wanted, and needed, to know. But Gunnar had no words.

Adonica stared blankly at him for a few more seconds, then turned away.

"Berex and Ptolemec," she said. "See if there are any more first-floor points of egress and do to them what you did to that one. Estoq, watch their backs. Ucydotus and Elzirda, upstairs. Find somewhere with a good view of the street. The sun's going down. It seems like we'll have to dig in here for the night."

Ordinarily, Gunnar would have taken a moment like this to make some sort of offhanded comment to lighten the tension. Maybe say something about the fine décor of this place and how you couldn't have asked for a nicer location to hunker down and kiss your arse goodbye while the jaws of death closed around you. But somehow, he just wasn't in the mood.

"You okay, Nimbus?" asked Adonica.

Again, it was her professional manner and lack of personal judgment that struck Gunnar.

"I don't know," he said.

CHAPTER 17

Whether it was his situational awareness, some sort of subconscious instinct, or simple blind luck, Hook reached out and pulled Olorus back behind the cover of the mossy rock just in time—only a split-second before the guard below stretched his neck and would have looked precisely in their direction.

Hook's hand pushed Olorus down behind the rock a bit harder than he meant to, and the older man gave out a small grunt as he went down on his behind next to Megara. Hook gave Olorus an apologetic pat on the shoulder. Olorus cleared his throat in slight annoyance but nodded his understanding.

Hook had peeled back a section of the blanket of moss growing on the stone that he, Olorus, and Megara were currently ducked behind. He used the peeled moss like a curtain, leaving a gap at the end so that he had a narrow field of view along the side of the rock, down to the fortress below.

The sun had set about an hour before, but there was still enough light for Hook to see the guard at the fortress finish his stretch, giving no indication of having seen anything, and go back to looking the other way.

Carefully, Hook moved back from the curtain of moss and turned to face Megara and Olorus. After questioning the soldiers who had spoken to the refugees from whom the rumors of this fortress had originated, the three of them had set out in search of this place. They'd left their steeds about a mile back and proceeded the rest of the way on foot to mitigate the risk of being spotted. One of those steeds, a black mare named Stormbringer, had been with Hook since Hartla.

Presently, Olorus was rubbing at his lower back where he had hit the rock beneath Hook's push. "When they told us it was a fortress," he growled in what passed as a whisper for him, "I expected *a* fortress. Not this!"

The same thought had been going through Hook's head. This place that Leah had gone off in search of, in the hopes of finding Justin somewhere within it, was not simply a fortress. Rather, it appeared to be an entire complex of structures—several fortresses built into one.

The complex was situated between a set of rocky outcroppings that utilized the high surrounding peaks as natural defenses. The area leading up to the entrance was another one of the region's characteristic stands of thick hemlock forest, bordered by a set of shadowy chasms dropping to unknown depths, which was equally as characteristic of Central Erum. The resulting narrow approach made it impossible to get anywhere close to the gate without being spotted. If they tried, they would easily be seen coming from half a mile away.

"How many soldiers do you think there could be in there?" asked Megara.

Hook shook his head. It was impossible to guess. From here, he could only see four guards at the gate. But the complex was so large that it could contain ten thousand, for all he knew.

Hook, Olorus, and Megara were armed with their preferred weaponry. Hook and Olorus both had their Nolian kite shields. Olorus carried his Nolian spear and side-sword, and Hook had his golden, a'thri'ik-tipped Ancient Ellenean lance. Megara had her sunstone gauntlet, her trident, and a belt knife made of volcanic rock from her homeland. And all three of them wore full sets of the a'thri'ik plate armor that had been found in the Armory of the Ancients in Cymorikka, beneath the Shifting Mountains back in Athacea. Their helmets sat on the ground beside them.

Against most enemies, the three of them would have been a force to be reckoned with. But even fully armed and armored as they were, there were limits to what they could hope to do here.

Olorus, who had remained uncharacteristically level-headed about Leah's decision to strike out on her own until actually laying eyes on this place, let out a deep, growling sigh.

"I hope she didn't really go *in* there!" he said. "King Darius would be rolling over in his grave if he knew the risks his daughter was taking!"

For a man who had gained such a thorough education of the vocabulary of the hand-sign language, Hook wished that Olorus would *use* it once in a while.

"You agree with me, don't you?" said Olorus. "Look at that place! Leah is in far more danger than we anticipated. So I ask you, how long do we wait before we go in *swinging*?!"

"Longer than five minutes," Megara answered, her blue facial tattoos shifting with an antagonistic grin.

"We have been here longer than *five minutes*, and you know it!" Olorus snapped. Wincing a bit, he adjusted his seated position behind the rock in a none-too-graceful fashion. "Blast it, I'm not built for crouching like this for so long. You know I've had a bad back ever since Gaius."

"I thought it was your arse," signed Megara.

Olorus glared. "It is my *lower back*, thank you very much."

Megara signed, *"You worry too much. Leah is a more capable fighter than any of us."*

"I don't doubt her capabilities as a fighter," said Olorus. "But the hydstone provides *strength*, not invulnerability! Just because Leah can go around ripping her enemies apart doesn't mean she can't get hurt!"

Hook had the same concerns. He was not a spirit warrior and didn't know much about aurym or its associated powers. But based on Zechariah's explanation, hydstone abilities were so powerful that the wielder could block a direct sword-strike with their bare hand—but *only* if they saw the strike coming with enough time to properly prepare their defenses.

As Hook understood it, Leah's strength came through concentrated bursts of power through the stone—not a steady, constant flow. To perform a feat of strength, a carefully calculated surge of power had to be sent to the appropriate muscles, bones, and tissues. The muscular strength to punch through a stone wall was worthless if one's bones were crushed to powder by the impact or the flesh stripped from one's hand by the abrasion of a violent meeting with solid stone. Or an adjoining tendon could be overtaxed and its elasticity pushed beyond its breaking point by the strain. The entire muscle group and all its associated parts had to be strategically strengthened. And it had taken Leah a great deal of training, trial and error, and injuries to learn how to use it effectively.

When it came to protecting herself, Leah had to see an attack coming with enough time to access her power, apply it, and bolster her defenses in the correct part of her body. And although the hydstone could, through muscular strength, also provide its user with inhuman speed, it did not give them proportionate speed of perception or reaction times; Leah's body might be able to move faster than almost any other person alive, but her thoughts were still limited by the speed of human synapses.

In the end, even Innocen—the hydstone user who had killed many people back at Cervice and nearly kidnapped Leah—had been stopped by a single, ordinary arrow fired from the bow of a Cru archer who had, thankfully, happened to be in the right place at the right time. If Innocen had simply seen that arrow coming in time, he could have strengthened his body enough for it to bounce off his skin like a dart against plate armor. Instead, it pierced through his flesh and injured him enough that Leah was able to escape from his clutches.

Now, Leah had those same powers.

"We came to help if needed," signed Hook. *"But we have to trust that she knows what she is doing."*

"I'm sorry," Olorus grumbled impatiently. "You know how I worry about the girl. No matter how powerful she becomes, part of me will always see her as that same little whipper-snapper adventuring in the palace gardens with a toy sword." Before Hook or Megara had the chance to comment on this, Olorus demanded, "So, we came to help, but she knows what she's doing, eh? So, why are we here? What are we to do now?"

"Watch and wait," signed Hook.

Olorus shot him a withering glance.

"You have never been what one would call 'patient,' have you, Olorus?" signed Megara.

"No, I—!" Olorus began, almost at full volume, before seemingly remembering where he was. He hastily dropped his voice to a strained whisper. "*No!*" he said. "I have *not!*"

Hook raised a hand and added, *"Neither have I."*

Megara's smile widened enough to show the gap of her missing canine tooth as she signed, *"We three are kindred spirits, then."*

"Leah would not have entered that place without a plan," signed Hook. *"And I would not have our hasty actions, good-intentioned though they might be, be the undoing of it. We will wait a while longer."*

Megara made a sympathetic face at Olorus. *"Think your bad arse can handle it?"*

"Lower back," Olorus hissed through gritted teeth.

"Let us not forget that Leah is a diplomat," signed Hook, doing his best to ignore the two of them and focus on the matter at hand. *"She is a daughter of kings, trained in the arts of politics and rhetoric. She is probably negotiating peace even as we speak."*

CHAPTER 18

The flat of Leah's hand struck the guard in the back of the neck. Through daily practice, she had developed enough control over the flow of her hydstone power that, despite the adrenaline coursing through her, she was able to reduce the speed and force of the strike just before it landed. As a result, the blow only dropped the man to his knees instead of shattering his vertebrae like brittle seashells underfoot.

The guard made an admirable effort to remain standing, fought a losing battle against blacking out, and fell motionless among the rest of his comrades on the floor. She'd made short work of the five of them and had tried to do so as humanely as possible.

She turned to assist Kallorn with the last of the guards in time to see him spin his iron cell bar in a full circle and land a strike to his opponent that made his knee buckle sideways. His cry of pain was cut short when Kallorn followed it up with a rap to the top of the head. He, too, fell motionless.

Kallorn exhaled deeply and mopped at his brow. "I did what I could to keep my stamina up while in my cell," he said, "but I am still woefully out of practice."

They had descended several staircases, proceeding deeper and deeper into the maze beneath the Warlord's dungeons. Now, they were in the underground city below. Like Cymorikka beneath the Shifting

Mountains, this place contained monumental architecture, as if the city had been built for, or by, giants. Veins of a'thri'ik in the walls, some left in their natural state and others set in manmade patterns, illuminated the underground world. So far, there was hardly a soul to be found down here except for a few soldiers unlucky enough to have gotten in Leah's way and unwise enough not to get out of it.

Leah checked each of the fallen men and each time, was relieved to find a pulse. Most of them hadn't even had time to draw their weapons.

Kallorn's strike to the final assailant had been hard enough to separate his patellar tendon. It would make for a rather unpleasant experience when he woke up later, and Leah wished she had her healer's aurstone with her to heal him. At the very least, she could have mended the worst of the injury so that it would not cause him lasting problems. If they managed to find Justin, recover Leah's belongings, and come to some sort of agreement with the Warlord, she would offer her services to these people and request that she be allowed to heal anyone she had hurt.

"Back in Athacea," said Leah, "I found an underground city much like this one. It contained an armory filled with weapons and armor dating back to the time of the Ancient Elleneans. If there is a similar cache here, my people will be able to. . . ."

But Leah trailed off, realizing that Kallorn wasn't listening to her. She turned and found him kneeling to take a sheathed longsword from one of the guards. At first, Leah assumed he was simply selecting a weapon from the fallen that would prove more suitable than an iron rod. But then Leah noticed the design of the weapon's crossguard and the runes etched in the hilt.

"That sword," she said. "It looks like Ahlund's."

Kallorn nodded. "It is a Ru'Onorath blade. Mine, in fact."

Kallorn pulled his longsword from its sheath to examine the blade. He flexed his fingers around the hilt. Leah held back a gasp of surprise as threads of white lightning jolted to life and danced up and down the blade, illuminating Kallorn's grim, bearded face. Any lingering traces of the haggard, bent prisoner whom Leah had met in the cell above were driven out, replaced now by a warrior in his full glory standing before her.

"Until I die, I will not be relieved of this weapon again," he said. "I swear it."

Leah smiled.

"We must be getting close," said Kallorn, sheathing his weapon and tightening the sword belt around his waist.

"We are," said Leah. "I can feel it."

Beneath the green glow of the a'thri'ik in the walls, Leah and Kallorn stepped over their fallen assailants. She almost pitied anyone else who was waiting for them down here.

CHAPTER 19

The part of Innocen that was still Innocen—a remnant of his consciousness shackled in a tiny, partitioned corner of his mind— watched as the hand that had once been his hand caught a man's wrist in mid-swing of a sword. He was a middle-aged fighter of some sort, in patchwork armor.

Bones broke under Innocen's grip, and the man dropped his sword. Then Innocen's opposite hand came up and grabbed the attacker by the throat.

Innocen's hand squeezed. And squeezed. And squeezed.

There were other soldiers around him, outfitted in similar assortments of mismatched armor, also wielding swords. But at the sight of a demon creature in black throttling their companion, they turned and fled through the hemlocks as if coblyns were right on their heels. It was becoming increasingly rare to find humans in Erum. But it seemed they were still around, here and there.

Who are these men? Innocen wondered. *A wandering patrol belonging to a remnant of the local population? People who somehow managed to escape demon attention all this time?*

Whoever they were, they were not who the Nameless One was looking for. It had been a simple stroke of bad luck for them that they had come across the wraith that had once been Innocen of the Cult of the Hyd.

Slowly, the aurym-light in the body within Innocen's grasp dimmed. When the feet stopped kicking, and all the light was gone, Innocen's hand released its grip. The body dropped and lay, unmoving, on the forest floor.

"With my strength, we could have crushed his bones to powder!" Innocen screamed from his place locked inside himself. "With my speed, we could chase the others down! *Do you hear me?!*"

But, as usual, the Nameless One either did not hear Innocen or ignored him.

Innocen's body sniffed at the air.

"HE IS NEAR," growled the voice of the Nameless One through Innocen's throat. "WE ARE CLOSE NOW. . . . VERY, VERY *CLOSE!*"

Only now did Innocen notice the sensations of daemyn coming from multiple sources around him, converging on his location. Cythraul. And cythwraiths. It seemed he wasn't the only one of the Nameless One's slaves being sent to do their master's bidding.

Innocen kept writhing and screaming in his position of eternal pain deep within. And his commandeered body kept walking.

"YOUR FRIENDS WILL BURN, JUSTIN," the voice said. "TOGETHER, WE WILL *BURN* THE *SHEEP!*"

CHAPTER 20

Gunnar hopped out of the crow's nest and slid down the *Gryphon*'s main mast. "See up ahead there!" he called out, pointing to an eddy along a wide elbow of the Greenspring River. "That's where the fish are, boys! Bring us in on the shadowed side and put the anchor down! We'll be eating good tonight!"

"Aye-aye, Cap'n!" Vick called from the wheel.

As Samuel saw to the nets and Borris and Pool rushed to prepare the anchor, Gunnar checked over his shoulder to judge the wind. He had nearly forgotten that Adonica, Leah, Lycon, and Justin were on board, too.

Adonica was smiling at him. With her blonde hair flowing in the wind instead of tucked up inside of a helmet, her shoulders relaxed instead of tensed with the effort of gripping a sword, she looked every bit as beautiful as Queen Anavion standing beside her. In fact, she might make a nice queen herself someday.

It was a crazy notion. Adonica's feelings for him seemed to fluctuate between playful fondness and outright disapproval of just about everything he stood for. There were times when it felt like she *detested* him. But wasn't that just the way love went sometimes?

It was while Gunnar was contemplating his future plans, or lack thereof, that another member of the crew emerged from below deck. A short man with a compact frame, wearing a hessian tunic that bulged in the shoulders and arms. He may have been little, but he was all muscle. His hair was black as the ocean depths, and it came to a sharp point at a severe widow's peak at the front of his forehead.

"Ragny?" said Gunnar. "What are you doing here?"

"Don't you remember?" the little man said with a smile. "You brought me with you. And what happens next is your fault."

Ragny shot forward in a burst of speed that didn't make sense. There wasn't enough time to cry out a warning before he reached the helm of the *Gryphon* and drove his hand deep into Vick's back.

"*No!*" screamed Gunnar.

Ragny pulled his dripping hand free, and Vick dropped to the deck, dead. The little man was a blur as he crossed the deck and punched Samuel in the stomach—no, *through* the stomach, as if the flesh he was made of was no sturdier than raw dough. Borris and Pool were next. Ragny killed them in a single motion, stepping up between them and driving the fingertips of both hands into the base of their necks. Only then did Gunnar remember.

There is no Ragny, he realized. *There never was. His name is Innocen.*

There was nothing Gunnar could do as Innocen grabbed Leah and threw her like a doll. She hit the mast of the ship with an audible snapping of bones and fell in a limp, wrongly angled heap. Before her body hit the ground, Innocen grabbed Justin and lifted him over his head. He slammed him down in front of him, over and over again, until the deck boards were broken, wet, and red, and Justin's body was a ruin.

Innocen stepped up behind Adonica. Gently, almost lovingly, he took her head in his hands, flattening his fingers against the contours of her face.

Adonica's eyes turned to find Gunnar. Her face wasn't fearful. Instead, she wore an expression of bitter disappointment.

Of course you would fail to save me, her look seemed to say. *Of course you would let this happen to us. You never were able to be the man we needed you to be.*

"Thank you for the ride, Cap'n," said Innocen.

His fingers flexed against Adonica's head, and he squeezed—

Gunnar sat bolt upright so fast he didn't have time to course-correct before smacking his head against the underside of the desk he had chosen as his resting place for the night. Not only was the impact enough to daze him to the point of seeing stars, but it knocked loose the aurstone from beneath his eyepatch. The stone, solid black and polished to a mirror sheen, fell out and rolled down onto his chest.

For a few seconds, Gunnar sat there, blinking stupidly in the dark, breathing heavily, trying to recover, trying to remember where he was. He was not on the Greenspring River aboard the *Gryphon*, that was for damn sure. It'd been a long time since he'd fished those waters. The *Gryphon* lay at the bottom of the Greenspring. And even its successor, the *Gryphon II*, had met a similar fate. Since then, Gunnar hadn't taken any new flagships. If he ever did, he was going to pick a different name.

The vertical city, he realized. *That's where I am. In Erum. Looking for Lycon.*

Gunnar drew in a deep breath. It was not the first time he'd had that dream. It was just one of several versions of the same nightmare that had recurred many times since Gunnar befriended a volunteer soldier and cook who called himself Ragny.

Gunnar had brought Ragny aboard his ship and ferried him to Leah's capital city of Cervice. It was there that Ragny had revealed himself as the one called Innocen.

Not only was Gunnar haunted by the fact that he had personally, inadvertently aided Innocen in his mission, but dozens of soldiers had been killed by Innocen in his attempt to capture Leah. Their deaths, all that blood, was on Gunnar's hands.

Gunnar had always heard that no soldier really escaped from war unwounded; there were things that one brought home from the battlefield below the surface. Wounds of the mind that festered and putrefied, unseen, and could not be remedied even by an aurym-healer's touch.

He grabbed his godsbreath aurstone from where it had fallen onto his chest. He could move, at least. He wasn't stuck in that sideways place where he couldn't move his body. It was a condition that was becoming a real problem.

You aren't supposed to be here, he thought. *That is the real problem. You were raised in a palace. You weren't built for this life.*

Everyone seemed to think that being a Mythaean Royal Admiral qualified him to be a leader. But the truth was, in his former life, he had been a ne'er-do-well disgrace to the royal family.

Before joining up with Ahlund and Zechariah and the others, he'd only ever been part of a few real battles, and each of those had gone just about as poorly as a battle could go, short of getting an up close and personal look at your own entrails.

Since then, most of the fighting he'd done in Leah's Army of Light had involved him being on the front lines. As it turned out, fighting was one of the things he was best at—*him*, a spoiled son of kings who had been raised in a palace and educated by the finest tutors in matters of politics. He wondered if any of the stuffy old teachers who had seen to his and Yordar's education back in Eppex were still alive, and what they would think if they could have seen him now, as he shoved his aurstone back into his empty eye socket and lay back down to try to readjust himself underneath a desk in a demon-infested city.

Talk about a fall from grace, thought Gunnar.

"You all right?"

He propped himself back up on one arm and looked across the room. They had all decided to sleep with their armor on, as removing it in a situation like this seemed very unwise indeed. Accordingly, thanks to the glow produced by a'thri'ik in the absence of light, they had to keep themselves covered up as best they could with their heavy, hooded cloaks to prevent potentially giving away their positions. Thus, Adonica, across the room, had just a small bit of green light peeking out of her cloak to illuminate her face as she watched him.

"I wish you'd stop asking me that," said Gunnar.

"I wish you'd stop giving me reasons to," said Adonica.

Gunnar felt his cheek twitch in annoyance at her tone. She was positioned beside a partially barricaded window, giving her a view of the street outside. She had been more beautiful in his dream in the classic sense. But here, in the real world, the way the glow from her armor caught her features in the dark made for a far more striking vision than Gunnar's imagination ever could have conjured.

"What happened today," said Adonica. "That's not the first time I've seen you freeze up."

She waited, but Gunnar wasn't taking the bait. He remained silent.

"It happens," she said, "but if it happens when it counts, you're going to get someone killed. I'm sorry if you aren't ready to hear that, but I've got to think practically about these sorts of things, for the sake of the mission."

"For the sake of the mission," said Gunnar. "You say that as if you were *given* a mission. But, so far as I can remember, you and your fellow soldiers came here against direct orders. You are technically deserters, and all of you may be subject to a court-martial when, and if, you ever return to the Army of Light."

"I wasn't just going to leave Lycon out here to die," snapped Adonica.

"Neither was I," Gunnar snapped right back. "I would have figured something out if you'd given me the chance instead of running off like a brat."

"I don't need you to figure anything out for me. I take action when action needs to be taken."

"And how's that working out for you?"

Adonica's nostrils flared. She started to say something, then turned to glare angrily out the window. Damn it, she even looked good doing that.

"The demons have mostly dispersed," she said. "By morning, it may be safe for us to continue moving."

"Swell," said Gunnar, crossing his arms behind his head and lying back down beneath the desk.

A few quiet moments passed.

"You didn't have to come," said Adonica.

Of course I didn't, thought Gunnar.

But it's no accident that you did, said the other voice in his head. *You'd rather plunge headlong into a demon-infested city than step up and be the ruler that all those tutors trained you to be.*

I just don't like giving orders that put others *in danger*, he shot back.

Yes. Better to die than have to take responsibility for your actions, right?

Gunnar gritted his teeth in annoyance.

"Did you hear me?" said Adonica. "I said you didn't have to come—"

"Yes, I know, I'm a real dumbass," said Gunnar. "You don't have to rub it in."

He rolled over and closed his eye, making a mental note not to sit up so quickly the next time he woke up.

A creaking floorboard announced a bit of movement from upstairs. A moment later, Gunnar heard a hushed voice from the curved set of steps that led to the second floor.

"Captain Lor," said Estoq. "You'd better come see this."

Adonica stood from her place by the window and went upstairs. After slipping on his boots and sword belt, Gunnar followed.

The home's second floor was less ransacked than the first, but there were still signs of violence. Adonica's team had covered themselves in their cloaks to snuff out the light of their a'thri'ik armor, except for one helmet set at the center of the room to serve as a sort of makeshift lantern. In that light, Gunnar could see the marks of coblyn claws dug into stained floorboards.

At one window were Ptolemec, Berex, and Elzirda. At another were Estoq, Ucydotus, and Adonica. By now, Gunnar had given up on the notion that he was in any way in charge and didn't expect to be saluted. He would have been content for someone, anyone, to simply acknowledge his presence, but none of them so much as looked at him as he entered. He cleared his throat, then crossed the room to stand beside Adonica at the window.

"What are we looking at?" he asked.

"Up there," said Estoq, and she pointed out the window.

Gunnar had to duck a bit to follow the trajectory of her gesture. She was pointing up. Way up. Above the third level of the city entirely.

It was difficult to see much on such an overcast night, with no light from the moons, Cnidus and Nun. It didn't help that here in Central Erum, the mists often hung so heavy that the nights became oppressively dark. But somewhere up there, on the next terraced section of the city, the darkness was broken by a light source. A dull glow. It could have been anything—if it hadn't been the same shade of emerald green as the helmet lamp in the center of the room.

"Cat's eye," said Gunnar. "You can't tell me that's a coincidence."

"A signal?" said Estoq.

"Gotta be," said Adonica.

Gunnar decided not to point out the obvious possibility that even if the source *was* Lycon or a member of his missing team, that didn't make it a signal. Just because they could see the light of a piece of armor did not mean that whoever was wearing it was alive.

Instead of saying as much, Gunnar shrugged and said, "Don't be rude. Answer the man."

Berex passed Adonica his a'thri'ik-forged shield. After carefully checking the street below, Adonica raised it to the window. A'thri'ik did not shine so bright that the light of the shield would be a gleaming beacon. It was not even as bright as a torch flame. But it was distinctive. And it was more than bright enough to be seen from up there.

A few seconds passed, and nothing changed. Then the green light high above them seemed to go out, reveal itself again, go out, and come back.

"Someone *is* alive up there," said Ucydotus.

"Yes," said Adonica, "but something must be wrong. If they're willing to risk a signal light, they must need help."

"I haven't seen any demons for the past hour," said Ptolemec from the other window. "We can set out at first light as long as the streets remain clear."

"Even if they aren't," said Adonica flatly. She tilted the shield back and forth to return the message, then turned to the team. "Get your gear together and be ready to move at first light."

Ptolemec started to acknowledge the order, but he came up short as his eyes darted to Gunnar.

"Sir?" Ptolemec said as if asking for confirmation. It was rather refreshing.

Gunnar gestured deferentially toward Adonica. "You heard the woman."

As Ptolemec, Berex, and the others backed away from the windows to ready their things, Adonica directed an exaggerated look out the window at the faraway signal, then cocked an I-told-you-so eyebrow at Gunnar.

"Don't look so smug, Captain," said Gunnar. "It wasn't *finding* them I was worried about."

Come first light, another chance to die, said an unbidden voice in his head.

No matter what Gunnar did, that voice was always there, nagging him. Usually, it was best to just ignore it. But there were times when he could almost swear that voice wasn't his own.

CHAPTER 21

The deeper they delved into this world beneath the Warlord's fortress, the more Leah realized that this place was almost an exact duplicate of Cymorikka. Clearly, the two underground cities had been designed and built by the same ancient civilization.

In Cymorikka, they had entered via a central chamber, from which many halls extended like the spokes of a great wheel. Here, it seemed that they had entered the city from a point that had been tunneled inward from above to meet one of the outer spokes, and they were making their way inward toward the center. The monumental architecture grew in complexity and size as they proceeded, and soon, Leah noticed a theme that had been prevalent in Cymorikka as well: images of giant, tusked cyclopes.

Presently, she passed beneath a stela constructed of glowing a'thri'ik veins that depicted cyclopes in battle against creatures that were clearly cythraul. She noted that the cyclopes stood nearly one and a half times as tall as the cythraul.

In a way, she wished Itzacoatl, the elderly soldier she had found guarding the ancient city of Cymorikka and who was now an advisor in her Army of Light, were here to see this. He was a native of this part of the world, and he and his brothers had traveled halfway across the Oikoumene to find the legendary city of Cymorikka, apparently unaware that another one just like it existed so close to home.

Then again, maybe it was better that he was not here. The irony might have been a bit shocking to the poor fellow.

If we cannot topple Avagad's demons, thought Leah, looking around at the massive, labyrinthine corridors, *maybe there remains some hope for humankind. Maybe human populations can survive in places like this city.*

Leah, for her part, did not intend to hide. She had brought her people across the world to fight. But perhaps, if all else failed, even as the demons defeated her and her armies and ravaged the world above, all the way from Erum to Otunmer, humankind might manage to survive in hidden sanctuaries like these. The possibility gave Leah a glimmer of much-needed hope.

Suddenly, Kallorn slowed to a halt. He remained motionless long enough that Leah almost spoke up to ask him what was wrong. Then she heard voices coming from somewhere ahead.

Kallorn tightened his grip on his sword. Leah nodded at him, and they proceeded forward.

She had long ago stopped wearing armored boots. With hydstone abilities, simple, light shoes were much more practical. The ones she wore were more like slippers, really, and she was grateful for them now as she padded quietly over the ancient cut-stone floor. Ahead was an open doorway. She heard the voices again, closer now, followed by the laughter of multiple men. How many were there? Three at least, she guessed.

Near the doorway, Kallorn came to a halt. He inched forward until he could see in, and something in his body language changed. Without looking, he gestured for Leah to join him.

Leah tried not to make a sound as she stepped up beside Kallorn at the edge of the doorway and peeked past him. Inside, beneath the light of glowing veins of a'thri'ik, three soldiers sat at a table. One of them raised a brown jug to his lips, took a long pull, and then passed it to the man beside him with a hearty smacking of his lips. Two more guards were positioned along one of the walls. And at the far end of the room, beyond them, was a single cell of iron bars much like the cells where Leah and Kallorn had been detained. And there, inside the cell, was—

Leah placed a hand over her own mouth to prevent herself from gasping aloud.

The fact that five soldiers had been posted to guard this room would have been enough alone to indicate its importance. But even from here, she could see the occupant of the cell: a young man lying on a blanket on the floor. The boy had sandy blond hair. He looked tall. And although he currently lay with his back turned to Leah, she could see that there seemed to be something wrong with one of his arms. The abnormality had been covered up with wraps of dark cloth.

"Justin . . ." whispered Leah.

"I can hit the three at the table before they even know we're here," Kallorn whispered. "If you can reach the other two—"

Whatever else Kallorn had to say, Leah didn't hear it. She wasn't listening. Calling on aurym, she sent spirit energy pulsing through her hydstone.

The power flowed through her muscles like coal to a furnace, and without waiting for Kallorn, she shot forward and entered the room.

CHAPTER 22

"*Longer than five minutes,*" grumbled Olorus, sitting with his back to the stone, shifting uncomfortably to ease the pain in his aching *lower back*, or so he claimed. "Isn't that what you said? Five minutes?"

Still crouched behind the same rock above the fortress, in the same positions they'd been in at sundown, Megara made a sign that needed no translation: a tilt of her head to the side, signifying a begrudging acknowledgment.

"By the look of the moons, it is closer to dawn than dusk," said Olorus. "And still, there has been no change."

Hook made no reply, opting to focus instead on the guards at the entrance of the fortress. He had to admit that his patience was wearing thin, too.

An intelligent woman trained in the arts of diplomacy was formidable enough. Add to that the fact that Hook had lost track of the number of times he had seen Leah tear the heads off of coblyns or disembowel bone-armored cythraul with her bare hands, and he no longer questioned what she was capable of. But he still didn't like this situation. He kept trying to remind himself that this was probably all part of Leah's plan, and she simply needed more time.

But maybe not. Maybe, despite Leah's best precautions, the occupants of that fortress had found her hydstone and taken it from her. The possibility did not make for a pretty picture.

Adding to Hook's growing sense of unease was the fact that the skies had cleared, and the moons were almost full.

He never felt quite right when that purple moon was out.

It had first happened following an otherwise typical lunar eclipse. Nun, the smaller of the two moons, which, as far as Hook was aware, had *only* ever been observed in the night sky in occasionally varying shades of blue, had changed. Its color had transformed to a strange, deep purple hue.

At first, the color change had been taken as a passing anomaly. A trick of the light caused by unfamiliar environmental phenomena. But months passed, the two moons waxed and waned, and the color persisted. Even Zechariah didn't know what to make of this and claimed that there was no precedent for it.

Popular opinion among the Army of Light was that the purple moon was an ill omen. It was said that when Nun was full, the demons fought all the harder, and daemyn was all the stronger. Hook didn't know if this was true. His Islander mother had always been a rather superstitious soul, and try as he might to remain practical, it was sometimes difficult for Hook to shake her influence, especially when some of her superstitions—even if they were not strictly *true* in the objective, black-and-white sense of the word—had helped to keep him alive through many close calls in the past.

And, in a roundabout way, if superstitions *worked*, didn't that *make* them true?

Hook couldn't always put words to what he believed. What some might have called faith, religion, or superstition, he called pattern observation. If something *was*, it didn't matter *why* it was. And, as far as the moon of Nun was concerned, he could not deny that some of the Army of Light's most colossal failures in recent memory had occurred when that moon was shining its brightest, its fullest, and its most violet.

Perhaps it was just his imagination, but with each passing cycle of the moons, Nun's purple shade seemed to grow deeper and stronger.

"These are either some *lengthy* diplomatic negotiations," Olorus spoke up when he could stand it no longer, "or Leah has been thrown into a cell! Or *worse*! We have waited long enough! I say we go in there now!"

"Me too," signed Megara.

Hook felt his eyebrows raise in surprise. It was not every day that Megara agreed with Olorus on matters of tactics.

"If we go in," signed Hook, *"we go in fighting."*

"Good!" Olorus spat. "And if, in doing so, we interfere with Leah's plans, I am prepared to take responsibility for my mistake, as long as it means ensuring her safety!"

"What if we kill someone important?" signed Megara.

Olorus pulled his Nolian sword from its sheath. It was a machete-like blade with a single cutting edge. He patted the edge that wasn't sharp and said, "Use the dull side. Aim for the back of the neck, and hope they wake up a few hours from now with nothing worse than a headache and most of their mental faculties intact."

Megara looked circumspectly at the triple points and barbs of her trident, trying to find the dull side.

Charge in and hope for the best, thought Hook. It was the sort of plan he himself might have come up with in his former life, when Jocasta had fought by his side.

Hook had changed since then. But not quickly enough to have saved his beloved.

"See those clouds?" Hook signed. He pointed up toward a mass of clouds that was moving slowly across the night sky, toward the moons. *"We wait for their cover. We will be spotted. But the closer we can get before that happens, the better."*

"Finally," growled Olorus.

Hook took another look down at the entrance to the fortress and the guards at the gate. Then he reached over his shoulder and drew the lance of the Ancient Ellenean king, tipped with a razor-sharp shard of pure a'thri'ik.

Hiding and fighting. Hiding and fighting.

Maybe someday, the cycle would stop for Hook Bard.

But not today.

CHAPTER 23

Leah entered the room. But it would not have appeared that way to the men inside the room. To them, it would have been as if one instant, all was well. And the next, in a blur of motion, a small-statured young woman suddenly stood in the midst of them.

The young woman wore only a simple tunic and slippers. She carried no weapons. In fact, the only thing she carried was the brown jug that one of the men at the table had been in the process of lifting to his lips a split-second before. This man looked down at his suddenly empty hand in shock, then back up at the girl.

For a few tense seconds, the guards only stared at Leah, and she stared back. Finally, one of the guards standing along the wall pulled his sword from its sheath and stepped toward her.

In a flash, Leah shot forward and grabbed the man's sword by the blade with her free hand. He tried to pull it back, but it was stuck fast in her grip. In dumb amazement, he took a double-handed grasp on the sword's hilt and threw his entire body weight backward. But the sword did not budge. It remained in Leah's hand as firmly as if it had been melded into a smithy's anvil.

Leah studied the look of shock on the man's face. She allowed the moment to sink in, then she twisted her wrist. The blade bent, then snapped in half in her bare hand.

The breaking of the sword seemed to jolt everyone to action. Chair legs squealed against the floor as the men at the table pushed back to stand. The soldier who had attacked jumped back in surprise, now holding half a sword. The second guard on the wall charged forward, but Leah sidestepped him and smashed the brown jug against his head, sending wine spraying across the room and dropping him to the floor.

Leah was fully aware of the next-closest attacker coming at her with a dagger in his hand. She was preparing to dispatch him when there came a sharp crackling sound from behind her, and a flash erupted that bathed the room in light as bright as midday. A bolt of energy like lightning struck the charging soldier's hand. The dagger went flying across the room and clanged against the bars of the cell. The soldier who'd been holding it dropped to his knees, cradling his hand.

Leah turned to find Kallorn standing in the doorway. He held his sword in a fighting stance unlike any Leah had ever seen. The sword was held up horizontally, with the hilt resting against his cheek. His opposite arm was extended, with the blade of the sword in the crook of his thumb and forefinger. His head was tilted with one eye closed, the other looking down the length of the blade at the men in the room. It was like the stance of an archer taking aim. Threads of electrical power danced along the blade, and bright sparks occasionally jumped from the tip.

The soldiers in the room who were still capable of moving came to a sudden halt. They hardly dared draw breath.

There was a sound of rattling chains from the cell as the prisoner inside attempted to turn to see what was happening. But he had been cruelly chained to the wall by shackles on his arms and his wrists so short and so tight that they prevented him from even turning around. The Warlord probably hadn't wanted to take any chances when it came to the potential power of an ethoul. Better to keep him on a short leash, limit his movement, and keep him weak.

Anger flared up within Leah at the thought of it. Nevertheless, had she been capable of speaking the language of these soldiers, she might have assured them that she had not come here intending to hurt them, and that she was only there for Justin. Instead, all she could do was look them in their eyes and hope that her intentions were made clear by her actions.

With a single finger, Leah pointed to the keys hanging on the wall. Then she pointed at the cell door.

It was the man whose sword had been broken who complied. Without breaking eye contact with Leah, he set aside his weapon, got the keys, and backpedaled carefully to the cell. He inserted a key into the lock of the cell door, and he opened it.

"Have you got them covered?" Leah asked over her shoulder.

"I do," replied Kallorn. "Go ahead."

Leah stepped through the cell door to approach the prisoner lying on the floor. Her sudden appearance startled him, and he crawled desperately away from her, trying to flee, pulling himself as far from her as his short chains would allow.

"No—no, *please!*" he pleaded in a voice so hoarse that it was beyond recognition.

He held his shaking hands up toward Leah in pitiful defense, cowering in the shadows. He was malnourished. His musculature had eroded. His fingers were narrow and knobby. Even his hair was thinning.

How long? wondered Leah. *How long have they kept him like this? He was already here when Kallorn arrived, and that was several weeks ago, at least. He's probably sick. Surely nutrient deficient. Probably hasn't had sunlight in—*

A blinding flash lit up the room, accompanied by a sound like a tree trunk being split down the middle.

Leah turned to see one of the soldiers hit the floor, writhing in pain. Kallorn's blade pulsed as he pointed it threateningly at the other guards.

"That's what happens to poor wretches who find their courage," Kallorn announced, speaking to the guards. "The rest of you had better not find yours." Then he called out to Leah, "Is everything all right in there?"

For a moment, Leah couldn't bring herself to answer. She realized her hands were shaking nearly as badly as those of the prisoner before her. After everything she'd been through, she hadn't expected to find him like this, curled up on a cell floor, cowering, almost whimpering, arms raised and folded over his head like a frightened child. . . .

Something caught Leah's eye, and she stepped forward. She grabbed the prisoner by the wrist, causing him to cry out in fear.

The hand at the end of the boy's left arm had only a thumb and forefinger. The rest of the fingers were fused and malformed.

Like a woman possessed, Leah grabbed the black wraps of fabric on the prisoner's left arm and frantically tore them off. The limb beneath was shriveled. The skin seemed to cling almost directly to the bone, as if the arm were devoid of the muscle structures that should have been beneath the flesh.

But *flesh* was indeed what the arm was made of. And, stretched unnaturally thin over the bone though it was, it *was* covered in skin, not the chitinous black material of a demon arm.

A birth defect, Leah realized, turning the arm gently this way and that to examine the fused fingers, the atrophied muscles, the shortened tendons.

Carefully, she pulled the prisoner's raised arms away from his face to get a better look at him, causing his fearful whimper to grow even louder. The face that looked back at Leah was that of a scared young man, perhaps a year younger than she was. His frantic eyes looked sunken. The pale skin of his face formed hollows beneath the sharp cheekbones. He had a bulbous nose, spotty facial hair, and freckles.

It was not Justin. Leah had never seen this person in her life.

C H A P T E R   2 4

"It's not me! I'm not him!" cried the young man. "I'm not the fallen angel! Please don't kill me!"

Leah, still holding him by the arms, felt her grip on him tighten in spite of her best effort to keep her head. "Who *are* you, then?" she demanded.

"My name is Justus!" cried the boy, and he was truly crying. "I'm from Darsida!"

"Justus?" Leah let him go. "Then where is—?"

A commotion from behind drew Leah's attention to the room outside the cell. One of the soldiers had drawn a sword and was making a move toward Kallorn. This time, the Guardian allowed the attacker to get within arm's reach, at which point he met him in a forward rush, leading with the butt end of his sword. The pommel connected with the soldier's jaw, and a blinking spark jumped from the point of impact. The soldier went limp and crumpled, falling to the floor with a black scorch mark on his face. A ribbon of smoke trailed from the wound.

"Don't make me," Kallorn warned the others.

Leah turned back to the boy on the ground, Justus. He was once again cowering from her in abject terror.

"I'm not him! I swear!" he sputtered.

"Obviously!" snapped Leah. "So, where *is* he? Where is Justin?!"

"They think I'm him!" Justus cried, tears spilling from the corners of his eyes. "I keep telling them they've got the wrong person! But they won't listen—they don't believe me!"

Leah's heart sank.

The name. The arm. The rumors.

All of her hopes. Everything she'd been through. Could all of it really have been based on nothing more than a case of mistaken identity?

"No," Leah said. "I sensed him!"

Out of pure frustration, she took a step toward the boy named Justus with her hands squeezed into fists. It was more aggressive and more threatening than she had intended it to be, and the boy recoiled with such fright that he rebounded against his short chains and gave a pained yelp.

"He is here!" said Leah. "He. . . . He has to be!"

"I sensed him, too," said Kallorn from outside the cell. He set his blade sizzling brighter than ever, aiming it at the nearest guard. "Tell us where he is."

The guard at the business end of Kallorn's blade said something in the Aznochti tongue and pointed in desperation toward Justus, cowering beneath Leah.

At that instant, Leah had something akin to an out-of-body experience. She saw herself before this prisoner in chains, a boy who had been taken against his will and held here, of no fault of his own, starved and perhaps tortured at the hands of these captors. She saw the way she was standing, so threatening. She saw the expressions of the frightened guards and remembered the faces of those she had attacked and hurt just to get here.

Leah blinked, snapping herself out of it, and the urgency and devotion to her purpose were replaced by something simpler. Disappointment. And a sorrow so deep that it made her feel like a thin shell floating on top of it.

You didn't sense him at all, she suddenly realized. *You and Kallorn only thought you did. . . . Hoped you did.*

"Kallorn, stand down, please," she said.

Kallorn's head turned in her direction. He seemed confused by her tone, but he stepped away from the soldier, keeping the aim of his sword cautiously trained on him.

Leah looked down at the frightened boy with the withered arm and took a deep breath. Then she grabbed his shackles and, one by one, ripped them open, freeing him from his bindings.

The boy called Justus gazed in confused wonder at the rings of wrinkled, whitened skin around his wrists and ankles where the shackles had been. His hands were shaking.

"Justus," Leah said gently. "Follow me. We'll get you out of here. I promise."

"Lady Leah?" said Kallorn.

"It's time to go," said Leah. "This was all just a mistake."

"A mistake?" said Kallorn. "My Lady, this is not Justin, but he is here somewhere. I'm certain of it."

"A friend of mine, a man named Zechariah, once told me that the real power of the fallen angel was what people made *of* them," said Leah. "Belief can make a symbol become divine, and hope can lead people to do strange things."

She trailed off, looking at her own hands. Hands that only a moment ago had been shaking a malnourished boy with a birth defect for information. How deeply the Warlord must have hoped that this boy represented the salvation of her people.

"It can lead people to do awful things," said Leah.

"I sensed him," said Kallorn, though he no longer sounded so certain. "My Lady, *you* sensed him."

"You heard what Nefari said," said Leah. "She is *desperate* to keep her people safe. Just like I am for mine. And then, someone found a boy with a bad arm, with a name that sounds like Justin." Leah gestured to the guards in the room. "After everything these people have been through, is it any wonder that they would latch on to any small chance they could find? Or that you and I would be willing to hurt, kill, and even die for the same thing when we were at the end of all hope?"

Kallorn's face seemed to harden at this. "At the end of all hope," said Kallorn, "is the place where one is given the privilege to act on faith. Perhaps it is time to ask yourself, Lady Leah, have you any faith left? And have you still the courage to act on it?"

Leah opened her mouth, but she promptly closed it again. She had no answer.

CHAPTER 25

As soon as the clouds rolled over the moons, the three warriors stood from their hiding place. Hook gripped his a'thri'ik lance. Olorus raised his Nolian kite shield and held his sword at the ready. Megara wielded her trident, which was as long as Hook was tall, and the gauntlet on her arm contained an aurstone that imbued her with the power of the sun. All three wore cloaks dark enough to obscure them in the night by shrouding the glow from the a'thri'ik armor they wore beneath.

And yet, even together, with all our strength combined, we would not rival Leah Demonsbane, thought Hook.

The logical question, then, was what made them think they could rescue *her* from anything?

Olorus made to step out first. Hook placed a hand on his chest to stop him and signed a reminder: *"Dull sides."*

"If I can help it," agreed Olorus.

"All right," signed Hook. *"Let's—"*

But Hook abruptly broke off his signing. Because something down at the fortress had caught his eye. Something he was sure hadn't been down there a few seconds ago. A new arrival.

Perhaps the thing he now saw had, just like the three of them, been waiting for the clouds to cover the moons to obscure its approach. Where it had come from, Hook could only guess, as he hadn't thought there was any way to get much closer than he and his companions already were to that fortress without being spotted.

The guards at the gate appeared to notice the new arrival's presence at the same time as Hook: a figure in black, stepping out from beneath the shadows of the hemlock boughs down below. With slow, deliberate steps, it walked toward the fortress.

"What is that?" signed Megara.

Hook found his grip on his lance tightening as he watched the figure's approach. It was too big for a coblyn. Too small for a cythraul.

"A cythwraith," said Olorus.

One of those poor souls cursed by the touch of a cythraul, transformed into a half-demon and enslaved under the control of Avagad.

But it was not *a* cythwraith. The figure was less than a dozen paces out of the shadows when another cythwraith emerged, following it. Then, a third, a fourth, and a fifth.

Then came the giant form of a cythraul. Followed by three more of them, pushing through the trees, pushing hemlocks over, uprooting them from the ground as if they were only minor nuisances as they walked toward the gate.

The blast of a horn echoed from within the fortress. An alarm to alert its inhabitants of an attack.

"Zechariah was right . . ." said Olorus. "It *was* a trap."

PART IV

BURN AN

ETERNAL FLAME

CHAPTER 26

A long, low noise reached Leah's ears, reverberating down the dungeon hallway. It was distant but distinct, and the confines of the underground city's passageways caused it to echo on for what felt like an unnatural length of time. A blast from a horn.

The guards grew visibly upset by the sound, but they refrained from making any movements.

"An alarm?" said Kallorn.

"Our escape has been noticed, it would seem," said Leah.

One of the guards on the floor said something in the Aznochti language, and a second guard replied.

"It's not for you," said Justus from his place on the floor of the cell. "They say it's the alarm that indicates an attack at the gates."

More horn blasts. More chatter among the guards in Aznochti. Their words and body language were growing increasingly tense. She had a feeling that despite her and Kallorn's displays of power, these guards would not stay idle much longer.

"Tell them we mean them no harm," Leah said to Justus. "Tell them we do not know who is attacking their gates, but we will help them defend this place if they let us. We will help them protect their people, their families."

Justus seemed confused by her words at first but then relayed the message. Looks of relief and wonder spread across the faces of the guards.

Kallorn shot Leah a look. "We will?"

"If there is any faith left in me, Kallorn," said Leah, "it is in the act of protecting people from harm. It is. . . . It is the only thing I know to be right. Always."

Kallorn wore a grave expression. For a few moments, Leah thought he might argue with her on the matter.

"Then let us act on it, together, with all our mind, body, and spirit," said Kallorn, "and count it every bit the privilege it is."

CHAPTER 27

Hook heard three horn blasts sound from inside the fortress by the time the first cythraul raised its hand, and a ball of concentrated blackness, sparking with violet energy at the periphery, appeared within its palm. The guards outside the fortress turned and tried to run. Not one of them was fast enough.

The daemyn blast shot from the cythraul's hand, hit the doorway, and exploded outward in a pulse that Hook felt half a second before he heard the sound of its report.

The front of the fortress blew inward. Only one of the soldiers escaped being turned to dust. He was rewarded instead by having the flesh pulled from half his body in a haze of red. What remained of the man dropped, rolled once, and lay motionless.

Rubble fell in the wake of the blast. When the cave-in at the front of the fortress had stabilized, leaving a gaping hole in the stone wall, the first cythwraith that had appeared stepped forward, leading the way. The rest followed.

On a good day, Hook, Olorus, and Megara might have been a match for a single cythraul. There were five cythraul down there, plus five cythwraiths.

No communication was needed between Hook and Olorus. Long before they'd been generals on the warpath, they'd been men of the High Nolian Guard, the personal bodyguards of the royal family. The two of them were moving down the hillside in an instant, followed closely by Megara.

Odds be damned. Their queen was in trouble.

CHAPTER 28

At first, there was resistance. At first, several soldiers bravely stood their ground and attempted to stop Innocen as he led his force of cythraul and cythwraiths into the front of the fortress.

All who resisted paid the Nameless One's price.

Now, Innocen was in a central courtyard, open to the night sky above. He could sense many human lives in this place. Hundreds. Perhaps over a thousand. He could sense them through the fortress walls, could see the distant auras of their life forces visible through the walls ahead of him. And he could see a mass of them below him.

Fleeing, thought Innocen. *Evacuating through some other exit point of the fortress.*

Innocen guessed it was a series of underground tunnels, judging by the relative distance and location of their visible auras. They were moving in a large group, like a panicked herd of livestock. A fitting comparison, for they would, all of them, be hunted down to feed the insatiable hunger of the Nameless One.

Innocen watched as the Nameless One used his body to raise the dripping scythe in his hands and flick it clean. The splatter it left across the courtyard in front of him was bright with the lingering life essence of aurym before quickly dissipating to nothingness in his spiritual sight.

Now, there was no resistance left. The last living soldier lay writhing on the ground near the wreckage of the walls where the cythraul had broken through. The little soul managed to get to his feet for a second, then slipped and slid in the puddle of what had leaked out of himself and his compatriots and fell back down. His movements slowed, and the life force faded from him. If any other fighters remained, they were fleeing along with the rest of the human herd.

The only person still alive who had not run was a single individual standing before Innocen in the center of the courtyard.

This person was impressively large, as far as humans went. They held a long, cleaver-bladed voulge, but it did not seem as if they intended to use it. And it was a credit to their mental fortitude that, left alone to stand and face Innocen, five cythwraiths, and five cythraul, the aura of energy radiating from them carried determination and single-minded purpose. Innocen might have almost called it hope.

What, Innocen wondered, *could this person possibly have to hope for in the face of the monsters standing before them?*

Innocen's mouth opened, and a voice that was not his own growled, "WHERE IS HE?"

"He is here," said the person ahead. "I have him. Do you represent Avagad?"

Innocen's mouth released a sound that was almost like a laugh but closer to a hellhound's bark. "AVAGAD REPRESENTS *ME.*"

The tall human faltered a bit. Perhaps it would not have even been noticeable to someone whose perceptions were limited to physical sight. But the Nameless One saw all.

"I will offer him to you," said the tall person, a woman, judging by the sound of her voice, "as a token of subservience to. . . . To you, the master of Avagad and the master of the demons."

"I ACCEPT YOUR OFFERING," said the Nameless One.

A strong emotion rippled through the tall woman's aura. If Innocen could have put it to words, he would have called it relief strangely mingling with a sense of horror at what she had just done.

"There are people here in this fortress who follow me," said the woman. "They call me their Warlord, and they obey my commands. They will not stand in the way of your demons. If I give you the fallen angel, you must spare my people in exchange."

If she gives *us the fallen angel?* thought Innocen, almost pityingly. *The poor fool.*

In the heavy silence that followed the words of this self-proclaimed Warlord, the wind whistled through the open-air courtyard of the fortress. High above, the clouds were pushed aside, and Innocen bathed in the nourishing glow of Nun, the purple moon. It felt like kindling had been heaped upon his inner fire. His grip on his scythe tightened.

As the moments passed, the Warlord squirmed nervously. Her hopeful aura was diminishing.

"*Will* you let my people live?" she finally said. "I. . . ."

She hesitated, then dropped heavily to her knees. She cast her weapon on the ground in front of her, beyond her reach, and she lowered her head in submission.

"Please," she said. "I . . . I beg you! Spare them, and I will call you My Lord. I will do anything you ask. My people will not stand in your way, I swear it!"

The Nameless One walked forward in Innocen's body until he stood directly in front of the Warlord, his long scythe in his hands. Such was the disparity of their height that on her knees, this giant woman would have looked almost eye to eye with Innocen, had her face not been pressed to the ground.

The Nameless One opened his mouth and said in a near-whisper, "DEAR CHILD. . . . ALL WHO *LIVE* STAND IN MY WAY."

The Warlord's emotions changed drastically, shifting from desperate supplication to panic, failure, and, finally, hostility. But it was too late for that. Even as she lunged forward, her hand extended toward her discarded weapon, Innocen's scythe was already coming down. It passed through the woman's neck, separating her head from her body.

The Warlord's great body slumped like a puppet whose strings had been cut. Her abnormally large head landed face-first, producing a hard snapping sound of teeth cracking against the courtyard's flagstones. Then the head rolled with muffled thumping noises and came to rest a few feet away from her neck.

"I ACCEPT . . . YOUR *OFFERING*," the Nameless One said again.

Locked within his stolen body, Innocen asked through his eternal agony, "Why didn't you turn this one? She could have been an asset to you. Why don't you turn *them all?!*"

The Nameless One flicked the scythe clean, aurym-light fading from the sprayed droplets it cast. And in a voice like the grinding of stones, mixed with the roar of a tall flame, the Nameless One said, "NOT ALL ARE WORTHY OF MY BLESSING."

Shock ran through Innocen. Shock and twisted hope.

Had the Nameless One just . . . answered him?

The words could have been dismissed as a comment on this Warlord's misguided attempt at striking a bargain with him. Perhaps they were. Vague and possibly coincidental as the statement was, it was the first possible indication that the Nameless One might be hearing him after all. The first hint that there might still be a chance for Innocen.

There came a sudden flash of aurym from nearby—a source of energy that was deliciously distinctive. The fallen angel.

But Innocen felt a brief twinge of confusion run through the Nameless One. That flash of power. . . . Its source was coming not from the depths beneath the fortress, as he had at first thought.

It's somewhere above ground, realized Innocen. *He isn't down there. He never was. He's outside the fortress.*

And he was coming their way.

CHAPTER 29

Leah thought she could feel faint sensations of daemyn coming from the world above as she and Kallorn backtracked through the underground city, along the tunnels leading to Warlord Nefari's dungeons. But this time, they were not alone. The prisoner named Justus followed, along with any of the guards still fit enough to travel after their rough treatment at the hands of Leah and Kallorn.

What awaited them above ground, Leah could only guess.

"The alarm has stopped," Justus said nervously.

Only now that he pointed it out did Leah notice that it had been several minutes since she'd heard the last blast from the horn above.

"I can't imagine that's a good sign," she muttered as she ran.

Finally, they emerged from a tunnel and passed the cells where Leah and Kallorn had been kept, and they reached the door at the far end of the hall, which Leah had barred prior to their descent into the underground city. She could hear fists beating against it from the other side.

Leah grabbed the rod she had used to barricade the door and pulled it free from the lock. Through it poured several soldiers, leading a rush of men, women, and children. The soldiers hesitated and looked prepared to fight at the sight of Leah, Kallorn, and Justus, but after some quick words were exchanged between them and the guards accompanying the freed prisoners, the aggression left them. It took so little convincing to satisfy them, in fact, that Leah surmised that things up above were worse than she might have imagined. The soldiers proceeded through the doorway, past the cells, leading the people deeper into the dungeons, back the way Leah and the others had just come.

"What are they saying?" asked Kallorn.

Justus, weak and shaken after all that had happened to him so quickly, took a moment to find the words.

"I—I only understand bits of their language," said Justus. "The fortress has been breached, and Warlord Nefari has ordered them to evacuate through the underground city."

"Evacuate *through* the city? Or *from* it?" said Kallorn.

"I think they said through," said Justus.

"Cymorikka had several hidden entrances and exits," said Leah. "There must be a way out, through the city, for these people to escape. Justus, do they say *what* breached the fortress?"

Justus listened for a moment to the words of the guards and the passersby, and his face paled a bit.

"I think they're saying something like 'ghosts,'" he replied.

Ghosts, thought Leah, feeling daemyn flare up again from the fortress above her. Justus had said he was originally from Darsida, not Erum. For a non-native speaker, it would not be much of a stretch to mistranslate a word like "ghost" for a similar word, such as "demon."

"Justus," she said, "go with them."

Justus didn't need to be told twice. After spitting out a hasty "Thank you" almost as an afterthought, he joined the mass of humanity streaming down the halls and quickly vanished from sight.

"We both know I'm only slowing you down, Queen Anavion," said Kallorn. He gestured toward the open doorway. "Go ahead. I'll catch up as soon as I can manage."

Leah nodded once. Then she sent aurym flowing through the hydstone in her shoulder. A burst of power flowed through her, into the muscles of her legs, her ankles, and her feet, and she raced through the open doorway and up the stairs like an arrow loosed from a bowstring.

This was her first time seeing these passageways; she had been blindfolded when they'd brought her down here. Using the directions she had memorized during her descent, Leah navigated through the corridors and saw that they were lit by bits of scavenged a'thri'ik that had been inserted into wall sconces and ceiling fixtures, likely harvested from the city below when this much newer, connected complex was constructed.

The surroundings raced by Leah like swiftly flowing water as she ran, and in seconds, her aurym-fueled muscles had taken her all the way back to the central courtyard—a distance that would have taken her normal human body several minutes to traverse. A sense of urgency took over, and she abandoned any thoughts of stealth, racing straight out into the open.

Beneath the purple light of Nun, ten demons stood. Five cythwraiths and five cythraul. All of them turned as one to look at her as she emerged into the courtyard.

As usual, the cythraul all carried gigantic weapons. Three had swords that were larger than Leah's entire body. A fourth carried a club that appeared to have been whittled down from an entire tree, though what species of tree the strange black wood had come from, she could only guess. The fifth cythraul wielded a pair of hooks similar to the kind Leah had seen used to pick up and haul heavy blocks of ice. The bodies of all five were armored in black bone exoskeletons, with heads reminiscent of human skulls but massive and deformed, with empty eye sockets that glowed with red light from some unseen source deep within.

The cythwraiths, like all of the turned, had the appearance of charred skeletons, with varying amounts of damaged flesh still intact. Like Justin's demon arm, which had been transformed by a cythraul's touch, it was as if their human exteriors had been melted away to reveal these monstrosities beneath. The clothing of their former lives still hung from them in some places, mostly in tatters, and they carried the weapons of soldiers: swords, shields, spears.

All except one.

One of the cythwraiths, a small one standing barely five feet tall, carried a scythe.

As the small cythwraith turned to face Leah, she noticed the headless corpse lying on the courtyard floor in front of it.

Leah felt her jaw clench. Nefari, the Warlord of the Deep, had been beheaded. One of her muscle-bound arms lay outstretched in death toward the cleaver-bladed voulge that lay on the ground in front of her.

As Leah focused on the small cythwraith standing over Nefari's fallen form, her breath caught in her throat. There was something familiar about this demon who had once been a man.

The creature wore a simple hessian tunic, torn and badly stained. Sections of its scalp had been peeled back or flayed off entirely, but some dark hair still clung to the front of its head, forming a sharp widow's peak.

These features alone would not have been enough for Leah to come to an objective conclusion. But sometimes, when you listened hard enough, aurym gave you the answer. And when that happened, it went beyond logical deduction; you knew it deep in your core.

It's him, realized Leah. *Or rather, it was him.*

"They got you, I see," said Leah. "Innocen."

The small cythwraith that had once been Innocen stared at Leah with pupil-less, whited-over eyes.

There had been several times when she had thought that she'd sensed this man's presence during the Army of Light's journey across the Oikoumene, but she had never been entirely certain. Back in Cervice, when he'd attacked and attempted to kidnap her, Innocen had claimed to be acting alone, pursuing his own ambitions, with no affiliation to Avagad. But now, his transformed body stood before her, a servant of the demons.

He has become the monster he always was.

"WELL, WELL," said ten deep, grating voices—all five cythraul and all five cythwraiths, speaking in unison. "PRINCESS ANAVION. I DID NOT EXPECT TO FIND YOU HERE."

"I came looking for someone," said Leah. "But he isn't here."

Despite the communal nature of the voices, she directed her words at the small-statured cythwraith that had killed Nefari. But even as she spoke, the cythraul and the cythwraiths in the courtyard began to spread out slightly. Leah did not know how a cythraul's vision worked in the absence of any discernable sight organs, nor how the whitened, glazed-over eyeballs of cythwraiths were able to see the world around them, but all ten of the demons watched Leah carefully as they took up strategic positions around her.

Attempting to flank me, she realized.

She and her allies had discovered long ago that cythraul and cythwraiths somehow shared a common mind. They had called her by name just now, which meant that they knew what she was capable of. Every encounter in which Leah had fought and killed a cythraul or a cythwraith was remembered. Each time she fought them, they learned from their mistakes, and they adjusted their approach.

"YOU HAVE NEVER FOUGHT SO MANY OF ME BEFORE," said the voice of daemyn.

Despite her resolve, Leah had to suppress a chill at the sound of those ten voices, speaking in a demonic choir, directed at her from ten different directions at once.

"I WILL ACCEPT YOUR SURRENDER, MY LADY," they said.

"Like you accepted hers?" asked Leah, gesturing toward Nefari.

The thing that had once been Innocen used the butt end of its scythe to prod cruelly at Nefari's neck. Its human features contorted into a smile, causing what remained of the flesh of its cheeks to crack and break open at the corners of its mouth.

"PRECISELY," said ten voices at once.

Leah hoped that the demons didn't notice her swallow hard and take a deep breath to try to calm herself down.

It was true that she had never faced this many of them at once before, alone. Her hydstone gave her great strength and speed. But so had Innocen's, in life. And she didn't know if this turned version of him had retained those powers. If so, it was uncertain how she would fare against him in single combat, let alone against the rest of them, all at once.

All I have to do is distract them long enough for the Warlord's people to get away, thought Leah. *Then, if I can make it over the walls, maybe I'll have a chance.*

It had been a long time since she'd felt fearful enough for her own safety to consider running away from a fight. There was a strange degree of comfort about it. Nostalgia, perhaps, for simpler times.

"Innocen," said Leah, her eyes darting from one corner of the courtyard to the other as the demons continued to spread out, trying not to lose track of their positions. "If there is anything left of the person you once were and you can hear my words, I want you to know that I have pity in my heart for all who have suffered the torture of being transformed by a cythraul's daemyn touch." She paused, then narrowed her gaze at the small figure. "All except you. I pray that somehow, some small part of you is still alive in there, somewhere, so you can feel it when I kill you a second time."

"IT WILL PLEASE YOU," said the ten demon voices, "TO LEARN THAT THE SOULS THAT INHABITED THESE BODIES . . . STILL LIVE, LOCKED IN PERPETUAL TORMENT. IT WILL BRING ME GREAT PLEASURE, MY LADY, TO BLESS *YOU* WITH THE SAME . . . *ETERNAL FATE!*"

Leah called on aurym, sending spirit power flowing through the hydstone in her shoulder and into the muscles of her body. Even as she charged at the first of the demons, she could feel the cythraul around her calling on daemyn—could sense the concentrated "black aurym," as it had once been described to her, forming in their hands—explosive blasts preparing to be fired at her from five different directions at once.

But, simultaneously, she also felt Kallorn appear behind her. Until this moment, he had kept himself concealed as he watched from the shadows of the doorway leading from the courtyard into the dungeons. But now, his aurym presence leaped into sharp focus.

There was a bright flash and a burst of power as Kallorn fired a lightning bolt from his sword at the nearest cythwraith. Leah, her hands clenched into fists, darted at Innocen, eager to do to him as he had done to the Warlord and to do it as slowly and painfully as prudence allowed.

CHAPTER 30

Hook's tendency was to be shrewdly calculating. Olorus was wont to be enthusiastically daring. Megara, meanwhile, tended to represent a sort of middle ground between the two. Normally, this made them a well-rounded trio. But, under the current circumstances, all three of them entered the broken front gates of the fortress with the same level of devil-may-care recklessness, to hell with the consequences. The life of their queen, their commander, and, more importantly, their friend, hung in the balance.

The alarm horn had gone eerily silent. The clouds they had planned to use as cover were gone, and it was beneath the full light of the purple moon of Nun that they breached the smoking ruins of the front gate of the fortress, blown asunder by the daemyn blasts of cythraul.

Hook could smell smoke and charred stone. That haunted sensation of unease that he had come to associate with the presence of cythraul—an ethereal, almost undefinable feeling of dread, comparable only to stagnant air in the room of a sick person—hung heavy thick in the atmosphere all around him.

What can we hope to do against cythwraiths and cythraul working together? wondered Hook.

He tightened his grip on his a'thri'ik-tipped lance as he ran, and he tried not to think about it. They knew they didn't stand a chance. But if this was how it ended, Hook Bard was prepared to die the way he'd lived. Not just fighting but biting, scratching, and gouging—fighting as dirty as he had to.

"Watch out!" Olorus shouted, skidding suddenly to a halt.

Hook stopped his charge not a moment too soon.

Where the dark figure that suddenly stood before them had come from, he could only guess. It seemed as if it had materialized out of the very shadows. No matter. Hook wasted no time. He hauled back and threw his lance. It whizzed through the air.

Hook's aim was true. But when the lance was halfway to its target, the dark figure raised its arm. The sailing lance shuddered in the air, and, defying all of the laws of physics with which Hook was familiar, it turned end-over-end in mid-flight, like the needle of a compass. Its blunt end landed firmly in the grasp of the figure's outstretched hand.

Megara leveled her gauntlet at the figure, and a blast of concentrated sunlight, so bright that Hook had to shield his eyes, erupted from the aurstone embedded within it.

Megara's aurym attack was not a projectile. Or, if it was, it was too fast for its movement to be observed; the beam drew an instant connection between its source and its target. How the target managed to block it in time—creating a sudden wall of energy that caused the sunlight to disperse harmlessly into a cone around it—Hook couldn't begin to guess. But that was what Hook saw, all in less than a quarter of a second.

Olorus, true to form, had thrown caution to the wind and was already rushing at the figure as wildly as a charging elasmoth with sword and shield raised despite the clear results that awaited him. If Hook could have had his tongue back for just one second, for just one word, he would have used it to shout at Olorus to stop. If the creature before them could call a flying lance to its hand and render moot even an attack as powerful as Megara's, then what would it do to Olorus?

But there was nothing Hook could do. He could only watch his friend sprint forward, with one last war cry, to his inevitable death.

Olorus had his sword raised behind his shield and primed to strike when the figure made a sweeping arc with its arm. Not the arm that now held Hook's spear, but the other one, which appeared to be holding a short sword.

A gout of flame erupted from the end of the weapon. Even from here, the wall of heat was so intense that Hook found himself taking a step back.

Olorus, caught in such close proximity to the attack, involuntarily halted his charge and fell backward with his arms raised to cover his face. His sword and shield hit the ground beside him.

But the flames did not touch Olorus. They only blocked his path to the figure, halting his charge and forcing him to remain at a distance.

Olorus tried to scramble for his sword. But the wall of flames suddenly dispersed, the figure stepped through, and it intercepted him, stepping between him and his weapon.

Beneath the shroud of a black, hooded cloak, a face looked down at Olorus, and Olorus looked bravely back up at it. Hook's lance was still in one of its hands. In the other, it held the weapon that Hook had at first mistaken for a short sword. But in fact, he now saw that it was a longsword whose blade had been fractured.

At the sight of the face looking down at him, Olorus's expression, contorted in rage and defiance a moment before, transformed into disbelief and something that might have been terror, wonder, or a bit of both.

"By the spirit . . ." Olorus whispered.

CHAPTER 31

Even as Leah closed the gap between her and the cythwraith that had been Innocen in a few leaping steps, she felt the daemyn blasts forming in the hands of the five cythraul behind her. She had seen such attacks destroy entire buildings and tear through the brick and mortar of city walls as if they were no more substantial than a child's pillow fort. What they did to flesh and bone was far more terrible.

Innocen stood still, watching Leah as she advanced. If he had lost his hydstone powers when he was transformed, she could tear his head off his shoulders before the cythraul let loose their first attacks. But if he did still have those powers, the two of them would be equally matched, at best.

At the last moment before Leah reached him, she made as if to lunge forward but adjusted her trajectory to sail past him instead, snatching the Warlord's voulge from the floor of the courtyard as she went. She had been hoping that this would draw an attack out of Innocen if he still had his hyd powers.

But if he did still have his powers, he didn't take the bait. He did not so much as move a muscle.

Leah hit the ground in a sprint toward a cythraul whose hand was raised with a ball of concentrated darkness growing in its palm. Despite their size, cythraul were far deadlier at a distance than they were up close—to someone like Leah, anyway. Engaging them in close quarters was her best bet. But she had to proceed with caution. The hydstone was a dangerous tool. When you could move faster than you could think, you were only one wrong move away from killing yourself at any moment.

Warlord Nefari's voulge spun like a windmill in Leah's hands as she reached the cythraul. The cleaver-like blade would not be strong enough to cut through its bone armor. But that was not her intention. She slammed the face of the blade into the monster's extended hand, batting it to the side to get past it.

Leah jumped and clung fast to the cythraul's shoulders. Entangled so closely with the eleven-foot monster, she could feel the heat emanating from the unseen fires burning deep within it, illuminating the red glow from its empty eye sockets. She sent hydstone power flaring through her right arm as she jabbed. If the High Demons could be said to have a weak spot—and that was a *relative* term only—it was the front of the neck.

Leah's bare fist, its flesh, sinew, and bones momentarily strengthened by the power of the hydstone, punched through the cythraul's throat. The daemyn blast in its hand, only half-formed, went sailing skyward as Leah, her arm plunged elbow-deep into its neck, dug blindly through the connecting tissues within. Finally, her fingers closed around the object of her search.

Leah pulled.

With a crack, the cythraul's head collapsed backward like a flower whose stem had been bent. Still riding the creature's shoulder, Leah ripped the black, viscera-coated vertebra out and discarded it.

Leah knew from experience that the creature's own power would turn on it as it died. Its body would collapse inward as if imploding, then explode outward in a final blast. She would have to be clear of the blast radius, but there was also a chance to put it to good use if she could only get the dying body close enough to one of the other—

Leah saw Innocen coming with enough time to register the incoming attack but not enough to move out of the way. Panicking, she dropped everything else and redirected the full flow of the hydstone's power away from her arms and into her midsection, strengthening her abdominals, pectorals, skin, and bones—the instant before his fist struck her in the sternum.

Leah heard herself make a noise that was half gasp and half gag. Even with her hyd-powered defenses, pain jolted through her that rivaled any she had ever known. It felt like her guts had been hit with a broad-headed mallet. If she hadn't seen him coming in time to mount a defense, she was certain that his hand would have gone straight through her abdomen, up beneath her ribcage, through her heart, and out her back, perhaps taking a handful of her vertebrae in its grasp in an ironic homage to how she had dispatched the cythraul.

The force of the strike carried her backward. The voulge was thrown from her grasp. And as she sailed through the air, any doubt that Innocen could still call on his hyd powers was erased from her mind.

She struck the courtyard wall and dropped hard to the ground. She could barely breathe, but she forced herself to roll quickly to the side and take stock of her situation.

Leah could move at highly increased speeds while under the influence of the hydstone, but its power did not increase the rate of her perception. She had time to register three things: that Kallorn, across the courtyard, appeared to have dispatched one of the cythwraiths and was now engaged in combat with three all at once, that as the first cythraul writhed in its death throes, the remaining four cythraul were *all* aiming daemyn blasts at her, and finally, that Innocen was already only a few yards away from her, lunging toward her, leading with his knee raised and aimed for her skull.

Leah scrambled, propelling herself by her fingertips to roll through the dirt. It was anything but a graceful escape, but it did the trick. Innocen's intended strike ended with his knee buried in the stone of the courtyard wall instead of taking her head off at the shoulders or crushing it like an egg.

Evading his attacks isn't an option, she realized. *I'll run out of luck eventually and get myself killed. The only choice is to press him.*

Before Innocen had the chance to extricate himself from the wall, Leah was there. With one hand, she grabbed him by the back of the neck, causing him to emit a demonic roar. With the other, she unleashed a barrage of punches to the lower back. But he was prepared, and his defenses were up. So she turned, braced herself, and threw him, sending his body sailing across the courtyard.

It was at this point that the four remaining cythraul let loose their fully charged daemyn attacks. Leah was prepared to dodge four daemyn blasts aimed directly at her. But they weren't loosed all at once, nor at a single target. Instead, they fired them one at a time: the first directly at her, another at the courtyard floor a span in front of her, the third to her right, and the fourth to her left.

The attacks were thoughtfully interspersed so that dodging them became almost impossible, even for her. She felt a brief moment of panic before selecting the only direction available.

Up!

Leah kicked her feet off the ground and sailed skyward, twenty or twenty-five feet off the ground. The daemyn blasts erupted in a series of sucking, swirling, ear-splitting explosions against the courtyard's floor and wall below and behind her. Only at the height of her jump—in the long moment before her upward momentum gave way to the downward pull of gravity, did she realize her mistake.

Leah looked down. Below, the cythraul she'd mortally wounded was beginning to implode, portions of its exoskeleton being sucked inward, causing gouts of black blood to splash across the courtyard floor.

And Innocen was standing down there, slightly to the side, the shredded rags of his tunic flapping in the expelled energy of the daemyn blasts, quietly regarding Leah as she dropped, observing her fall and measuring her trajectory.

Leah's arms pinwheeled as she attempted to gain some control of her descent. But all the strength in the world was nothing against empty air. No amount of force was useful without something against which to enact it.

Innocen bent his knees like a runner preparing to begin a race. He seemed to be bracing himself, waiting for the proper moment.

And soon, it came. Leah's momentum caused her to turn over in her fall, and she lost sight of him.

She knew it was coming. She braced herself and tried to disperse her hyd power as evenly as possible across her entire body, not knowing where the strike would land—only that it would.

A kick. Directly to the back of the neck.

Her aurym-powered defenses were enough to prevent the blow from breaking her back but not enough to prevent her from uttering a cry of pain as her body was sent flying.

Leah felt herself spinning through the air. In the midst of her spiraling flight, she realized what Innocen had done. He hadn't just kicked her to harm her. He had kicked her to redirect her toward the dying High Demon.

Leah barely managed to get her hands up in time to brace herself against the exploding cythraul directly in front of her. But this time, even hyd-powered defenses weren't enough.

C H A P T E R   3 2

A shockwave expanded outward from the dying cythraul in a veil of violet bolts and rearing flames. Leah felt a sucking sensation against her eardrums, felt the concussive force press so hard against her chest that her ribcage seemed to compress against her insides, felt a bolt of energy arc sizzle up her arm, boiling the blood in her veins and leaving a streak of blackened flesh in its wake, felt violet flames sear her face and burn her scalp.

When Leah's body hit the courtyard floor, she found it strangely forgiving for a solid stone surface. An instant later, she realized why. The exploding cythraul had compromised the foundation.

She felt a shudder. The stone gave way beneath her, and she was falling, falling, falling. Falling into shadow, into the darkness of the dungeons beneath the fortress.

Leah had no memory of landing. One moment, she was hurtling downward amidst a shower of broken stone. The next, she lay looking up at a hole in the ceiling fifteen feet above her. There was pain all over her body, but none of her injuries seemed as pressing as the dancing heat coming from above her head. It was a bit surreal, coming to the conclusion that one's hair was on fire.

Leah rolled, raising her hands over her head and beating out the flames. The pain of her hands against the burns on her scalp was dizzying and nearly blinding.

When the fire in her hair was out, she looked up at the hole in the ceiling where she had fallen through the courtyard floor. Nun, the purple moon, shone down through it perfectly, as if it were watching her. She could still hear and sense fighting going on above, but with Innocen up there *and* multiple other demons, Kallorn did not stand a chance.

Leah stood. She could jump that high, as long as she wasn't too badly injured. She just hoped she could make it back up to the courtyard before it was too—

The figure emerged from the shadows so fast she couldn't react. She hadn't even realized Innocen had jumped down here.

A bony black hand grabbed her by the neck. Before she could get her defenses up, the fingers squeezed her windpipe shut. She hastily got some power into her neck to prevent it from being crushed any further.

All at once, Leah was hanging suspended above the ground, looking down into the pupilless white orbs of Innocen's blank eyes in the purple glow from the moon. She clawed at his fingers with her hands. She kicked at his arm. But ninety percent of her power was being used just to keep her neck from being crushed within his grip. What remained wasn't enough to give her the strength to break free.

Her healer's training gave her unnerving insights into precisely what was happening and what would happen next. The compressed carotid artery was reducing the amount of blood flowing to her brain. That explained the growing dizziness she felt and the haziness at the edges of her vision. The longer this went on, the quicker she would fade. Soon, she would black out. And without the hydstone's power actively defending her body, her neck would be turned to pulp within Innocen's grasp.

Leah continued to claw and kick, but her hands and feet felt heavy. She seemed to be having trouble moving them at all, let alone mounting an effectual counterattack. She felt limp. And tired. Very, very tired.

The desiccated flesh of Innocen's half-demon face split open, revealing a blackened, deformed cheekbone lined with loose teeth as he smiled up at her.

I'm sorry, Leah thought as the world faded around her. *Zechariah, Olorus, Hook, Gunnar, Megara, Sif. . . . I never should have come here. I'm sorry . . . everyone.*

Leah heard and felt a surge of aurym power from above, distinct from anything she had felt so far. Innocen's partially intact nostrils flared, and the white orbs of his eyes widened. His focus appeared to have been broken, for she felt his grip on her neck loosen a bit, and she knew it was the only chance she was going to get.

Redirecting some of the power from the muscles of her neck into her arms, Leah slammed her fists against either side of Innocen's head. Weakened as she was, she could only muster the strength to stun him, but that was enough. He staggered backward, a stream of mostly human-looking blood leaking from one ear, and Leah was free.

Innocen was already reaching out to try to grab her again as she kicked downward with both legs and shot up in the air. She gasped for breath as she sailed upward and through the open hole in the ceiling, back up into the courtyard.

The first things she saw as she landed were two ragged halves of a cythraul pouring black blood as they fell apart from one another. For a moment, she thought she had underestimated Kallorn. But then she saw him lying on the ground, clutching a wound in his side, surrounded by three cythwraiths. True to his word, his sword was still in his hand, but he wasn't getting up. He was out of the fight.

Yet the cythwraiths stood stock still, staring. They were not attacking Kallorn. Neither were the cythraul. They were all focused on someone else. Or something else.

Leah turned. Beneath the purple moonlight, a tall figure stood in the center of the courtyard—smaller than the cythraul and not nearly as tall as Nefari the Warlord had stood, but taller than average, nonetheless. A dark cloak hung from his shoulders, and the hood was drawn over his head.

It was a man. That much, Leah could tell. And his body language bespoke a calmness that bordered on serenity, even when surrounded by demons on all sides. It was a calmness that communicated the implied promise of a threat.

It was difficult to describe how you knew you were looking upon a dangerous man. You just knew. And as the man shifted his grip on his weapon, allowing Leah to see for the first time that he held a sword with flames dancing along the blade, Leah's intuition was confirmed. Her heart leaped with hope.

"Ahlund!" she called.

The figure looked toward her.

The closest of the three remaining cythraul took action. It was the one wielding a club that appeared to have been whittled out of an entire tree. It hauled back and threw its weapon at Ahlund.

Leah tried to run but was too drained and battered from Innocen's attacks to get there in time. She could only watch as the club—a thousand pounds if it was an ounce—hurtled toward Ahlund....

And stopped.

Leah skidded to a halt in mid-step, staring at the tree-sized club. It had stopped before it could hit Ahlund. He had his hand raised toward it.

He . . . caught it? thought Leah.

But no. His hand wasn't touching it. It was still several feet away from him. It hung, suspended by an invisible force, floating in midair.

Ahlund lowered his hand, and the tree-sized club fell to the courtyard floor with a ground-shaking thud.

A sound from behind drew Leah's attention back around. She turned to see Innocen leap up out of the hole in the courtyard. He landed sure-footedly, blood still dribbling from the ear that Leah had wounded.

Ahlund made a calculated survey of the demons that surrounded him. Three cythraul, three cythwraiths, and now, Innocen.

"FINALLY," said the remaining seven at once, in the same chorused voice. "YOU COME OUT OF HIDING."

Silence hung over the courtyard. Ahlund said nothing. He only watched the demons.

"FOOL," said the demons. "YOU SHOULD NOT HAVE—"

The seven voices were cut off as Ahlund swung his sword and a volley of fireballs jumped from it. At dazzling speed, they shot across the courtyard and rained down like comets, carrying away the cythwraiths before they could so much as take a step.

The three cythraul raised their hands and fired daemyn blasts. Without the benefit of hyd powers, Ahlund was unable to evade them. Leah could only watch as they bore down on him.

A flame erupted from Ahlund's sword. But instead of striking outward at the demons, it enveloped him, closing in over his own body until it formed an elongated spheroid of fire—not the raging red or orange type that Leah was used to seeing, but a steady, brilliant blue-white.

The daemyn blasts struck the flaming spheroid, where they erupted. But Leah knew she couldn't afford to watch any longer. She turned to face Innocen.

Leah blinked in surprise. She scanned the courtyard, searching every corner, but Innocen was gone.

Hiding somewhere, she thought. *Waiting for a chance to strike from the shadows again.*

When Leah turned back, she saw that the daemyn blasts were dissipating. The smoke cleared, revealing the blue-white spheroid, still intact. It opened outward from the center, like a flower with petals of flame, and peeled back to reveal the same figure standing at its center, holding up the source of the power: a Ru'Onorath sword that had been broken, leaving only half the blade.

The figure did not speak. It surveyed the courtyard, then swung the sword.

The blast of blue-white energy that poured forth from the blade was like a solid entity, so blinding that Leah had to raise a hand to shield her eyes. It rushed forward like an ocean wave and was met with no resistance as it pushed through the cythraul. Leah heard two roars of agony as the blue-white fire burned them to ash.

"Behind you!" Kallorn cried from his position on the ground, clutching his wound.

Ahlund turned. The last remaining cythraul had unleashed another daemyn blast that was coming straight for him.

Ahlund raised his left arm. The blast of daemyn slowed, swirled like water circling a drain, and seemed to shrink as if collapsing inward on itself.

But it was not collapsing. It was being sucked inward by something.

Into . . . his arm? thought Leah.

Just like that, the attack was gone, and the figure stood, untouched. The last of the cythraul seemed to falter as if fighting the urge to take a step backward.

The figure—a figure that Leah now realized was not Ahlund after all—raised its free hand. Something came flying through the courtyard and landed perfectly in his outstretched palm without looking. This was not a lucky catch; he had drawn it to himself like metal filings to a magnet. Leah recognized it instantly. It was Hook's a'thri'ik-tipped lance. The one he had plundered from the tomb of an Ancient Ellenean king. Leah turned and, for the first time, noticed Hook, Olorus, and Megara standing on the opposite end of the courtyard.

The figure pushed the hood of his cloak back from his head, and Leah gasped.

Beneath the hood were features that were still quite boyish, even if they had hardened since the last time Leah had seen them. His sandy-blond hair was longer and unkempt, and a surprisingly thick layer of facial hair coated his jaw, cheeks, and upper lip. His blue eyes seemed to flash as he stared at the cythraul.

"There's no need to send any more of your servants to find me," said Justin Holmes, pointing the lance at the cythraul. "I am coming for you."

The fleshless, skull-like faces of cythraul allowed for only a limited palette of expressions to emote. But today, Leah saw one that she had never seen on the face of a High Demon before. It was fear. And it was the last expression the cythraul made before a beam of concentrated aurym energy shot from the a'thri'ik tip of the golden lance in Justin's hand and burned through the center of its head.

Justin swung the spear gracefully sideways as if he were painting the air with a brush, and the beam of energy separated the top of the cythraul's head from the bottom, cutting the skull in half just below the eye line.

A cocktail of black ichor and gray brain matter spilled down the front of the beast's skull. Its body dropped to its knees and imploded.

With the last of the demons defeated and Innocen nowhere to be found, Justin placed the butt end of the lance against the ground at his side like a walking stick. He let out a deep sigh, turned, and smiled.

"Hey, Leah," he said.

Leah ran to him. Justin let the lance fall with a clatter and came toward her, too.

They met in the center of the courtyard, where Leah jumped into him so hard that it almost knocked him off his feet. The momentum carried her in a half-circle in his arms, which locked so tightly around her that it would have taken hyd-powered strength for her to have broken free. If she'd wanted to. But she didn't.

Leah's face was pressed against his chest. She felt his hand run gently through her hair and down her cheek. He touched her chin, and she looked up at him.

Justin's eyes moved back and forth, taking in the look of her. But he wasn't examining the scar across her head, the injury to her ear, or any other features of her face. He was looking at her eyes, switching back and forth between them, taking turns looking deeply into each one. The expression on his face was akin to astonishment, like he couldn't believe what he was seeing.

Leah moved her face closer to his, until she could feel the heat of his skin. He tilted his neck and rested his forehead against hers, letting out a sigh of relief. Relief that she was alive, perhaps? Relief that he had found her? Whatever it was, she felt it in his body against hers, like a release of tension, as if a great weight had suddenly been lifted off him, even as his arms tightened around her all the more. It was not a grip of possession. Not even one of passion—at first. It was the grip of someone holding on to something they never wanted to lose again.

Their foreheads were still touching. Neither of them seemed to want to pull away. His arms were wrapped around her, and her hands cradled his face, her thumbnails scraping gently up and down along the line of his jaw. It felt only natural that the next thing to touch would be their lips. It was only incidental contact. A slight graze, without plan or purpose. But, yet again, neither of them pulled away. For a moment, their lips lingered there, only touching. Leah opened hers first. Then Justin. And they kissed, long and deeply.

Leah was vaguely aware of the carnage around her, of the injuries she had sustained in battle, of the other people present in this courtyard. But only vaguely. It was, for practical purposes, as if the rest of the world had fallen away, leaving Leah and Justin together.

Finally, they had found one another.

CHAPTER 33

Innocen's body limped as it fled through the cleft between the rocks. There, under the Nameless One's control, it moved into the shadows, ducked low, and remained still.

Hiding, thought Innocen from his place trapped within the partitioned corner of his consciousness. *Has the fallen angel become so powerful that even the Nameless One hides from him?*

The Nameless One had driven Innocen's body to retreat while the fallen angel was busy with the others, escaping from the courtyard and racing up one of the rocky escarpments surrounding the fortress beneath the purple moonlight.

Presently, Innocen's body repositioned itself until, with its extrasensory perception, Innocen could "see" the glowing outline of several life forces far below.

The princess of Nolia, thought Innocen, *using hyd powers.*

That had been an unexpected surprise.

I underestimated her, he thought. *If I had known what she was capable of, our first meeting might have gone differently. I might have taken her on as an apprentice rather than merely attempting to use her as leverage to get to the ethoul.*

But then again, there were many things he would have done differently if he'd had the chance.

Innocen had gotten quite good at reading the emotions of his master. And at the moment, the Nameless One felt . . . unsettled.

Innocen's body had been brought here because the Nameless One had sensed Justin. The young man's presence, therefore, could not have been what had the master of demons so unnerved. It must have been something else.

I would not have expected him to be able to stop us, thought Innocen. *Perhaps the boy has grown more powerful than the Nameless One anticipated.*

Innocen felt a wave of disgust at his own thoughts. *Us.* When had he started thinking of himself as belonging to this collective of the Nameless One's forces?

The Nameless One continued watching the scene below. Several life forces entered the fortress courtyard. Nearby, the spirit warrior wielding lightning powers still lay wounded. In the center of the courtyard stood the princess. Her aura was quite distinctive and quite strong.

Only now did Innocen notice that she appeared to be standing alone.

But that wasn't right. The ethoul was with her. Or he had been. Now, there was. . . .

"Nothing," Innocen said within his mind.

So, that was what had surprised the Nameless One so much.

"You cannot sense him as you can others," said Innocen.

"HE HAS LEARNED TO MASK HIS PRESENCE WELL," replied the Nameless One.

Innocen felt a thrill. The Nameless One again appeared to have responded to his words. Further confirmation that his master could hear him.

"The girl is still the key," Innocen quickly added in an attempt to maintain momentum and further test the waters. "The boy cares for her. We can separate them, capture her, take away her power, and draw him to us."

"WE NEED NOT *DRAW HIM* TO US," said the Nameless One. His voice was like the grinding of great wheels. "HE SAYS HE INTENDS TO COME TO ME. SO BE IT. WE SHALL LET HIM THINK THAT HE IS A THREAT. IT WILL MAKE HIM OVERCONFIDENT IN HIS MISSION. HE WILL WALK, WILLINGLY, INTO THE SAME TRAP IN WHICH HIS *FATHER* WAS ENSNARED."

Innocen hesitated, planning his next words carefully. This would be a gamble. But it was one he had to take.

"The hyd powers of this body were compromised in the transformation," he said. "This body would have been enough to defeat the princess easily, and perhaps the boy too, if I had been in control."

A noise emanated from Innocen's throat: a dangerous sound, like the warning growl of a predator. "I DO NOT CEDE CONTROL OVER THE BODIES OF THOSE WHO HAVE BECOME MY SERVANTS."

"I wish to *remain* your servant, My Lord," said Innocen.

It was a lie. But what other choice did he have?

"Give me full control when we are in battle, and take it back afterward," offered Innocen. "All my skills and abilities, I offer you freely. Simply give the command."

Another noise bubbled up from the throat that had once been Innocen's and Innocen's alone. For several long moments, the Nameless One's attention remained focused on the life forces in the fortress below. Enough time went by that Innocen's hope faded, and he felt certain he wasn't going to get an answer. But then, the Nameless One spoke.

"I AM SENDING THIS BODY TO ROHGHOST," said the Nameless One. "THERE, YOU WILL JOIN MY LIEUTENANT, AVAGAD, AND PREPARE FOR THE ETHOUL'S ARRIVAL."

"Yes, My Lord," said Innocen.

"IN THE MEANTIME," said the demon's voice. "YOU WILL SHOW ME WHAT YOU CAN DO."

And suddenly, standing there in the rocky cleft, Innocen realized that, for the first time in over half a year, he was in control of his body.

Innocen took a step forward—of his own accord. The torment of constant pain that had wracked his soul, though it did not disappear, had cooled to a more manageable form of agony. He raised a hand and held it in front of his face, flexing the individual fingers at his command.

He felt a smile pull at what cracked, desiccated flesh still remained on his face.

This, thought Innocen, *changes everything.*

Innocen sent aurym flowing through the hydstone embedded deep within his body. With strength and speed belying his small form, he leaped from the hiding place in the rocks and ran along the near-vertical cliffside like an insect, punching straight into the rock to create handholds and footholds where necessary. He was moving as he used to.

He felt almost alive. Or, at least, closer to living than he had felt in a very long time.

CHAPTER 34

By the time it occurred to Justin that he ought to let Leah go, he could hardly remember how the two of them had gotten themselves into this position: standing in the center of the fortress courtyard with their bodies entangled, their mouths pressed together in eager passion. There was no learning curve to kissing her; it came so naturally that it was like he had done it a thousand times before and could do it a thousand times more without ever getting enough.

But finally, their faces parted, and he was staring into her eyes again. They were green, with little gold flecks in the irises that he imagined few people ever got close enough to see the way he saw them now. The lips he had just tasted so thoroughly curved upward at the edges as she stared back at him. Her lower lip curled inward, and she bit it as if trying to hold back a laugh.

When he'd sensed her here, so close to his location, he had hardly dared believe it to be true. Coming out of hiding this early hadn't been part of his plan. But it had been worth it.

It was with some chagrin that Justin suddenly realized Leah was not standing. After lifting her up, he had neglected to lower her back down again, and she was still suspended off the ground in his arms. He bashfully lowered her to her feet, but even then, he did not let go—*would* not let go. He kept his hands on her hips, and to his relief, she kept hers on the sides of his face.

"I . . ." Justin said quietly, "wasn't planning to do that."

The grin that had been tugging at Leah's mouth spread. He remembered her as beautiful, but not *this* beautiful.

"I was," she said.

Leah's eyes flashed toward the others who had entered the courtyard. She stepped away from him, and for a moment, Justin was seized with the crazy impulse not to let her go, lest he lose her again—

Justin was blindsided from behind, struck with the force of a tackle and lifted clean off his feet. Suddenly, it was *he* who was suspended above the ground, with Olorus Antony's thick arms wrapped around his midsection so tightly that he couldn't hold back an involuntary and thoroughly undignified "*Hurmph!*"

"By the spirit, lad!" Olorus growled, turning Justin around and around like a dancer, barking out gleeful guffaws that echoed through the fortress courtyard. "Do you know how good it is to see you alive?! Where have you been all this time, you big—?"

"Kallorn!" said Justin urgently, suddenly spotting him across the courtyard.

Sir Kallorn Rhodos was bent low, propped on one knee. One hand held his Ru'Onorath sword. The other clutched a wound in his side. He appeared to be shaking.

Olorus hastily let Justin down, and Justin turned to Leah. "Leah, can you help him?"

Leah nodded. But instead of rushing toward Kallorn, she first ran where the headless body of a large woman lay sprawled on the ground in the courtyard. She gently turned the body over and retrieved a chain the dead woman was wearing as a necklace. Attached to it was a ring, which she quickly pulled from the chain and slipped on her finger. Then, together, she and Justin ran to Kallorn.

Justin acknowledged, in passing, the other two new arrivals in the courtyard: Hook Bard and the big woman with him. Both of them, along with Olorus, had tried to kill him a few minutes ago outside the fortress. But, in their defense, Justin was pretty sure they had thought he was a demon at the time. Or at least he hoped so.

"Kallorn," said Justin as he slid to a stop in front of him.

In the light of the violet moon, Kallorn looked up. Justin noted a splash of red across the ground in front of him.

"It's . . . really you," Kallorn said in a pained voice.

The yellow-haired Guardian of the Oikoumene was a shell of the man Justin had known back at Esthean before the hidden city's fall to Avagad's forces. He was propped on one knee. He held his sword in one hand, but he wore no armor, and the simple clothing he did wear had not done him any favors. He clutched tightly to his side.

"I never thought I'd see you again," said Justin.

"Likewise, my old student," said Kallorn.

Kallorn shook with a sudden spasm of pain and fell forward. He would have hit the ground if Leah, moving at a speed that defied human limits, had not dashed to intervene, catching him.

"Try not to move," Leah told Kallorn as she lowered him to a prone position. "Let me see it."

Kallorn tilted his hand away from his side. The hand that had been cupping the wound was a bowl of dark red blood. His arm trembled badly.

Leah got quickly to work. Borrowing Ahlund's broken sword from Justin, she began to carefully cut away Kallorn's shirt to better expose the wound. Justin lingered to the side, watching Kallorn, and watching Leah.

I have so many questions to ask her, he thought. *And she probably has twice as many for me. That will all have to come in time.*

Justin closed his eyes and reached out with the extrasensory perceptions of aurym. He always kept his perceptions up, sensing everything around him to some degree at all times. But when he focused, he could feel—and, in a way, see—from a broad distance. He could sense the occupants of the courtyard around him. But he could also sense the people beneath this fortress, and other life forces further down that were difficult to identify. He could sense the wildlife in the wilderness surrounding this place, from the largest mammal to the smallest insect. And he could sense that there were no more demons, not for many miles.

Except for one, thought Justin. *The one that got away.*

He could sense the lone cythwraith that had fled the battle rather than fighting to the death, already a mile from this place. It seemed to be wasting no time putting significant distance between itself and Justin.

Leah had removed Kallorn's shirt and was touching the gash in his side to examine the severity of the wound. Kallorn looked up at Justin.

"What are you doing here, boy?" he asked.

"Looking for you," said Justin.

The answer seemed to surprise Kallorn. It looked as if he might question Justin's statement, but another spasm of pain rocked him, and he gritted his teeth and closed his eyes.

"Is it bad?" said Justin.

"Yes," said Leah. "But not beyond the skill of a healer. Kallorn, you'd better lie down for this."

Justin and Leah helped lower Kallorn to a position more conducive to Leah's work. To Kallorn's credit, he did not cry out. Neither did he let go of his Ru'Onorath sword.

"This won't feel good, but it will be over quickly," said Leah, and she extended her hand over Kallorn's wound and called on aurym to speed the healing process.

By now, Olorus, Hook, and the third member of their group—a tall woman with blue, geometric facial tattoos—had approached from behind and were surveying the scene from a respectful distance.

Justin promptly stood and ran at Olorus. He gave the man quite a start as he wrapped his arms around him for a more proper greeting now that he was not so distracted. He squeezed him tightly enough that Olorus made a sound very nearly as undignified as the one Justin had made within *his* grasp. When he'd caught his breath, Olorus returned the embrace with a joyful, growling laugh.

"We are a long way from our first meeting in the Shifting Mountains, my friend," said Justin, releasing Olorus. "Thank you for having the patience to only *threaten* to kill me that day."

At Justin's words, Olorus wheeled to address the woman standing beside Hook. "Did you hear that?!" Olorus demanded with a smile. "'Thank you for having the *patience*,' he says! I told you I can be patient when I want to be! But when it's time to act, I act!"

Returning his attention to Justin, Olorus nodded to him. "You're most welcome," Olorus said. "Rarely have I regretted it!"

Justin studied the man's face. He could not tell if Olorus was just older than he remembered him or if the days since he'd last seen him had been so unkind that they had dramatically altered his physical appearance. The physical state of the man notwithstanding, it was good to see him.

A few steps away was Hook Bard. He stood with his lance in his grasp, having retrieved it from the place where Justin had dropped it to embrace Leah. As usual, Hook was silent, watching Justin.

Justin raised his hand to make one of the only hand signs he could remember: *"Hello."*

An amused look came over Hook's face. He stepped forward, raised one hand, and gave Justin a good-natured smack on the shoulder that very nearly knocked him over. Justin replied with a friendly smack of his own—and didn't manage to make Hook budge a fraction of an inch.

The big woman with the tattoos snapped her fingers to get Olorus and Hook's attention, then began signing something.

"Yes, good point," said Olorus. "There could be more demons nearby. We'll take up positions at the gate and—"

"The danger is gone for now," said Justin. "One got away, but there aren't any other demons within fifty miles of here."

Justin focused his perceptions and turned to gaze through the very walls of the fortress, through the mountains, toward the tiny, dark figure still racing away, off to the east. Demons fleeing from battle was an unprecedented occurrence in his experience, and he wasn't quite certain what to make of it yet.

Olorus, Hook, and the warrior woman responded to Justin's assertion of their safety with dubious looks. Justin smiled at them with understanding.

"Trust me," he said.

Leah stood from Kallorn's position, wiping blood from her hands. What had a few minutes ago been a deep, open laceration in the man's side was now a strip of scar tissue that might have passed for a years-old injury if not for the still-drying blood on the surface of the skin surrounding it.

"Will I live?" asked Kallorn. He had never been one to mince words.

"You will," said Leah. "In a perfect world, I would tell you to rest for a week while the deeper damage, below the surface, heals itself."

"There are no such luxuries anymore," said Kallorn.

Leah handed Ahlund's sword back to Justin. They shared a silent look. Then Justin slipped the broken sword into the scabbard hanging from the baldric slung over his shoulder.

A part of Justin still expected to wake up and find that this had all been a dream. He had never expected to see Leah again. Especially not after the disaster at Esthean that forced him to flee aimlessly across the ocean and into the east. There was much about her that had changed. Her hair was longer than he remembered it, except for a portion that appeared to have been burned off in the battle here in the fortress minutes prior. He saw that an aging scar running across her face and a partially missing ear were souvenirs of what he could only assume had been a nearly fatal wound. But the biggest difference was the hard, haunted look in her eye, a testament to wounds of a more hidden nature. He could only imagine everything she had been through.

And what about me? thought Justin. *How different I must look since the last time she saw me.*

Moments ago, they had been so close. But a lump formed in his throat at the thought of the gulf that separated them. How could he possibly hope to tell her everything that had happened to him, everything he had done . . . and everything he hoped to do?

"Thank you, Leah," said Kallorn.

"I had assumed introductions would be in order," said Justin, "but I see you've already met Princess Anavion."

"Princess Anavion?" Olorus spoke up from behind. "You *have* been gone a long time, Master Holmes! You look upon Queen Anavion, High Commander of the Army of Light, better known to some as Leah Demonsbane."

Justin turned to regard Leah impressively.

"Dang," he said, scratching his head. "Good job."

Leah snorted a laugh at this, and it was just about the nicest sound Justin had ever heard. Judging by the surprised reactions of Olorus, Hook, and the big woman, it was not the sort of sound they were used to hearing from their princess—or queen, or commander, or whatever else Leah was now. Seeming to grow a bit self-conscious of the attention, she cleared her throat.

Hook signed something. Leah nodded in reply, then began to heal some of her own injuries.

Not only does she look different, but she is tougher than I remember, thought Justin, watching her heal a deep burn in her scalp that had taken a portion of her hair with it. *Far more suited to the role of a warrior than me.*

With no small degree of effort, Kallorn managed to get himself up to a seated position and looked up at Justin. "Did you really come here looking for me?" he asked.

The answer to that question was somewhat convoluted. Justin had first sensed Kallorn almost two weeks ago, from many miles away, and the weakened state of the man's aurym presence had been enough to tell Justin that his old teacher was in some sort of trouble, though he had no way of telling what kind.

It had taken Justin some hard traveling and a few major adjustments to his plan to get here. Today's encounter with the demons had undone a great deal of what he had been working toward over the past few months. Nevertheless, he wasn't going to leave a friend in need. It wasn't until he was much closer to this fortress that he sensed the presence of Leah and the others as well.

To say that finding Leah here had been a surprise would have been an understatement. Justin had assumed that she, along with all of his former companions, were still back in the far west of the Oikoumene, if they were still alive at all.

But instead of explaining all this in answer to Kallorn's question, Justin simply said, "Yes."

Kallorn gave a small, single-note laugh. "You're getting to be just like him."

Justin did not need to ask whom Kallorn was referring to. Even Leah had at first mistaken Justin for Ahlund.

"Time will tell if that's a good thing or not," said Justin. "I haven't sensed any of the rest of the Guardians. Are they all right?"

"We got separated," said Kallorn. "I'm not sure."

Justin nodded. It wasn't the answer he'd been hoping for, but at least it left a chance that Cyaxares and the rest of the Ru'Onorath were still alive.

Cyaxares and I have a lot to talk about, thought Justin, *if I ever manage to find her again.*

"The Guardians!" said Olorus, looking upon Kallorn with newfound respect. "But where is Master Ahlund? Is he not with you, Justin?"

Justin opened his mouth to answer but found that he couldn't. Shamefully, he looked away. He had relived Ahlund's last moments a thousand times in his mind. Visions of it haunted his dreams.

"I am not traveling alone," said Justin, clearing his throat. "But no, Olorus, Ahlund is not with me."

A moment of heavy silence followed.

"You told those demons you were coming for them," said Leah. "What did you mean by that?"

There was so much to tell that Justin didn't know where to start. The full truth would have to come in time. For now, he simply smiled at Leah and said, "I have a plan."

PART V

PROCLAMATION

CHAPTER 35

At first light, Gunnar and his group departed.

His group. Who was he kidding? These were Adonica's people, and everyone knew it. He was just along for the ride.

The vertical city was deathly quiet, which made for an unnerving sensation in a place that, at its height, must have been home to several hundred thousand people, though Gunnar didn't really know how to estimate something like that. It was only recently that he'd begun to understand the extent of his ignorance when it came to anything outside of his own small corner of the world, of the many civilizations and different ways of life on the other landmasses of the Oikoumene.

Not a day had passed during Gunnar's time in Erum when the mists didn't limit visibility to a mile or less, and today was no exception. Mornings were particularly bad, and on this morning, it was as if the group were traversing through clouds carrying the promise of rain. Outfitted in their a'thri'ik plate armor and cloaks, they followed Adonica through the fog-shrouded streets. There was less conversation between them this morning. In general, they observed a greater degree of caution today, the encounter with the demon horde the night before having shaken all of them.

Now that they knew that demons roamed the city, there were too many hiding places for comfort. Every darkened, broken building front was a possible nesting place for coblyns. Every blind corner was a chance to encounter a wandering cythwraith.

Or cythraul, thought Gunnar.

If a High Demon showed up in these close quarters, their only chance would be to make a run for it.

Gunnar pulled out a bottle he'd found and procured for himself from the domicile where they'd spent the night, and he removed the cork. He sucked down two quick swigs of the contents, feeling it burn against his throat and warm his belly. He wasn't sure what sort of exotic spirits he'd found. Some sort of wine, he had initially assumed, but it was too strong for that and had a fragrant, earthy taste to it. Whatever it was, it would do for now.

As they traveled, Gunnar was once again struck by the surprising difficulty of navigating the narrow, claustrophobic city streets. He had taken care to mentally mark the location where they had seen the green light the night before, along with the distinguishing features of the intervening rooftops to use as markers along the way. Keeping those landmarks in a relatively straight line would lead them toward the right place, in theory. But it was easy to lose track of the proverbial mountaintop when you were at the bottom of a canyon.

Their objective was one level up within this shelved city. And, just like the previous level, they found multiple options for ascent: a platform on wheels and chains that could be raised and lowered using a winch system, and a switch-backing staircase. The stairs seemed the safest and least conspicuous choice. But the mist was so thick that by the time they were halfway up them, Gunnar could see neither the level above, toward which they climbed, nor the level below, from whence they had come.

By Gunnar's guess, they were about a hundred feet above the streets of the city section below when the stairs abruptly ended at a broken section.

For a moment, all seven of them stopped and simply stared at the dead end. It was a straight drop down to the mist-veiled city below. A gulf of at least fifty feet separated them from the next intact portion of the staircase.

Finally, Adonica stepped forward to take a look, venturing perhaps a bit closer to the broken edge than Gunnar would have dared, personally. When she stepped back from the edge, she took off her helmet, placed it on the ground, and sat on it like a small stool.

"Damn," was all she said.

Gunnar took the opportunity to take out the bottle for another quick nip as he surveyed the damage. It seemed clear that it had been no accident. He had always been a lackluster student as a young noble beneath the instruction of the private tutors of House Nimbus, but one of the first things you learned in the study of warfare was that an effective invasion required the destruction of extant infrastructure. Disrupting the enemy's ability to move from place to place affected their capacity to mount a proper defense.

Gunnar could almost imagine the looks on the faces of the families attempting to traverse the stairs from one level of the city to another to flee from the assault on their homes, only to find that their escape route had been cut off, forcing them to funnel toward whatever *other* direction the enemy desired.

Most telling of all were the unnatural-looking scorch marks around some of the broken pieces of the stairs. The scorches did not look as if they had been produced by fire. The very stone seemed almost to have melted at the edges.

"A daemyn blast?" asked Ptolemec, his battle hammer propped upon his shoulder.

"Uh-huh," said Gunnar, slipping the bottle back into his pack.

Elzirda, who had been using her spear as a walking stick, raised it to gesture toward the lift system not far from their position, just barely visible through the mists. "We could try that thing," she said.

"It would give away our position to everyone and everything below us within a one-mile radius," said Ucydotus. "Possibly even farther, depending on how loud it is."

Elzirda shrugged. "What does it matter? They can't follow us up a broken staircase."

Gunnar, who had seen coblyns scale vertical surfaces like insects on walls and witnessed cythraul punch handholds into solid rock in order to climb up the sides of cliffs, scratched at his neck and said, dubiously, "Meh. . . ."

Adonica, too, had seen more than her fair share of demonic persistence and ingenuity in action. She propped her elbow on her knee and rested her chin in her hand.

"Damn," she said again.

Estoq, who had been walking with her crossbow on her hip for most of the morning, slung it over her back and took off her a'thri'ik great helm to shake out her dark brown hair. She noticed Gunnar looking at her but ignored him. To his surprise, she reached into her pack and pulled out a bottle that looked mighty similar to the one he had taken from the home. She took a quick drink, showing hardly a bit of reaction to the potency of the stuff.

"These can't be the only stairs," said Estoq as she pushed the cork back into the top of the bottle. "These city levels are so wide that it wouldn't make sense for there to be so few ways for people to go up and down."

Ucydotus nodded in agreement. "It would take some time, but we could go back down and scout the base of the wall."

Gunnar tilted his head, examining the gap between the broken sections of the staircase to estimate the distance. He stroked his hanging mustache in thought. "Well," he said, "I could do that thing I did in For'qan."

Adonica shot Gunnar a sideways glance, considering. The rest of the group, having not been present for that particular escapade, only looked on, confused.

Adonica scratched her head and sighed begrudgingly. "Yeah, okay."

Gunnar grinned. It was as close as she was likely to admitting she needed his help, short of actually asking for it. And although it wasn't much, he still found it somewhat gratifying.

Especially after she made it clear last night just how little faith she has in you after your freeze-up.

Gunnar shrugged off the inner voice and began looking around for a suitably secure anchor point. It would have to support a substantial amount of weight.

As the others watched, Gunnar backed away from the edge of the destruction, to a place well removed from the worst of the damage. He pulled his satchel from his belt and began rifling through his many seed pouches.

Now, it was Berex, the ax-wielding Mythaean, who removed his great helm. He was the youngest of the bunch, yet his blond facial hair had come in thickest of all of the men since departing the day before.

"No offense meant, Sir," said Berex. "But if you think I am going to cross *that* gap on a rope bridge made of vines, you are out of your ever-loving mind."

"No offense taken, soldier," said Gunnar. "And you may rest assured that we are not doing any such thing. Completely impractical and dangerous, that would be."

Berex breathed a sigh of relief. "Good."

"What we'll do is," said Gunnar, "I'll snake a vine from down here all the way up to there. I'll tie it around something or other on the opposite end, and I'll snake it back down again. Then we cinch the end around your waist, give the old heave-ho, and hoist you on up there across the gap, just like water in a bucket. Couldn't be simpler."

Berex looked suddenly pale.

Gunnar found the pouch he was looking for, undid the drawstring, and pulled out a single seed.

"Now," he said, looking around, "who's first?"

Everyone's shoulders seemed to have gone tense. None of them moved. Only Adonica, still seated on her great helm, seemed unfazed. She shot Gunnar an impatient look. In a past life, Gunnar might have winked mischievously back at her, but when you only had one eye, that was one particular gesture that tended to get lost in translation.

Suddenly, Estoq stepped forward, her shoulders back and her jaw set. "I volunteer, Sir."

"No!" said Ucydotus, so quickly that it made Gunnar double-take. The Enden phalanx man came forward, nearly stepping in front of Estoq. "I'll do it."

"I said *I* volunteer," said Estoq.

"Please, Admiral Erix Nimbus," said Ucydotus. "Send me instead."

"U!" said Estoq, turning swiftly to face him.

Ucydotus—or, apparently, just *U* to some people—turned and looked deep into Estoq's eyes.

"I can't let you take such a risk," he said. "Once I'm on the other side, I'll help you get across."

"You don't think I can do it myself?" said Estoq, her tone growing icy.

"I know you can," Ucydotus said. "Of course, I know that. But, please, I can't...." His voice lowered to a whisper. "I can't lose you, Estoq."

Adonica's face stretched in a look of surprise. Judging by everyone else's reactions, she and Gunnar weren't the only ones blindsided by this public declaration.

So, thought Gunnar, *that explains why she's been pretending not to know me.*

"Splendid, *two* volunteers! Even better!" said Gunnar, breaking the silence that followed. "You know, that's a good idea anyway. I *think* the vine will hold two, but it'll be good to find out for certain, for future reference—"

"Would you put these poor kids out of their misery and get on with it?" Adonica cut in.

"Oh, you're no fun . . ." grumbled Gunnar.

Adonica sighed dramatically, as if she were dealing with a troublesome child, and stood from her seated position. She backed away from the edge of the stairs as Gunnar took the single seed from his hand and placed it on the ground.

Gunnar took a step back, raised one hand, and focused on the lifeline between him and the seed. All joking aside, this was no small feat. It would take a great deal of energy to make this happen.

Gunnar called on aurym and fed it through the lifeline. The seed split open. A stem stood upward, sprouting leaves. Tiny tendrils of roots spread outward from the bottom, growing across the surface of the stone, and although they were unable to burrow into the surface, they found every possible crack and gained purchase by gripping tightly to the uneven surfaces.

Behind each inch of growth was Gunnar's will, delivered through the power of aurym. He sent the root system expanding outward until it reached the edge of the broken walkway, wrapped over it, and gripped the underside of the stairs. All the while, the stem grew taller and thicker.

Within a few seconds, the plant was a stem no longer but a trunk as big as a years-old sapling. Branches extended from it, and he took care to direct their growth into a sort of cradle that wrapped around the main trunk.

The older and stronger a plant was, the less willing it was to bend to the will of another. That was just the way of the world. So, naturally, the bigger this plant got—not a vine, as he had led the others to believe, but a deciduous tree with parchment-like bark, which tended to grow well along steep riverbanks—the more energy it required from him.

Already, Gunnar felt sweat beading on his forehead and dampening his shirt along his lower back. It was one thing to grow a plant from seed to maturity when its maturity only represented a season, as was the case with the crops he was often required to produce for the Army of Light's provisions. It was another matter entirely when maturity was the equivalent of half a century of growth in the wild.

The sound of a few decades' worth of growth in less than a minute was like the groaning of many old trees in strong wind, its melody magnified into a curious chorus. To increase the tree's stability, he directed it to hug the rock wall as it grew outward. By the time the tree spanned the gap, with its leafy canopy a lush blossom of green at the base of the upper portion of the broken staircase, Gunnar was gritting his teeth with the effort of keeping his lifeline connected.

Finally, his work complete, he severed his connection and cut off his flow of aurym. The tree stopped growing.

What now lay before them was a sort of living bridge, with a mostly flat trunk spanning the fifty-foot gap from the lower portion of the broken stairs to the upper section. The trunk was only wide enough for a single person to cross at a time, but with the wall on one side and his strategically arbored cradle of branches on the other to form something akin to a banister, it was in many ways safer than anything the architect of a manmade structure could have hoped to construct.

Gunnar sucked in some air to catch his breath and fought a wave of dizziness. He had the strong urge to drop to his knees and rest there for a while.

Used to be able to do things like that without overexerting myself, he thought. *Part of getting older, I guess.*

Not just older, returned his inner voice. *Weaker. And not just physically.*

Gunnar managed to stay upright. He squared his shoulders, cleared his throat, and casually removed a handkerchief from his pocket to mop his brow.

"Not bad, Admiral," said Berex, stepping up beside him. "Should we go one at a time, or can it hold us all?"

Gunnar nodded his thanks. "The strength and flexibility of this species makes it ideal for this sort of thing. Just watch your step. That bark has a tendency to peel underfoot."

"Better than being hauled up like water in a bucket, at any rate," muttered Ptolemec with a chuckle.

Turning, Gunnar found Estoq and Ucydotus positioned close to one another, surveying his handiwork. Ucydotus furrowed his brow, clearly annoyed at Gunnar's fun at their expense. Estoq shook her head in mild amusement.

"Proud of yourself?" asked Adonica, shouldering past Gunnar.

"Almost constantly, my dear," said Gunnar.

She put her great helm back on and led the group up the newly grown walkway.

The seven of them were only a few steps up Gunnar's newly grown bridge when it all went wrong.

CHAPTER 36

At first, Gunnar thought he heard the shriek of a human voice, like a young child wailing in terror. But that was only how the sound began.

It continued to rise in pitch and volume for several seconds until it either faded away or its pitch surpassed the limits of human hearing. Either way, it was clear to Gunnar that it was coming from somewhere between their current position and the section of the city beneath them.

The shriek halted all seven of the humans on Gunnar's living bridge. Estoq pulled her crossbow from her shoulder. Berex's boarding ax was in his hand and shimmering with the promise of aurym. Adonica, at the front of the procession, almost to the crown of the tree-bridge, looked the least frightened and yet somehow also the most ready.

"Something's coming!" said Elzirda.

"*Down!*" said Adonica.

Everyone did so—except Gunnar. He remained standing so he could get a better look as a swift shadow flew toward them from over the city.

The creature came sailing in their direction, emerging out of the dishwater-colored mists. It was too big to be any bird of prey that Gunnar was familiar with. Too big to fly at all, he would have said, if he weren't seeing it with his own eye. But it was sailing toward them, leaving spiraling trails of disrupted mist behind it.

The closer it got, the more of its features were revealed, and Gunnar soon realized it was a bat. But calling this thing a bat would have been like calling a lion a kitten. Its body was a thin, skeletal frame, six feet long from claw to snout, supported by a fifteen-foot wingspan. Unlike most common bats with which Gunnar was familiar, it did not beat furiously at the air to stay airborne. Instead, it sailed almost motionlessly, silently, on a pair of thin, membranous flaps of skin.

Sailing toward Gunnar's tree bridge. Toward him.

For a moment, Gunnar imagined the bat-like creature attacking them, envisioned dozens more appearing out of the mists behind the first one, diving at the humans, great talons clamping down on arms or legs, picking them up to fly them off like mama birds carrying home breakfast for the brood. But he quickly shook off that fear. This creature made for an intimidating sight as it swooped toward them, but regardless of how sharp its teeth or talons were, the laws of physics prevailed. Even very small birds could only achieve flight by the grace of hollow bones that kept their anatomies lightweight. For a creature of *that* size to stay airborne, it would have to weigh next to nothing; it wouldn't possess enough muscle mass to lift much of anything, let alone a human body.

And if it's lightweight enough to fly, it's more prone to injury, thought Gunnar. *So it's probably not the sort of animal liable to take unnecessary risks, like attacking a group of creatures as large as us.*

These thoughts came courtesy of all those private tutors of his youth, back at the palace in Eppex, and he had to admit he begrudgingly appreciated his education at times like these. The conclusion he was able to reach in a few seconds of quick thinking eased his mind . . . to some extent. But then again, a larger-than-man-sized bat was flying at him, and he *was* still human.

The string of imaginative vulgarities that trailed from Gunnar's mouth as he threw himself down on the parchment-like bark of his living bridge was mostly incomprehensible, except that it culminated in ". . . one big son of a mother!"

He landed next to Estoq, who had a bolt fit to her crossbow's drawstring and was preparing to stand and fire. Gunnar reached out and gently gripped her arm to stop her.

"Don't, Essie," was all he said.

Estoq looked at him. The familiarity of the nickname made Ucydotus's head swivel in their direction, and Gunnar felt Estoq's arm tense beneath his hand. He quickly pulled away.

The wailing screech sounded again, so close that Gunnar winced against its piercing call as it echoed against the face of the cliff. Through the cradle of branches, he saw the great bat swoop within twenty-five feet or less of their position before finally banking to the side, so close that he heard the air catch in its fleshy, membranous wings, like sea breeze catching a flag.

The great bat rose high and began to circle back around toward them.

"Some new type of demon?!" Ptolemec said in a growling whisper.

"No, just an animal," said Gunnar. "A weird animal, I'll grant you that. But just an animal."

"Doesn't make it any less dangerous," said Adonica. "Estoq, do you think you can—?"

"It won't do us any harm," said Gunnar. "Leave it alone."

Adonica shot him a threatening look, and Gunnar made a face right back at her.

"Trust me, all right?" he said. "I know *some* things."

Adonica seemed prepared to argue the point, but this time, mercifully, she let it go.

The airborne creature returned and swooped even closer, then banked sharply again and veered off, this time in the opposite direction. It did not turn back but kept on going until it disappeared silently into the mists. In its own way, it was rather beautiful.

A few seconds after the creature was gone, Gunnar heard the collective exhale of several nervously held breaths let loose beneath several helmets. He pushed himself to his feet, brushing flaky bits of bark off his cloak.

"See?" he said. "Just a curious fella, checking in on some strange creatures edging in on his territory. Nothing to worry. . . ."

Gunnar trailed off at the sound of another screech. With the eyes of the whole group on him, he could only hope that his face didn't fall quite as badly as his spirits. Because this screech did not come from the sky. It came from the city below them. And there was no mistaking this one for a bat.

The screech was followed by a howl. Then more screeches, yelling, a chorus of sounds that was a bit like the raspy giggles of children, and the scratching and slapping of many clawed feet against stone.

Gunnar leaned over the banister of the living bridge to look down. The mists had cleared enough that he had a blurred but good enough view of the level of the city below them. What he saw in those hazy streets looked like a rush of black ink flooding toward the staircase.

Yes, just a curious fella, thought Gunnar. *Whose curiosity just alerted the entire city below to our presence and position.*

Gunnar could see where the flood of black in the street ended, but he couldn't see where it began, which meant they might already be on the stairs and climbing.

"Coblyns," said Gunnar. "Lots of 'em! Go—*now!*"

CHAPTER 37

Running up a tree wasn't as hard as one might have expected. At least, not when it was a tree that had been expertly grown with that very purpose in mind. With Gunnar's branch-constructed banister on one side and the cliff face on the other, it wasn't even a particularly dangerous endeavor.

The danger was what was coming up the stairs beneath them.

Gunnar, who had scaled a tree or two in his time, made it up to the other side with the least amount of slipping on the flakey, papery bark underfoot. Before long, the group broke through the leafy canopy of the minutes-old yet fully grown tree and stepped onto the solid ground of the upper portion of the broken stairs. Here, Adonica and the others kept running, taking the steps two and three at a time. But Gunnar turned back. He faced his living bridge, took a deep breath, and waited.

"What are you doing?" came a voice from up ahead.

Gunnar glanced over his shoulder. The rest of the group was still moving, but Adonica had skidded to a halt and was watching him as the echoes of raspy giggles and the slapping of clawed feet against the stone below grew ever louder and ever nearer.

"The more mature a tree is, the less you can influence its growth," said Gunnar. He shook his hands a bit and flexed his fingers, cracking his knuckles. "I won't be able to alter what I've already done. But I can improvise."

He took another deep breath. This was not going to be fun. Attempting to output so much energy like this, so quickly, would likely drain him of aurym. Best-case scenario, he would be fatigued to the point of worthlessness for the rest of the day. Worst-case scenario, he would black out from the stress it put on him. But it didn't seem like he had much of a choice.

"Go on ahead without me," he said. "Don't worry, I'll be. . . ."

At the sound of boots pounding against the stone, Gunnar turned and realized that Adonica was already sprinting up the stairs. She hadn't even stuck around long enough for him to insist that she leave him behind.

"Sheesh, some friend," mumbled Gunnar under his breath.

The noise from below was getting louder by the second, intensifying into a dull roar. Alone on the stairs, Gunnar ran a hand over his bandolier of lobber-balls, trying to decide on the best approach here. But instead, he opened his satchel, found the pouch he was looking for, and pulled out a single seed. He tossed it down upon his living bridge and once again called on aurym and fed his power through the aurstone lodged in the socket beneath his eyepatch.

Gunnar urged the seed to grow. Its roots spread across the trunk of the tree-bridge, and its stem expanded and grew longer until it was a tree of its own—not the same species as the living bridge, but a long-needled pine with deep ridges in its bark. He grew it downward until the bulk of its trunk hung suspended above the staircase.

Gunnar's chest began to sweat, and dark spots danced before his vision. With hands raised, he kept a tight hold on his connection to the newly grown pine tree. The coblyns were getting louder and closer. And—

Gunnar's world went sideways again, and he froze.

No. . . ! thought Gunnar. *No, not again. Not now!*

As always, it came without warning. As always, it left him feeling detached from his body. The way a muscle might seize up from a sudden cramp and cease to function—it was like that, except it was happening inside his brain. Terror, déjà vu, and the smell of burning wood.

Why so surprised? said the voice in Gunnar's head. *This has been happening for months, after all.*

It's never happened twice in two days before! he shot back.

Whatever this was, it was getting worse.

The sound of the approaching coblyns was so loud now that Gunnar was certain they would appear on the stairs below him and begin climbing up his living bridge at any moment.

In seconds, taunted the voice, *your belly is going to be torn open, and you will still be frozen in place like this as you watch your entrails being feasted upon, for as long as you can cling to life. After all you've been through, for it to end like this. . . . Embarrassing, really.*

Gunnar's hands were locked in the air where he had raised them to orchestrate the tree's growth, but no aurym was flowing through them. His heart was racing. And all he could do was stand there, frozen in place.

There was never any pain when the world went sideways like this, not even any real confusion. He maintained an acute awareness of everything around him. But he was a spectator to it, trapped inside of himself, the victim of a sudden inability to do anything. The first time this happened, he thought he was dying.

And this time, said the voice in his head, *you're right.*

He could see them now. The coblyns. They had crested the stairs and were bounding up the steps, coming straight toward his tree. First, a dozen of them. Then, fifty. Then, a hundred or more. Child-sized bodies with lanky limbs, galloping along on all fours, knuckle-walking, whiplike tails trailing behind them or raised up for balance. Leathery flesh stretched over round faces, slits for nostrils, and mouths full of spittle-coated teeth. And here Gunnar was, frozen, just standing in place like a—

As suddenly as it began, it ended. The world shifted back into focus, and all at once, Gunnar was let go.

There was no time left to be cautious about overexerting himself. It was all or nothing now.

He pushed every ounce of aurym he could muster into the pine tree. Under his influence, its great trunk swung downward like a hammer to an anvil, not into the crowd of coblyns but into the staircase itself. New branches shot out and went down into the stone like spears. At the same moment, he sent another branch outward horizontally to push against the rock wall of the cliff face.

The first of the coblyns had reached the branches and were climbing over them or slipping through. They would be on him in seconds. But this was no barricade he was building.

Gunnar became aware of someone nearby shouting so loudly that it hurt his ears, and he suddenly realized it was *his own* voice, almost roaring with the effort of pushing his power into the tree. He pushed it against the wall, burrowed branches into the stone, tried with everything he had to wrench and twist and pull. He had dropped to his knees, though he didn't remember them hitting the stone. The muscles of his forearms and hands flexed so hard that he could feel them beginning to go into spasm and cramp, yet he persisted. If the first few coblyns managed to reach him before his work was complete, his armor would just have to keep them away from his vital organs long enough for him to finish the task.

Rethinking your policy on helmets yet? asked his inner voice.

"Shut up!" Gunnar shouted aloud.

There was a deafening *crack*. The pine tree's outward force against the cliff wall, combined with the downward force against an already damaged staircase, finally did the trick. As soon as the stone split, Gunnar sent new branches through the opening, growing and expanding them as fast as he could. And, like many fingers prying open a clamshell, his arboreal servant broke off the lower section of the staircase.

Gunnar saw the staircase break free from the wall but didn't get the chance to admire his work any further. Because that was when the first of the coblyns reached him.

Dinnertime, said his inner voice.

CHAPTER 38

Knocked to the ground by several lanky bodies, Gunnar immediately felt their claws shredding through his cloak. He felt a set of jaws clamp down on his upper arm, where the teeth broke against his armor.

With his connection to the tree now severed, he fumbled to pull his cutlass from his sheath. A claw caught him across the face, slicing deep into the skin across the bridge of his nose and up under the ridge of the orbital bone—of the eye that was already missing, fortunately. His entire experience became a mess of swiping claws and gnashing teeth.

"Little bastards!" Gunnar growled, feeling the blood running down his face.

Finally, he freed his cutlass from its sheath. He shoved it blindly into the bodies on top of him, stabbing again and again. He felt one go limp. But the nightmarish, sunken face of another one, with eyes like red pearls, was bearing down on him with a mouthful of ape-like teeth open wide.

The head suddenly snapped back. The feathered fletching of an arrow protruded from the face where it had embedded itself in the coblyn's slitted nostril. The creature fell dead atop Gunnar, leaking black blood.

Gunnar heard the whizzing of another arrow as it flew by close overhead. It hit one of the other coblyns, knocking it backward. And, in a moment of shock, Gunnar realized he was free. A great crash erupted from far below, mingled with the wailing of many coblyns— the sound of a great chunk of the staircase and Gunnar's two trees slamming down into the city beneath them.

He scrambled to his feet, but after the effort of expending so much aurym power, his legs felt like they had run many miles without rest. Where his living bridge had been a few seconds before was nothing but empty space. The second tree had toppled it, along with a large portion of the lower staircase, and all that was left were some bits of the canopy that had been ripped free and still clung to the upper edge of the stairway. Across the intervening span, a mass of night-black bodies churned and writhed, so desperate to cross that those in the back were pushing those in front over the edge, causing them to fall into the abyss and topple out of sight.

"I'll be damned," he muttered. "It worked."

He glanced down at the arrows in the dead coblyns at his feet and turned. He expected to see Adonica, Estoq, and the other soldiers standing triumphantly on the stairs, having returned at the last moment to save him in his time of need. Instead, what he saw was the lift system they had earlier elected not to use, no longer at ground level but in the process of being raised up toward the next level of the city.

Four men rode the deck of the lift. Standing at the edge of the platform, with a Cru bow in his hand and currently in the process of pulling another arrow from his quiver, was Sif. Beside him, with sword drawn, was Tel. And, working as a team to furiously crank the wheel that controlled the winch and gears were his fishing buddies.

Borris and Pool, you beautiful sons of aurochs, thought Gunnar.

He did not have the energy left in him to shout to them, so all he did was point to himself, point to them, and then raise one finger in the air, followed by a tiny salute. He hoped the meaning was clear: *I owe you one, thanks*.

Breaking the staircase had bought them some time, but he had paid a heavy price for it. The day was too young and the danger too near for him to be this exhausted.

Here I thought Adonica was starting to like me, he thought, taking the bottle from his inner pocket and emptying the last of it down his throat. *Then she goes and leaves me to be torn to shreds*.

He tossed the empty bottle over the edge of the stairs.

It was then that Gunnar realized he could hear the sound of battle. Not from below but from overhead.

Gunnar put his head down and ran.

Once he got moving, his muscles loosened up a bit and some of his strength seemed to return. A few moments later, he made it to the top of the stairs, reaching the next level of the city. The spires and points and flying buttresses here looked like great bone shards, standing up like spines along the backs of giant, extinct creatures. He had taken careful mental note of which direction they needed to go once they reached this level. But remembering was no longer necessary. All he had to do was follow the sounds of fighting.

He looked over his shoulder, seeing that Sif, Tel, Borris, and Pool, on the lift system, were coming up about a hundred yards from his position.

Can't afford to wait for them to get here, he thought. *Just have to hope they can catch up with us*.

Gunnar took off running, turned a corner, and discovered quite quickly why Adonica had not come back for him.

Adonica lay motionless in the middle of the street. Her cloak was in tatters. The entire side of her cat's eye armor was scorched black. Her helmet was still on, and blood ran down from beneath it to be channeled into the seams between the bricks of the street like red-stained canals.

Ahead of Adonica lay a second body: Ucydotus. Gunnar wasn't sure if Adonica was dead, but he was *quite* sure Ucydotus was, because only half of him was left. Where the rest should have been was a black crater in the street, still smoking from the impact of a daemyn blast.

Farther up the street, the battle raged. The other four soldiers were squared off against the massive figure of a cythraul. As Gunnar watched, Elzirda barely managed to avoid the swipe of a mace that was as long as she was tall, with a flanged metal head the size of a wine cask. Instead of hitting her, it struck the side of a nearby building to cleave through the wall, sending a shower of bricks and dust across the street. At the same instant, Ptolemec brought his battle hammer down. The aurym power that surged through it emitted a shockwave strong enough to drop the cythraul to one knee, but not for long.

Berex, on the other side, was calling on aurym through his boarding ax and attempting to build up ice along the creature's feet. With each swing of his weapon, he drove icicles the size of cave stalagmites into the demon to try to pin down its movements. But the cythraul seemed to hardly notice. Estoq, meanwhile, hung further back, firing her crossbow not at the cythraul but up. It was only then that Gunnar noticed arrows strewn throughout the street that did not match the size or style of her Darvellian bolts. He looked up to see several archers atop the heights of the buildings. But these archers were not human. Or at least, they weren't anymore.

Cythwraith archers, he realized.

Demons that had once been men and women fired down at Gunnar's group as quick as their arms could draw, and their shots were accurate. One arrow bounced off Elzirda's back, dead center between the shoulders. If not for her a'thri'ik armor, that shot would have killed her. Another hit Adonica's motionless body and broke against her breastplate.

An arrow struck Berex in the front of his great helm, dangerously close to the eye slit. The blunt force knocked him off balance, interrupting his assault on the cythraul. The beast took its chance. It turned toward Berex and raised its flanged mace to strike.

Then, a new figure emerged from behind the demon, wielding a cythraul weapon of its own: a giant black blade.

Lycon Belesys swung his demon blade and caught the cythraul across the back of the leg, sending a spray of black blood across the street. The creature roared in pain and dropped back to one knee again, giving Berex enough time to recover and move to safety.

So, Lycon was alive. Maybe Adonica had been right after all.

Gunnar made to dash forward and join the fight. But just then, another arrow hit Adonica's fallen body, and he faltered. He knew it could be the death of the others if he didn't help them, but for some reason, he couldn't leave her here. He grabbed her beneath the armpits and dragged her away from the center of the open street, under a bit of cover.

Once they were protected from the archers, he pulled the great helm off of Adonica's head as gingerly as he could. Beneath it, he found the source of the bleeding. The helmet had protected her, and she was alive, but she must have been hit hard, for her nose had been badly broken, and she was out cold.

Happy? said his inner voice. *She's alive. For a couple more minutes.*

Gunnar ignored the voice. Somehow, his Mythaean royal admiral's hat was still on his head. He removed it and sat it beside Adonica.

"Hope you don't mind if I borrow this for a minute," he said as he took up Adonica's great helm.

Only now did he realize that his eyepatch had been torn off by the slash that had cut him across the face, leaving exposed the polished, pure black aurstone lodged in his eye socket. The fresh gash in his face was deep enough that the skin of his cheek had a detached sort of sensation and was still bleeding. He could feel it dripping.

He didn't like helmets. But at least it would cover all that mess. He slipped on Adonica's great helm.

"Admiral!"

He turned. Sif and Tel had found their way to the battle from the lift and now came rushing up the street behind him. Sif, hindered by his bad leg, moved as quickly as he could manage.

"Are you all right?" said Sif, staring at the blood dribbling out from beneath Gunnar's borrowed helmet.

"No time not to be, I'm afraid," said Gunnar. "Where are Borris and Pool?"

"At the lift," said Tel. "Guarding our escape route."

"Thank you men for coming," said Gunnar. "Sif, try to bring down some of those bastards firing on us from the rooftops. Tel, is your furnace nice and hot?"

Tel nodded and raised his hand. With a burst of aurym, a small tower of flame jumped up from the armored glove where he wore his fire aurstone.

"Good," said Gunnar. "We'll try a little maneuver Ahlund and I once used. Fair warning, I'm almost spent, so if I pass out halfway through this, you'll have to make do without me."

"Yes, Sir," said Tel.

Gunnar pulled one of the lobber-balls from his bandolier and tested its weight in his hand. Then he stepped out from their place of cover.

He didn't have the energy to run, so he settled for walking, which made for a rather incongruous sight as arrows rained down at him. Tel was at his side. And behind them, Sif fired up at the cythwraith archers.

As if it could sense his presence—and perhaps it could—the cythraul, even in the midst of fending off attacks from Lycon, Ptolemec, Berex, and Elzirda, turned its full attention on Gunnar.

The empty sockets of a skull-like face, burning with an unseen fire within, locked on him, and the dagger-toothed maw split. It was almost as if the thing recognized Gunnar, even with Adonica's helmet covering his face. Gunnar supposed that if what Zechariah claimed was true, that each of these high demons and wraiths had a way of knowing everything that all the other ones knew, then perhaps it really did.

In a way, this wasn't a new foe. It was the same one, in a different body, that Gunnar had faced many times before.

Which means, thought Gunnar, *it's learned from its past mistakes.*

The creature raised its mace. Practically ignoring the onslaught of the others' attacks, it brandished its weapon at Gunnar and bellowed a gut-shaking, eager roar.

"That's right," said Gunnar. "It's little-old me again."

He called on aurym, gently at first, to test it, and spots danced before his eyes. He blinked to clear them, nearly lost his balance, and kept moving.

"I've got news for you, gruesome," said Gunnar. "One of us is staring death in the face, and it ain't me."

And Gunnar attacked.

CHAPTER 39

Justin, Olorus, Hook, Leah, Kallorn, and the big woman named Megara sat on the ground in a circle around a small cookfire in the courtyard, sharing a meal of provisions that had been scavenged from the fortress's stores. All of them were still outfitted for battle, with weapons within arm's reach. But Justin could have told them there was no need. The nearest demon was many miles away.

Smoke still rose from the places where Justin's flames and the cythraul's daemyn attacks had damaged the courtyard. Not far from their position, they had respectfully covered the body of the deceased Warlord Nefari. Justin knew something would have to be done about the people who had dwelt here, whom he had sensed fleeing into what he presumed were tunnels beneath the fortress. But there were questions that needed answering before any action, one way or another, could be taken. The first of which, to Justin's dismay, had been to share what had happened to Ahlund. Leah had already learned of his fate from Kallorn. But for Olorus and Hook, the news struck them a grievous blow.

As he concluded his story, Justin felt his hands shaking, and he tucked them behind his legs, hoping no one had noticed. Every time he thought of the way Ahlund had died, it was as if he went right back to that moment, as if he had never left, as if a part of him remained forever trapped there, unable to escape from that small boat where he had cradled Ahlund's bloody and blackened body, begging him to stay with him, and gradually realizing that it was hopeless.

"Sir Ahlund," said Olorus in a low voice, staring into the fire. "It cannot be."

Leah sat directly across the fire from Justin with her legs hugged against her body. "I can't believe he's gone," she said.

"Neither can I," said Justin.

"Ahlund followed a dark path," said Kallorn, "and yet, he returned from it and gave everything he had in the name of the light, when it mattered. I'm sure he would be proud of both of you."

"He is," Justin said. He cleared his throat and changed the subject. "Tell me about this Army of Light. You brought them all the way from Athacea?"

"Some of them," said Leah. "We started this journey as a smaller force, but our army has grown."

"*Our* army, she says! She means *her* army!" said Olorus, some of his joviality returning. He was cooking some meat over the fire. It looked like the leg of some kind of big game mammal—Justin had long ago given up on trying to remember the names of the unfamiliar species of wildlife in the Oikoumene, let alone on this strange continent of Erum. "It was Leah who founded the Army of Light and led us all east. Each time we encountered a human settlement or a population in trouble, we helped them and, if they were willing, brought them into the fold for their own protection. Those who were willing to fight began drilling with our soldiers. There's something like one hundred thousand of us now, and Leah is High Commander over them all!"

Megara raised her hands and signed something, prompting a smile from Olorus, Hook, and Leah.

"Megara says," said Olorus, "'Yes, Leah commands them, when she is not disappearing on one-woman quests in the wilderness.'"

"I, for one, am glad she did," said Kallorn. "I was growing weary of that dungeon."

"You know you didn't need to follow me," said Leah, exchanging looks with each of the trio. "With that said, I thank you all the more for coming anyway."

"Naturally," said Olorus.

From what Justin had seen, Leah didn't need *anyone*'s help. He had reached the fortress in time to witness part of her battle and could hardly believe what he was seeing. It was clearly an aurym ability, but he had never seen any human being move so fast or strike so hard. She had gone toe-to-toe with multiple cythraul and a cythwraith that was somehow just as fast and just as strong as she was, and she had held her own.

"With one hundred thousand people, I'm surprised these were the first demons you encountered in Erum," said Justin. "How do you hide a force of that size?"

"You don't," said Leah. "We had many run-ins with demons in Darsida, including a few near-catastrophes. But since reaching Erum, nothing."

Hook signed, and Olorus translated, "Due in no small part to the rough terrain, no doubt. Easier to go unseen in these canyons and chasms shrouded in mist."

"That is part of it, I think," said Leah. "But perhaps not the whole story."

Leah paused for a moment, and the allies assembled around the fire waited for her to elaborate.

"The kingdoms of Erum were the first to fall to Avagad's forces, and from there, they moved westward across the Oikoumene," said Leah. "With a few exceptions like this fortress, all humans seem to have been either driven out or eradicated from these lands. We can see evidence of it; the Army of Light is currently camped not far from a city that, according to our scouts, is many times larger than the *largest* city in Athacea. And I am told that its streets are silent and empty, purged of all life, desolate. For how long, who can say?

"When a human army conquers an enemy's lands, they occupy the place. They gather from the fields. They plunder and reap. But demons require no crops, no supplies, no rest. They seek no riches or comfort. What sustenance they do require comes from the act of destruction itself, not from its aftermath. There is, in short, little reason for them to occupy the lands they conquer. Without any local opposition left here, why would Avagad need to maintain a strong presence on this continent?

"To me, it stands to reason that the bulk of Avagad's forces would be at the *front* of his war machine, driving westward into places like inner Athacea, Darsida, and Raeqlund in northern Otunmer. If we had remained in the west, our fate would have been to defend against the relentless attacks of the demons until we were eventually, inevitably, overwhelmed. We came to these lands hoping that the last thing

Avagad would expect us to do was take the fight to him. The fact that there appear to be so few demons here in Erum is encouraging."

As Leah concluded, she was met with nods of agreement from everyone around the fire.

Everyone but Justin, who simply didn't have the heart.

Avagad's forces. The last thing *Avagad* would expect. They all still thought *he* was the enemy. How could Justin explain that all of the enemy's forces, all the demons, even Avagad himself, were only the servants of a far more powerful master?

The Nameless One.

"So," said Justin, "your plan is to invade and take Avagad down from the inside?"

"To be honest, it was Zechariah's plan," Leah said. "But he insisted that I take the credit for it."

Justin did his best not to visibly react to these words. But the truth was, the admission sent a chill down his spine.

Zechariah's plan, thought Justin.

The words of Cyaxares ran through Justin's head: "This man, Zechariah . . . Remarkable that he, alone, survived Avagad's betrayal. . . . Maybe he escaped Avagad's assault on the Brethren, and maybe he now mentors you with righteous intent. Or, considering the trickery that this enemy is capable of, maybe the apparent opposition between Avagad and Zechariah is nothing but their greatest stratagem yet."

And then, there was what Avagad had told Justin in his own words: "I had a partner. I still have a partner. A fellow member of the Brethren who worked with me to destroy the rest of them. And has continued to work with me in service to our master. Keeping a close eye on you. Protecting you when necessary. Teaching you. You know of whom I speak. . . . What's the matter? Your wise teacher who just happened to be in the right place at the right time to take you under his wing—is he not the unassuming, kind old hermit you thought he was. . . ? Zechariah has always been so adept at bending people to his will."

"Justin?" said Leah, leaning to get into his line of sight. "Are you all right?"

Justin suddenly realized that he was staring into the fire, lost in thought. He shook himself back to the present.

"I'm fine," he said.

It was clear by the look on her face that she did not believe him, but to Justin's relief, she let the matter drop for now.

Hook made a series of signs toward Justin, and Olorus translated, "You have told us about Ahlund and much more, but surely, you did not come all this way alone."

Justin looked at Leah, hesitated, then looked away. He wasn't sure yet how to answer that question.

Kallorn spoke up, breaking the awkward silence. "After Justin disappeared, we waited for several days on the island. But every day that we tarried put us in greater danger of being discovered by the demons who were surely searching the surrounding seas for us in the aftermath of the disaster at Esthean. When we could wait no longer, we put together a small cache of supplies and left them in a boat in case Justin returned, and we departed.

"It was not until weeks later that we sensed what felt like a ripple of aurym power. Cyaxares guessed it was the reappearance of the fallen, but we were waylaid by demon ships before we could return to search the island, forcing us to flee from their pursuit and sail far north around the tip of Ythia." He paused to look at Justin. "I am just as curious as everyone else. Not only about how you got here and who you are with, but about this plan of yours."

"That's right!" agreed Olorus. By now, the leg bone in his hand was sucked almost clean. "You say you have a plan, Justin! So, what is it?"

All eyes turned to Justin. They were fair questions. But still, he hesitated. He couldn't help but feel that now was not the time to go into the details.

His eyes found Leah's, and he tried to push everything aside and focus his thoughts on the here and now. The rest would have to come in time.

"How I got here is . . . a long story," said Justin. "And no, I'm not alone. I'm sure all of you probably thought I died or ran away. But I haven't been idle. I've been fighting in the shadows, trying to make a difference, but also trying to stay hidden. I had hoped to get a bit deeper into Erum before the demons learned I was here, but when I sensed your presence, Kallorn, I had to adjust the plan and call a bit of an audible."

"An audible?" said Leah.

"Sorry," said Justin. "Something we say where I come from. It means improvising your strategy on the fly. It's a sports term."

"Ah!" said Olorus, leaning forward eagerly. "Is it from that game you told me about? The one where everyone slobbers?"

"It's called *dribbling*, actually," said Justin. "And that's a different game."

"The one with the ball and the two baskets," said Olorus, raising his index finger in confident assertion.

"You got it," said Justin.

Olorus nodded sagely and leaned back, crossing his arms over his belly.

Megara signed, and Leah translated, "Did you also come here to kill Avagad, then?"

"I came here," said Justin, choosing his words carefully, "to find the source of the demons."

This was evidently not the answer the group was expecting, as none of them seemed to know what to say in response. Leah watched him closely. She wore an expression that he couldn't quite place. Hesitancy? Caution? Disappointment?

They wouldn't understand, he thought. *They couldn't. Not yet.*

"That woman," said Leah, gesturing to the covered body a stone's throw away. "Warlord Nefari. She showed me something while I was her prisoner. She had an aurym ability that she referred to as farseeing, and when she took my hand, I saw. . . . I don't know what you would call it. A *vision*, I guess. In the vision, I saw legions of demons crawling up from the shadowed depths of a great—"

"Pit?" said Justin.

Leah's head snapped up. "That was exactly what Nefari called it," said Leah. "The Pit."

Justin thought back to the words he had found written on sheets of parchment in Avagad's tower, back in the Kharon.

Mu. The Pit. Beloved Son.

On his person, even now, were the copies he had made of those sheets of parchment. And a set of maps. One was a map of Erum. Another was a map of lands that matched no landforms found within the Oikoumene at all.

"Did she say anything else about this Pit?" asked Justin. "Where it's located? How to get there?"

"She told me she led an army against Avagad and invaded his capital city," said Leah. "Rohghost, she called it. She said that the demons were endless, her army was defeated, and she lost everything. Perhaps the Pit is somewhere in that city."

Megara signed something, and Leah chewed the inside of her cheek uncomfortably.

"Yes," Leah admitted, "that does sound a lot like what we are trying to do. I think she showed the vision to me because she hoped to dissuade me from trying the same thing."

Justin turned and looked across the fortress courtyard to the shrouded body of Nefari the Warlord.

"I wish I'd gotten here quickly enough to help her," said Justin.

"I would not mourn overly much for her," said Kallorn bluntly. "That woman imprisoned me, along with a poor boy who did nothing wrong except to have a bad arm and a name similar enough to be mistaken for you. The demons came here this night because she sought to give that boy, who she thought was you, to the demons as tribute to Avagad."

"But she's been to Avagad's city?" said Justin. He pushed himself up from the fire. "That could be helpful. If she's willing to talk. I wouldn't blame her if she's not in the mood."

It was clear by the dubious looks the others exchanged with one another that they thought Justin had misunderstood something.

Justin strode across the courtyard to the covered body of the Warlord. He paused to look back toward the cookfire. Leah, Kallorn, Olorus, Hook, and Megara watched him in cautious silence, the way one might observe a person who had taken leave of their senses.

He smiled at them. "Still," he said. "It's worth a try."

Justin reached into his pocket and pulled out a ruby-colored stone about the size of a chicken's egg with a rough, uneven surface. He closed his eyes and fed his aurym power into the stone his father had given him.

CHAPTER 40

Hook watched Justin across the courtyard. He held a red stone in his hand as he stood over the beheaded body of the big woman lying in the courtyard. In the perpetual twilight of the Mistlands, there was no mistaking the resulting shimmer in the air for a trick of sunlight.

Aurym, thought Hook.

A bluish vapor, quite unlike the natural mists characteristic of the region, suddenly manifested above the ground in front of Justin. It coalesced as it was drawn inward, creating a transparent, shadowy blue figure. It was the figure of a large human—a woman who matched the proportions of the dead woman on the ground. Her transparent blue visage stood before Justin, blinking her eyes in shock.

Hook did not even remember rising to his feet, but he had to steel himself to keep from taking an involuntary step backward at the sight before him.

"By the spirit. . . !" he heard Olorus mutter.

All his life, Hook had wrestled with the legacy of his Islander mother and the belief system she had done her best to impart to him. Many would have considered it less a religion than a set of superstitions, and much of it, he had abandoned over the years. Nevertheless, portions of it had become a part of him; he still regularly thanked the departing spirits of the creatures he hunted for game. He held deep respect for the dead and places associated with death—not necessarily for the arbitrary plots of land where lifeless bodies were laid to rest, but rather, for the places where people had fallen. His mother, along with many Islanders on the Raedittean Archipelago, believed that the spirit of a person lingered at the location of their passing, even if the body did not. It did not seem altogether implausible.

It was one thing, however, to believe in ghosts, and quite another to see one.

"Nefari," said Leah, her voice barely a whisper.

Nefari the Warlord was the tallest human that Hook had ever seen. Even under normal circumstances, the sight of her would have turned heads. But to see her as a semitransparent blue figure towering over *her own* dead body made the sight all the more memorable.

The Warlord raised her hands to look at them—or perhaps through them—while Justin stood calmly before her, the red stone in his grasp.

Despite having spent a fair amount of time with Justin, Hook had never actually witnessed the power of the ethoul, the fallen angel, firsthand. He had only heard the accounts of others who had seen Justin in action. Leah had told him that she'd seen Justin destroy an entire group of cythraul with just a few swings of his sword. Lycon and Adonica claimed that back in Hartla, he had unleashed a power unlike any they had ever seen to help them escape from the demons' attack on the city. After that, Justin had disappeared.

All the other accounts of Justin's power, firsthand and otherwise, had quickly turned into hearsay and legends, leading a part of Hook to wonder how much of it had ever been true at all. Today, he had witnessed for himself the destructive power of Justin's aurym in the fight against the demons in the courtyard.

And now, he was watching him raise the dead.

Hook glanced over his shoulder and saw that Olorus, Megara, and even Kallorn looked as thunderstruck as he felt. Leah, on the other hand, was moving slowly toward Justin and the apparition. Hook quickly stepped forward and placed a hand on her shoulder. Every instinct told him to stop his friend from getting any closer. He couldn't have stopped her if he'd tried, of course. Neither he nor any other ordinary man or woman alive had the strength to stop Leah Demonsbane unless she allowed herself to be stopped. But she humored Hook by halting at his touch, giving him a look to wordlessly reassure him that she would be careful, and then proceeding forward.

"It's okay," Justin told the Warlord. "Don't be afraid."

"I'm dead," she said in a deep, slightly echoing voice, still staring at her transparent hands.

"Yes," was all Justin said.

The ghost of the Warlord—or the image or the memory of her, or whatever it was that Hook was seeing—shifted her gaze toward Justin.

"It's you," she said. "*You're* the one. The ethoul."

Justin nodded.

The Warlord closed her eyes and seemed to sigh heavily, which only raised more questions in Hook's mind about the nature of the manifestation he was seeing. How did somebody sigh when they had no lungs to take in air?

"Then, that boy," said the Warlord sadly. "All that time, he was the wrong person. Everything I did to try to save my people. . . . My people! The demons! They were here! What happened? Did my people—?"

"They're safe, Nefari," Leah spoke up, stepping up to stand beside Justin. "They evacuated through the tunnels, just as you planned."

The Warlord's shoulders relaxed in relief at this news, but she seemed surprised to recognize Leah. Her surprise faded into a sad smile as her gaze wandered downward to take in the covered body at her ghostly feet. Her body.

"In all fairness," echoed the Warlord's voice, "I suppose you did warn me I would die if I didn't let him go."

"I'm sorry this happened to you," Leah said. "I would have stopped it if I could. Justin, is there some way to. . . ?"

As Hook watched, Justin shook his head. "This is only temporary," he said. "It will last only for as long as I keep aurym flowing through this stone. It requires a lot of focus. But once I establish a connection, I can call to someone from many miles away, and their aurym can reform. The problem is, the more spirits are called back, the harder it gets. And I can't pick and choose who does and doesn't come back. See?"

At this last word, Justin gestured around the courtyard.

For the first time, Hook realized that the Warlord wasn't the only new arrival. There were a dozen other ghostly figures, looking just as confused as her, at the edges of the courtyard or from the adjoining passageways. All of them were watching Justin intently as he spoke.

Of particular note were four spirits very close by: two men and two women dressed in ordinary civilian clothing. Unlike the rest, they did not seem confused. They seemed overjoyed, almost to the point of tears. They were assembled in the general location where four cythwraiths of similar size and stature had recently been killed.

People who were turned, thought Hook. *They are freed.*

The Warlord bent over, pulled back a corner of the covering that lay draped over her body, and gently removed a ring from the finger of her own dead hand. Despite the fact that her semitransparent form looked no denser than a patch of fog, she picked the ring up as if she were no less physically present than Hook or Justin. She studied it lovingly, slipped it onto her incorporeal finger, and caressed the stone set in its band with her thumb.

Even as Hook marveled at what he was seeing, the implications loomed heavy in his mind.

What will this ability mean for the Army of Light? he thought. *His power in battle could change our strategy, but to call back the dead and speak to them at will. . . . This could change life as we know it.*

"I can help your people, Nefari," said Leah. "With your blessing, I will find them. The Army of Light will take them in and protect them if they wish."

The Warlord's face hardened, and her voice gained an edge. "To fight for you?"

"Or to be fought for," said Leah. "The choice will be theirs."

Nefari thought for a moment, then said, "The dungeons beneath this fortress connect to an ancient underground city. It has tunnels that lead northeast. If disaster ever befell us, our plan was to rely on our benefactors."

"Benefactors," said Leah. "You used that word before."

"A remnant of the people who lived in that city beneath the ground in ancient days," said the Warlord. "A few of them yet survive. We have a tenuous alliance with them, only out of necessity, but it is an alliance nonetheless. You will find my people there."

The Warlord blinked hard, then winced a bit and rolled her shoulders as if fighting a stiff neck.

"Sorry," said Justin. "I know it's uncomfortable to be called back like this, but I must ask for your help, if you are willing to give it."

The Warlord looked herself over and shrugged in amusement. "A little late for that. Of what help can I be in this state?"

"Leah told me about the Pit," said Justin.

At Justin's words, a troubled look crossed the Warlord's face. Hook wondered if the boy had gone too far. But after a few moments, Nefari said, "What of it?"

"You can call on aurym in this form," said Justin. "Just as surely as you can pick up a ring and place it on your finger. I've seen it done."

"And?" said the Warlord.

"I want to ask you to show it to me," said Justin. "Show me the Pit."

PART VI

SANCTUARY

CHAPTER 41

Ever since winning the Brig in a card game, Gunnar had spent many a half-coherent night gracing its makeshift wooden-planked stage with his musical talents. Few would have guessed that his ability to pick along with the local fishermen's bawdy drinking tunes had its basis in courtly training from the most renowned bards that Mythaean royalty could afford, nor that his skills on the picking-variety dulcimer were nothing but a bastardized form of his classical knowledge of the lute.

On most nights, his choice of personality lubricant was wine. Tonight, it was something a bit stronger, and the room was spinning as the barmaid ended a solo on a miniature harp to the raucous applause of the entirety of Gunnar's Brig. She stepped back, and it was Gunnar's turn at a solo.

Seated on a stool with the dulcimer in his lap, feeling lightheaded and lighthearted, Gunnar began with an arpeggio that climbed upward from the note the harpist had left off on. It never ceased to amaze him that even with drink dulling his logical mind, the creative side somehow didn't seem to suffer. If anything, it prospered.

He made a show of repeating a series of triplets, pausing to look up at the room.

His lone eye immediately found her. Estoq.

She smiled at him, and he did his best not to smile back. She'd come to Lonn hunting a two-timing merchant with a price on his head and had ended up at the Brig. It would have been a lie to say that the past few days with her hadn't been a pleasure. Neither knew the other's intentions. Neither seemed to have any. And that was just fine with Gunnar. Just a bit of fun. And there was nothing wrong with that, was there?

Movement in the crowd drew Gunnar's attention over Estoq's shoulder, and he was surprised to see that Adonica was here tonight as well.

This might complicate things, he thought. *She shouldn't even be here, should she?*

Why? thought the second voice inside him.

Because I don't know her yet, he answered.

Adonica stepped up to stand alongside Estoq. They exchanged a look, and there was a degree of familiarity about their proximity to one another, but they didn't say anything. They only watched Gunnar as he performed.

If you don't know her yet, thought Gunnar's inner voice, *what's she doing here?*

I . . . don't know, thought Gunnar. *I can't remember.*

A shadow at stage right distracted Gunnar from the two women in the crowd.

His fingers slipped against the neck of the dulcimer, producing a twang of sour notes, for he saw that the harpist was no longer a barmaid but a short man, clothed in shadow, with shining red eyes.

The little man opened his mouth, causing the flesh from his cheeks to peel off and reveal rows of sharpened teeth lining a fleshless jaw within. Ragny, the man or demon or creature who was really Innocen, lunged at Gunnar. The sharpened teeth clamped down on Gunnar's throat and *tugged.*

"Admiral!" growled Ragny's monstrous voice, muffled through a mouthful of Gunnar's dripping flesh. "Admiral!"

Panicking, Gunnar tried to pull away from the tugging of teeth against his flesh.

"Admiral!"

"Cap'n!"

The explosive pain of his throat being torn open was devolving into full-body numbness. His vision faded to black. But he could still feel the tugging. He threw his hands up and flailed, trying to free himself.

"Cap'n! It's all right!"

His vision had *not* faded to black, he suddenly realized; his eye was just closed. He forced himself to open it, and what met him was dim morning sunlight through the hanging vapors of the Mistlands, dispersed into a spectral array. The sensation of tugging against his neck was actually someone trying to pry Adonica's great helm off his head.

Gunnar lay there, stunned, blinking up at Borris, Pool, Sif, Tel, and Lycon, who were all looking down at him. There were others there, too, but Gunnar's vision was blurry. He couldn't tell who they were or where he was, although he was aware that they were not in the middle of the street, nor engaged in battle with demons. They were on a flat surface that was moving. Moving down, to be precise.

"He don't look hurt," said Pool.

"I see no major injuries," concurred Tel.

"He passed out from overexertion," said Lycon in that deep, raspy voice of his. "Too much power. It's like that for aurym users when we overdo it."

"Adonica?" Gunnar asked.

One of the figures at the periphery of Gunnar's vision leaned in closer. The hair that was usually pulled up in a tight ponytail was a wild mess. Her nose and mouth were ringed with dried blood, and one of her eyes was blackened. Her face was grave. Adonica made her presence known to Gunnar, but she said nothing.

"Did we kill that thing?" said Gunnar.

"You don't remember?" said Sif. "You made short work of him, my friend. But it seems it took everything you had left in you."

Gunnar touched his face, feeling the area of his left eye. The stone was still there in its socket, but with his eyepatch lost, it was exposed. He pulled the bandana off his head, letting his usually tied-back, long black locks spill out, and tied it diagonally around his head to cover his missing eye.

He blinked to clear the remaining haze and had a vague memory— far less detailed than the dream or nightmare or vision he'd just woken from—of charging the cythraul alongside Sif and Tel. He remembered throwing one of his lobber-balls into a wound that had been opened up in the monster's stomach and calling on aurym to set the payload of seeds into full bloom. Perhaps that explained why Sif and Lycon's armor was coated in a slimy layer of chunky black viscera.

He could now see that they were on the lift system and were riding it down toward a lower section of the city.

Gunnar pushed himself up to a seated position to get a better look around, and he immediately regretted it. His head felt like it was in a vice.

"Ow—mother. . . !" he grumbled.

"Easy," said Lycon, taking him by the shoulder to steady him. "You landed hard when you passed out. Good thing you were wearing that helmet."

"I don't suppose anyone thought to grab my hat," said Gunnar.

He'd been hoping to get a laugh, but nobody so much as cracked a smile, not even Borris or Pool. Then he remembered finding the body in the street near Adonica. Or half of a body, anyway.

"I saw what they did to Ucydotus," said Gunnar. "Did we lose anyone else?"

"Berex," said Adonica.

"Damn it," said Gunnar.

Adonica turned away. She looked sick.

Gunnar scanned the lift. Sif and Tel were beside Lycon and Adonica. Nearby was Lycon's scout team. Elzirda was currently working the large crank of the lift's winch system to lower it toward the city level below. Beside her stood Ptolemec. As usual, he had his battle hammer propped over his shoulder, but in his opposite hand, he held Berex's marine-style boarding ax. His head was lowered as he stared at the ax.

In the opposite corner of the lift, Estoq sat cross-legged with her crossbow cradled in her lap. On her back was an Enden-style phalanx shield, the one that had belonged to Ucydotus. Her face was smeared with dirt, her expression blank. Her eyes seemed to stare into the distance, seeing nothing.

More of the same, thought Gunnar. *More fighting. More killing. More dying.*

Did you expect anything less? came the response in his mind. *Pain is life. Pain was your past, is your present, and will be your future.*

Gunnar mentally shrugged at the thought. At least he was consistent. But his inner voice wasn't done.

The two who died today might have lived had you not frozen up.

Gunnar squeezed his eye closed and shook his head, trying to shut out the voice.

And the day is still young, it said. *Soon enough, your turn will come. Pray it is a quick end. But know that it will not be.*

"Lycon," said Gunnar, "how many of your people did you lose?"

Talk over me all you want, said the voice. *I am going nowhere.*

"Zero," answered Lycon, unaware of the argument going on within Gunnar's head. "All ten of them are alive and accounted for. We accomplished our mission of finding a route through the city that leads up and over the cliffs and into the north country, and we were on our way back down when those cythwraiths found us. We were pinned down until your team's arrival, which provided a chance for us to escape. I must be honest with you and with myself: This disaster is my fault, Sir. The blood of the two men who died today is on my hands."

"As long as we're being honest with each other and ourselves," said Gunnar, "you can thank Adonica for the chance to escape. I'm only here because I was fool enough to tag along when she and the rest of these soldiers openly defied my orders *not* to come and find you."

Lycon's mouth fell open a bit, and his brow furrowed. He looked at Adonica, then at the rest of the group. He appeared to be in disbelief.

"I told them," said Adonica, "you would do the same for any of us."

Lycon squared his bearded jaw. His furrowed brow went hard. "I would."

But you wouldn't, hissed the voice inside Gunnar's mind.

It pained him to know that it was right.

"We're almost to the bottom," announced Elzirda from the lift's crank.

"No sign of demons yet," said Ptolemec, looking over the side, "but we know they're down there. And there's no way all that commotion went unnoticed."

"We'll have to be ready to move," said Lycon. "Admiral, can you walk?"

"Walk, yes," said Gunnar, "but that's about it. Don't expect me to be any good in a fight for a while. More like a hindrance, probably."

"Business as usual, then?" said Lycon, flashing a small grin.

"Well, look who found himself a sense of humor while he was gone," said Gunnar.

"If it comes to anything more than a jaunt, we'll carry you," said Lycon. "We may not all survive this, but no one gets left behind."

In response, the rest of the soldiers either voiced or nodded their agreement. All except Adonica, who was staring at Ucydotus's phalanx shield on Estoq's back.

To Gunnar, Adonica's change in mood was a surprisingly unnerving development. He couldn't think of a time he had ever seen her confidence shaken.

"Right, Captain Lor?" said Lycon, quietly but firmly.

The words jolted Adonica to attention. "Yes, Sir," she said.

A quiet moment passed. Too long for Gunnar's liking.

"That reminds me," he said, scratching his head. "Lycon, maybe you can settle a disagreement. When Leah's gone, who's in charge?"

"I would assume you, Sir," said Lycon.

"We've been through this," said Gunnar. "An *admiral* is supposed to be in charge of *boats*. Since when am I second in command of this entire army?"

"It has always been inferred, Sir," said Lycon.

"Well, no one inferred me about it," said Gunnar. "As soon as we're back, I'm delegating the hell out of my duties. What rank are you anyway, Lycon?"

"I believe I'm still technically a major," said Lycon. "I think."

It seemed to upset Lycon to realize that he wasn't sure.

Gunnar was about to further rock Lycon's world by promoting him to General Lycon Belesys on the spot—he had the authority to do that, didn't he? But before anyone could say another word, the sound of a cythraul's roar came echoing down from a higher level of the city above. It was answered by another roar. This one sounded even closer.

"I hope all that talk about not leaving anyone behind was more than just inspiring rhetoric," said Gunnar. "Elzirda, would you be a dear and turn that crank as fast as you can, please?"

CHAPTER 42

It was difficult to tell the exact time of day, thanks to the usual mists covering everything, combined with weather that was even more overcast than usual, but Gunnar pegged it to be midday or early afternoon by the time they reached the ground level of the city. They stuck as close as possible to backtracking along their original route. So far, the only complications had come when they'd spotted a roving herd of coblyns from a distance. Fortunately, the creatures hadn't seen or smelled them and were easily avoided by taking a detour of a few city blocks.

Gunnar found himself wishing he'd taken more than one bottle from that home. It'd been hours since he'd had anything to drink stronger than water, and he was starting to feel it.

"Almost there, I think," announced Ptolemec from the front of the procession, still carrying his great battle hammer in one hand and Berex's boarding ax in the other.

"Thank the spirit for small miracles," said Lycon.

"What about Zechariah?" said Gunnar.

Lycon made a confused face at him.

"Why isn't *he* the one in charge?" said Gunnar.

The fatigue of overtaxing himself was wearing heavily on him, but it helped to keep talking. It distracted him. And he was good at it.

"Zechariah is only an advisor to Commander Anavion," said Lycon as they walked beneath a broken cathedral. "He has no military title."

"Oh, come on," said Gunnar. "He never hesitates to order *me* around. Though, admittedly, I've never been sure quite who or what he is."

Gunnar turned to look over his shoulder at Sif, Tel, Borris, and Pool.

"Speaking of Zechariah and his orders," he said, "what made you change your minds and follow us into the city? Conscience catch up to you or something?"

"Something like that," said Sif.

"Borris and I wanted to come with you from the start, Cap'n!" said Pool.

"I haven't forgotten," said Gunnar. "You have my gratitude, all of you. I'd be dead if not for you."

Gunnar's gaze wandered toward the front of the procession, where Estoq and Adonica walked together. With Ucydotus's shield strapped to her back, hardly any of Estoq was visible from Gunnar's vantage point except the top of her head and her armored legs from the calves down. The two women had been talking quietly, removed from the rest of the group, for the better part of an hour.

She blames you for what happened, said the voice in Gunnar's head.
Which "she"? asked Gunnar.

Both, came the answer. *Your list of friends is growing short. Remember when people used to love you, Gunnar? That was a long time ago.*

"Major Belesys, I apologize for asking," said Sif. "But was your mission a success?"

"Yes and no," said Lycon. "We did find what we were looking for. There is a route through the city that could be used to pass through to the north, but it would be impractical for the entire Army of Light to take it even under ideal circumstances. Now that our presence has been revealed to the demons, traveling that way will be too dangerous. And I fear they may begin to search the surrounding countryside for our encampment."

Gunnar had been thinking the same thing. That cythraul had recognized him. And if it was true that what one cythraul knew, all cythraul knew, the enemy was now aware that Gunnar, and perhaps other old adversaries, were in the area.

"As soon as we get back to camp, we start packing," said Gunnar. "And before anyone asks, that *is* an order. We just have to decide which direction we're going."

"About that, Sir," said Lycon, reaching into a bag he carried at his belt. "The building we found ourselves pinned down in was a house of records. In my downtime, I did some digging, and while none of my team can read the writing of this land, we did stumble upon these."

Lycon pulled out several sheets of folded parchment and handed them to Gunnar. As he walked, Gunnar unfolded them, revealing a series of maps.

One of the maps was a close-up view of the vertical city and its sections, with its streets and roads labeled, along with a relief map of the surrounding countryside. The relief map was limited in its scope, but it would be helpful to know where some of the chasms and cliff faces were *before* their entire army marched right up to them and realized they had reached an impasse. Another map showed the entire continent of Erum with rivers, borders, and cities marked.

"If I may," said Lycon. He leaned over and placed his finger on the map of the continent, indicating a labeled city amid what appeared to be a canyon with steep peaks. "We are here, I think. And over here. . . ."

Lycon ran his finger across the land and through what appeared to be a forest. Beyond that, the landmass of Erum ended at a great gulf. But beyond that gulf, a peninsula extended downward from the northern portion of Erum, creating a strip of land separated from the main landmass.

Upon that peninsula was a city.

"Lycon, you son of a mother!" said Gunnar, giving his back a slap. "Mark my words, when we get back to camp, I am promoting you so hard."

Lycon grinned in spite of himself.

At the core of Leah's plan to invade Erum was to find the rumored capital city of the demons, the seat of Avagad's power. Fleeing refugees had described to them a city on a peninsula in the far east, but up until now, its existence was only a theory based on some outdated maps from halfway across the world and backed up by some rather dubious anecdotal evidence. And even if those old maps could be trusted, they hadn't been detailed enough to provide a route.

With these, they might not only be able to navigate their way through the maze of the Mistlands but also formulate a plan of attack.

Gunnar noticed that on the map, beside the city on the peninsula, notes had been scribbled in the margins by hand.

"Any idea what it says here?" said Gunnar, pointing to the handwriting.

"Not a bit," said Lycon. "Perhaps Itz will know the language and be able to translate. In any case, these are better than any of the maps we've been working with so far."

Gunnar was about to say something else about the maps when a bit of movement up ahead caught his attention. Adonica and Estoq, walking together, parted ways so suddenly that there could be no mistaking it for a coincidence. Estoq increased her pace to march ahead, hefting Ucydotus's shield higher on her back as she went. And Adonica, clearly shaken by something that had been said, slowed her pace considerably. Her hands seemed to be locked in place. She closed them into tight fists and kept moving, in the middle of the group and yet alone.

"The city gates," announced Tel.

Gunnar breathed a sigh of relief. The end of this nightmare was in sight. He handed the maps back to Lycon and increased his pace to keep up with the others, revitalized by the promise of escape.

Do not fool yourself, said the voice. *You may escape this city of the dead, but nowhere is safe.*

That's why we're fighting, Gunnar reminded himself. *So that there can be such a thing as safety again someday.*

But you won't live to see it, said the inner voice.

"You think that changes anything?" he whispered.

He noticed, out of the corner of his lone eye, Lycon shooting him a sidelong glance. He had heard him talking to himself.

Gunnar increased his pace, putting some distance between him and the major before any questions could be asked.

CHAPTER 43

The instant that Justin returned from the Warlord's vision, Leah knew.

He saw it, too. He saw the Pit.

A few minutes later, after saying farewell to Nefari, Justin withdrew his power and allowed her spirit to disperse and depart. Then Justin turned away from the others and stood alone, deep in thought.

Leah exchanged uncertain glances with Hook, Olorus, Megara, and Kallorn. Even after Justin's sudden reappearance and her reunion with him, she was finding it difficult to convince herself that he was really here, that this wasn't a dream or an illusion.

After so much time apart, they were finally together again. Her mission in pursuit of a rumor hadn't been a lost cause after all. She had finally found him.

Except, it was he who found me, thought Leah.

So much about him had changed. He looked different, and he carried himself more like a man than the boy she remembered. He had always been nervously talkative and lighthearted. Now, he was quiet and severe. As Kallorn had earlier implied, being around Justin was, in many ways, like being around Ahlund.

But the most striking change of all was the air of power about him. Leah could feel it. Just being near him was unnerving and somewhat startling. And seeing it manifested had been nothing short of frightening. Like a flame, she knew that it could burn and destroy. But it also gave off a powerful, life-sustaining heat, a savage comfort.

After several minutes of silence, Justin still appeared to be consumed in deep, solitary thought. Finally, Leah stepped up to address him, speaking quietly so that only he could hear.

"Are you all right?" she asked.

Justin turned to face her. He took a deep breath and nodded. "I'm fine."

"You keep saying that," said Leah. "But you don't seem fine."

Her words clearly caught Justin off guard. After composing himself, he smiled flatly and gave her a deferential shrug. "I guess I probably don't."

"Now that you know where we're going," said Leah, "what happens next? Are you coming with us?"

"Is that an official invitation to join your army?" asked Justin.

"That depends," she said. "Can you follow orders?"

Justin grinned. "I would come with you," he said. "But I've been traveling with some friends. When I set out by myself to find Kallorn, I promised them I would come back for them. They're miles northwest of here. Far from your army, by the sounds of it."

"If you can't come with me," said Leah, "then I'll just have to go with you."

"You'll just have to *what*?" said Olorus.

Justin blinked at her in surprise.

"I didn't go through all this to find you," Leah told him, "only to let you get away again. I'm not letting you out of my sight."

He blushed a bit at that. It was a refreshing sight. It reminded her of the old Justin.

"What about your army?" he asked.

"Olorus, Hook, and Megara can return to camp and relay my orders," said Leah. "You and I will find your friends and catch up with the army later."

"Easier said than done," signed Megara. *"How will you find us on the move?"*

"If Justin can sense Kallorn's presence from miles away," said Leah, "I'm certain he'll be able to find a force as big as our army. You three and the others can run things for a while in my absence. If there are any problems, you'll have Zechariah there to advise you."

An odd expression flashed across Justin's face at the mention of Zechariah's name. Hook seemed to notice, and he shot Leah a look.

"What is it, Justin?" Leah asked.

"Nothing," Justin said. "Leah, are you sure about this?"

"I am," said Leah. "But before we depart, would you be willing to help me with something first?"

"Anything," said Justin, and this time, it was Leah's turn to blush.

"Nefari's people, beneath the fortress. I want to fulfill my promise to find them and offer help and protection, even if they don't accept it."

Justin turned and looked downward, squinting slightly, as if he were seeing through the very floor. "They're not far, and they seem to have stopped," he said. "It shouldn't take us long to catch up to them."

"It's settled then," said Leah.

She stood from the fire, crossed the courtyard, and picked up Nefari's voulge from where she had dropped it. With a burst of hydstone power, she snapped the haft of the polearm at the midpoint, cutting it down to a more manageable size for her much shorter stature. She spun it in a flourish to test its balance and, satisfied with the results, planted its dull end in the ground like a scepter as she addressed her soldiers. The three of them stood from the fire.

"Orders, My Lady?" said Olorus.

"Return to the Army of Light and take command," said Leah. "If longer than a fortnight passes and I have not returned, proceed with the invasion as planned, without me."

Hook leveled a concerned gaze at her that spoke volumes.

"I will be careful," Leah said, dropping the tone of a commanding officer in favor of the warm reassurance of a friend.

"Do not be careful," signed Hook. *"It is better to be mindful. And ruthless."*

Kallorn stood. "With your permission, Your Highness, I would like to come with you. There are some matters of importance that I need to discuss with Justin."

"Then we have something in common," said Leah. "I'll allow it."

Kallorn bowed to her.

Justin opened his mouth as if to say something, but he was distracted when Hook tossed his a'thri'ik-tipped lance in his direction. Justin grabbed the weapon out of the air and shot a glance at the silent soldier.

"Keep her safe," signed Hook.

"He says—" began Olorus, but Justin cut him off.

"I think I got the gist of it," said Justin.

Justin tested the weight of the lance in his hand, then fed a tiny bit of power into its a'thri'ik tip, causing it to flare with a brilliant green light.

"Thank you," said Justin, nodding to Hook. "I'll do my best."

Olorus approached Justin and extended his hand to him. Justin grasped it.

"To victory over darkness!" said Olorus. "Death to the demons! And death to Avagad!"

The others, encouraged by Olorus's words, did not seem to notice what Leah saw: a strange look that crossed Justin's face at the words "death to Avagad." It was there and gone in an instant, so quickly that she almost felt as if she may have imagined it.

There is something, realized Leah, *that he's not telling us.*

CHAPTER 44

It didn't take long for the dungeons beneath the fortress complex to end and a distinct and altogether different underground realm to begin. Even to Justin's unknowledgeable eye, it seemed clear that the monumental underground city through which they passed had been here long before the fortress above, which must have been built at a later date and connected with this preexisting city.

The a'thri'ik that lit the underground realm had been shaped into light fixtures in some places and set in the walls in thin green lines to form murals and artistic depictions in others. He had never seen anything like it.

Although Justin could sense the presence of the Warlord's people, many twists and turns still had to be navigated to reach them. Kallorn, a skilled tracker, led the way, following the signs of the refugees' passage while Justin and Leah walked side by side behind him.

Justin wore simple clothing, a black cloak, and no armor. Upon sensing Kallorn in trouble, he had taken immediate action, bringing a satchel of basic supplies and nothing more. The only weapon he'd brought with him had been Ahlund's broken sword. He'd left everything else behind, including the armor his father had given him—his panoply, Benjamin had called it.

Justin walked with Hook's a'thri'ik-tipped lance in his hand. He cast a sidelong look at Leah, hoping to get some idea of her current mental state.

The first few hours of travel down here had been spent with many questions being asked and many long answers given in return. But it had now been at least half an hour since any of them had spoken a word, and the silence was starting to weigh heavily on Justin.

For so long, he'd hoped to someday be reunited with Leah. The anticipation of the moment had loomed so big in his mind that he had gone from wishing for it to fearing it, almost dreading it. So much had happened to him that he was no longer the same person he'd been, and the same was probably true for her. He'd imagined that their reunion would be like meeting for the first time all over again.

Leah noticed him looking at her, looked back, and smiled.

He'd been wrong. Thank everything holy, he'd been wrong. It was like no time had passed between them at all. The connection had been instant and intense, and now that he felt it, he had something new to fight for.

When they reached an intersection where the fifty-foot-high, glowing green tunnel they were following split into three different directions, Kallorn finally broke the long silence.

"Ahlund was always the better tracker," he said as he came to a halt. He bent to examine the ground before him. "Even bare stone could not keep its secrets hidden from him."

Almost without thinking about it, Justin rested his hand on Ahlund's broken sword, which hung from the baldric over his shoulders.

"You said you were separated from the rest of the Guardians," said Justin. "What happened to Cyaxares and the others?"

"They are here in Erum, somewhere," said Kallorn, still examining the ground. "For hundreds of years, Cyaxares lived in hiding within Esthean, building and commanding her Ru'Onorath in an effort to protect the world from darkness. Her Guardians could act in secrecy, forgoing the need for all-out war. But Avagad's attack on Esthean changed her perspective. I do not know where they are now, but Cyaxares seemed intent on finding Avagad. I think. . . . I think, despite all her insistences to the contrary, that she still holds out hope that he can somehow be dealt with peaceably."

Mu, thought Justin. *The Pit. Beloved Son. . . .*

"We'll find them," said Justin.

"Perhaps," said Kallorn.

Kallorn had been pleased to see Justin at first. But there was also a distance there.

Is it any wonder, after what I did? thought Justin.

"I am sorry that I left you, Kallorn," said Justin. "You and Cyaxares and the others were right not to wait for me on that island. When I returned there, I had to fight off a group of cythraul. I managed to commandeer a ship. But I had only been sailing a short time when a fleet of demon ships surrounded me. I was ready to fight to the death if I had to. But instead of demons, it turned out to be a bunch of Raedittean Islanders, some of them former Mythaean slaves, in stolen demon ships.

"They boarded my ship and shared some much-needed food and supplies. When I told them my story and who I was, they offered to help me reach Erum. Along the way, I sort of became like a leader to them, second only to their admiral, who's an escaped galley slave like Hook. They've been my only allies all this time."

That was the abridged version of what had happened. Since joining them, that band of Islanders and former slaves had become like a family to Justin. They'd been through a lot together. It had pained him to leave them behind in order to find Kallorn, and unfortunately, he didn't seem to be able to sense their presence this far southeast from where he'd left them.

If anything happens to them while I'm gone . . . he thought.

He had been trying not to think about that possibility.

Something caught Kallorn's eye, and he took a few steps into the far-left tunnel. He bent over and picked something up off the floor. Justin stepped forward to take a look and realized it was a piece of wood that had been shaped and sanded into a smooth, oblong shape. At the bottom, a dried vegetable husk was tied to it in the form of a lady's dress. At the top, a smiling face was drawn. After examining it, Kallorn slipped it into the satchel at his belt and led the way up the tunnel.

"I almost feel bad about sending Hook and the others back to face Zechariah without me," said Leah. "I'm sure he wasn't happy that I left the army, with only a note to tell him where I was going and what I planned to do."

Again, Leah's mention of Zechariah's name gave Justin pause. And again, he decided not to say anything. He set his jaw and continued to walk.

There are so many things I don't know how to tell her about yet.

Over the past few hours, Leah had shared the origins of her Army of Light, its many key players, and some of the many battles they'd fought to get here. Justin hadn't been surprised to learn that Zechariah was among her trusted advisors. But it was unnerving to learn that invading Avagad's lands had been *his* plan.

How can I tell her, wondered Justin, *that, according to Avagad himself, Zechariah has been working with the enemy all this time, manipulating us all from the inside?*

She had also told him that her nongovernmental, independent Army of Light had come to Erum with the sole purpose of defeating Avagad to stop the demons. How could he explain that the demons had invaded the Oikoumene before, and that Avagad and Justin—and Justin's father before him, for that matter—were only small parts of a cycle that had been repeating itself since the beginning of time?

Even if they did manage to defeat Avagad, it wouldn't stop the demons. The cycle would continue to repeat itself.

Leah was shocked to find out that Justin's father had been a fallen angel like him, thousands of years ago on the timeline of the

Oikoumene. But how was he supposed to explain that after defeating the demons, his father had established himself as a tyrant while under the control of the Nameless One?

How could he explain his suspicions about his father's close relationship with Cyaxares, one of the immortal Brethren and the founder of Kallorn's order?

How could he explain the significance of the note he had found in Avagad's tower that appeared to be from Cyaxares—a note that read, "Beloved son"?

How could he hope to explain what those two relationships possibly implied about who Avagad really was, and what that meant about Justin's connection to him?

And how can I hope to tell her, wondered Justin, *that I didn't come here to kill Avagad?*

Justin felt a flash of something. A surge of power so strong that he closed his eyes against it and yet could still see it within the darkness through perceptions that went beyond physical vision.

Spiritual sight was not like eyesight, limited to a small field of view. Instead, one could see everywhere at once, three-hundred and sixty degrees, in every direction. There was no need for Justin to look toward it for him to see it. Still, out of force of habit, he found himself automatically turning his head in its direction: up.

The crackling, demonic energy was like a purple flame, ever present, hanging above him. To anyone around him, it would have looked like he was staring blankly up at the dark ceiling of the underground passageway. They could not see what he could see: a ball of violet energy, turning, swirling, so powerful that Justin could sense it, could see it, through thousands of miles of atmosphere and through the very earth, down here in this underground world.

The moon called Nun. Its daemyn power was growing ever stronger with each passing day.

What did it all mean?

"I hear something," announced Kallorn in a hushed tone. "Voices."

CHAPTER 45

Leah could tell that they were close. The echoing of voices was getting louder.

"We'll reach them in a few minutes," said Kallorn. "We had best prepare ourselves. Lest we forget, Leah and I are not on good terms with these people."

Leah nodded and once again caught Justin looking at her. But when she turned to face him, he did not look away. He stared into her eyes.

He was bolder than she remembered.

"You haven't asked about my face yet," said Leah.

"I didn't mean not to," said Justin.

"It happened when we first entered Cymorikka back in Athacea," she said. "There was a fight, and an aurym-powered a'thri'ik blade caught me across the head."

Leah used her finger to trace the line of the scar from the height of her head, where the blade had peeled back part of her scalp, down over her brow, frighteningly close to her eye, and across her temple. These days, she did her best to let her hair cover that side of her head, but she pushed it back so Justin could see, revealing that she had only half an ear there.

Leah didn't think she was a very vain person. Still, part of her was afraid of what Justin would think when he saw the injury.

"That looks like it sucked," said Justin seriously.

To Leah's own surprise, she snorted a laugh. "Does 'sucked' mean something is bad?"

"Oh, yeah," said Justin. "Like, you'd say, 'losing Ahlund sucked.' Or, 'Olorus's stories suck.' Don't tell him I said that. Or, when I first got to the Oikoumene, I sucked at pretty much everything."

"Ah," said Leah. "Then, yes, it sucked. It also hurt like a bitch."

This time, it was Justin who laughed.

"Poor Lycon felt terrible that he couldn't fully heal it. When he told me he couldn't reattach the missing piece of my ear, I said, 'Say again?'" Leah leaned forward in an exaggerated fashion, cupping her hand to her ear.

"You did not," said Justin.

"It fell a little flat," said Leah. "Too soon, maybe?"

"Perhaps we should be a bit wary here," suggested Kallorn, interrupting the exchange and making little effort to hide his annoyance at the two of them. "We are about to encounter a group of people who think they are being pursued by demons, and we don't know if there are any aurym users among them. I daresay it would *suck* to be caught unaware, and it could *hurt like a bitch* if one of them decides to defend themselves first and ask questions later."

"Right," said Justin, chuckling a bit. "Sorry, Kallorn."

"What'd you say?" said Leah.

"Honestly . . ." said Kallorn.

A few minutes later, they rounded a corner and encountered a rudimentary encampment of about one hundred and fifty people huddled together around a rounded mass of stone.

At first, the Warlord's people did not even notice their approach. The fact that they had not posted guards behind them to watch for pursuers told Leah that these were not people used to being on the run. Kallorn raised both hands to signal that he came in peace, and Justin and Leah followed his lead as they walked slowly forward. It still took several seconds before anyone in the group saw them. When they did, gasps of alarm rippled through the group.

Most were unarmed. Those who did have weapons stepped forward to place themselves between the civilians and the newcomers. Children and the elderly were quickly ushered to the opposite side of the rounded mass of stone.

Some of the civilians were people Leah had seen in the fortress courtyard. She also recognized a few of the soldiers who had dragged her before the Warlord.

Not far from them was Justus, the prisoner and false ethoul.

"We do not mean you any harm," said Leah, raising her voice in hopes of being heard over their rising panic. "The demons are not pursuing you. We have come to—"

At this point, Leah lost all words. Because the rounded mass of stone before them . . . moved.

To be more precise, it stood. To be even more precise, it towered.

A creature larger than anything Leah had ever seen in her life, including Raeqlund war elephants and cythraul, stood up from the midst of the Warlord's people. It had been seated in the middle of the crowd, facing away from them, which had led Leah to mistake its rounded shoulders for an amorphous rock formation.

The giant creature was dressed in rags. Its skin was a dull, grayish color, and its head, chest, and face were coated in animal-like black fur. It had two arms and two legs like a human, but it was almost twice as big as a cythraul. As its massive shoulders turned and its body came around to face them, the light of glowing a'thri'ik reflected in a single, great eye set in the center of its face.

The eye was fixed on Leah.

A mouth as wide as a wheelbarrow opened up with a snarl. In everything except size, the teeth inside were quite human. However, in addition to those human-like teeth were two elephant-like tusks that protruded from the upper jaw.

The cyclops puffed out its chest and rose to full height: twenty feet tall. It raised two six-fingered hands as big as tabletops and then clenched them into fists. The mouth opened wide, and the flesh of its throat vibrated like a rain-beaten sheet as its snarl transformed into an inhuman roar that shook Leah deep in her guts.

"This," said Leah, "sucks."

CHAPTER 46

Neither Justin nor Kallorn voiced any disagreement with Leah's assessment of the situation as the cyclops reached upward, snapped a full-sized a'thri'ik stalactite from the cave ceiling as if it were no sturdier than an icicle, and hefted it like a club primed to come down on the three of them.

Leah shook herself from her stupor and called on aurym. Power pulsed through the hydstone implanted in her shoulder, fueling her muscles. Kallorn drew his sword with a flash like lightning and a crackle of sparks.

The cyclops stepped forward. The impact of its six-toed foot shook the very ground.

"It hardly needs to be said," said Kallorn, "but aim for the eye."

"Justin," said Leah, "can you use the lance that Hook gave you?"

But Justin didn't respond. In fact, he was completely silent.

Leah turned to look at him. He was rooted to the spot, just staring at the cyclops.

"Justin, stay with us," she said, fearing that the sight of this creature had him in the throes of panic.

"Look out!" shouted Kallorn.

The cyclops raised the a'thri'ik stalactite high above its head, preparing to attack. Leah readied herself to leap toward Justin, to grab him and pull him out of harm's way if he didn't move on his own.

But before Leah could act, a visible shimmer appeared in the air, accompanied by a feeling of aurym that was unlike anything she was familiar with.

All at once, the cyclops's fury was replaced with a look of shock. Or perhaps it was alarm. The monstrous creature stopped moving and blinked its huge eye.

Leah turned to face the source of the aurym power. Justin was still just standing there, now with one hand calmly raised toward the cyclops.

This was not the look of a man in the throes of panic. Justin's expression was . . . confident. Almost casual.

The cyclops slowly lowered the stalactite club to its side. It tilted its head a bit as if listening to something it could not quite hear. Leah saw that the Warlord's people were just as confused as she was as the cyclops stood there, its great, furry chest rising and falling with breaths so heavy that Leah could feel the breeze against her face when it exhaled.

Another sensation of unseen aurym power came from Justin. The cyclops's brow furrowed. It looked suspicious. Then it gestured to the Warlord's people huddled behind it, and it uttered a series of grunts and growls.

It's speaking, Leah suddenly realized. *To Justin.*

CHAPTER 47

The tusks that protruded from the cyclops's jaw were large enough to have belonged to a mastodon. The pupil of its single eye was like that of a goat, elongated to the point of being almost rectangular.

Justin kept steady eye contact with that pupil as he let his aurym flow, speaking to the creature.

Of course, to call what he was doing *speaking* was inaccurate. It really wasn't anything like speaking at all. The first time he'd managed it had been in the jungles outside of Esthean, when Kallorn had tasked him with navigating back to the city of the Guardians alone. What had *not* been intended to be part of the test was an attack by a giant blue tiger in the dark.

In that hour of need, Justin had realized that through aurym, he could communicate with the animal.

It was not telepathy; the communication did not use words at all. It was more like connecting on a life-force-to-life-force level, pushing pure thoughts and emotions into another creature's soul. With this technique, he had successfully convinced the tiger that he was not for eating. Since then, he had utilized the trick a few more times, including an incident on the Altirin Sea. In each case, he had essentially imposed his will on the animals in question, coercing them or forcing them to obey him.

But this creature was not an animal. Based on the emotions he felt radiating from the cyclops, it was clear that this thing was not a mindless monster. It was a being with intelligence. If not quite as intelligent as a human, it was close.

This cyclops seemed to be about as close as you could get to something being a *person* without being human. He couldn't impose his will on such an intelligent mind. But he could at least try to calm the creature down by communicating his intentions.

"Justin," said Leah from beside him. "Are you. . . ?"

"It's okay," said Justin without breaking eye contact with the cyclops. "Just give me a minute."

The cyclops's initial emotional reaction to their appearance—single-minded purpose toward *immediate* violence—had changed to feelings of confusion upon Justin's mental connection. And hesitancy. Nevertheless, alarm and aggression still radiated from the creature like heat from red coals.

It would have been impossible to tell a lie while using this technique; communicating this way meant opening oneself up and laying one's emotions completely bare, and Justin did just that.

We do not want to hurt anybody, thought Justin through the connection.

The cyclops must have understood Justin because its emotional state shifted in response. The creature's cautious curiosity seemed piqued by this human's nonverbal intrusion into its mind. The clench of its six-fingered fist eased a bit.

The collection of refugees behind the cyclops murmured apprehensively.

Benefactors, the Warlord had said. A people who lived in the city beneath the ground.

Is this your home? asked Justin. *Are there more of you?*

They were the wrong questions. The creature's great, protruding brow furrowed, and the cyclops took a step toward him, snarling, raising the stalactite club again.

Through the tenuous vibrations of aurym, Justin felt Leah sending power through the aurstone embedded in her shoulder. Without looking, he could "see" the flash as Kallorn prepared his Ru'Onorath blade for its deadly work.

"Stop!" Justin shouted at them, still keeping his gaze trained on the cyclops alone.

Reading the creature's emotions also meant Justin could, to a certain extent, know its intentions. And, just as he had anticipated, the lunge ended with a single step, albeit a step that brought the cyclops's giant foot too close for comfort to Justin's current position.

The advance had been a feint. A warning.

"Justin. . . !" said Leah, holding tight to her power, ready to take action at any moment.

"It's all right," said Justin. "Please, trust me."

The Warlord, Nefari, sent us, said Justin through aurym.

Like a note vibrating through a chord, a change went through the cyclops at that name.

Justin pressed his advantage, adding, *She asked us to help these people. To take them to a place that is safe.*

A noise rumbled from the cyclops's throat in tones so deep that they could be felt as vibrations in the air, so low that Justin got the impression his ears were picking up less than half of the sounds being produced. What accompanied the rumble was a thought communicated directly into Justin's brain: *This place IS safe.*

For just a moment, Justin's focus faltered. He had shared feelings and commands and messages through the connection of aurym before, but this was the first time he had ever received a message *back.*

Holy crap, it worked, was the gist of the thought that ran through Justin's mind at that moment. It was little wonder, then, that the cyclops tilted its head to the side in bewilderment and puffed hard from one cereal-bowl-sized nostril.

"Are you *speaking* to that thing?" Kallorn said from behind.

"Sort of," said Justin. "It's hard to explain."

Again, a throaty sound, deep from the cyclops's gullet, communicated a warning. The cyclops did not seem to need to open its mouth to produce these sounds.

This place may not be safe anymore, Justin replied. *Your friend Nefari was killed by demons.*

For a moment, the cyclops seemed to stop breathing. Through the connection of aurym, the stunned shock of sudden sorrow hit Justin like a pulse, so strong that he felt its grief for the Warlord by extension. It was like sharing the creature's emotions.

And yet, Justin realized that there was a slight degree of misunderstanding, or perhaps it was reduced comprehension. This was a being of high intelligence, but not quite at human levels. It understood death as the sudden cessation of life, but it also did not entirely fathom the enormity of its permanence.

Are you on the demons' side? asked the cyclops.

It was the creature's loudest communication so far. In addition to the bass notes of its throaty grumbles, it gave off an almost musical tone. To Justin, it sounded like someone warming up on a French horn.

So, the cyclops was at least aware of the demons. That was a start. The next part would be a bit of a gamble.

No, Justin told the cyclops. He patted his open palm against his chest. *My name is Justin. The demons are my enemy. I'm going to destroy their master, the Nameless One. It will require me to give up my own life.*

For a few tense moments, the cyclops only stared at Justin with its great, rectangular-pupiled eye.

The truth that he had just shared with this cyclops, he had not yet shared with any living soul.

The lips around the cyclops's tusks tightened suspiciously. Then, it shifted its weight and gave a groan and a huff. What Justin heard in his mind was, *How could YOU hope to destroy a master of demons, small one?*

Justin smiled. The cyclops wanted proof of his power.

He looked around. Tensions were high among his allies and the crowd of refugees huddled behind the cyclops. Using a weapon like Hook's a'thri'ik-tipped lance for a demonstration of his auyrm did not seem wise. Instead, he set the lance aside and held both hands up and out in as clear a gesture as he knew to indicate that he meant no harm. Then he turned his back on the cyclops, leaving himself defenseless, and walked across the cavern.

Justin stopped at the wall, where he reached out and touched a vein of a'thri'ik set into the stone. Lightly at first, he pushed a bit of aurym power into it.

The natural glow of the minerals in the wall brightened like a live wire. It extended upward and outward from the position of his hand. He could feel his power spreading through the stone, not just the visible connections on the surface of the wall, but in the places where the ore reached deep within the rock.

As he increased his aurym, the a'thri'ik grew brighter. The brightness moved upward along a natural vein, then met a great piece of wall art that depicted massive, one-eyed warriors wearing plate armor and wielding great weapons, clashing in battle against what were clearly cythraul. He could not help but notice how *small* cythraul looked when compared to cyclopes. His power set the scene blazing brilliantly.

The people watched in astonishment as Justin's aurym glow extended all the way to the ceiling of the underground city and outward, around the corners in every direction, creating an emerald light brighter than midday, far removed from the presence of the sun. Kallorn, watching the display, seemed almost impressed. And Leah, watching Justin, grinned in wonder.

The cyclops turned its one-eyed gaze on Justin. A bass note rumbled from its throat. In Justin's mind, he heard, *At last. An ethoul.*

Chapter 48

"I don't like these reports," said Zechariah.

With his good hand, the old man tossed the sheets of parchment down on the ground in front of his seated position in his tent. With his other hand, the one he had lost and replaced with a hook, he scratched at his beard.

Three men sat together in the command tent: Zechariah, Gunnar, and Itzacoatl. Itz was an Ecbatan, a native of these parts. A white, wiry ponytail hung from the back of his head—the only part of his head that wasn't bald.

The three of them sat on the ground, as they usually did if a nice rock or log wasn't to be found. By the seas, how Gunnar missed chairs. If he managed to survive this war, he vowed to never again take for granted a straight-back seat with a nice cushion for his arse.

It was late afternoon, and the reports in question were missives that had been written up by scouts at the front of the Army. The night before, they had been forced to engage a small force of demons.

Gunnar didn't know all the details of what had happened. All he really knew was that he could use a drink right now. It would help him feel. . . .

Normal? said the voice inside.

Gunnar decided to speak up, if only to distract himself from that line of thought.

"There's bound to be a few run-ins with coblyns from time to time," he said, gesturing to the reports Zechariah had just put down.

"At least we didn't lose anybody this time," said Itz.

Gunnar shifted uncomfortably to reposition his rear end on the ground. He didn't *think* Itz was referring specifically to the losses of Berex and Ucydotus in the city when he said "this time," but it was hard to tell, and the possibility only made Gunnar want a drink even more.

"We are in demon territory, after all," said Gunnar. "To tell the truth, I thought we were going to be waist-deep in the little devils the moment we stepped foot on Erum. It's a wonder we've gotten this far and come up against so few on this cursed continent—no offense meant toward your homeland, Itz."

"How's that?" said Itz.

Gunnar kept forgetting how hard of hearing Itz was. "I said, I'm surprised we haven't encountered more demons," he said more loudly.

"That," said Zechariah, "is precisely what I *don't* like." He leveled a look at Gunnar. "After your encounter with that cythraul in the city, the enemy knows someone with powerful aurym abilities is here. They should be seeking us out. We should be seeing more of them. Many more."

"I see," said Itz. "And if they aren't here, you are concerned about—"

"Where they are instead," finished Zechariah.

"Do you suspect a trap?" asked Itz.

"I suspect everything," said Zechariah. "Or at least I try to."

Gunnar tugged at his new eyepatch. He'd had one of the Army's tailors create a replacement for the one lost during his foray into the city to find Lycon. The fit was just right, but he wasn't used to the fabric. He'd been informed that it had been made out of the tanned hide of some beast that Hook and Olorus had killed. Supposedly, it was a very sturdy and reliable substance. But it was also itchy.

"Any word on those missing Raeqlu?" asked Gunnar.

"Missing Raeqlu?" said Itz.

"You hadn't heard?" said Gunnar.

"Several nights ago," said Zechariah, "before the catastrophe in the city. Some sort of disagreement between some of Gunnar's people and some Raeqlu infantry escalated into a brawl and ended in bloodshed. The Raeqlu in question left camp the next night and haven't been seen since."

"How many?" asked Itz.

"Fifty or a hundred, depending on who you ask," said Zechariah. "Our census-taking has been notably poor." He looked at Gunnar. "And, no, there is still no word on them."

"Where do you think they went?" asked Gunnar.

Zechariah let out a great puff of exasperated breath. "I have not had much time to ponder that question in the days since this army's commander and half its officers wandered off to pursue their own ambitions, leaving me to pick up the pieces! I still can't fathom what Leah was thinking."

If pressed on the subject, Gunnar would have had to admit that he agreed with that last point. It was odd that their princess turned queen turned commander would so abruptly leave an army that she had, until now, been so single-mindedly devoted to leading.

Days had passed, and Leah was still missing. And to top it off, Olorus, Hook, and Megara, all of whom had departed against Zechariah's wishes to attempt to follow her, hadn't been heard from since then, either.

Adonica, Lycon, and Sif had only recently returned. And as for Gunnar, he knew he certainly hadn't been much help recently.

Cracks are forming in the foundation of this army, said his inner voice. *It's only a matter of time until it all crumbles.*

"Itz," said Zechariah, clearing his throat in annoyance and changing the subject, "you said you had some concerns about the maps Lycon brought back?"

Itz took out said maps. He laid them flat on the ground in front of him and indicated the peninsula in the far east of Erum. On which was the city that Lycon had pointed out when he'd first shown the maps to Gunnar.

"This map was annotated relatively recently," said Itz. "The notes scrawled in the margin label this entire portion of the continent 'demon lands.' It seems possible that this peninsula beyond the Bay of Anemoi is where we should be headed."

"Possible?" said Gunnar.

Itz nodded. "But there's something else. The traditional land route to the peninsula," said Itz, tracing his finger over the map, "is up through Central Erum here, toward my homeland of Ecbata, around the Bay of Anemoi, and down along the peninsula. It's a long route through a great deal of open country and leads to the Thunder Corridor, a strip of land bordered on both sides by high walls, which acts as a bottleneck to any invading force, funneling them into closer quarters and heavily favoring the defenders. However. . . ."

Itz moved his finger to the bottom of the peninsula and the place where the peninsula stuck out, separating it from the main landmass of Erum by a narrow strip of ocean. As Gunnar examined it, he realized that a series of circles had been drawn there, presumably by the same hand that had made the notes.

"These symbols here gave me pause," said Itz. "At first glance, they appear to indicate a chain of islands. But, in all my life growing up in this land, no map of Erum that I have ever seen had any islands here. The more I studied it, the more I realized that it, like the margin notes, was a recent addition to the map: a late annotation added by hand.

"I began to look further and realized that there were other places where alterations were made to this map. You can see that the coastline has been amended here. And a narrow strip of land has been inked over here where, to my knowledge, none existed before."

"Ocean levels were not always as they are today," said Zechariah. "Perhaps the lowering waters prompted the keepers at the house of records to amend their maps."

"Do you think it's accurate?" asked Gunnar.

"There are too many changes, and they have been added too skillfully to have been done by an amateur without purpose," said Itz. "I suppose we won't know for certain until we see for ourselves. It could be that whoever altered these maps inadvertently did us a great service, rest their souls."

Zechariah nodded. "Thank you, Itz. I'm sure Leah would thank you for your scholarship as well if she were here." He grumbled something under his breath in annoyance.

CHAPTER 49

Leah might have expected the cyclops to appear less intimidating in a seated position, especially the peculiar way it chose to sit: its legs folded beneath it, with its bottom resting on its feet. It was more of a childlike kneel than a sit, really.

The cyclops was *not* any less intimidating in this stance. Not at all. The creature appeared to be male, and even with his palms resting facedown on his lap, Leah could not shake the reminder that her entire body could have fit within one of his six-fingered hands. The long, chipped, plaque-spotted tusks protruding from his jaw didn't do much to put her at ease either.

Leah, following the procedures of intercultural diplomacy, had adopted the same seated position. Mirroring the body language of the other party, so long as it did not come across as mimicking or antagonistic, had a way of putting others at ease. She hoped that it demonstrated her willingness to meet the cyclops at its level . . . so to speak.

On the one hand, Leah couldn't believe what she was seeing. On the other hand, it all added up.

How many times she had wondered about the connection between the giant gates in the fortifications around the Shifting Mountains and the massive architecture of the underground city of Cymorikka—far too large to be practical for regular human beings, with a statue of a twenty-foot-tall cyclops, carved of pure a'thri'ik, in its main hall.

Not to mention, thought Leah, *the impossibly oversized pieces of arms and armor we found in that city.*

Swords as long as barn beams. Breastplates the size of castle doors. Helmets as big as rain barrels, with oddly centered, singular eyepieces.

"Does he have a name?" Kallorn asked bluntly.

In contrast to Leah's technique, Kallorn remained standing. He had sheathed his sword, at least, but one hand remained rested on its hilt.

Beside Leah, Justin turned his attention to the cyclops. She could tell from the feel of the aurym emanating from him that he was once again communicating with the cyclops, though there was no outward indication of what he was saying. In response, the cyclops replied in a voice like the bleat of a rutting stag, punctuated by intermittent, higher-pitched tones like an elk's bugle.

"I don't know how you'd pronounce it," said Justin, "but his name means something like 'Little Brother.'"

Kallorn blinked. "Little?"

"I get the impression he's short for his kind," said Justin.

Not far from their position, Justus, the boy with the withered arm who had been mistakenly imprisoned by the Warlord of the Deep, made a sound as if he were trying not to faint.

The rest of the refugees from the fortress observed these negotiations from afar. Leah, aware that Justus spoke both Waelik and the local Aznochti tongue, had selected him from the crowd to aid in translating. With his help, she had even gotten her satchel of healer's herbs back from the guards who had detained her.

"What is 'Little Brother' in Aznochti?" Leah asked Justus.

"Ye'Eeh Grae," replied Justus.

"Yeegrae, then," said Leah. "Will that do?"

Justin relayed Leah's question, and the cyclops seemed content.

The place where they were gathered was a great, cavernous chamber with hallways extending outward in all directions, much like the central chamber of Cymorikka back in Athacea. Leah now noticed that where there ought to have been a large statue of a cyclops, there was instead a shattered ruin of broken pieces.

With the help of Justus acting as translator, Leah had learned from the Warlord's people that retreating into this underground city had been the contingency plan if their fortress was ever compromised. They were nothing if not prepared; she could see that they were well provisioned, with plenty of food and rations. Even now, a small cookfire was being lit, and kettles were being brought out for tea.

Nefari had been thorough. Down here, her "benefactors" would protect her people.

Benefactors, thought Leah. *Plural.*

"Justin," she said. "Can you ask him if there are more people like him down here?"

Justin nodded. He rubbed his eyes and yawned, then called on aurym to relay the message.

There was a low growl from Yeegrae's throat, followed by a sound like a blast from a brass horn.

"He says," said Justin, "there *were*."

Yeegrae shifted in his seated position. His attention was turned away from the humans, and for a few long moments, all was silent.

"Maybe we should give him a minute," Justin whispered to Leah. "The topic seems to have upset him."

Upon being informed that this massive being was "upset," Kallorn made no discernable change in stance, yet Leah seemed to be able to sense the increased tension radiating from him.

"Upset him?" said young Justus. He shifted where he sat and swallowed so hard that Leah could hear it. "I, uh, think I'll go get something to drink." And he hastily excused himself.

Leah watched the boy go, feeling pity for him. He had been through great trauma, possibly literal torture at the hands of Nefari the Warlord.

Everything Nefari did, thought Leah, *she did for her people. To keep them safe.*

Did that excuse the boy's treatment at her hands?

And what about me? Does it excuse everything I have done?

Leah didn't know.

Returning her attention to Yeegrae, she realized that he was not staring blankly into space as she'd assumed. Rather, he was staring at the broken pieces of a'thri'ik on the cavern floor. The pieces that had once been a statue of a cyclops.

"He's remembering something," Justin whispered. "A conflict between members of his kind."

"A *recent* conflict?" asked Kallorn.

"I don't think so," said Justin. "But I think there was a recent disagreement that was an echo of the bigger conflict from long ago. Maybe not a full-scale war, but there was bloodshed."

"How do you do that?" asked Leah.

Justin, still watching Yeegrae, shrugged without looking at her. "It's an aurym thing. I can just sense it."

"That's not how aurym works," Kallorn spoke up.

Justin squinted at him. "What do you mean?"

"You talk about sensing the presence of others and communicating like this as if it comes naturally to you," said Leah. "I'm a healer, but I can't heal without my ring. And Kallorn can't use his powers without his sword. No one can. You shouldn't be able to do these things without an aurstone."

"Or call a weapon to come to your hand, out of the very air," said Kallorn.

Leah had almost forgotten the way Justin had done that back in the fortress. Hook's lance had flown into his grasp as if of its own accord.

And it wasn't the first time such a thing had happened. She recalled a conversation between the two of them long ago. "I never got to thank you for throwing me my sword back there," Justin had told her in the palace of Hartla after their victory over the demons. To which Leah had replied in confusion, "I didn't throw anything."

"You need an aurstone," said Leah, in the present, "to be able to do the kind of things you're doing."

Justin gave another small shrug. "I guess I don't really know how it works," he said. "Maybe it's an ethoul thing?"

"Was your father able to do it?" asked Leah.

Justin hesitated. "Actually, when I told him about it, he seemed as surprised as you are."

The boy named Justus returned holding a wooden platter with steaming teacups. He took one for himself and gave one to each of the rest of them, except Yeegrae, for whom a teacup would not have held a teardrop.

"Can you do that to coblyns?" asked Kallorn. Even with a cup of tea in one hand, he kept his other hand on his sword. "Communicate with them? Make them do as you wish?"

Justin shook his head. "I've tried, and it doesn't work. But I can stun them with it. It seems to overload their senses. It blinds them or something."

Leah's gaze wandered to the Warlord's people again. They were restless and confused, and the news of Nefari's death had shaken them. Despite Leah assuring them, through Justus, that they were here to help, she got the impression that few of them were convinced.

Maybe, she thought, *if they could hear it from Nefari herself. . . .*

"Justin," said Leah, "would it be possible for you to call on the Warlord again?"

"I think I could do that," said Justin. He took a sip of his tea and, for a second time, rubbed his eyes and yawned.

A thought occurred to Leah. "Justin, how long has it been since you last rested?"

He made a face. "If by *rested* you mean *slept*, it's been a couple of days. But I'll be fine, really."

Leah grinned as she watched him fight against another yawn. Somehow, even his stubbornness was endearing.

It was a bit frightening to feel such things. As a princess back in Cervice, she hadn't had many romantic relationships, not real ones, anyway. And now, with the war and her place in it, well, there hadn't been very much time for such things. Or perhaps she had intentionally not made the time for it. She was used to maintaining a necessary distance from people, even those whom she cared for like family.

A few more moments passed in which Leah, Justin, Kallorn, and Justus waited quietly. Finally, Yeegrae seemed to snap out of it and remember that the humans were there. He turned back to face them. He gave a low growl, followed by a series of elk bugles and gut-shaking rumbles.

"He says," said Justin, "that his people used to rule this part of the world. Their kingdom extended not only through the underground cities but above ground, where they rode ... something. Big mammals."

"Indricos," said Leah. Those were the great, long-necked mammals that cyclopes herded in myths, sometimes called land whales.

"They once rode them all over the Oikoumene," said Justin, "but there are now few of Yeegrae's kind left, and the indricos might be gone entirely."

As Yeegrae spoke, he pointed at the wall art above and around him, and Leah realized that much of it depicted scenes that matched his descriptions.

"They once lived in cities like this one, by the hundreds and thousands," said Justin, relaying Yeegrae's meaning as the cyclops continued to speak. "They fought against the demons when they invaded the Oikoumene. A great plague wiped out many cyclopes. Changes in weather killed their indrico herds, and it became difficult to live in populations greater than a few dozen. In those difficult times, they turned on one another for resources. Now, there are few of his kind left."

Justin paused to allow Yeegrae to finish sharing a long, complex thought.

"And with the rest of his people having now left this city after their falling out," said Justin, "Yeegrae fears that the demons learning of this place means the Warlord's people may no longer be safe here."

This was the moment Leah had been waiting for. She set her teacup on the ground and leaned forward, her hands clasped.

"Justin, please tell Yeegrae," said Leah, "that they are welcome to find refuge among my Army of Light."

Justin, whether intentionally or not, mimicked *her* stance by placing his empty teacup on the ground and doing the same thing with his hands. He rubbed his eyes and shook his head against weariness, then relayed the message to Yeegrae.

It was difficult to read the facial features of this creature, but Leah noticed a shift in his expression, even if she was not sure what it meant.

"My Army is about one day's march from here," she continued. "We are a military force on the warpath against Avagad, the master of the demons. Although we are heading toward danger and not away from it, we are one hundred thousand strong and have powerful warriors who can protect these people."

Leah waited long enough for Justin to finish this message. Then, before Yeegrae could respond, she added, "I am the army's commander, Leah Demonsbane. And I want Yeegrae to know that he is also welcome to join us."

"Bold of you, Commander," muttered Kallorn.

Justin raised his eyebrows in appraisal. He started to translate, then hesitated. He yawned, blinked hard, and rubbed his eyes again. He let out a deep breath, like a low moan.

"Justin?" said Leah.

Justin's eyelids fluttered. His arms went limp. All at once, his body crumpled, and he tumbled forward. He would have cracked his face against the cavern floor if not for Leah. Calling on her hydstone, she fed power through her muscles and shot forward like an arrow from a bow, catching Justin before he could hit the ground. He was dead weight in her arms.

"Justin? Justin!" said Leah, shaking him.

He did not respond.

Leah's concern was steadily intensifying into panic. Yeegrae leaned forward, trying to see what had happened. Kallorn stepped toward them, and Justus backed away in fear as murmurs spread through the crowd of refugees.

"What's wrong?" said Kallorn. "What's happened to him?"

"I don't know," said Leah.

She tilted his head from side to side, checking his pulse and heart rate. His breathing was regular but shallow. She pulled back his eyelids and found his pupils heavily dilated.

Then, her eyes found the empty teacup on the ground in front of Justin.

She looked up at Justus, still backing away from them in fear, now with his hands raised and shaking.

"Please," said Justus. "I'm sorry."

"The tea," said Leah.

Kallorn was on Justus in an instant, grabbing the boy by the collar of his prisoner's rags and raising his sword to his throat.

"No, *no!*" the boy screamed. "Please!"

"What did you do?" demanded Kallorn.

"It was only his!" Justus squealed, the tip of Kallorn's sword at his throat. "I didn't do anything to yours! Only his!"

By now, the unease in the crowd of refugees had evolved into an uproar. Yeegrae was standing, looking around in confusion and apprehension. The last thing they needed right now was an agitated cyclops, but Leah didn't have time to worry about that. Depending on what had been in the tea, she might have only a few minutes to prepare a countermeasure.

"What did you give him?" Leah shouted.

"I'm sorry—I'm *so* sorry! He made me do it!" said Justus. "He shows me things—talks to me in my dreams!"

"Who?" said Kallorn, shaking him.

"Avagad!" said Justus, his words falling apart into barely comprehensible babble. "I try not to listen, but I can't! I can't! *I can't! I CAN'T!*"

Where would he have found something to poison him? thought Leah, trying to reason through things logically despite the circumstances. *What substances are even available to him down here?*

Leah looked down at her healer's satchel at her side, which had been returned to her only a few moments ago—thanks to Justus.

He'd had it in his hands before giving it back to her.

Leah grabbed the teacup from the floor, sniffed it, ran her finger along the bottom, and tasted the residue.

Grilcin.

"Justin!" she said, slapping him lightly in the face. "Justin! Wake up! *Justin!*"

PART VII

IMAGINARY

VOYAGE

CHAPTER 50

Justin zipped his coat up as high as it would go against the snow, all the way to the top of the collar, so that the scratchy nylon was unpleasantly tight against his face, covering his lips.

The wind hit the remaining unprotected parts of his face like a dry boar-bristle brush. It was the kind of snow that fell in salt-like pellets instead of flakes but still small and light enough that, in addition to the usual direction that snow tended to come at you from, the swirling wind sent it moving right, left, and up, too.

In short, it was the kind of day that made residents of places like western Pennsylvania look at one another and say, "Why do we live here?"

Justin drew a tighter grip on his weapon of choice: a plastic-bladed ice scraper. He had started the truck to let it warm up, and the defroster was on high, but it was still an uphill battle. A mild morning with a light rain shower had been followed by a precipitously sharp drop in temperatures at midday. That, combined with the bitter afternoon snow squall presently rolling through the region, had resulted in the truck's windshield being covered not only by a layer of snow but a skim of ice on the glass under that. It was the sort of problem only elbow grease could remedy.

He ran the scraper in a few quick horizontal lines across the windshield of the little red pickup truck and braced himself against a particularly strong gust of wind. As if the weather wasn't bad enough, here in the high school parking lot, it always seemed several standard deviations outside the norm in terms of general misery. The school had been built on a flat hilltop, with nothing to break the wind as it came rushing through the parking lot.

Justin muttered a few choice words, profaning everything from the snow to the truck to the school to his cheap-ass ice scraper with the broken handle—and, most of all, himself for forgetting his gloves at home this morning. His hands were bare, and his fingers were already going numb.

It figures, he thought. *I would have gotten home before all this bad weather hit if I hadn't had to stay late for—*

Another gust of wind. Another wild swirl of snow. A spray of ice crystals, loosened by his scraper's blade, got caught in the updraft and peppered him across both cheeks.

God! Can't even remember what I had to stay late for—so effing cold, I can't even think!

With the driver's side of the glass mostly cleared, Justin had to resist the urge to say "good enough" and get in. Dad would be angry if he caught him driving with a half-cleared windshield just because he was too lazy to do the other side. He shuffled through the snow, along the edge of the truck's hood, to the passenger side of the vehicle and continued scraping. Thankfully, the defroster was starting to do its job, and his first scrape got under the ice and cleared a nice, straight row.

The newly cleared portion of the windshield gave him a line of sight through the glass at Kate, sitting in the passenger seat, her long hair tucked up beneath a knitted beanie cap, her hands held over the blower as if the meager warmth it put out were as life-sustaining as a roaring hearth.

Justin knocked against the glass with the butt end of his scraper and pulled the collar of his coat away from his lips to shout, "Okay, your turn!" through the windshield.

Kate looked away as if something interesting had suddenly caught her eye.

"Hey! I know you can hear me in there!" Justin said.

She looked one way, then the other, whistling with a dimpled grin as she continued to stare off into space in an exaggerated fashion.

"What talented acting!" Justin shouted. "Really an award-winning performance!"

Justin pulled his collar back up and continued scraping. When it really came down to it, that was what he liked about Kate. She had the type of personality that. . . .

Justin's vigorous scraping of the windshield slowed, then stopped entirely.

Wait, Kate? thought Justin. *We broke up a month ago. No, even longer ago than that.*

There were times when he forgot. They had been together since Junior year. And when you were together with someone for a while, that person became a part of you. You forgot how to function without them, in some ways.

So, why was she in his truck? He was giving her a ride home, but he couldn't remember why.

Oh, well. Just because they were broken up didn't mean he couldn't give her a ride home. He had to stop acting like her boyfriend, though. It was over. It was. . . .

Come to think of it, it wasn't just that he couldn't remember why he was giving her a ride home. He couldn't remember much about school that day at all. Or walking out here to the parking lot to scrape the truck. Or much of anything before this very moment, in fact.

"Why am I here?" whispered Justin.

It seemed like a very significant question. One he had asked himself many times before.

Justin looked around. Only now did he realize that his truck was the only vehicle in the entire high school parking lot. He wondered how, until now, he had failed to notice that for at least a hundred yards in every direction, there was nothing but a no man's land of empty spaces. Beyond that, the snowstorm was like a solid wall of white, obscuring his vision of everything except the doors of the school beneath a large glass overhanging pyramidal structure, very modern in design. He remembered how big that glass entryway had seemed to him just a few years ago. And now, it felt. . . .

Don't get distracted, he thought, shaking his head. *What's going on? How did you get here? Why is Kate—?*

He looked through the truck windshield again and saw only a bare polyester seatback. Kate was gone.

Justin gently put the ice scraper down on the truck's hood. He was now starting to notice other anomalies, all of which should have been obvious but had somehow escaped his attention. Like the fact that it had suddenly stopped snowing, yet he still couldn't see past the white-shrouded border of the parking lot. Or the fact that the wind had died, and it was now silent. Or the fact that it was night, not afternoon, and the only light he could see was coming from the inside of the school.

But it wasn't like normal lights. It was a pulsating glow.

None of this was right. He knew that. But he couldn't remember why. Couldn't even remember what *right* was anymore.

Something like this happened to me once before, thought Justin. *Didn't it?*

He was already up to the sidewalk in front of the school before he even realized that he had started walking—not of his own choice but as if his feet were moving automatically beneath him. He walked, alone, to the school doors. At the place where he should have reached them, he kept walking; the doors were almost twice as far away as he'd thought and almost twice as big. When he reached them, he pushed them open to the tune of impossibly loud, unoiled hinges.

The doors should have opened up to a common area and an attached main office. Instead, Justin stepped through them straight onto the wood-paneled floor of the school gymnasium. His tennis shoes squeaked, but that wasn't right either. He looked down. He was no longer wearing his winter coat with the scratchy collar and the zipper all the way up. Instead, he was dressed in his school basketball uniform and game shoes. And there was a basketball in his hands.

A cheering crowd met him as he stepped out onto the court beneath white lights and hanging banners embroidered with the years of past district and state championships and the names of thousand-point earners. He *heard* the crowd—their shouts and cheers were deafening. But he didn't know where it was coming from because the stands were empty.

Except, they were not quite empty. Not entirely.

Justin's breath caught in his throat. There, in her usual spot on the bleachers, her hands cupped over her mouth as she cheered, looking and behaving more like she was part of a crowd than the only person in the stands, was Claire Holmes.

"Mom," Justin said. "Mom!"

He dropped the ball and ran to her. But as soon as he took a step, the shouting of the crowd changed. It took on an eerie, discordant tone. The yelling continued, but it was no longer cheering; it was screaming. Wails of terror, then sorrow, then pain, intensifying into agony.

Claire Holmes raised her hands to her mouth, and instead of cheering, she said, "We'd better get home. Supper's ready."

The words were like a spike through Justin's heart.

That was the last thing she said, thought Justin.

Or, at least, it was the last thing he'd heard her say. She'd said those words just seconds before the crash.

"Mom!" Justin yelled as he ran.

One by one, with great thudding reports, the banks of overhead lights in the gymnasium shut off.

Clank.

Clank.

Clank.

The brightly lit gym, row by row, was plunged into utter darkness until only one light was left.

The last thing Justin saw was his mother, her expression still as pleasant as if watching one of his basketball games. But it looked for a second like she was illuminated not by the overhead lights but by the headlights of an oncoming vehicle.

"We'd better get home!" she yelled. "*Supper's ready!*"

"No!" Justin cried, reaching for her. "Wait! *Mom!*"

Clank.

Blackness.

Justin's hand, reaching out for her, found nothing but cold, empty air that seemed to congeal against his skin like a solid entity. And there, alone in the total blackness, it all became clear to him.

All at once, Justin knew where he was.

CHAPTER 51

"The Kharon," he said.

The world between worlds, he thought. *A sideways shift instead of a jump. A place able to be entered physically, or spiritually while the body remains behind.*

Justin lowered his arms to his side, clenched his hands into fists, took a deep breath, and let it out slowly to steady his nerves. He raised his voice to speak into the darkness surrounding him.

"How is it that you do all this?" he said. "How are you able to show me things that you yourself have never seen?"

At first, there was no response. Only silence in the darkness where, moments prior, Justin had been running and crying out for his mother. And yet, despite that darkness and its uncertainty and the danger Justin knew he was in, he felt no fear. Because he was not that boy running for his mother anymore. He hadn't been for a while now. He couldn't afford to be.

Finally, a voice spoke from somewhere ahead.

"I *show* you nothing," said the voice. "Everything you see is an invention of your own mind. All I provide is the general . . . theme."

The darkness was broken in an instant by the light of a single purple tongue of flame hovering over an outstretched palm. The violet glow illuminated a sharp-featured face.

Oddly, Justin thought, only for a second, that that face was his own. He blinked to clear his vision.

Ornate, glistening steel armor, colored scarlet and white with sharply upturned shoulder plates and armguards as sharp as blades. Light brown hair. A thin crown of silver atop his brow, with a trio of diamonds set in the shape of a triangle.

"What is it that you saw this time, son of Benjamin?" said Avagad.

"Ghosts," said Justin.

Avagad's face was a blank canvas.

That high-ridged nose. The jawline. The hair. The overall stature. Yes, the features were strikingly similar, now that Justin thought about it.

"Friends of yours?" asked Avagad. "Family? Or . . . a *mentor,* perhaps?"

An image flashed in Justin's mind of the last time he had seen Avagad in person. He had been holding Ahlund's broken and bleeding body in place. The Guardian had been half-changed by a cythraul's transforming touch. But Ahlund had driven his own sword through his body to pierce Avagad, to allow Justin to escape, sacrificing his own life in the process.

In the past, Justin might have cursed Avagad for all that he had done. He might have spoken to him with defiance, with brave determination and bold promises. He might have been a bit scared. Or full of rage. Probably both. But instead, he was just curious.

"How were you able to bring me here?" said Justin.

"I admit, I had a bit of outside help," said Avagad. "Fortunately, it is not overly difficult for a man in my position to arrange such things. I have servants everywhere."

Servants everywhere, thought Justin.

Although Justin now knew this place for what it was, the influence of the Kharon still made his recent memories foggy. He was having trouble pinning down the details. The last thing he remembered was being somewhere with Leah. He tried not to let it show on his face how disturbed he was by that thought. Whatever had happened in the Oikoumene to bring him into the Kharon like this, he just prayed that Leah was all right.

More light had begun to filter into the darkness as the illusion faded. As Justin gained a better view of his surroundings, he recognized this place.

It was a single, circular room. Toward the center, a large globe sat on a stand. Justin had learned enough about the Oikoumene by now to recognize its landmasses as Athacea, Otunmer, Darsida, and Erum. The room's windows looked out on skies that were gray yet seemed to carry a hint of the same purple hue as the color of the flame in Avagad's hand. There was a desk with a candle burning on it. There was a finely upholstered chair. And, set against the far wall, there was a bookcase.

The little room at the top of Avagad's tower was just as Justin remembered it.

"It's an aurym ability, right?" said Justin, thinking back to the Warlord using her power to show him the Pit. "The far-seeing stone can show people visions. But with your level of power, you can use it to *create* visions."

"Very good, Justin," said Avagad. "Many aurstones, as you yourself have discovered, can be used in more advanced forms if the wielder is capable of calling on enough power. By entering the Kharon physically and using this aurstone's advanced form, I am able to enter the dreams of my servants across the entire Oikoumene and communicate with them. Or . . . I can change those dreams into nightmares."

By entering the Kharon physically, thought Justin, taking careful note of Avagad's choice of words.

It hadn't occurred to Justin until now, but finding Avagad's tower in the Kharon should have tipped him off earlier to a very important fact.

Avagad can use a keystone like I can, thought Justin. *He, too, can travel between worlds.*

Justin pushed aside that thought, vowing to return to it at another time.

"You once tried to make me walk through a doorway in this place," Justin said, idly strolling through the tower. "I now know that most of what I saw was an illusion. Like right now."

"What makes you think *this* is an illusion?" asked Avagad.

As was often the case with this man, Justin had a hard time telling if his interest really was piqued or if it was just an act. But it didn't really matter either way.

Justin turned to face Avagad. "Well, for one thing, I'm sure you don't look like that anymore. Not after what my . . . *mentor* did to you."

A look crossed Avagad's face. It was like a combination of outrage and satisfaction, as if he did not appreciate the remark but savored being challenged.

For a moment, everything seemed to blur, as if Justin were seeing the world through incorrect prescription lenses. Then, it all came back into focus, and he saw the man's true form.

Armor badly damaged, marred, and blackened with scorch marks. Cheeks of web-like scar tissue. An empty, hollow socket where his left eye should have been. A mouth that had no lips, only rounded humps of flesh that ringed a mouth that looked too small for his face. Where his nose should have been was a dark recess, with the interior structures of his nasal cavity visible within.

This man fancied himself a king, and it seemed he would wear his crown forevermore; the silver, diamond-studded diadem on his brow was fused into his flesh, melted into a misshapen, uneven ring where it had been melted by aurym fire. Perhaps even the ornate armor he wore was now a permanent feature of his body, for it seemed to have been melted inward, twisted, and misshapen to the point that Justin could not imagine a scenario where he could remove it without causing catastrophic, possibly fatal damage to the body beneath. Below the sternum and just off-center, there was a split in the armor. It looked like Ahlund had been only a few inches from stabbing him straight through the heart.

Perhaps most remarkable of all, a dull reflection of steel could be seen within the armor's split.

Ahlund's broken sword, Justin realized. *Still embedded in his body.*

Justin might have expected to take satisfaction from the sight of what Ahlund's final attack had done to this man. Instead, he found himself just wishing it had never happened, that it had never needed to happen, that none of the death and violence and hate and darkness that he had been through since arriving in this fallen world had happened.

It all had a single source. And that source was not the man standing before him.

Avagad let the purple flame in his hand go out. The shade of violet from outside the windows continued to burn and pulse like an unseen storm. He seemed to be waiting for Justin to say something about his appearance. Instead, Justin decided it was finally time to lay everything out on the table.

"I know who you are, Avagad," said Justin. "Who you really are."

It was a bit of a challenge to discern emotion on Avagad's scarred face, but it did not appear as if Justin's words surprised him.

"Secret's out," Avagad said.

Now that he had dropped the illusion of his former form, his speech was changed as well. The damage to his mouth gave his speaking pattern a lisping quality, and his voice came out sounding hollow.

Avagad casually reached into a pouch hanging at his belt and drew forth an object. He held it out so that Justin could get a clear view. It was the wooden box Justin had found when he had last entered this tower, a wooden box with a telling description on the inside.

Avagad admired the box for a moment, then looked at Justin and said, "Brother . . . have you been going through my things?"

CHAPTER 52

"So," said Justin. "You do know."

"Of course I know," Avagad said, "although great pains were taken to keep the truth from me."

Avagad turned and crossed the room. There was a pronounced limp in his gait now. He stopped at the bookcase, where he placed the wooden box back on the shelf. But instead of turning to face Justin, he remained in place, staring at it.

"The fallen angel who united the world by defeating the demons, only to replace them as a tyrannical overlord," said Avagad. "It took the combined might of all the immortal Brethren to finally defeat him and expel him from the Oikoumene. . . . That man was gone long before I was born. I was raised by my mother among the Brethren, with their leader, Amphidemus, as a sort of surrogate father. When the time came, I, too, accepted their gift of long life and joined their ranks. The truth of my lineage, however, was hidden from me."

Only now did Avagad turn away from the bookcase to face Justin again. The remaining eye beneath his melted silver crown pierced like a needle.

"It was the Nameless One who finally revealed to me that the blood of the fallen ran in my veins." Avagad stroked his scarred chin. "My servant informs me that you have been reunited with that little shrew, the princess of Nolia. You must be so happy. I know you two are quite close. But are you really? Traveling companions for all of, what? A few days? A *year* ago? How much do you even know about her? How much does she know about you? Do you have *anything* in common— do you even know her well enough to answer that question?"

"Your game never changes, does it?" said Justin. "You bring me to this place, and then you poke and prod to try to find a weak point. You lie. You manipulate. All to try to get me on the Nameless One's side. My father . . . *our* father . . . told me that the Nameless One changed him. He somehow made him his slave. Is that what happened to you, too? He made you his slave and then made you kill Amphidemus and the rest of the Brethren—the only family you had ever known. Only Cyaxares and Zechariah escaped."

"*Made* me?" said Avagad. He shook his head as if he pitied Justin for his simple-mindedness. "I am no slave, Brother."

Justin shrugged. "Brainwashed sycophant, then."

"I prefer to think of myself as a willing servant. You should carefully consider your own options, boy. Willing servant, like me. Or slave, like that fool, our father."

"It took you a while to figure that out, didn't it?" said Justin. "That we shared the same father."

Avagad did not seem thrown by the pivot in subject matter. "I was aware from the start."

Justin leaned back casually against the wall and crossed his arms. "Nah, I don't think you knew."

Avagad sneered at him.

"You knew the name Benjamin Holmes," said Justin, "and you knew I had the same surname. You may have suspected we had the same lineage, but you didn't know about the time difference between worlds. You didn't know that despite the passage of thousands of years, you and I could share the same father. There are a lot of little things like that, things you must not have known. Otherwise, you would have done things differently. Either that or you made some very unwise choices."

Avagad's sneer sharpened, but he still said nothing.

"Somewhere along the line," said Justin, "you pieced together that your father, Benjamin, was, in fact, my father as well. Probably through your spies and servants. The funny thing is, I'm the firstborn."

"I have lived for two thousand five hundred years," said Avagad.

Justin nodded. "And I was only a year younger than I am now when your life began."

"Well, *elder* brother, I defer to your wisdom, then," said Avagad. "I long to know: Does our father still live?"

Justin chewed on this for a moment, wondering if it would be wiser to conceal this information from Avagad, but he could see no reason not to tell the truth.

"He is alive," said Justin. "But he can't return. He was cut off from aurym by the Nameless One. The first time you brought me to this tower room, you tried to make me go through a door. A portal. If I had gone through it, I assume the Nameless One would have done the same thing to me that he did to our father. But there's one thing I don't quite understand.

"Why didn't the Nameless One turn me into a wraith when he had the chance? He could have used his cythraul to do it when he changed my arm. And why didn't he do it to dad? Or to *you*, for that matter? The only reason I can think of is that something is lost when the process occurs. There must be some reason why a willing—or, at least, *almost willing*—servant is more effective than a slave."

"Perhaps you will soon find out personally," said Avagad.

"The portal to the Nameless One," said Justin. "To the demon realm, a world called Mu. Could you make another one? A doorway that would take me to him?"

"Why?" demanded Avagad, suspiciously.

Justin shrugged again. "He seems so interested in me. Maybe I should introduce myself."

Avagad's lipless mouth peeled back in what now passed for a smile, revealing a mostly toothless lower gumline. "You have grown very bold. But you are as foolish as ever."

"Yeah, as far back as I can remember, I've always been pretty dumb," said Justin. "I'm not sure about bold, though. I think it's just that nothing surprises me anymore. Still, I am glad you brought me here. I wanted to talk to you one last time, before the end. To see if there was any hope for you."

An odd sound bubbled up from Avagad's throat. A wet-sounding laugh that grew wetter and wetter until it devolved into a coughing fit that wracked his body. He took a wobbly step backward and nearly fell but managed to steady himself. The laugh turned to a shout of pain, and he clutched at the broken sword piece in his body, gritting his teeth and wincing.

He must be in constant agony, thought Justin.

"Hope? For me?" said Avagad when he managed to regain his composure. "Dear Brother, that is what you do not understand. I am the *only* hope humanity has."

"You?" said Justin.

"You speak as if you know all," said Avagad. "But you have neglected to consider one key aspect in this story. I am not trying to destroy humanity. I am trying to save it. And I brought you here because this is the only place where we can talk without the Nameless One hearing our words."

Justin tried not to let it show, but he found himself thrown for a loop by that one.

"The cycle of Aurym has continued for tens of thousands of years," said Avagad. "For as long as the Nameless One has existed in his realm of Mu, he has influenced the Oikoumene through daemyn, an extension of his very spirit. His influence has grown over time. Periodically, he unleashes his demon armies. In response, aurym intervenes and sends a champion, in the form of a fallen angel, to aid humanity in driving the darkness out again. Slowly, the Nameless One rebuilds his armies, daemyn's influence increases, and it happens all over again. But have you ever stopped to wonder where daemyn comes from? *What* it really is?"

"I . . . no, I guess I haven't," admitted Justin.

It had been implied to Justin that daemyn was like aurym. An energy source: the opposite side of the same coin.

Avagad made a satisfied face at Justin, or at least, he did so as best he could with his scarred features. "Daemyn is corrupted aurym."

Justin squinted at him. "*Corrupted* aurym?"

"That's right," said Avagad. "The Nameless One takes the life force of aurym, distorts it, taints it, and recycles it as his own. He gets it from many places. From willing servants like me, who commune with him and sacrifice a portion of our life force. From people like the Brethren, whose immortality stemmed from a ritual that, unbeknownst to most of them at the time, pledged a portion of their eternal aurym to him. From slaves like cythwraiths, whose spirits become locked in perpetual torment and slowly feasted upon, even as their bodies are made his to command. And. . . ."

Here, Avagad paused. He looked hard at Justin.

"And he gets it from all the aurym that is used against him, through his High Demons."

Justin blinked. "What?"

"You have seen how the cythraul can absorb aurym attacks, have you not?" said Avagad. "That is the collection process in action."

Justin felt a coldness creep into his stomach at the implications.

But that would mean, thought Justin, *every time I've ever attacked one of them. . . .*

"I don't believe you," snapped Justin.

"*Oooh*," purred Avagad. "I see that I finally struck a nerve. I think you know, deep down, that I'm telling the truth. Consider that within it lie the answers to your own questions; fallen angels have the potential to be the conduits for unspeakable aurym power. Killing an ethoul would be a devastating loss to the Nameless One. As a fully turned cythwraith, you could be his slave, but you yourself stumbled upon the reason why the Nameless One would prefer not to do this: there are limitations to that form. The amount of aurym power you could give him as a cythwraith, while substantial, would be far less than if you, like our father, were influenced at a soul-deep level."

Justin felt his certainty faltering. Avagad was a master of deceit and manipulation. But he had once told Justin that the only thing more effective than a lie was a well-aimed truth. And as Avagad explained all this, Justin could sense no deceit behind his words.

"But Dad said the Nameless One cut him off from aurym," said Justin.

"Not quite," said Avagad. "It was more like the Nameless One established a mechanism that would divert aurym from him. He would have become like a waterwheel. Every bit of his power, from that point on, was channeled to the Nameless One and fueled *him* instead, bringing the Nameless One ever closer to his ultimate goal."

"The destruction of aurym," said Justin.

"Not destruction, Justin," said Avagad. "Absorption."

A small, misshapen tongue extended from Avagad's mouth to moisten the lipless edge of his mouth before he continued.

"The Nameless One aims to install himself, and daemyn, in the place of aurym. But all life is, at its core, aurym. To absorb it *all* is a monumental task. And he cannot achieve such a goal from a distance. He must come to our world. Personally."

Justin's chest went cold and hollow with the dread of sudden understanding.

The Pit, he thought. *The place where the demons are coming from. It's not just for coblyns and cythraul to enter this world. It's a doorway for the Nameless One himself.*

"Are these lies, Avagad?" said Justin.

"It is, all of it, true."

"Then why would you, a self-proclaimed 'willing servant' of your demon master, tell me all this?"

"Because, as I explained," said Avagad, "I am the hope of humanity. I am trying to stop it."

CHAPTER 53

For a moment, Justin didn't know what to say. He almost thought he had misheard Avagad.

"It all started when Cyaxares discovered that the immortality of the Brethren was unintentionally funneling power to the Nameless One," Avagad went on. "She shared this revelation with me, her son, thinking that I would follow her in her decision to renounce the order and leave. Instead, I opened myself up to the Nameless One, hoping to learn more, pinpoint any weakness he might have, and defeat him. I was righteous in my cause. But in my search for an answer, what I found . . . was that he had no weakness. His power was indomitable. He is the king of the demons, Justin, but he is not a demon himself. He is more like a god."

"So you betrayed and killed the very people who raised you," said Justin.

"Have you heard nothing that I have said?" demanded Avagad. "What good would it have done the Nameless One to kill them? Their power was too valuable to be wasted. As I have told you, daemyn is recycled aurym.

"The Nameless One's demons entered our citadel with my help. The Brethren were overwhelmed. There were some, like our leader Amphidemus, who had to be killed. But the rest, we transformed through the touch of daemyn."

Justin felt his lip curl in disgust and horror.

"Their immortal souls, to this day," said Avagad, "are held captive in eternal torment within cythwraith bodies, feeding power to the Nameless One."

Living power sources, thought Justin.

"All of them except your mother, Cyaxares," said Justin. "And Zechariah."

"Hmm, yes, about that . . ." said Avagad, stroking his scarred chin.

"What?" demanded Justin.

"That *was* a lie, Brother."

Justin decided to proceed cautiously. "*What* was a lie?"

"I told you that the old man whom you call Zechariah was working with me," said Avagad. "I knew from my spies, as well as from prying into your own mind, that there was a 'scholar and scribe' assisting you in your journey. He claimed to be one of the immortal Brethren, and this . . . vexed me. I had never heard of the man. Still, I could leverage his presence and bend it to be useful to me. Claiming that he was my ally seemed like a well-placed, strategic falsehood to destabilize you. But that falsehood no longer serves my purposes, so I now must recant."

"Or *this* is the falsehood," said Justin.

"You never know," admitted Avagad with a shrug. "But hear me: Not only is Zechariah not my ally, I don't even know who he is. I knew all the Brethren, and there was no one by that name among us."

Justin furrowed his brow. Hadn't Cyaxares made a nearly identical claim?

So, thought Justin, *does this mean* . . . no one *knows who Zechariah is?*

He would have to file that one away for later.

"That still doesn't explain what you said a moment ago," said Justin. "That you're trying to stop the Nameless One. Becoming his servant, being the commander of his war machine, ravaging nations, murdering the only family you ever knew, spreading war and chaos and destruction among your fellow humans. . . . Seems like a funny way to go about it."

"Simpleton." Avagad sighed in annoyance. "My master's ability to overhear my words while I am in the Oikoumene has made it necessary to behave in certain ways. Originally, it was power I was after. He promised that I would rule as king of the humans whom he allowed to survive his invasion. For those who died, it would be a tragic loss. But for those who survived to live under my reign, it would be prosperity and stability the likes of which the world has never seen. I . . . wasn't aware of the Nameless One's intentions to come into this world personally. Until recently. It complicates matters. His ambition to corrupt *all* aurym is a particularly troublesome matter. But I have a way to fix that."

What way? thought Justin. *That's what he wants me to ask him.*

But Justin wasn't taking the bait. It was time for a little strategic falsehood of his own.

Justin endeavored to keep his acting subtle as he shook his head regretfully and said, "For the life of me, I cannot see why your mother still thinks there's hope for you."

He pretended not to notice the look of shock that crossed Avagad's scarred face. It vanished almost the instant Justin clocked it.

"Do not try to deceive me," Avagad said in a playfully scolding tone.

Justin shrugged. "Someone once taught me that the only weapon more powerful than deceit is the truth."

"Then consider this truth," said Avagad. "We both want the same thing. To stop the Nameless One. It will require sacrificing a bit more of humanity, but in the end, we can save a remnant and rebuild the world anew. I brought you here to propose a partnership to that end."

"I'm sure you did," said Justin. "And I don't even want to hear it."

Avagad squinted his one remaining eye in what appeared to be genuine confusion.

"Even if you choose not to accept my bargain," said Avagad, "you would be a fool not to at least hear what I have to say—"

"My goal isn't to stop the Nameless One," said Justin.

Avagad made a face.

"My goal," said Justin, "is to protect people and keep them safe. Stopping the Nameless One is only one element of that equation. Sacrificing more of humanity? To save a remnant? I can't trust anyone who thinks like that. If stopping the Nameless One will protect people, I'll do it. The same goes for stopping you."

The muscle beneath Avagad's empty eye socket twitched. "Do you really hate me so much, Brother?"

"No, Avagad, I have no hate for you," said Justin. "But I am done with you. And I think I'll leave now."

Justin raised one hand and called on aurym.

A quick pulse of power from within him was all it took for the entire image surrounding him to warp and destabilize, like the picture on an old TV that had gone funny.

Avagad's eye went wide, and he recoiled in shock.

"After I realized this was an illusion, I could have left anytime," said Justin. "But I didn't want to seem rude."

Justin flexed the fingers of his raised hand and increased the flow of his power. The walls of the tower on all sides cracked as if under intense pressure from outside, causing the bookcase to shake so violently that the contents of its top shelf fell and spilled across the floor.

"How can you. . . ?" Avagad began, but he caught himself and trailed off. "This is a mistake."

"You have my word, Avagad," said Justin, "that I will try to save you if I can. But if not, I will do what I have to do."

Avagad straightened up and regained his composure. "The Nameless One will find you, boy," he said.

"Tell him not to bother," said Justin. "I'm coming for him."

Justin squeezed his hand into a tight fist, and the tower room caved in on itself from all sides. The last thing he saw before the illusion failed was a look of disbelief on Avagad's face. Disbelief and fear. Real, genuine fear.

CHAPTER 54

Gunnar had never been able to decide whether it was worse to have a nightmare you thought was real and then wake up from it, or to be *aware* that you were having a nightmare and helpless to make it stop.

This nightmare was of the second variety. He knew it to be a dream because Yordar had been dead for almost a year, and as Gunnar stood upon the pinnacle overlooking the capital city of Skyre, he turned back and found his brother standing behind him, very much alive.

Their assault on Skyre had been an unmitigated success. He and Yordar had taken the city. Their forces had broken through the naval defenses, set aground, and fought their way through the city to the royal palace complex. There, Gunnar and Yordar had cornered their uncle at the end of this narrow walkway on the edge of a precipice.

All of this had really happened ten years in the past. But this time, things didn't follow the course of the true events.

Instead of Yordar betraying Gunnar—drawing his sword and slashing him across the face in what *would* have been a killing blow, had Gunnar not reacted just in time for the attack to take only his eye and not his life—Yordar just looked at Gunnar with a smile.

"We've done it, Brother," said Yordar. "All will be right soon enough."

And then, from behind, a pair of hands grabbed Yordar by his wrists and ripped his arms out of their sockets.

Yordar stared at Gunnar in shock as he dropped to his knees. His body rolled forward into a twitching heap, revealing Ragny—no, Innocen—standing behind him, holding his arms.

Yes, Gunnar knew it was a nightmare. But he was helpless to stop it.

"You are broken inside," said Innocen. He tossed the leaking arms of Gunnar's brother over the edge of the walkway. "It's your mind, Gunnar. Your mind is broken."

Innocen raced at Gunnar, moving faster than any man should have been able to move. Gunnar took an involuntary step backward, slipped, and tumbled off the edge of the walkway.

He fell, rolled over in midair, and kept falling, falling, falling.

"Broken inside," echoed the words. "Broken. *Broken. BROKEN!*"

Gunnar woke, sitting up so hard that his forward momentum nearly carried him into the cookfire he had fallen asleep sitting in front of. He managed to reach out and catch himself before his face reached the flames. In the process, some of the contents of the open bottle in his hand sloshed out. The liquid hit the fire and ignited in a sputter of flames, and Gunnar pulled back, shielding his face.

After a quiet moment, sitting on the ground where he'd fallen, alone in the darkness of another night he was having trouble remembering, Gunnar looked down at the bottle in his shaking hand. Somehow, he'd managed not to drop it. He found that there was a certain degree of muscle memory that prevailed when it came to things like that, no matter what sort of state you were in.

He raised it to his lips and drank from it. A lot.

Gunnar coughed, barely getting the bottle away from his lips in time to avoid sputtering all over himself. His throat was raw, his vision was swimming, and his stomach, which already felt like a roiling sea, pitched more furiously as the newest addition was added to the mixture.

Days had passed since he, Adonica, Lycon, and the others had returned from that accursed cliff-side city of the dead. To Gunnar's surprise, Leah had been missing, and she still had not returned from her search for Justin. Not only that, but Olorus, Hook, and Megara had gone looking for her. Now, they were missing too.

Zechariah may not have been so off-base when he said we should stop taking unnecessary risks, thought Gunnar. *Our officers keep disappearing. And I've been on one too many rescue missions recently to feel like risking another.*

In Leah's absence, Gunnar, Zechariah, Lycon, Adonica, and others had reached a consensus. Attempting to take the Army of Light through the vertical city wasn't an option. But with the demons now aware of their presence in these parts, staying put wasn't either. Luckily, Itz had been able to read the maps Lycon had found in the city. Using them, they had moved the army through the maze of canyons and cliffs, leaving scouts and messengers behind to inform Leah of where they'd gone, when and if she finally did return.

Gunnar took another painful drink. He lowered the bottle and tried to set it down beside him. Instead, it slipped from between his fingers, hit his chest, and spilled across the front of his trousers. He managed to get ahold of it again before all of it was lost, and he set it aside, making a verbal noise that, even in his own ears, sounded like disgust in himself.

You're a mess, said that same old voice in his head.

He stood and removed himself from the fireside but lost his balance in the process, this time coming closer than ever to falling into the flames. Wouldn't that have been a fun experience, with a lap full of spilled liquor?

Only now did he notice that he was not alone at the fire. Several members of the Army of Light had joined him and were sleeping or passed out in the firelight. Most of them were lower-level soldiers; Gunnar's fellow officers never joined in. Fortunately, no credentials were required to get into this party. He really didn't know any of them all that well. Their common ground was the choice of hobby they indulged in to help pass the evenings.

He used to drink with Borris and Pool, but they had stopped joining him for some reason.

Yes, for some reason, said his inner voice. *Best not to try to think about that too hard.*

Gunnar made it to the edge of the firelight's influence and had opened up the front of his liquor-soaked trousers to answer the call of nature when he realized the edge of the firelight's influence was not actually the edge of the clearing. He was only a few steps away from a man and a woman, seated and in mid-conversation, who looked up in surprise at his unexpected arrival.

Hastily, Gunnar buckled back up—too hastily. The movement was too much. He lost his balance and dropped straight down, landing hard on his back.

"He's drunk again," said an exasperated female voice.

Adonica.

"Better help him up," said a raspy male voice.

Lycon.

Gunnar shook his head, trying to clear the cobwebs and pull himself up on his own. Before he got the chance, a pair of hands grabbed him under each arm and pulled him to his feet.

"Let's get him inside before someone sees him like this."

"Do I detect a hint of *judgment*?" said Gunnar. His words came out unslurred and without a single syllable misspoken. He had always been an articulate drunk.

"Where's his tent?" asked Lycon on one side of him.

"Over here," said Adonica on the other.

"It's just a bit of fun, you know," said Gunnar. "A man's got to be able to unwind once in a while."

"Once in a while," said Adonica.

"We all have our vices," said Gunnar. "Except you, Lycon. You're as squeaky clean as a freshly buffed hull and just as boring."

"Would you shut up, Admiral?" said Adonica.

Gunnar knew he should take her advice, but he couldn't seem to keep his mouth shut.

"What were you two doing out here in the middle of the night, anyway?" said Gunnar. "Oh. I think I know. A little tryst, eh?"

"Captain Lor," said Lycon. His raspy voice was still patient, but it had gained an edge. "Would you give me a private moment with the Admiral, please?"

Gunnar could feel Adonica staring daggers at him. But finally, she did as Lycon asked, and she walked away. Lycon waited a few seconds longer before he spoke.

"Not that we owe you any explanation," said Lycon, "but Adonica and I were discussing what happened back in the city. Two men are dead, two men who were there because of her, because she wanted to help me, and because they trusted her enough to follow her. She blames herself for their deaths. Especially Ucydotus. Estoq, acting out of grief, has hardly spent a moment sober since we returned from the city, and she is making Adonica feel—"

"Somebody should have told me," said Gunnar. "I could use a drinking buddy."

Lycon cleared his throat. "Estoq, in her words and actions, is making Adonica feel—"

"Adonica should have listened to me," said Gunnar. "*That's* the problem. She should have known her place and done as I said."

"You are a mean drunk, Gunnar," said Lycon. "I've known angry drunks, and I've known violent ones. You are nothing but mean."

"I hate to bring rank into the conversation, Soldier," said Gunnar, "but you forgot to call me 'Sir.'"

Lycon stared at Gunnar for a moment before speaking.

"Be kind to Adonica. All she cares about is defending the defenseless. In her pursuit of that goal, she has lost many, perhaps even most, of the people who were close to her. She would never admit it, but I know she is lonely. There have been several times she's thought she found something deep and lasting with the right person, but each time, the world has cruelly proven her wrong. *Sir.*"

"Are you trying to tell me I have a secret admirer?" said Gunnar.

"No, I am not," said Lycon. "And with all due respect, Admiral, if she does see anything in you, I can only hope that your continued disgraceful behavior will be enough to sour her opinion, because she deserves a hell of a lot better, and you deserve a hell of a lot worse."

Gunnar laughed. "Only you, Lycon, would feel the need to say '*with all due respect*' before giving a friend some good-natured ribbing. Besides, the lady could do worse than royalty, don't you think?"

Lycon looked Gunnar up and down. "Indeed. A fine piece of work upon which we must rest our hopes for the future of the Thalassocracy."

Up until now, this conversation had struck Gunnar as rather humorous and inconsequential, but Lycon's words and the tone he used to deliver them told Gunnar this was a bit more than good-natured ribbing.

"All right, take it easy," Gunnar said. "You know it's the drink talking when I act this way. Why pick a fight when I'm like this?"

"There isn't much choice when you're always like this."

"Now you're just being petulant."

"Keep your voice down," said Lycon.

"What for?" Gunnar said, speaking even louder, just to annoy him.

Lycon's jaw clenched. "You know what? Go ahead. If you don't care, why should I? Shout it out, let everyone know what a fool you are. I'm tired of trying to hide it."

Gunnar's mocking antagonism was, to his surprise, steadily being replaced by real anger. It was sobering him up, and he didn't much like it.

"What's gotten into you, Major?" he snapped.

"I am growing weary, Admiral, of trying to paint *you* in a positive light to all these people who follow you, only to have you make such a pathetic display of yourself night in and night out."

"Then stop," said Gunnar. "I never asked you or anyone else to follow me or sing my praises. Talk about a pathetic display! No need to get your knickers in a twist just because I caught you and one of your soldiers in a little midnight rendezvous—"

Gunnar had started to turn away when Lycon's great fist grabbed him by his shirt collar and spun him back around.

Lycon pulled Gunnar close, so close that Gunnar could see his clenched teeth beneath his bird's nest of a beard. It took Gunnar a moment to realize that his feet were not touching the ground. The big Hartlan was holding him suspended in the air—with one hand.

"You have my attention," said Gunnar.

To say it was shocking to see a man like Lycon Belesys rankled enough to lay hands on a superior was an understatement.

"If we win this war, we will one day march for home again," Lycon said. His raspy voice had become a deep growl through his clenched teeth. "The seas only know what's going on back there in the Thalassocracy, even as we speak. Perhaps our cities are under demon rule, or perhaps what remains of your brother's confederacy has taken over in our absence. Either way, there will be work to do. But I want you to know, Admiral, that I care too much about my home and our people to let things go back to the way they were before."

"What are you talking about?" demanded Gunnar.

"Slaving. State-sponsored piracy. The bruised egos of spoiled brats raised in royal palaces, leading to betrayals that spill innocent blood instead of one another's. The Thalassocracy was a broken system. People like you, and even me, were thriving under it, but at what cost? The suffering of thousands, maybe millions. What we need is a new Sovereign King, one who will rule with a just hand, like the one who once united the Raedittean Archipelago."

"And you think it should be me?" said Gunnar. "A one-eyed drunk who fell victim to his brother's plots and abandoned his home to become a fisherman in some little backwater village while everything fell apart?"

"No," said Lycon. "If you are going to make me say it, hell no, I do not think it should be you. In fact, I think it is downright *unfair* for it to be you when there are so many better people for the job. But I think you are the closest thing we've got, and you'll have to do."

Gunnar felt his nostrils flare. "Well, Lycon, since we're all being so honest with each other tonight, it might as well be said: The odds are slim to none that we will ever get the luxury of having to deal with this problem you're so worried about. The operative word is *if. If* we win the war. *If* we make it home. *If* you and I don't die before then. No use worrying about it until we get there."

Lycon's grip on Gunnar tightened. "Can't you set yourself aside? For *our people*, can't you find it within yourself to be the leader they need? If the thousands who follow you heard what you are saying right now—"

"*You're* hearing it." Gunnar wrenched himself free of Lycon's grip. He nearly fell over in the process but managed to keep his footing. "So do all of them a favor. Find yourself another king. The name Erix Nimbus should be stricken from the history books, not elevated even higher. Just ask the ghosts roaming the streets of Hartla if—and I do mean *if*—you and your little love-bird Adonica ever get the chance to return to the smoking ash heap that's left of your home—"

It happened so quickly that Gunnar couldn't have reacted in time even if he *had* been in his right state of mind. He was quite experienced at agitating men and women to the point of making them want to strike him—experienced enough that he knew to be ready for a swinging fist or a sweeping slap when things got heated. What he was not ready for was the gut punch that Lycon nailed him with. The big man's fist was as hard as an iron ball, and it struck Gunnar with such force that it felt like his abdominals went in two separate directions.

Gunnar doubled over and stumbled backward several steps, clutching at his midsection. He did everything within his power to remain standing, if only for pride, but it was impossible. All the strength seeped out of him, and he dropped to the ground and rolled over on his side.

"Holy hell, was that a good hit," he wheezed.

He looked up, bracing himself for the next strike. Adonica, who apparently hadn't gone very far after all, rushed over in response to the commotion and grabbed Lycon to hold him back, but it did not seem as if the man had any intention of following up with another hit. Lycon only glared down at Gunnar, looking as angry as Gunnar had ever seen him.

"If only you cared half as much for your people as you do for yourself," said Lycon.

With that, Lycon left.

Adonica lingered for a moment, looking down at Gunnar as he writhed on the ground. The look on her face was something halfway between disappointment and resignation.

Gunnar reached a hand up for her. "A little help, if you would be so kind?" he said.

Adonica set her jaw. Without a word, she turned and walked away, leaving him there with his hand still outstretched.

Gunnar dropped his hand to his side and, reeling from the pain, rolled over onto his back. He lay there, gasping for breath and staring up into the stars, alone except for a voice in his head that said, *You would be a great king.*

To Gunnar's surprise, it was not spoken with irony but with sincerity.

"No, I wouldn't," Gunnar replied, speaking into the air.

"You will. And I will help you."

Those last couple of gulps of drink must have really been catching up to Gunnar, because he could have sworn that he had just heard those last few words spoken aloud.

CHAPTER 55

Justin woke beneath deep, dark water. But he did not panic. He had been here and experienced all this before.

For some reason, the first thing on his mind was the lengthy instrumental intro of a song from his father's prog rock record collection: an over twenty-minute-long track with spacey guitars, layered synths, and a driving bass. It began as an echoing din in his head, then faded into the background as he calmly resurfaced from the depths of unconsciousness and opened his eyes to find himself not in an illusory memory, not in Avagad's tower, not even in underground ruins. He was outside, beneath the boughs of a hemlock tree, on a misty morning.

Justin shifted his head and found Leah Anavion asleep in a seated position beside him. Judging by the look of her, she had drifted off while keeping vigil at his side.

Justin looked around and saw that they were camped at the exit to what appeared to be the mouth of a large cave. The Warlord's people were there, and so was Yeegrae the cyclops, seated on his haunches, with his shoulders rising a foot or higher with every deep, bellows-like breath. Kallorn stood guard a few yards away, his hand resting on the hilt of his sword.

And beside Kallorn was a pitiful sight: the boy called Justus with the bad arm. Under the Warlord, he had been a prisoner. Now, he was a prisoner once again, his hands bound with cords behind his back.

Servants everywhere, thought Justin, harkening back to Avagad's words.

He would have to be more vigilant in the future.

Justin's movements caught Kallorn's attention.

"Leah," Kallorn called out.

Leah stirred. At the sight of Justin looking back at her, relief flooded over her face.

"Are you all right?" she asked.

"Fine," said Justin, stretching as he sat up. Leah's cloak had been folded and laid beneath his head as a pillow. "I feel ... refreshed, actually."

"You ought to be," said Kallorn. "You have been asleep for a night and a day."

"It was the tea, I'm assuming?" said Justin.

Leah nodded. "Drugged with grilcin, stolen from my satchel of healer's herbs."

A few yards away, the boy called Justus squirmed.

"I guess we're lucky he didn't use it on the two of you, too," said Justin.

"All that I carry, he used on you," said Leah. "The boy says he was acting on Avagad's orders."

Justin looked around. "How did we get out here?"

"The underground city is connected to this cave system," said Leah. "Yeegrae led us out."

"I would apologize for you having to carry me," said Justin, looking at Leah, "but after what I've seen you do, I can't imagine it was any more difficult than lugging a small bag."

"You were like a little child being carried to bed," said Kallorn with a smirk.

Justin grimaced.

Leah smiled and offered him her hand. Justin took it, and she helped him to his feet.

"Were you. . . ?" Leah began. "Did anything happen to you while you were unconscious?"

"Nothing serious," said Justin, groaning a bit as he rubbed a sore spot in his neck. "I'll tell you about it later."

Justin turned to level his gaze on Justus.

"I'm sorry!" the boy blurted out. He started to stand, but Kallorn stepped on the back of his ragged shirt, roughly pinning him in place. "He made me do it. I can't say no. I've tried! I've *tried*—!"

"You," said Leah imperiously, "are doing yourself no favors by further annoying me."

A thought occurred to Justin.

"Justus," said Justin. "Does he tell you to do things often?"

Justus nodded quickly. "He talks to me in dreams. I don't want to do what he says, but the dreams turn into nightmares when I don't. And there's pain. Real pain. I know it's not really happening, but it hurts!"

"I understand," said Justin. "He's done the same sort of things to me. These things he tells you to do. Be honest with me. Was coming to the Warlord's fortress one of them?"

Justus gave a slow, sad nod. "And he—he made me do this to my arm!"

As the boy broke into a sob, Justin found himself looking at his bad arm.

"Made you. . . ?" said Leah, a note of pity creeping into her voice. "You weren't born with your arm that way?"

"No," said Justus. "Justus isn't even my real name. He made me hurt myself, then told me to call myself by another name, go to that fortress, and say I was the ethoul—the fallen angel."

Kallorn took a threatening step forward, causing Justus to cower back. "Why?" said Kallorn.

"I don't know!" wailed Justus.

"I think I do," said Justin, but he left it at that.

Leah turned away, and Justin could sense the waves of frustration emanating from her. She squeezed her hands into fists and stared at the ground.

"Of course," she said. "Zechariah told me it was all just a trap, to try to draw out allies of the ethoul." She tilted her head toward Justus. "When I found him, I assumed it was a case of mistaken identity, that the Warlord found a young man with an injured arm and a similar-sounding name and thought it was you, Justin. I didn't consider that it was intentional—that the mistaken identity was *part* of the trap."

Kallorn exhaled a bitter sigh. "It worked on me."

"And me," said Leah.

And what about Cyaxares and the rest of the Guardians? thought Justin. *Where did they end up? Snared in similar traps?*

But that wasn't at the front of his mind at the moment.

"And when Avagad speaks to you," said Justin, his attention still solely on the boy. "You speak back to him?"

Justus nodded.

"And you tell him things," said Justin. "Answer his questions. Report to him."

This time, Justus did not nod or answer. He looked away shamefully.

A quiet moment passed. Beside Justin, Leah cursed under her breath as she realized what Justin was getting at.

Justin stroked his thin beard, trying to recall how much Leah had said during their conversation with Yeegrae: *"My Army is about one day's march from here. We are a military force on the warpath against Avagad, the master of the demons. Although we are heading toward danger and not away from it, we are one hundred thousand strong and have powerful warriors who can protect these people. . . . I am the army's commander, Leah Demonsbane."*

"Are we certain about how this form of communication works?" said Kallorn. "Is it possible that the boy has not yet had time to tell Avagad what he has learned?"

Justin thought about this. In addition to his own long-distance encounters with Avagad, he was aware that Avagad had servants whom he communicated with. Not only had he himself boasted about this, but back in the Drekwood in Athacea, Lisaac, the first human Justin had ever been forced to kill, had described Avagad coming to him in dreams.

"Can he see what his servants see?" asked Leah. "Or do they have to purposefully convene with him?"

"I don't know exactly how it works," Justin had to admit.

"Then perhaps," said Kallorn, "there is still time to prevent any damage from being done."

The Ru'Onora's hand, already resting on the hilt of his sword, tightened around the weapon's grip. Justus noticed, and his chin quivered.

"Yeegrae?" Justin called out.

The sentiment went out through his thoughts, too, and the cyclops, previously seated and ignoring the conversation, turned to face him. He grunted from his tusked mouth in a sentiment that Justin understood as, *I see you are still alive.*

The thought he used was not *alive*, however. It was closer to *moving*. Justin got the impression that *moving* and *alive* seemed to be synonymous in Yeegrae's mind, and perhaps also in the cyclops language. There was, when Justin thought about it, not all that much difference, when it came right down to it.

Justin gave a small shrug. "I am for now."

That, replied the cyclops, *is all any of us can ever hope for.*

Justin blinked, slightly taken aback by the depth of the answer. Perhaps he had underestimated the intelligence of this creature—no, this person.

"Have you considered Leah Demonsbane's offer to join her army?" asked Justin.

Yes, answered Yeegrae, and Justin realized he would have to ask more directly.

"Will you join her?"

The response from Yeegrae was a clear negative. Justin, throwing a glance toward Justus on the ground, decided to proceed with the rest of the conversation silently.

Where will you go, then? he asked Yeegrae.

To rejoin my clan, said Yeegrae in his mind. *If I can find them.*

I understand, replied Justin. *But first, could you travel with these people for a short time? To help protect them on their journey?*

Yeegrae considered, then grunted in the affirmative.

Thank you, said Justin. *I have just one more request. If you do find your people, would you be willing to relay Leah Demonsbane's message to them? An offer of an alliance between your people and hers?*

Justin sensed hesitancy. He wondered if he might be pushing the limits of good manners a bit too far with someone he had just met. Then the cyclops spoke in a series of deep rumbles and bugles, and through the extrasensory perceptions of aurym, Justin could read his meaning.

We are not a warlike people, said Yeegrae. *This city once contained an Armory, but it was plundered long ago. Most among us will want to continue to stay hidden, I think, rather than face the demons in open battle. Not all of us have the foresight to know what hiding will cost us in the long term.*

Please tell your people, replied Justin, *no matter what their answer may be, that Justin the ethoul wishes them the best. Tell them that there is still hope, and that I'm going to try to stop this at its source, forever.*

I have heard your words, said Yeegrae.

Yeegrae looked at Justin, held a six-fingered hand out toward him, and squeezed it slowly into a fist. Guessing that this was a symbolic gesture, Justin held his own hand out and did likewise.

Justin returned his attention to Leah and the others. "Yeegrae is choosing not to join the Army of Light. But he has agreed to escort the Warlord's people for a time and help keep them safe." He looked at Leah. "Considering what we have just learned and the danger your people may be in, you should probably—"

"I would remind you," Kallorn spoke up, "that every word we speak right now, including our plans and strategies, may be reaching the ears of the enemy." He gestured meaningfully toward Justus at his feet. "Unless we deal with this problem. *Now.*"

Justus closed his eyes and trembled.

"Right," said Justin. He pulled Kallorn and Leah aside, out of earshot of their prisoner.

"Before you ask again," said Leah, speaking in a low voice. "I'm still coming with you."

"Okay," said Justin. He knew better than to try to argue with her. "Kallorn, if Leah explains how to find her army, would you be able to help escort these people there?"

Kallorn didn't look happy with the idea, but he ran a hand over his gray-streaked yellow beard in thought and said, "I will do as you ask."

"And would you take Justus with you?"

Kallorn looked almost affronted by that final request.

"I know, I know," Justin said hastily. "But I think the damage has already been done. And he could prove useful."

"How?" asked Kallorn.

"I'm not sure yet," said Justin. "Just intuition, I guess."

Frowning, Kallorn turned to face Leah. "Lady Demonsbane, do you approve of bringing a *spy* into the very midst of your army?"

"I trust Justin's judgment," said Leah. "And a direct line of communication to Avagad, should we have need of it, may be worth the risk of keeping him around. We'll have to inform the others of the situation and be mindful about what is said around him."

"Very well," whispered Kallorn.

Justin breathed a silent sigh of relief. His idea had been received better than he'd anticipated.

Justin returned to Justus and stopped directly in front of the boy. Justus tried to scramble away across the ground at first but gave it up as a hopeless endeavor.

"I want you to know," said Justin, "that I understand. I'm sorry for what you've been through because of me. And I forgive you for what you did."

The boy cowered at Justin's words. A small whimper escaped from his lips.

He thinks there's a "but" coming, realized Justin. *I guess I can't blame him. Kallorn would kill him if I gave him the chance. And Leah. . . .*

Would Leah do something like that? She was a commander and a queen, after all. Maybe she had to do such things sometimes. He'd had to kill people, too. But not like this.

She wouldn't.

Would she?

Avagad's words rang in Justin's head: *"I know you two are quite close. But are you really?"*

"How much do you even know about her? How much does she know about you?"

Justin shook it off.

"I'm afraid you're going to be a prisoner for a while longer, Justus," said Justin. "But you'll be safe. No one is going to hurt you."

Justus sank to the ground in disbelief.

"We'd better get home," rang Justin's mother's final words in his head. *"Supper's ready."*

Justin suppressed a chill, then exchanged looks with Leah and Kallorn.

"We'd better get going," he said. "I have a feeling that things are about to start moving very quickly."

PART VIII

NO DISGRACE

CHAPTER 56

Shielding his eyes against the late-morning sun, Gunnar made his way through the Army of Light encampment. He was unsteady and unwashed and could smell the aftermath of the night seeping out through his pores.

He'd woken up with an aching head, but it didn't hurt half as bad as his stomach, where Lycon's fist had connected. He remembered the hit, along with most of their conversation. Or at least he thought he remembered most of it. The constant problem with piecing things together from nights before was not knowing how much you didn't know.

He was thankful for the reprieve from the sun as he entered the command tent. There, he found Zechariah seated cross-legged on the ground, alone.

Gunnar looked around at the otherwise empty tent. When the messenger had come to summon him for an "urgent meeting," he'd been expecting to find the rest of the officers already assembled. He wasn't used to being early. Why arrive early when you could arrive on time? He was too smart to wait.

"I was told we were meeting here," said Gunnar.

"We are," said Zechariah. "Have a seat."

Had he been feeling a bit more himself this morning, Gunnar might have given in to his contrarian nature and remained standing, just because. But sitting sounded so much better than standing, so he did as he was asked and sat down at an appropriate distance from the old man.

It took only a few moments for Gunnar to suss out the situation.

"No one else is coming to this *urgent meeting*, are they?" he said.

"Does that make it any less urgent?" asked Zechariah.

"You tell me."

The old man glared at Gunnar. "Do you have anything you would like to tell me?"

In the silence that followed, Gunnar looked away from Zechariah to examine the interior of the canvas tent, this place that had been Leah's for so long but had belonged to Zechariah ever since she'd gone off in search of Justin.

He's referring to the drinking, thought Gunnar.

Or Adonica told him about the freeze-ups, piped in his inner voice. *Or Lycon told him about your behavior last night. Or he knows about the nightmares.*

How could he know about my nightmares?

You never know with this crafty old meddler.

That voice. . . . It was driving him crazy.

For a moment, Gunnar actually considered telling Zechariah about the freeze-ups, the dark thoughts, and the nightmares.

"I can't stop thinking about Ragny," said Gunnar. "Or *Innocen*, as he called himself. The powers he had—and that Leah has."

"What about him?" asked Zechariah.

"If he's still alive and he, or someone like him, shows up. . . ."

He trailed off. A stab of pain went through his aching head, and his mind hearkened back to all the nightmares he'd been having recently of Innocen appearing and making short work of his allies and friends.

"Hyd powers are formidable," said Zechariah, "but not infallible. All it takes is a single arrow."

"I guess so," said Gunnar. "That was how Leah got away from him, back at Cervice."

"True," said Zechariah. "But that's not what I was referring to. It is ironic that a single arrow made the difference in Innocen's attack as well, because that was also the case in the story of Xanthicles, the founder of the Cult of the Hyd."

Zechariah reached into his robes and pulled out a small glass bottle filled with amber liquid. He pulled off the stopper, took a short drink, smacked his lips, and was about to put it away again when he noticed Gunnar's eye on it. Wordlessly, he offered it to him.

Gunnar looked at Zechariah suspiciously. "I would have thought you'd be trying to stop me from drinking."

"You're the type of man who gets what he wants," said Zechariah. "Until what you want changes, neither I nor anyone else could hope to stop you."

Gunnar found that he had already taken the bottle from Zechariah before he'd even finished speaking. He took one drink, then another, and handed it back.

"The story dates back nearly to the time of the Ancients," said Zechariah, tucking the bottle away. "Xanthicles led an order of zealots devoted to dark rituals of his design. They were the architects of a reign of chaos and terror that spread through northern Darsida. They believed that the practice of feasting on the living entrails of a human being could give them sustenance, as it does to coblyns. Coincidentally, it was the founder of *my* order who finally defeated Xanthicles."

"Your order?" said Gunnar. "You mean the Brethren? The legendary immortal men?"

"The Brethren were not all men," corrected Zechariah. "Nor were they . . . *we* . . . technically immortal. Just immune to the wasting effects of time."

"So?" said Gunnar. "How did a single arrow kill this Xanthicles guy?"

"Well," said Zechariah. He cleared his throat. "I suppose I should elaborate. Perhaps I shouldn't go so far as to say that a single arrow killed him. The founder and leader of the Brethren, a man called Amphidemus, hunted Xanthicles down. Amphidemus had an aurym ability that allowed him to move objects without touching them. By studying the fighting tactics of the Cult of the Hyd, Amphidemus realized that their incredible strength protected their bodies from harm. The result was a sort of aurym-fueled armor.

"Amphidemus realized that this phenomenon only manifested when they were actively exerting force; when they were not in the process of executing a focused action, their flesh remained as vulnerable as anyone else's. And although their physical prowess allowed them to dodge an arrow fired straight at them, they still had to see it coming in time to react. So, Amphidemus did something Xanthicles did not expect. He challenged Xanthicles to meet him on the field of battle, to allow him to fire just one single arrow at him. He would raise no other weapon against him. He gave his word that if his arrow did not hit

Xanthicles, Xanthicles could feast upon him, and he would offer up no resistance. Xanthicles was nothing if not prideful. He agreed to the bargain.

"The two of them met on the field of battle. Amphidemus brought with him a bow, one single arrow, and no more. Xanthicles stood before him. Amphidemus raised his bow, nocked his arrow, drew aim, and fired. Xanthicles could have easily sidestepped the arrow or allowed it to break against his body. But there was no need. The shot missed him, sailing high and wide.

"Amphidemus lowered his bow. Xanthicles laughed at his challenger's foolishness, and he approached, prepared to claim his prize. He was boasting mightily about his win when the arrow, which had not hit the ground, circled back around on its aurym-influenced flight, under Amphidemus's command, and struck Xanthicles in his exposed and quite vulnerable spine, dropping him to the ground."

Zechariah smiled and nodded as if recounting this bit of cleverness satisfied him greatly.

"But it didn't kill him?" said Gunnar.

"Ah. Well," said Zechariah. "In truth, the arrow only brought Xanthicles down. What killed him was Amphidemus subsequently separating his head from his body. I suppose this technically violated the original agreement of the battle. . . ." He stuck out his lower lip and shrugged. "But the victor writes the history books."

"He kept his true power hidden until he needed it," said Gunnar.

"Precisely," said Zechariah.

The thought gave Gunnar pause. Zechariah was one of the mythical Brethren. They were said to have been powerful aurym users. But, other than immortality, what power did he have?

I can't remember a single time when I've seen the old man use any kind of aurym power, thought Gunnar. *Not outwardly, anyway.*

What sort of abilities might he be hiding . . . until he needed them?

"This Amphidemus," said Gunnar. "Avagad killed him when he betrayed the Brethren?"

Zechariah's gaze went distant. "That was a dark day. Avagad led a host of demons into the sanctuary of the Brethren. Now, he and I are all that remain of our order. There was a third, one of us who left the order prior to Avagad's betrayal. But that was long ago, and I do not know if she yet lives. Avagad may have long ago found her and finished the job."

For a few moments, neither said a word. Finally, Gunnar opened his mouth to ask a question—to force Zechariah to explicitly state why he had asked him here this morning—when the flap of the command tent was suddenly pushed back without warning. Looking down at Gunnar and Zechariah were the impassive, dark eyes of Hook Bard.

"Welcome back," said Gunnar.

"You have returned not a moment too soon," said Zechariah, pushing himself to his feet with a small grunt of effort. "It is high time Her Highness resumed her command of this army."

Hook only looked at Zechariah.

Zechariah's thick, white eyebrows drew together in a scowl. "Don't tell me she's not with you."

Hook raised his hands and signed, *"Olorus, Megara, and I have returned. Leah is not with us because she is with Justin."*

Gunnar watched Zechariah's mouth slowly open in shock.

"She found him," signed Hook.

CHAPTER 57

Hook crossed his arms and waited. Normally, it was highly boring work to watch someone *think*. But, at the moment, it was rather entertaining to see the conflicting emotions battle across Zechariah's face. Gunnar, meanwhile, reclined back on the ground, took out his pipe, and began to chew thoughtfully on the tip of its long stem.

"So," said Gunnar. "After all this time, Justin is—"

"Quiet!" Zechariah snapped. "We do not know who might be listening." He shot a stern look at Hook. *"Who else knows about this?"* he signed.

"Olorus, Megara, myself, and a member of Ahlund's order whom we met by chance," signed Hook.

"A member of Ahlund's order," signed Gunnar. *"The Guardians?"*

"Yes," signed Hook.

Hook followed this up by signing phonetically to form the name *Kallorn Rhodos*. He wasn't sure how well Zechariah knew the phonetic signs, but he knew Gunnar had spent time getting to know them over the course of their travels.

Zechariah stroked his beard, staring at the floor of the tent. Hook could practically read his thoughts: *She did it. She actually found him.* Hook found it thoroughly enjoyable to see him humbled for once.

"And what about Ahlund?" signed Zechariah.

"Dead," signed Hook. *"Killed by Avagad himself."*

Hook watched Zechariah and Gunnar, measuring their reactions. Zechariah went from shocked to sorrowful to angry, all in the span of just a few quiet seconds. Gunnar, however, could only stare at Hook.

"Damn that betrayer!" hissed Zechariah under his breath.

Gunnar's eye went distant. He removed the pipe from his mouth and lowered it to the ground as he looked at nothing, sitting, staring in stunned, silent disbelief.

"Justin has found other allies," signed Hook. *"Kallorn was separated from him, but the Guardians are led by a woman called Cyaxares."*

The change in Zechariah was subtle. So subtle that if Hook hadn't happened to be looking directly at him at the time, he might have missed it. But something flashed across the old man's face at the mention of that name that was too distinct to be Hook's imagination.

Zechariah turned away and ran his good hand over his mouth and down his beard, almost as if. . . .

Trying to hide his reaction, thought Hook.

"But, why didn't Leah and Justin come back with you?" asked Gunnar, forgetting to sign.

"I will tell you all that I know," signed Hook. *"But we should call the rest of our officers here first. There is much to explain."*

"I can't believe she really found him," said Gunnar. "But Ahlund. . . ." He trailed off, shaking his head. "It doesn't seem possible."

Hook had felt the same way. But he'd felt that way about others before, too. How many times did he need to learn the same lesson: that life was not fair and death made no exceptions?

Well, thought Hook, eyeing the immortal man standing in the tent in front of him. *Almost no exceptions.*

"This Cyaxares I mentioned," signed Hook. *"Someone you know?"*

Another look flashed across Zechariah's face. And once again, he quickly quelled it.

When Zechariah had recovered, he focused his attention solely on Hook, studying him with an equal degree of scrutiny.

"I, too, will explain all," Zechariah said flatly. "In time."

CHAPTER 58

So, this is where it comes from, thought Leah.

Tentatively, she reached one hand out and touched the trunk of the tree before her. It was a species of long-needled evergreen unlike any with which she was familiar. It stood much taller than she would have thought possible for its narrow girth and grew almost perfectly straight. Unlike most evergreens, its boughs grew at an odd, slightly upward angle. From a distance, it looked like an arrow stuck deep in the ground with its feathered fletching exposed.

But most noteworthy of all was the fact that, at a place where a recent wound to the tree had peeled away a strip of bark, the wood beneath was so dark that it was almost black.

"I guess they missed this one," said Justin.

Leah nodded, removing her hand from the tree. It was the only plant life taller than ten feet that had been left standing for at least a mile in every direction. Thousands of black stumps bespoke the mass logging of what had once been a great forest. Enough time had passed for a thick layer of secondary growth to have emerged: some young trees, but mostly bushes and brambles that normally wouldn't have been able to survive in the shadows of the giant evergreens.

Leah had often wondered about the strange, black ships used by the demons. She'd wondered what kind of wood they used to build them and whether it came from the Oikoumene, from some faraway land, or from another world entirely. Now, it seemed she had her answer.

Justin stepped past her and hopped up onto one of the flat-topped stumps to get a better view of their surroundings above the undergrowth. The mist was uncharacteristically thin this evening. The sun even provided a bit of warmth as it streamed in from its low position in the sky.

Justin planted the a'thri'ik-tipped lance, which he had been using as a walking stick, on the top of the stump beside him. Ahlund's broken sword was sheathed in the baldric slung over his shoulder. Leah, meanwhile, carried no weapons and wore no armor at all.

Justin put a hand to his eyes to shield them for a better view, looking one way and then another.

"Are you sure you know the way?" asked Leah.

"I think so," he said. "I know I saw this area from a distance while I was on my way south toward the fortress. Just trying to figure out. . . . There." He pointed. "That hillside looks familiar. I think."

Neither his words nor his tone inspired much confidence.

It was just the two of them now. Yeegrae had gone his own way. And, after resting for the night with Nefari's people, Justin and Leah had departed toward the north while Kallorn escorted Nefari's people south, toward the Army of Light's encampment.

Or at least, he was taking them to the place where the Army of Light had been camped when she had left them. If Hook, Olorus, and Megara had returned and relayed her commands for the army to resume marching without her, Kallorn would have to track the army's advance to find them.

She and Justin, with meager supplies and only a vague idea of the way, had walked nonstop through the morning and into the afternoon. In that time, Justin had shared much with her that he had previously held back while they'd been in the presence of the others. Details about his journey across the Oikoumene. Details about Avagad.

And details about his father.

Justin told her how he'd traveled back to his home world and discovered that his father had been a fallen angel before him, thousands of years ago in the timeline of the Oikoumene. Benjamin Holmes had driven out the demons. But then, a being called the Nameless One, the god-king of the demons, took control of his actions, cutting him off from aurym.

The Nameless One. According to Justin, he was not only the master of the demons. He was the master of Avagad.

Justin stepped down from the stump. "I bet we can make it up that hill before the sun goes down. It should only take us a few hours tomorrow morning to find my people."

With that, Justin pushed through the brush and kept moving.

His people, thought Leah as she followed.

She could remember a time when the very thought of Justin as a leader would have seemed absurd. She remembered him as good-hearted and brave, but also impulsive, uninformed, and woefully uncertain of himself. To see the changes in him was fascinating. Not just his power and his confidence but the way he carried himself and the way he spoke.

There were times when he was like Ahlund. Yet there was a humility within Justin that had never been present in Ahlund. And gentleness, almost meekness. It all amounted to a person whom Leah felt she could trust. Maybe even with her life.

"So, what happened with the shipwreck you were telling me about?" she asked. "You never finished that story."

"Oh, yeah," said Justin.

He hopped down from the stump like a fun-loving kid, using Hook's lance to guide his descent.

"Well," said Justin, "after the storm passed, it took some time for us to find one another again. For a while there, I thought we'd lost the admiral. It turned out that two of our ships had hit some rocks, and the crews had taken lifeboats to shore. By the time I got there, they'd been captured by some locals."

They started walking as Justin continued his story.

"They tried to hold our people for ransom," said Justin. "When they realized we didn't have anything of worth, they demanded one of our ships, which wasn't an option. I didn't want to hurt anybody, but they weren't making things easy. Somehow, the subject of a sea serpent came up—"

"Sea serpent?" said Leah.

Justin nodded. "Yeah. Big and nasty. I guess it had been a problem for the locals for something like two hundred years, stealing livestock, turning over boats, sometimes eating old ladies who were too slow to get away from it. It wasn't really a *serpent*, per se. More like a dinosaur."

"Dinosaur?" said Leah.

"Like a really big lizard," said Justin. "One that swims. Anyway. I told these people that if I took care of their sea serpent problem, they had to let my friends go."

"And?" said Leah.

"And I went and took care of it."

Leah pushed him lightly from behind.

"I did!" said Justin, laughing. "After that, we loaded up the ships, and—"

"I want to hear the end of the story."

"Nah, you don't want to hear the end."

"*Yes*, I do."

Justin stopped walking for a moment. He turned to look at her. "It's a little anticlimactic."

"You fought a sea serpent," said Leah. "How is that anticlimactic? Did you kill it with Ahlund's fire?"

"Remember the way I talked to Yeegrae?"

"Yes."

"I did that."

"Huh?"

"I told it to go away, please."

Leah blinked at him. "And it did?"

"Yes."

Leah stared at him for a moment, then shook her head, scrunching up her nose in distaste.

"I warned you it wasn't very exciting," Justin said defensively.

"Yes, but you can make it sound more exciting than *that*, can't you? Build up the drama a bit? Maybe you had to beat the sea serpent in a game of riddles? Or you had to demonstrate your power to him in some way, maybe to earn his respect before he would leave?"

"You want me to lie?"

"It's not lying. It's the art of tale-telling."

"If you help me workshop it into a more interesting version," said Justin, "we'll do a test performance for Olorus and see what he thinks."

They had been walking for a few more minutes when Leah remembered something from the day before. An odd moment in a conversation they'd had.

"Justin," she said. "It seems like there's something you're not telling me."

"Huh?" he said.

"About Avagad."

"Oh."

That was all Justin said.

His reaction was such a stark change from the good-natured storytelling they had been sharing up until now that Leah wondered if she had said something wrong.

For several minutes, there was silence between them as they traveled through the black stumps and the secondary growth. Justin led the way, using the lance as a walking stick, and Leah followed. There were few sounds. Just a lonely-sounding bird calling from within a stone's throw of their passage. And still, Justin said nothing.

"I shouldn't have asked," Leah finally said.

"No," said Justin. "It's all right. It's just . . . a difficult topic."

"If you ever want to talk about it," said Leah, "you can talk to me."

"It's not that I don't want to talk about it," said Justin. "It's just—shoot, watch out!"

Justin lost his grip on a branch he had pushed aside to pass by, and it came whipping back at Leah's face.

With a quick burst of hydstone power, Leah raised her left arm in front of her face, moving far faster than the velocity of the branch. She caught it between her forefinger and thumb, an inch from her eye.

"Wow," Justin said, and he swallowed hard. "Sorry about that."

"No harm done," said Leah.

The interruption was, to Leah's dissatisfaction, enough to distract Justin from the topic at hand, and he pressed on without finishing his thought. Leah decided not to bring it up again. For now, anyway.

Half an hour later, they were mounting the crest of a hill when Justin slowed, turned to face Leah, and raised one finger to his lips. He pointed up over the hill. The meaning was clear. He could sense something up there or on the other side.

They proceeded in crouched positions, picking their way through the underbrush as quietly as possible.

At the top of the hill, Justin pointed. "They caught a whiff of our scent and took off before we even got to the top," he said, "but you can still see them. There. Running off through those trees."

Leah followed his gesture and spotted them: a group of large, brown-haired mammals fleeing between tree trunks, making not a sound as they ran. In form, they were like steeds, but they stood easily twice as tall, and their long faces lacked the opposable trunks of steeds. Most noteworthy of all, they had eight legs instead of four.

"Slepes," said Leah.

"They look like the horses of my world," said Justin. "Except horses have four legs like steeds. And they're not nearly as big."

Leah watched the intricate yet marvelously natural way the front four and rear four legs worked in tandem with one another as the last of the slepes disappeared into the woods. She found herself wondering if Justin could have communicated with them to tell them to stay. She glanced at him beside her and saw that he looked troubled again.

"I've never seen a normal one before," said Justin. "Only the ones the cythraul ride. And they were all, you know, turned."

The thought gave Leah pause.

"Turned," she said. "You mean cythraul can transform *animals* into cythwraiths, too?"

"I didn't think so," said Justin. "But I didn't even know until now that a *slepe* was an animal in your world. I've only ever seen demon ones, ridden by cythraul." He shook his head, staring at the place where the slepes had disappeared. "There's so much I don't know about this world. So much I don't understand. And yet, I have to. . . ."

Justin trailed off and turned his gaze skyward as if something high above had caught his attention.

Leah looked up. The sun was only just starting to sink below the highest of the surrounding peaks, and the moons, Cnidus and Nun, were already visible in the sky. Nun's glow, even in the daylight, shone with a dull violet hue.

"Justin," said Leah, trying to pull his attention back to ground level. "I won't keep bothering you about this, but I mean it when I say that if there's something wrong, you can tell me."

"Leah," said Justin in a low voice, almost as if he hadn't heard her. "Whose idea was it to come here? To leave Athacea and travel east to invade Avagad's lands?"

"Zechariah's," said Leah. "I told you that, remember?"

Justin nodded almost absentmindedly. Then he turned away from her without a word, and he kept walking.

CHAPTER 59

Gunnar was hard-pressed to think of the last time so many key representatives of the Army of Light had been in one place. Tucked beneath the tall walls of a deep canyon, on a characteristically misty evening, were a thousand or more leaders representing one hundred thousand humans—or at least roughly that many.

Everyone kept claiming that that was how many of them there were, but he wanted to know who was doing all the counting.

There were Athaceans, Mythaeans, Endens, Lundens, Raeqlu, Cru, Rorrdvuuk, Raedittean Islanders, Darvellians, Castydocians, Darsidans, and people from a dozen other civilizations of the Oikoumene, many of which Gunnar hadn't even heard of until recently.

These individuals were those who had been chosen from among their respective groups to be present for meetings of importance. Many of them were soldiers, but some were not. They all, however, had one thing in common: this volunteer-based mobile militia, unified by need and hope, had brought them all very, very far from home.

Several of the Army's oxen-pulled carts had been pushed together to form a makeshift platform, upon which stood the leaders of the Army of Light and Commander Anavion's most trusted advisors.

The canyon through which the Army of Light traveled was a long, deep fissure, so deep in the earth that the sun was visible above them for only a few hours of the day. According to Lycon's maps, it would still be several days of travel before they emerged from it into what appeared to be mostly open country.

On the one hand, Gunnar was looking forward to the change of scenery. On the other hand, open country would make it easier for them to be seen. More vulnerable to cythraul and whatever else might be out there waiting for them.

Zechariah was at center stage, flanked by military leaders from Raeqlund. Hook, Olorus, and Megara were there, with several captains from Athacea and Endenholm, as well as those who represented the formerly enslaved peoples among their forces. Lycon and Adonica stood with other Mythaeans and Sif and Tel of the Cru. Itz was up there, too. Hell, even Gunnar's old fishing crew and drinking buddies, Borris and Pool, were present.

The one leader of the Army of Light who wasn't there, besides Leah herself, was Gunnar Erix Nimbus.

Either Gunnar hadn't gotten the memo about this meeting, thanks to an oversight, or he had been intentionally kept out of the loop. So, instead of standing up there on that platform with the rest of them, he lingered at the rear of the crowd of onlookers, trying to make himself inconspicuous by leaning partially behind one of the region's many rock formations. It was about as far as one could be from Leah's inner circle.

Maybe they did tell you, said the voice in his head. *The way you've been the past few days, would you remember it if they had?*

Gunnar swallowed hard against a throat that suddenly felt dry. In the past, he'd always been able to convince others, and himself, that the drinking was just a way to have some fun and relax. It wasn't harming anybody.

He'd already been indulging a bit more than usual leading up to the incident at the vertical city. Since returning, it had gotten worse. And after learning that Ahlund had been killed, it had reached a new level. That news had rattled him. And there had hardly been a moment since when he'd been sober.

Zechariah raised his hands to quiet the crowd, then started speaking.

"I will not mince words," said Zechariah. "Several days have passed, and Commander Anavion still has not returned to the Army of Light. However, let any unsubstantiated rumors of her whereabouts be put to rest now. Leah Demonsbane went in search of the fallen angel, the ethoul called Justin. . . . And she has found him."

At this, surprise rippled through the crowd. The response only grew as translators for various groups relayed the message into their respective languages. It was half a minute before the crowd had calmed down enough for Zechariah to even attempt to continue speaking.

"Leah Demonsbane and Sir Justin the ethoul plan to join us soon in our assault on the demons," Zechariah continued. "The Commander has sent word that the Army of Light is to proceed as planned. When we reach. . . ."

As the briefing proceeded into specifics, Gunnar found himself hardly listening. The old man reminded the officers and leaders of their mission and their duty. He shared that Justin's return meant renewed hope for their cause. It was a stirring call to arms, an invocation of fate to stir the hearts.

In short, it was nothing Gunnar hadn't heard before.

He's not just delivering news, thought Gunnar. *He's practically pleading with them.*

Tensions are high, said his inner voice. *And the closer you get to the end, the more will be asked of these people.*

Zechariah was probably hoping that a show of solidarity among Leah's officers and a few words of hope and encouragement would prevent any further surprises, like that Raeqlu infantry unit that had disappeared in the night.

"Gunnar?" said someone beside him.

Gunnar jumped, snapping his head in the direction of the voice. His wits were dulled enough by a few morning drinks that he hadn't noticed Estoq's approach. She stood in the shadow of the same rock formation, quite close to him.

He took a deep breath to ease his nerves and attempt to look and act as sober as possible. He was very good at fooling people. Instead of the scrutinizing gaze that he was expecting to find, however, the woman's eyes were bleary.

Most of Gunnar's recent encounters with Estoq had been in moments when they were outfitted for battle. He wasn't used to seeing her in informal attire, with her hair tucked beneath a white headscarf in the fashion of Darvellian women, wearing a simple shirt and a long skirt.

But it was not her attire that had Gunnar's attention. It was the flush of her cheeks, the slight back-and-forth of her head.

By the seas, she's drunker than I am, he thought.

"Essie?" asked Gunnar.

"No," she said. "Don't call me that."

"Are you . . . feeling all right?" he said.

In the center of the crowd, Zechariah was, with rousing and impressive rhetoric, imploring the Army of Light's officers and leaders to stand firm in their mission, ensuring them that the invasion of the enemy's lands was at hand and that victory had never been as close as it was now.

"I came over here to tell you something," she said, swaying a bit. "Now I can't remember what it was."

Gunnar wasn't in much of a state to try to catch her if she started to fall, but he took a small step toward her, just in case. Up closer, he could smell it on her.

"Shouldn't you be down there with them?" she said.

Gunnar cleared his throat, stalling for time.

You shouldn't just be down *there*, said the voice in his head. *You are not some military officer. You are a son of kings. Leah is gone, and she isn't coming back. You should be in charge.*

I don't want to be in charge, Gunnar thought back. *I don't want to be this thing everyone wants me to—*

The time for what you want is passed, the voice cut in. *It is time to become what you were* DESTINED *to be.*

Gunnar blinked, taken aback. Had he ever been *interrupted* like that before? By a voice in his own head?

Power that is given can be taken away, said the voice. *It was correct of you to* REJECT *them. Now, they will overlook you, leave you in the obscurity you claim to desire, and assume you would sooner drink yourself to death than be a cause for concern. They will hardly be paying attention when you* MAKE YOUR MOVE *and claim the only power that cannot be taken away:* ABSOLUTE POWER, *taken by force.*

"Shut up," Gunnar whispered through gritted teeth. "Just leave me alone. . . ."

"What?" said Estoq.

He looked up, suddenly remembering where he was.

"Nothing," he said. "Never mind."

Estoq was staring off into the distance, blinking long and slow. "Would you like to have a drink with me?" she asked.

Gunnar was no longer listening to Zechariah's words, but the old man must have been making some thrilling points because a chorus of cheers went up from the crowd.

"Somewhere away from all this, this . . ." said Estoq, struggling to find the right word.

"Pomp and circumstance?" offered Gunnar.

"Interminable bull-scat is what I was going to say," Estoq said.
"Gladly," said Gunnar. "Follow me."

CHAPTER 60

They must have made quite a sight, the two of them walking unsteadily in the opposite direction of the crowd. Two or three times, Estoq took a wrong step, and Gunnar thought she was about to fall. He reached out to steady her each time and each time found himself woefully underqualified to provide support to anyone. Still, they managed to avoid falling over.

Gunnar noticed many eyes tracking their progress as they took their leave. They passed by the edge of the main section of the camp and moved toward a more secluded spot. Soldiers and civilians alike watched them with expressions that Gunnar recognized as curiosity, appraisal, judgment, disapproval, and shame.

As luck would have it, the first supply cart they encountered was abandoned. But even if anyone had been keeping an eye on it, who was going to say anything to Mythaean Royal Admiral Gunnar Erix Nimbus? These supplies were just as much his as they were anyone else's. Within moments, he and Estoq each had a full wineskin and had found a place beneath the boughs of a nearby hemlock where they would not be bothered as they imbibed.

This is the height of foolishness, thought Gunnar, suddenly realizing that he was not drinking but gulping as quickly as his throat could handle. *Or is it the depths of foolishness? Heights or depths, which one makes more sense? Either way, I shouldn't be—*

This is who you are, said the voice, interrupting him for the second time in the span of an hour.

So he drank more deeply, knowing if he got enough in him, the voice would go quiet.

When Gunnar paused to come up for air, he realized that Estoq, sitting with her back to the tree and her scarf-covered head resting heavily against its bark, was staring off into space. She had the look of someone just before the turning point of a severe illness. Her eyes seemed sunken, her face ashen.

Ignore her, said the voice. *She is* BROKEN.

Despite the increasing fogginess of his brain, Gunnar's brow furrowed.

If she is broken, he thought, *she is broken in some of the same places as me.*

"Are you all right?" he said.

"You already asked me that," she droned without looking at him.

"I'm still waiting for an answer."

Estoq gave no reply. Her eyes took on a sheen that warned of tears threatening to break free.

"Have you lost many people in your life?" she asked. "Ones who were close to you?"

Let's see, thought Gunnar. *My mother. My father. My brother. My uncle. Vick. Samuel. A dozen others. And now, Ahlund. . . .*

Isn't it exciting to predict who will be next? said the voice. *Perhaps Adonica.*

"I don't have many people I'm close to," said Gunnar.

"Because you lost them?" asked Estoq. "Or do you keep it that way, so you won't?"

Gunnar set his jaw, then raised the wineskin for another drink.

"What was the name of that place you had?" asked Estoq. "The one back in Lonn?"

"Gunnar's Brig," he said.

Estoq grinned. "Of course. Gunnar's Brig. . . . I went in there looking for a merchant with a price on his head for double-crossing somebody back in Darvelle. It would have been my first big payday after going independent if you hadn't snuck your nose into the whole affair."

Ah, yes, thought Gunnar. *I was wondering when we might finally broach this subject.*

"In the week we spent together," said Estoq, "how did it never come up that you were Mythaean royalty?"

"I was in hiding, you know," said Gunnar.

"So you put your name on the sign above the door."

"If you haven't noticed, my ego often gets me into trouble, Essie. Nobody from the Thalassocracy ever came that far upriver looking for me, except one fellow I had to take care of. It was smooth sailing after that, until a certain group of interlopers disrupted my life of freedom and ease."

"The *Brig*," said Estoq. "Funny choice of a name for your life of freedom."

"I had forgotten how dreadfully philosophical you get when you're this deep in your cups."

She closed her eyes and sighed. It took Gunnar several moments to realize that she was crying, in complete silence.

"Essie?" said Gunnar.

"He was there because of me," she said. "I chose to follow Adonica into the city. He only joined because of me."

The image came back to Gunnar's mind. Ucydotus, half of him lying in the street, victim of a cythraul's wrath. And Estoq, leaving the city with his Enden phalanx shield on her back.

Gunnar looked away. What Estoq didn't know, what nobody knew, was that Ucydotus had died during one of Gunnar's freeze-ups. He could have been there in time to help, maybe in time to save him, if he hadn't been back at his living bridge, standing stock still.

He's dead, said the inner voice, *because of* YOU.

"I . . . should have been firmer with Adonica about entering the city," said Gunnar. "We found Lycon, but the cost was too great. We should have taken a larger force. Or waited for Leah to return, like I wanted. I should've put my foot down. Instead, I was no better than any of you. I tagged along, too. Adonica was only trying to do what she felt was right, but being a leader is hard."

Coward, jeered the voice in his head, and it was right.

"You cared a great deal for him, didn't you?" said Gunnar.

Only now did Estoq's eyes finally snap open. There were trails of tears down her cheeks. But to Gunnar's surprise, she looked at him, and she sneered.

"What does *that* matter?" she spat.

Gunnar flinched. "I only meant," he said, "that it's hard to lose someone you care for."

Estoq looked at him as if he were the stupidest person she'd ever had the displeasure of interacting with.

"Did you even hear what I just said?" she demanded.

"Yes," said Gunnar, "and I was just trying to reassure you that I know how you must be feeling—"

"Me? You're thinking of *me*? Of how I *feel*?"

"Well, yes."

"Then save it, Admiral. You're not doing me any favors by caring about how I *feel*. Who cares about *me*? What about him? Think of him! He's the one who lost his life."

Estoq snorted hard, her breath catching in her throat as she choked on tears.

"He was such a good person, and now, everything that he was is gone and everything he was going to be is lost forever, stolen from him and stolen from everyone whose life would have been better just for knowing him, and.... And it all happened so fast! I—tried to help him—I didn't get there in time, I tried, I tried."

Estoq, now crying so hard that she could say no more, lifted the wineskin. It shook in her hands, spilling some of its contents onto her long skirt as she brought it to her mouth for another drink.

Gunnar reached out and stopped it before it could touch her lips. "Essie, stop, that's not going to fix it," he said.

"I am not trying to fix it, I'm grieving," said Estoq, tearing herself away from him. "What's your excuse?"

Gunnar's eye wandered, finding the wineskin in his own hand.

As Estoq took a long, hard drink, Gunnar found bitterness rising in him. Bitterness that bordered on hatred.

"They all say things like that," he said. "How I'm a disgrace and a waste of potential. How I'm meant for more. How I've disappointed the people around me. How I could be better and owe it to myself to be better."

"People tell you that?" said Estoq.

"All my life, I've heard those things."

"You spoiled little brat."

"As if I haven't heard that before," said Gunnar. "Prince of a noble family. Don't think you're the first to tell me how little I have to complain about because of who I am—"

"You think I'm talking about your *bloodline*? Bloody hell, you are thick!"

Gunnar bit his lip in annoyance. "What *are* you referring to then?"

"All of that—your title, your royal blood, I mean *all* of it—means blast-all," said Estoq. She threw her hands about as she spoke, and the fact that even in her wild gesticulating nothing spilled from the wineskin was testament to how little of its contents remained. "You're upset because the people around you judge you for being a disgrace? A waste of potential? A disappointment? For making you feel guilty because they want you to be *better*?"

"It's quite annoying to have people nose in on your business like that, yes," said Gunnar.

"Do you have any idea how lucky you are to have somebody around to tell you all that?"

Gunnar knew he must have been gawking at her in confusion by now, but he could do nothing to stop it. He had never been very good at masking his emotions.

"You, Lycon, Adonica, Leah, Hook, and the others," said Estoq. "You're like this little family. A dysfunctional one, sure. But a family, nonetheless. When people like that try to nose in on your business, it's because they're trying to save someone they care about."

Estoq paused here. It took her a moment to force her throat to unclench enough to form words again.

"Not all of us have that," she finally said. "Not all of us have someone, anyone, who cares enough to try to stop us from being a disgrace, wasting our potential . . . or destroying ourselves."

For a long time, neither of them said a word. Neither of them took a drink either. They just sat, alone with their thoughts.

"Maybe I'm grieving too, then," said Gunnar. "For myself and who I was supposed to be."

"Supposed to be, according to who?" asked Estoq.

The question gave Gunnar pause. But the drinks were catching up fast. His final clear memory, before everything became a haze, was pondering that question, and what it meant that he did not have an answer.

CHAPTER 61

The cloud cover was light, and the moons were high enough overhead that even in the depths of the rocky canyon where the Army of Light was camped, Hook could see the purple glow of Nun permeating through the ever-present mists.

It was just a moon. Just a shade of color, no different than any other. But there was something about it that made him uneasy. Something that made his skin crawl.

The evening's meal was long done, and most of the encampment had already retired for the night to prepare for an early start the next day. Hook and Olorus sat on opposite sides of a cookfire, keeping it burning with the occasional log and discussing the old days.

Presently, Olorus was relating a story about his time in King Darius's army before becoming a member of the High Guard. He and a company of soldiers had been tasked with hunting down a Nolian statesman accused of selling state secrets to Darvelle across the Gravelands. It was a story Hook had heard half a dozen times, and Olorus knew it, but it didn't seem to get in the way of his enjoyment of the telling.

A few hours before, Hook had been at center stage, in the middle of the gathered representatives of the Army of Light, as Zechariah revealed the return of Justin Holmes. Center stage was not a place Hook Bard had ever thought he would be, in any sense, let alone counted among the leaders of a force that had grown to such a size.

But, then again, thought Hook, *there are many things that have not gone the way I thought they would.*

Across the fire, Olorus took a swig of his ale and held it out for Hook. Hook shook his head. Olorus set it down.

"We found the bugger in the back of a wagon. He was having a diplomatic liaison with a Darvellian, all right," Olorus said with a chuckle, wrapping up his story. "It wasn't state secrets they were sharing, but it was all very new to me!"

It was the same punchline Olorus always used to end this story, and he seemed just as pleased with it as ever.

Only rarely did Olorus include in his telling what had happened afterward. How the Nolian statesman had panicked upon being discovered and attempted to flee. He had fallen from the wagon and broken his neck, dying instantly. It was not a happy ending. In fact, not many of Olorus's stories were happy. But he did his best to paint them in a more favorable light, for the benefit of the listener.

"It's strange, Hook," said Olorus, staring into the flames. "I've never believed in destiny. But the closer we get to the end, the more I feel I'm beginning to buy into it."

Hook decided not to reply. He watched Olorus carefully, waiting. This was rather heavy talk for a man whom he had known for so long yet rarely shared much about himself other than his war stories.

"If you'd asked me," said Olorus, "way back at the beginning, I'd have said that the deaths of King Darius, Queen Helena, and the princes were the greatest tragedies our nation could have endured, and I would have given anything to have been able to stop them. But now. . . . Spirit forgive me if I dishonor his memory, but King Darius *never* would have brought us here.

"The king was wise. But he was cautious. Perhaps to a fault. He never would have taken this sort of risk. Nor would Helena or any of the boys. Only Leah. That little troublemaker who used to skip out on her studies to roam the palace gardens on imaginary adventures. Her gamble to appeal to the Mythaeans for aid in retaking her country brought about the seeds of the Athacean League. And her reckless, idealistic, half-baked decision to break away from that League, form this Army of Light, and bring us halfway across the world instead of being overrun and feasted upon back in our homelands—I can't think of anyone else with such a balance of wisdom and, and utter. . . ."

Olorus trailed off, struggling to find the word. Hook raised his hands to sign, having to resort to signing phonetically to get his point across.

"Bullheadedness?"

"Exactly, thank you," said Olorus. "You'd be hard-pressed to find anyone else who would have led us to this place, in this state we're in. And yet, our being here may be the only reason the Oikoumene still has a chance. Strange to think that we couldn't have made it this far if the events I thought were tragedies hadn't played out the way they had."

The sound of heavy footsteps brought Hook's attention around to his side. Out of the shadows emerged two figures. One was the distinctive form of Admiral Gunnar Erix Nimbus, and judging by his stagger, the stain on his shirt front, his rolling eye, and the fact that a second figure was supporting him to help him walk, he had been up to nothing but more of the same. The second figure was Adonica.

"By the spirit, look at the state of him now," said Olorus, standing and moving to help. "What's he gone and done this time?"

Hook joined Olorus in helping Adonica by taking over support of Gunnar's barely vertical body.

Adonica rolled her shoulder and rubbed at a kink in her neck. "Damn, is he heavy. I found him behind a tree a hundred yards from camp with Estoq, surrounded by empty wineskins. Spirit knows how long they've been out there. They're lucky they weren't picked off by predators."

"Or scavengers, by the looks of him," said Olorus. "Who is Estoq?"

"Darvellian girl, good with a crossbow," said Adonica.

"Were they—erm, decent?" said Olorus.

"Yes," Adonica said impatiently. "Just comatose. I recruited a member of her company to help her back to her tent."

"And I suppose I ought to take this one to his," said Olorus, "though I've half a mind to find the tallest anthill in Erum and stake him down to it, stark naked as when his mother brought him into the world."

"I don't care what you do with him," said Adonica.

To Hook's surprise, she left it at that. No creative additions to the proposed punishment, no cursing or complaining. Just a sad look in her eye as Olorus led the staggering admiral away to help him toward his tent.

When Adonica turned and started to walk away, Hook snapped his fingers to get her attention.

"What?" she said, turning around.

"Something happened while you were in that city," signed Hook. *"You have not been the same since you returned."*

"Yes, something happened," said Adonica. "People died because of me. That girl, Estoq, lost her lover."

Hook nodded. He knew what it was to lose a lover. Departing from Athacea and traveling the Raedittean Sea had reopened old wounds.

Every time he saw a silver-haired Castydocian girl, a small part of him still believed, in spite of everything, that she would turn around, and it would be his beloved Jocasta.

The image flashed in his mind for the millionth time: Jocasta, looking down in stunned agony at the crossbow bolt through her chest, just before tumbling overboard into the churning waters of the Raedittean.

"Estoq hates me for what happened," continued Adonica, "and she is drinking herself into oblivion to compensate for the pain."

"I am sorry," signed Hook.

Adonica stared at him for a moment, stone-faced and nearly as silent as him.

"You should talk to your friend," said Adonica, gesturing toward the place where Gunnar had been dragged off. "He's the one you should be worried about. Something's wrong with him that is deeper than the drinking."

Hook squinted at her. *"You could talk to him, too."*

"People don't like to talk to me," said Adonica.

"I do," signed Hook.

Adonica gave a sad smile.

"Hook!" someone shouted, and Hook turned to see Olorus returning. But now, someone else was with him. To Hook's surprise, it was Kallorn.

"Leah?" signed Hook.

"She sent me here to join you," said Kallorn, "but she continued north with Justin. In the meantime, there has been a complication."

"Complication?" said Olorus.

"A spy. The false ethoul called Justus, from the Warlord's fortress. Justin believes he was communicating with Avagad. It seems likely that he informed the enemy about your Army of Light. Its size. Its location. Its intentions."

"How long ago was this?" asked Adonica, stepping into the conversation.

"Days ago," said Kallorn. "On Lady Leah's orders, I brought Warlord Nefari's people with me. The spy is with them. Justin seems to think he may be useful to us in some way."

Olorus gave a growl of displeasure from deep in his throat. "Take me to this spy," he said. "I would have a word with him."

Kallorn nodded, and the two of them departed.

Adonica made as if to follow Olorus and Kallorn. But she stopped herself. She turned back to face Hook.

"You should be the one leading us, you know," she said.

Hook cocked an eyebrow at her.

"In Leah's absence, I mean," she said. "Not someone like Zechariah, who sees people like pieces on a gameboard. Not someone like Gunnar, who only takes the reins when it's in his own best interest to do so. Certainly not someone like me, who wants to take action so badly that she charges off and gets people killed. You've got the head for it and the demeanor."

Hook shrugged and signed, *"Just not the right voice."*

"You are silent, Hook," said Adonica, "but you are not without a voice."

She marched off, leaving Hook alone with this thoughts.

CHAPTER 62

With no gear to set up a proper camp, Leah and Justin spent the night taking turns sleeping in the crook of a fallen hemlock. While one slept, the other kept watch. But for Leah, it had been a sleepless night.

Even while it was Justin's turn to stand watch, she lay staring up at the night sky for hours, watching the violet moon. Perhaps it was only her imagination, but its glow seemed to grow brighter with each passing hour.

There were moments in the night. Moments when Justin stepped into view, probably to check on her. Each time, she closed her eyes and pretended to be asleep.

Finally, the sky began to lighten with the coming dawn, and they set out again, moving in a northwesterly direction, toward the place where Justin said his allies were to be found.

After spending the morning traversing around one of the region's characteristically deep chasms, they descended down a steep, thickly wooded hillside. Partway down it, Leah began to hear the rush of a river, though she could not see it through the trees until they were practically right on top of it. It was narrow and ran swiftly between rocky banks.

"I think we're on the right track," said Justin, pausing to wipe the sweat from his brow. "I don't have any idea what this river is called, but I think it's the right one. It flows north, joins with another river, and then empties into the sea at an inlet. All we have to do is follow it downstream."

Leah walked to the water's edge and, using her hand as a cup, scooped it up and tested it in her mouth. Satisfied, she filled her waterskin, drank it dry, and filled it again. Justin did the same. For a few minutes, they lingered at the river's edge, standing close to one another.

"Justin?" said Leah.

"Yes?"

"Your plan, you said, was to find the source of the demons. But after that, then what?"

"Take care of it," said Justin.

"You going to ask it to go away, please?" said Leah.

Justin suppressed a laugh. "I guess we'll see when we get there." He cleared his throat, growing more serious as he busied himself with putting his waterskin back into his pack. "I usually try not to think that far ahead."

"Is that all you want?" said Leah. "To stop the demons?"

"When I came to this world," said Justin, "all I wanted was to go home, and I got it. But I chose to come back. Then, all I wanted was answers, and I got them. Now, I just want. . . ."

Justin trailed off. He looked away and breathed out so heavily that he seemed to deflate a bit in front of her.

"I'm tired, Leah," he said, staring out across the river. "I'm just so tired. I don't know what's coming, and I can't see how this ends yet. I guess I just want it to all be over. For better or worse, one way or another."

Justin turned to walk away from the riverside, but Leah touched him on the arm, prompting him to turn around.

"Justin," she said. "You can tell me anything."

Justin smiled. He placed his hand on hers. "Thank you, Leah," he said.

The sound of a raven cawing in the distance drew his eyes away from hers. He watched in that direction for a few seconds with that distant look in his eyes, the one that told her he was seeing through their surroundings, seeing things only he could see. Then he turned back to face her.

"I guess we'd better get moving," he said.

As Justin walked away, Leah watched him for a few paces without moving. She decided to ignore the feelings coming up, like she always did, and she kept going, like she always did.

CHAPTER 63

By late afternoon, Justin and Leah had followed the river north and found its confluence with a second river. Here, Justin got his first whiff of the saltwater of the inlet that was still several miles away.

On his journey south, following the echoes of Kallorn's presence, passing these waterways had required some treacherous swimming. This time, Leah's hydstone-powered muscles made short work of the river, pulling Justin easily along behind her.

He had told Leah much about his father's history in the Oikoumene during their travels, along with a great deal of what he knew about Avagad and the Nameless One. But there were certain details he hadn't been able to bring himself to speak of, even though she kept assuring him that he could be open with her. Details such as the relationship between his father and Cyaxares, and where Avagad had come from.

And, thought Justin. *That Avagad is my half-brother.*

It was early evening when they reached the inlet. It would have been easy to mistake this body of water for a lake; all that was visible were shorelines encompassing a broad expanse of water. But it was saltwater. And its depths changed along with the tides. For beyond those wooded shorelines, this body of water connected to the Altirin Sea.

Justin was relieved to see the shapes of thirteen ships of varying designs moored on the inlet, still in the same places they had been when he'd left. Some were demon ships, others were Mythaean galleons, and some were even small fishing boats. It had been a gamble to leave them tied off out in the open like this, but their options had been limited. He was also relieved, as they got closer, to sense several life forces in an overgrown structure near the edge of the water.

The structure, a stone temple, was mostly obscured from view by vegetation that had grown up its walls and penned it in on all sides from years of apparent neglect. This was where he had charged his allies to remain hidden until he returned.

"Is this the fleet that picked you up on the Raedittean?" asked Leah, indicating the boats as they proceeded along the shore where the river emptied into the inlet.

"What's left of it," said Justin. "I promise you, the fleet looked a lot more intimidating when it surrounded me on the Raedittean Sea. Since then, we lost those two in the storm I told you about. And there were a few other accidents."

"We had a few complications ourselves on the Altirin Sea," said Leah. "In the Ecbatan tongue, *altirin* means something like *woeful shipwreck*."

The foremost vessel was a blackwood demon ship: the one Justin had sailed on his own, with the guidance of Ahlund's spirit. Since then, it had become Justin's unofficial flagship, complete with a captain and crew.

"That one," said Justin, pointing to it, "is the *Gentle Giant*." He had named it himself.

"How many people are here with you?" asked Leah.

Justin opened his mouth to answer but immediately lost his train of thought. He nearly missed a step and had to come to a stop.

"Justin?" said Leah.

"You ask how many are here," said Justin, reaching out toward the temple with his senses. He turned to look at her significantly. "There are more than when I left."

PART IX

THE MOON SPEAKS

CHAPTER 64

Reaching out to the overgrown temple with his senses, Justin found all the life forces he had been expecting to find. But there were others, too. Why hadn't he sensed them until now?

Because someone was masking their aurym presence, Justin realized.

It was a difficult and advanced aurym technique, which meant whoever was behind it was very powerful.

The gentle sounds of the river flowing into the saltwater inlet might have been soothing if not for the tension in the air. He turned to find Leah silently watching him. She called upon aurym, keeping her powers at the ready, prepared to take action at a moment's notice if the need arose.

"You can tell how many there are?" said Leah. "Even from here?"

Justin nodded.

It was difficult to explain how his aurym-fueled perceptions worked. It was like a second form of sight. Even from behind closed eyelids, life forces showed up as bright spots in his vision, like shadows but in reverse. It worked with all forms of life. Plants, animals, and humans. If it was a person he'd spent a lot of time with, he could recognize their shadow and identify who they were. That was how he had been able to sense Kallorn from a distance.

Justin closed his eyes and focused on the light spots that formed in the darkness.

"They feel familiar to me," he said, "but I can't quite place them. Whoever they are, they're trying to intentionally block out anyone trying to sense them."

"That can be done?" said Leah.

"Yes," said Justin.

Not only could it be done, but it was a process he was doing almost constantly.

He hadn't told Leah all the stories of his journey to reach Erum, all the fighting he'd had to do. Masking his aurym presence so that he could not be sensed was so effective that there had been times when he'd been quite close to cythraul and cythwraiths, and they hadn't been able to see him.

"I'm getting tired of traps," said Leah. "Do you think this could be another one?"

Justin's mind flashed back to Esthean, the city of the Guardians, when Avagad had been able to shroud an entire demon army from being sensed by Cyaxares and her Ru'Onorath council.

He drew a tight two-handed grip on Hook's a'thri'ik lance. "Let's find out."

Using Hook's spear as a walking stick, Justin proceeded toward the temple along a rock-studded, sandy elbow of land between the river and the inlet's shores. Leah's thin, slipper-like shoes padded alongside him, staying close.

There were not so many of the region's characteristic giant hemlocks here. Instead, the temple was surrounded by a wall of foliage that was a mix of sumac and cherry trees, with thick brush choking the forest floor. Justin pushed his way through the brush until he found the decrepit stone-laid path leading up to the entrance of the temple.

Leah's hand touched Justin's shoulder. He stopped and looked at her.

"Are you sure about this?" she asked.

Again, Justin reached out with his senses. Again, he found that although he could sense more life forces within the temple, it was difficult to see them clearly due to someone's interference.

"I don't sense any demons," he said.

"But it's not just demons we have to worry about," said Leah.

"Right. Would you be willing to hang back a bit? Follow from a distance, just in case?"

"I'll stay back and remain unseen. If anything goes wrong, I'll be at your side in half a second." She nodded to him. "Go ahead."

As Leah stepped into the trees and disappeared from view,

Justin's apprehension was somewhat assuaged when he spotted a guard in one of the trees, an individual whom he recognized. He was a thick-jawed Mythaean convict who had been handed a life sentence at the oars of a galley ship as punishment for his crimes and subsequently freed by the people of this fleet. Like Hook, this man's tongue had been cut out, and he communicated in a language of signs. At Justin's approach, he smiled and waved, then turned and flashed a series of hand signals toward someone else, presumably a scout on the forest floor behind him.

So far, so good, thought Justin. *And thank God, because I'm starving. I hope they've got something to eat.*

He continued toward the entrance of the temple, an open gateway where there had once been a set of large doors. The beams of those doors, which had fallen long ago, now lay in piles of rotting wood on either side of the path.

More familiar faces emerged to watch Justin's approach. He exchanged nods and smiles with them all. He tried to read their faces. If anything was wrong, they would warn him. But by all accounts, all seemed well. They seemed happy to see him, and no one looked or felt as if they were under duress.

At the threshold of the temple, Justin slowed to a stop. He turned to ask, "Where is the admiral?"

"Scouting up the river," came the response, communicated in the language of hand signs. Justin was still learning that language; he knew enough to get by.

It was just before he stepped through the temple doorway that he finally broke through the spiritual barrier and recognized who was waiting for him inside.

Justin stepped in, and there she was.

She was dressed in plain robes: a small, unassuming-looking figure with dark skin and dark hair, except for a streak of white hair that ran along the front of her head like half a halo. Judging by the look on her face, Justin had been even more effective at masking *his* aurym presence than she'd been. Her face, usually impassive, took on an expression of surprise upon seeing him, followed by pleased relief.

She looked precisely the same as she had the last time Justin had seen her, which was to be expected of a person who never aged.

"So it *is* you, son of Benjamin," said Cyaxares.

CHAPTER 65

Son of Benjamin, thought Justin.

He'd always thought that Cyaxares called him that as a formality, or that it was a title that carried some sort of cultural significance. But now, after everything he had learned about who Cyaxares was, her relationship with his father, and who Avagad was. . . .

Justin decided not to fight his first instincts. He rushed to Cyaxares, and the two of them embraced.

"I am so glad to see you, my child," said Cyaxares.

"How did you find me?" asked Justin.

"Only by the will of aurym," she said.

As they separated, Cyaxares raised her hands to place them gently on either side of Justin's face, and she smiled at him. Her deep brown eyes were damp with joyful tears.

Her eyes flicked to the side, looking behind him. "And who is your friend?" she asked.

Justin turned. Leah stood in the doorway, having darted out of her hiding place. The Mythaeans and Islanders around her had recoiled in fright at her sudden appearance. No doubt, she would have appeared before them as a blur of impossible motion.

"Everyone," said Justin, speaking loudly so that all assembled could hear him. "This is Leah Anavion."

"The princess of Nolia?" said Cyaxares.

"Queen, now," said Justin.

"Among other things," said Leah.

"A pleasure, Lady Leah," said Cyaxares. "I am called Cyaxares of the Ru'Onorath."

"Cyaxares?" said Leah, her brow furrowed. "The leader of the Guardians?"

"Among other things," said Cyaxares. "I believe you were well acquainted with one of the greatest of our order."

"Ahlund," said Leah. "Yes, I was. He was my protector. And later, my friend. I was greatly grieved to learn of his passing."

The greatest of our order, thought Justin.

It was no small thing for Cyaxares to refer this way to Ahlund, a man who had abandoned the tenets of the Ru'Onorath, become a willing exile, and taken up the life of a mercenary. His actions had been in direct contrast to everything the Guardians of the Oikoumene stood for.

Upon returning to Esthean with Justin, Ahlund had been made Cyaxares's prisoner and had been facing a death sentence. But when Avagad's army attacked the hidden city, Ahlund made the ultimate sacrifice to allow Justin and the others to escape.

Only now did Justin take a good look around at the interior of the temple. Most of the people here belonged to the fleet—people he had expected to find upon his return. But there were others here with Cyaxares. He remembered some of them from Esthean and others from the island where the Ru'Onorath had taken refuge after fleeing from Avagad's attack. Most of them, like Ahlund and Kallorn, were warriors wielding aurstone-forged blades. But there were only about a dozen of them, no more.

"There are so few of you here," said Justin. "Only a fraction of those who escaped with us from Esthean. Where's everybody else?"

Cyaxares's smile faltered, and she did not answer.

"Perhaps we should step inside," said Cyaxares. "Your admiral should return shortly, but you must both be weary from traveling. And there is much to discuss."

Justin exchanged a look with Leah, and Leah nodded her agreement. *Much to discuss*, thought Justin. *Where do I even begin?*

CHAPTER 66

Leah was grateful for the food that Justin's allies were able to provide for them. But she was even more grateful for an unexpected luxury. In a dedicated room of the temple, a row of great stone basins were set into the floor. She was left in privacy to bathe in saltwater drawn from the sea and warmed over a fire.

It was while she washed her hair that she truly examined, for the first time, the damage done by the burns during her fight at the Warlord's fortress. Her scalp had been seared, and a chunk was missing from her dark hair, which had grown longer than she'd ever kept it before. As fortune would have it, the damage had been suffered on the same side of her head as the wound that had taken half her ear.

Father wore his dueling scar, a "smite," as he called it, with pride, she thought. *He never had a collection like this.*

There were scars from training. There were scars from battles. There was one at her hip, where an aurym attack had once burned her.

And then there was her shoulder, with the small surgical scar, self-implemented, marking the place where her hydstone rested in the hollow beneath her collarbone.

Leah washed her clothes in the basins as well and dried them over a fire. It gave her time to think. But the thoughts that came to her were mostly unwelcome.

After a light meal of fish brought in from the inlet, the light of the setting sun shone in through the gaps in the broken walls of the overgrown temple. Justin, too, had bathed and cleaned his clothing, and fresh strips of fabric had been wrapped around his demon arm.

As daylight faded, a species of bioluminescent insect emerged, first just a few of them, and then dozens. Leah had never seen anything quite like them. They seemed to be a cross between a common firefly and a moth, and their half-mad, silent trajectories through the shadows within the temple intermittently came aglow as they put on light shows for one another. The light seemed to shed from their wings like dust as they flew, leaving brief afterimages like runic figures hanging in the air.

It was in one of the shadowed, firemoth-lit corners of the temple, near a stone table that Leah surmised must have once been a sort of altar, that she, Justin, and the leader of the Ru'Onorath finally convened for a private meeting, away from all other possible listeners.

All three of them sat on the ground. Justin sat cross-legged, his gear within arm's reach. Cyaxares had her legs tucked beneath her and her robes draped over her, giving her the look of a bird on a nest. And Leah sat with her legs folded up in front of her, elbows resting casually on her knees, hands clasped. She knew it was not the pose of a queen but that of a soldier around a fire in a battle encampment, which was closer to how she thought of herself anyway.

"How did you manage to find my people?" Justin asked Cyaxares.

Cyaxares, who was watching Leah with great care, did not look away, even to ask, "Justin, are you sure about this?"

Her face was calm and her demeanor mild, but the hardness of her gaze as she studied Leah left no ambiguity to her meaning.

"Anything you can tell me, you can tell Leah," said Justin.

Cyaxares gave Leah a measured look, a look which Leah returned.

"Very well," said Cyaxares, and turned her attention to Justin. "I, and what remained of my Ru'Onorath, thirty-six in total, put ashore on Erum in the north and have been making our way south ever since. There are twenty-eight of us, now. All here in this temple."

"Ezon?" said Justin.

She shook her head.

"I'm sorry," said Justin.

"He was not killed by demons, mercifully," said Cyaxares. "Ezon was old, and the hard traveling was difficult on him. He passed away peacefully one night, on the northern coast of Darsida. Others were lost under less pleasant circumstances. And as for the rest of us, the will of aurym led us here to find you." Her eyes again came to rest on Leah. "Truly, I am eager to learn what twist of fate found you reunited with the Princess of Nolia."

"The short version is that I sensed Kallorn in danger and went to find him," said Justin. "Leah happened to be there, looking for me."

Cyaxares flashed him a curious look. "Kallorn is alive?"

"When last I saw him, yes," said Justin. "Though he had not been treated kindly."

"So," said Cyaxares, "twenty-*nine* Guardians of the Oikoumene remain. We have been separated from Kallorn for weeks, and I feared the worst."

"He led a group of refugees to join with my people," said Leah. "An army one hundred thousand strong, marching eastward to invade Avagad's lands."

"But the demons know Leah's army is coming," said Justin. "The element of surprise is gone. But there's another problem."

Justin seemed as if he wasn't certain if he should continue, and Leah watched him closely, wondering if he was finally going to share whatever he had been hiding from her.

Finally, he cleared his throat and spoke.

"For a long time, I have sensed a growing power." He gestured to his demon arm, covered by black wrappings of fabric. "This arm used to go numb when it wasn't exposed to daemyn. At one point, I lost all use of it and had to find a source of daemyn to fuel it, to get it to work again. But that no longer happens. Because daemyn has gotten so strong that it is everywhere, always, hanging in the very air. It is strongest when the moon is out and shining bright."

Leah did not need to ask which moon he was referring to.

"Since my arrival in Erum," Justin continued, "the power has grown exponentially. And after my discussion with Avagad, I feel that I now know what this buildup is leading toward."

"Discussion," said Cyaxares, "with Avagad?"

The tone of the woman's voice sounded strange to Leah, but she couldn't quite place the emotion behind it.

"Yes," said Justin. "I spoke to him. And he told me that the Nameless One, the god-king of the demons, means to break the barrier between this world and the demon realm of Mu, and come to the Oikoumene in physical form."

Leah suppressed a shiver. Cyaxares remained still where she sat. All the while, the firefly-moths silently danced above them, painting glowing figures in the air of the temple.

"I don't know if it can be stopped," said Justin, drawing out several folded sheets of parchment from his satchel. "But on Avagad's maps, there was a place called the Pit. Leah and I both saw it in a vision. A great hole reaching down into shadowed depths, with demons crawling out of it."

He handed the folded sheets of parchment to Cyaxares. Leah knew what the woman would see; Justin had shown her these copied maps during their travels.

"Cyaxares," he said as she examined the sheets of parchment, "do you know anything about this?"

It took a moment for Cyaxares to recover from Justin's words, but finally, she pointed to the map and said, "There is a city here, on this peninsula off the eastern coast of Erum. The Ancients built it around a geomorphic anomaly. A great fissure in the ground, almost perfectly circular, with sheer walls, that descended deep into the earth. Despite its depth and close proximity to the sea, groundwater never seeped in.

Its bottom, hundreds of feet down, if the rumors are to be believed, stayed bone dry year-round. It became a place of religious worship. A great pyramid was constructed around and over it to contain it and control access to it, for it also attracted those who pursued the worship of darker things. Forbidden rituals. Human sacrifices."

Cyaxares paused here and looked at Leah.

"Does she know?" asked Cyaxares. "About Benjamin?"

"Leah knows that Dad was an ethoul," said Justin.

Cyaxares nodded. "Benjamin defeated the demons on two separate occasions. Both times, the demons came from across the sea, not out of a Pit in the ground. Nevertheless, what you're describing sounds like the central complex in the city of Rohghost."

"Rohghost," said Leah. "Nefari used that name. She said it was Avagad's capital city. She led an army there, but they were defeated. After she escaped, her farseeing abilities were constantly clouded by visions of the Pit."

I wonder, thought Leah, *if Nefari knew her visions were of a place she had been so close to reaching.*

"So," said Justin. "We have a name to put to our destination."

"You mean to go there?" said Cyaxares. "And face Avagad?"

"I am going there," said Justin. "But not to face Avagad. I am going there to stop the demons, in whatever way is required of me. But before we make any more plans, there is something we must address." He turned and locked eyes with Leah. "Zechariah."

"What about him?" said Leah.

"Back in Athacea," said Justin, "when I first met Zechariah, he told me he was twelve hundred years old. He told Ahlund that he was a member of the Brethren, a group of immortal men and women. He told you the same, didn't he?"

"I have heard him claim that openly," said Leah. "Many times."

Justin gestured toward Cyaxares with an open palm, encouraging her to speak.

"No one by that name was ever a member of the Brethren," said Cyaxares. "To my knowledge, Avagad and I are the only surviving members of that order."

Leah's mouth almost dropped open, and she had to quickly clench her jaw to hide her emotions.

"My father had never heard of him either, when I asked him," said Justin. "But what's most concerning is what Avagad told me himself. At first, he claimed that Zechariah was, in secret, his ally, and that they had been working together since the beginning."

"What?" breathed Leah, feeling the bottom drop out from her stomach.

"I didn't know what to make of that claim at the time," said Justin, quickly pushing on, "and I still don't, because now, Avagad tells me that his original statement about Zechariah was a lie. Now, he claims *even he* doesn't know who Zechariah is. Somehow, I find that possibility even more disturbing."

"It's not impossible that he is one of the Brethren," said Cyaxares. "Perhaps Amphidemus took him on as a new member after I departed from their ranks. But if so, Avagad would have known him."

"Could Amphidemus have been taking initiates in secret?" asked Justin.

"Possibly," said Cyaxares.

So lost in her own thoughts was Leah that she found it almost difficult to follow their words.

Zechariah, thought Leah, feeling keenly the hollowness in her chest, *may not be who he says he is.*

She found herself trying to think of everything the old man had ever said to her, trying to replay every conversation they'd ever had. He was a skilled diplomat. She had seen firsthand how frighteningly adept he was at knowing just what to say and to whom, just what nerve to touch, to manipulate a larger body to perform according to his desire.

And I followed his advice to bring my people here. Into the heart of darkness. Into the demons' den.

"Justin," said Cyaxares, looking troubled. "You said you spoke to Avagad. But you also said. . . . You asked your father about Zechariah? Do you mean to say that you have spoken with Benjamin?"

"I have," said Justin. "That was where I went when I left you. I'm sorry about that, but I needed answers only he could give. He still cares for you greatly, Cyaxares."

Justin paused, as if hanging over the edge of a precipice, contemplating whether to jump. Leah knew Justin well enough to hear the deep emotion behind his words as he added, "I don't think he has any idea that Avagad is his son."

CHAPTER 67

The breath left Leah's lungs at Justin's words.

Cyaxares closed her eyes as if she were recovering from a physical blow. "Avagad told you," she said.

"No," said Justin. "But he has since confirmed it."

"You pieced it together yourself, then," Cyaxares said.

"His *son*?" whispered Leah, staring at Justin. "Avagad . . . is your father's son?"

"His," said Cyaxares, "and mine."

A jolt went through Leah, shaking her from her heart to the tips of her fingers.

Justin and Avagad shared the same father.

"The man you know as Avagad was born among the Brethren," said Cyaxares. "This was after Benjamin was sent away from the Oikoumene. He never knew I was with child. I named my little boy *Eth'oul'ad*. In my homeland, it means 'son of the angel.'

"Ethoulad was raised among our ranks, in a bastion in the deep south of Otunmer, where we lived as warrior-monks. A thriving community was built around us, with mortal humans attending to our needs in exchange for the protection and guidance we gave them. I was not alone in raising my son. But even from an early age, there were signs that he was more susceptible than most to the influence of daemyn, like his father had been.

"At the time, we still didn't know what daemyn was, or how dangerous it could be. Amphidemus, the leader of our order, and the other members of the Brethren believed that daemyn was an equal opposite to aurym, that there was nothing inherently dark or evil about it. As Ethoulad matured, so did his power. His aurym abilities, like those of his father, were extraordinary. When he grew to manhood, he undertook the initiation rites of the Brethren, and, like the rest of us, his body became immune to the effects of time. He ceased to age. But the process calls upon a certain amount of daemyn to siphon the power of timelessness from the realm of the Kharon. I never should have allowed him to undergo the ritual. After that, Ethoulad was never the same.

"My experiences with Benjamin had left me wary of daemyn. Now, seeing the changes in Ethoulad, I became convinced that daemyn was more than we assumed. There was a wickedness to it. A darkness that was growing, not just in my son but among the other Brethren, as well. I tried to convince them that we should renounce daemyn and devote ourselves to aurym and aurym alone. It caused a rift between me and the others. Amphidemus disagreed with me. And so did my son.

"By then, Ethoulad was older than most men ever become, wise far beyond even those many years, and frighteningly powerful. I did not want to lose him, but I felt convicted that if he, Amphidemus, and the others would not change their ways, I would have to leave the order. No one had ever done such a thing, and I suspected that if I announced my intentions, I would not be *allowed* to be the first to do so. So, I fled secretly, leaving behind nothing but a short note in a box, apologizing to my beloved son and urging him to flee from darkness.

"One hundred years after I left the Brethren, I received word that the immortals had been attacked and slain by a demon host. Only a few of the mortals who attended them escaped the slaughter, and they carried with them the story: My son, the son of the angel, had betrayed the Brethren and brought death to the immortals. He abandoned his birth name of Ethoulad in favor of a new name. *Av'ag'ad.* In my native tongue, it means 'son of the demon.'"

As Cyaxares concluded the tale, Leah felt the urge to comfort her somehow. But what could anyone say or do?

"I should not have kept the truth from you, Justin," said Cyaxares.

"I think you were right to," said Justin. "I'm certain I wouldn't have been strong enough at the time to hear all this. I'm not sure what it would have done to me, to learn that Avagad was my father's son. My own brother."

"Avagad may be our flesh and blood," said Cyaxares, "but the part of him that was your brother, and my son, died a long time ago. Now, he truly is what his name claims."

Cyaxares adjusted her position on the floor so that her hands sat folded in her lap. By now, the sun was down, and the moonlight was shrouded enough that the tip of Hook's a'thri'ik lance, leaning beside Justin, was glowing. That, combined with the light of the firefly-moths crowding into the room in surprising numbers, was enough to provide ample, eerie illumination.

"Justin," said Cyaxares. "In light of everything you've told me about the Nameless One, I can't help but wonder what it is you hope to accomplish by traveling to the Pit."

Before Justin could answer, there came a gentle knock from the adjoining doorway.

"It's me," said a female voice.

"Come in, Admiral," said Justin.

Leah turned toward the doorway, and in stepped a woman holding a lantern.

In the light of the lantern, Leah could see that the woman wore a patchwork of armor, high boots, and a short cloak wrapped about her neck like a mantle. It was easy to see that she was Castydocian by her striking silver hair, tied back in a knot. Her skin was light brown, a shade lighter than Leah's, and although she was older than Leah, she had the lithe figure and lean muscle of a young soldier. A Mythaean-style cutlass hung low at her side.

Rising from his seated position, Justin greeted the woman by clasping hands with her in a rough, soldier's fashion. She responded by pulling him in for an embrace and patting his back, also in a rough, soldier's fashion, before releasing him again. She flashed a wide smile of white teeth and huffed out a single-note laugh. "It is a relief to see you," she said.

"Likewise," said Justin.

In her younger life, Leah had been to many court functions. She had seen royalty from across the entirety of Athacea, some from Endenholm and Lundholm, and even from Raeqlund, where men and women alike were renowned the world over for their beauty. She had seen some of the most primped, well-bred, and well-groomed people in the inhabited world at their very best, wearing the most fashionable clothing that money could buy.

But the person whom Leah currently looked upon was, objectively, one of the most beautiful women she had ever laid eyes on—without any primping, grooming, or fashionable clothing required.

"Do you have a moment to join us, Admiral?" asked Justin, sitting back down and making room for her on his opposite side. "We're talking strategy, and anything you learned out there would be useful."

The admiral sat down crosslegged beside Justin and threw off her mantle. Beneath it, Leah noticed a badly healed scar near the top of her sternum. When she set the lantern in front of her to light the room, Justin looked up and gave a nonchalant flick of his hand. The firefly-moths suddenly ceased circling and dispersed through the cracks in the ceiling.

He was controlling them, Leah suddenly realized. *Communicating with them through aurym, to keep them here to light the room for us the whole time.*

"The northern arm of the river heads inland almost straight east for at least twenty miles, from what we can see," said the admiral. "If we were to head that direction, taking the ships with us would be tricky but not impossible. We'd have to pull them along from the shore by rope to get them upriver."

"Is that difficult to do?" asked Justin.

"It's not fun," said the admiral. "We've got enough strong backs to make it happen, but realistically, unless we know we're going someplace where we'll need them, it may be more trouble than it's worth."

"I could help with that," Leah spoke up.

The admiral shot her a curious look. In return, Leah offered her most diplomatic of smiles.

"Oh—introductions. Sorry," said Justin, shaking his head. "Admiral, it sounds like you've already met Cyaxares, but this is Leah Anavion, Queen of Nolia and Commander of the Army of Light."

The admiral's face changed. "This is Leah?" she said. She smiled and gave a hasty bow of her head—not an ironic one, either. "An honor to meet you, Your Highness. I've heard a lot about you."

"Please, just call me Leah," said Leah.

"Leah," said Justin, gesturing to the silver-haired woman, "this is the admiral of the fleet I was telling you about. She and her people are the ones who rescued me on the Raedittean Sea. Allow me to introduce Admiral Eos."

"Please," said the admiral. "You can just call me Jocasta."

CHAPTER 68

It was sundown, and Hook Bard stood alone amid a stand of long-needled white pines. Over the past day of traveling, the hemlocks were becoming less pervasive, as was the harsh terrain. For the first time in a long time, the land didn't rise or fall around the Army of Light in sheer, rocky escarpments or drop into chasms disappearing into the deep.

And, though the topography didn't give much indication of it yet, Hook knew they were nearing the ocean, just as Lycon's maps indicated.

Several had passed since Kallorn's arrival at the Army of Light with the refugees from the Warlord's fortress and the false ethoul, Justus. It had been several more days of travel. Several more days of navigating the mist-shrouded forests and canyons of Central Erum. Several more days of going either unnoticed or selectively overlooked by the demons in these lands.

But, most significant of all to Hook, several more days without Leah's return.

She had said to wait a fortnight. Just over a week had passed, but still, Hook couldn't shake the feeling that something had gone wrong. He and Olorus had several times debated backtracking toward the Warlord's fortress in an attempt to search for Leah and Justin. But so far, they had opted to respect her wishes and wait the full two weeks for her.

Hook flared his nostrils. He could feel salt in the air, high in his sinuses. It was a smell that many people found pleasant. But for him, all it did was bring back half a lifetime of bad memories.

The smell of saltwater would always raise his hackles. Getting sentenced to the oars in the guts of a ship until dropping dead from exhaustion had the tendency to do that to a person.

Hook stooped, picked up a handful of soil, and tested it between his fingers. There was a sandy quality to it that hadn't been present in Erum until now. If Lycon's maps were correct, there was a cluster of coastal towns to the south of here. Or at least, there had been. No doubt they would have been some of the first to fall to the demons.

Regardless, the Army of Light had no intention of going near them. Their destination lay straight ahead: the sea itself.

Hook heard Megara's approach and knew it was her without looking. He was a man who valued moments of solitude, and he didn't get many of them these days. But at least he could count on Megara not to annoy him with a lot of unnecessary words.

"Have the scouts returned?" Hook signed as he turned to face her.

Megara nodded. *"The map makes it look like a chain of islands,"* she signed, *"but according to their reports, it is more like a series of sandbars."*

Hook looked around at the hardwood forest. The Army of Light currently had no ships. It would take time to build rafts to get their soldiers across, but in theory, it could be done.

"There is plenty of wood," he signed. *"I will give the orders to begin making preparations."*

"Boats may not be needed," signed Megara.

Hook cocked an eyebrow.

"The scouts observed the waters through the morning," Megara signed. *"When the tide goes out, the waters lower. The sandbars connect, creating a land bridge. The water is no greater than ankle-deep in most places. If we synchronize our crossing with the tides, we could walk straight over the sea."*

Hook squinted a bit at Megara, posing an unspoken question. Most would have considered this new development to be good news. Megara, however, did not look happy. She ignored him for a few moments and then, finally, relented.

"If the waters lower before us," she signed. *"They also rise behind us."*

Hook nodded.

"We would be trapped," said Megara. *"Unable to retreat."*

Hook studied her. *"Do you plan to retreat?"*

Megara grinned. *"You know I do not."*

The big woman looked around to ensure that no one was watching her. Then she walked to a tree and leaned against it. She kept her signs close to her body on one side and used the tree to block any potential view from the other. Hook could empathize; relying on hand signs to communicate meant that one had to get a bit creative when it came to the equivalent of whispering.

"*Several of my people deserted last night,*" she signed.

Hook's brow furrowed. "*Why would they leave now?*" he asked. "*After coming so far?*"

Megara shook her head. "*The lack of a clear answer only further confounds and angers me.*"

A thought occurred to Hook. The Raeqlu deserters. The ones who had disappeared from camp in the night after a scuffle with some of Gunnar's people.

No signs of violence. No message left. By all accounts, it seemed they had just walked away.

"*It is possible,*" signed Hook, echoing Zechariah's earlier words in reference to the incident, "*that there are forces at work that influenced their decision.*"

Moving parts that we are unaware of. That's what Zechariah had said.

Megara frowned. "*I thought I knew them,*" she signed. Then, a moment later, "*I thought . . . they trusted me.*"

Hook hesitated, not accustomed to seeing Megara so deeply affected by something—by anything, really.

"*They would not be the first soldiers to give in to fear in the face of uncertainty and threat of death,*" he signed. "*It could be nothing more than that.*"

"*I do not know,*" Megara replied. "*But I do not think I have turned out to be the leader that Leah hoped I would be.*"

"*What sort of leader do you think she hoped for?*" asked Hook.

Megara glared at him. "*A good one. Do not patronize me.*"

"*And do you still want to be a good leader?*" asked Hook. "*Or should we find someone else to take the job?*"

This time, instead of glaring, Megara smiled. "*You are blunt.*"

"*It is the best way to draw out inner qualities. I have found it does not work on everyone, however.*"

"*I did not think I would want to lead,*" signed Megara. "*But I do. I greatly desire it. And I am trying my best.*"

Hook allowed for some silence to settle between them before he asked something he had been wondering for a long time.

"*How were you taken?*" he signed.

She tilted her head at him, startled by the question.

"You are Rorrdvuuk by birth," said Hook. *"But you were enslaved by the Mythaeans. Either they were a long way from home, or you were."*

For a moment, Megara looked as closed-off as Hook had ever seen her, but then her tense, muscular shoulders loosened a bit. Perhaps without consciously meaning to, her hand wandered to her belt knife with its black, volcanic-rock blade from her homeland.

"It was I who was the one far from home," she signed. *"I was with a Rorrdvuuk raiding party. We had sailed north to pillage the Darsidan coast."*

Hook cocked an eyebrow at her.

Megara shrugged. *"I never said my sentence at the oars was unjustly given."*

"I suppose you did not."

"We were waylaid by a Mythaean fleet that quickly bested us in battle. At first, we thought they were protecting the coastal towns we attacked. Instead, they took our plunder for themselves. We were pirates who had been out-pirated. Instead of killing us, they took us back to their islands. We became part of their bounty."

Megara gestured to the slave's brand scar across her head.

"I escaped, years later, during the siege of Skyre, in the War of the Nimbuses—the conflict between Gunnar, his brother, and their uncle— and eventually made my way south to Dvuuk-land again."

"Now you fight alongside one of those very Nimbuses," signed Hook, *"leading other escaped and freed slaves, and commanding Mythaeans, too."*

Megara wore a haunted expression. *"I swear, Hook, there are moments when I see faces among the ranks of this army whom I recognize as my own captors from my days at the oars."*

Hook nodded. *"Same."*

"And sometimes, it is all I can do not to. . . ."

Megara's next sign needed no interpretation. She raised her hand, clutched it into a fist, and punched the tree beside her three times so hard that its trunk trembled.

Hook nodded yet again. *"Same."*

"I believe I can be a leader," signed Megara, wiping blood from her knuckles. *"A leader to all of them, not just now but after the war, as well. If this war ends, that is. And if I live to see it."*

"None of us can be sure we will live that long," Hook added.

Megara nodded. *"What will you do if you survive?"*

It was a question Hook had been trying to answer for himself for some time.

What was waiting for him once this was all over? What were the things that mattered to him beyond the war? His country, Nolia. His friends, Olorus and Leah.

Fighting, he thought. *Fighting all my life. It feels like I've been doing it since the day I was born. How do you stop fighting when it's all that you know?*

"People like you and I," signed Hook, *"we are like knives. For now, these people need us to stay sharp. When we are needed no longer, perhaps they hope we will grow dull and rust."*

Megara frowned. *"Are you saying, do not think about tomorrow? Focus on the task at hand?"*

A fresh gust of breeze came pushing through the pines, bringing with it that same old aroma of salty sea air. Sickening.

"I am saying," signed Hook, *"one day, we may have our chance to do something about all those faces we recognize from our past. There will still be cutting to be done. But some cuts must be made with great care."*

Thunder rumbled in the distance, and the wind blew harder.

"Stay sharp," signed Hook, and he turned and walked away.

CHAPTER 69

The rain started soon after sundown and intensified as the night wore on. But, despite the soothing sounds of distant thunder and the rainfall against the roof of the overgrown temple, Leah still couldn't sleep.

She had been given her own private room in the temple, and although it contained nothing more than a blanket on the floor and her own pack as a pillow, it was a luxury compared to the accommodations most of the others had.

She rolled over and stared at the wall in the almost pitch darkness. Somewhere out in the main area of the temple, a fire had been lit, and its light from around the corner resulted in a barely distinguishable shadow of her prone body against the far wall. It had been a long time since she'd had trouble drifting off like this. Sleep was one thing she rarely struggled with. Despite the fact that her mind never seemed to be able to stop, despite the fact that she was haunted by visions of the horrors of battles past, despite knowing that one hundred thousand souls might rest in her hands at any given time, she was never incapable of getting at least a few hours of rest.

Sleep came even easier to her on days when she used the hydstone. She usually did not feel physically weary from the energy she expended during those times, but it was like any other aurym ability; you could overexert yourself if you weren't careful. When that happened, you paid for it. Now or later, one way or another, you paid for it.

Hours passed, and rest would not come no matter how hard she tried. Finally, she got up. If she couldn't sleep, she could perhaps relieve someone of their guard duties and allow them to rest for a time.

In her simple tunic and slipper-like shoes, Leah stole through the temple, following the light of the unseen fire. She passed through a room where Admiral Jocasta Eos shared her quarters with a few other women—her biological sisters, Leah had learned. In the far corner, she saw Cyaxares sitting upright but unmoving, with her cloak tucked around her. No one stirred or seemed to notice her passage.

Leah intended to move toward the temple's exterior to find the guards. But when she stepped into a small antechamber of the temple, the source of the light, she was not overly surprised to find Justin sitting by a hearth with a few logs burning within it.

Justin was alone. He seemed to be fidgeting with something small in his hand, but his eyes were directed toward the ceiling. Or perhaps through it.

For a moment, Leah stood still, quietly watching him. Given what she knew about him, she assumed he was aware of her presence and had sensed her coming.

But then, she realized Justin was speaking quietly, mumbling.

"I'm trying so hard to be like you," said Justin, in a voice barely above a whisper. "I thought what I did with Justus was the right choice at the time, but what if I was wrong?"

Leah hesitated, unsure whether to announce herself or take her leave. While she was still trying to decide, Justin kept speaking.

"I know what I should do, but I don't know if I can do it," he said. "There's so much at stake now, so many lives."

There was a shudder to his speech, and he inhaled shallowly, quickly, several breaths in rapid succession as if he could not get enough air in at once. He raised a hand to place it over his mouth as if trying to silence himself, and Leah could see that his fingers were trembling.

Leah took a step back, feeling very awkward for unintentionally eavesdropping. But then Justin opened his other hand, revealing what he was holding. An aurstone. And not just any aurstone.

A gauge, Leah realized. *Known to some as a keystone.*

The key that could open the way between worlds.

"What do I do?" Justin whispered.

He closed his hand over the stone, and Leah thought she felt aurym being called upon.

"Justin," she said, stepping forward, suddenly fearful.

Justin's shoulders tensed. He did not turn to look at her but instead focused his gaze on the fire before him. The flow of aurym power that Leah had felt ceased.

"I'm sorry," Leah said hastily. "I wasn't—I didn't mean to. . . ."

Justin pushed the gauge stone into a pocket. He took a moment to compose himself and managed to steady his breathing, but he had to clasp his hands together to keep them from shaking.

"It's all right," he said, still without looking at her. "I can usually sense people coming, but I guess I was distracted."

As Leah crossed the room, she found herself choosing her steps cautiously. Ever since his return, Justin had seemed so unshakeable, so solid. Almost too solid for her to relate to. But suddenly, she found herself worried that one wrong move might scare him off.

"I couldn't sleep," she said, stopping a few steps from the hearth.

"Me, neither," said Justin.

"I didn't know you were up," she said. "Otherwise, I wouldn't have. . . ."

"It's all right," he said.

"Do you want to talk?" asked Leah.

Justin continued to stare into the flames of the hearth. "Yes," he said. "But I don't know how."

"I've been there," Leah said, taking a seat beside him. "I've found that the first step is to not turn away a willing listener. They're hard to come by."

"Leah," he said, "how do you make decisions when you know people will be in danger because of your actions?"

"You're in luck," said Leah. "I think about that so often that I have an answer ready. I deal with it by reminding myself of the danger they would be in if I *didn't* act. It's not easy to think about someone getting hurt or dying because of my choices."

Images flashed through Leah's head. Soldiers disemboweled by coblyns. People turned to dust by cythraul. Cimon Endrus, with his arms ripped off by Innocen. Marcus Worth, turned into a cythwraith.

"But that's the burden of leadership," she said. "I have to think about what will give us the best chance of victory. In the long run, that's the best way to protect them."

"Victory," said Justin, and the word sounded hollow on his lips. "Leah, this has all happened before. All of it. Demons invading the Oikoumene. A fallen angel arriving to drive them back. It's happened before, and it will happen again. It's the cycle of aurym and daemyn. Even if we do achieve victory, the cycle will just repeat itself."

"Are you saying," said Leah, "that you think what we're doing doesn't matter?"

"It's not that it doesn't matter," said Justin. "All I mean is that it's not permanent. It will happen again, maybe in a hundred years, maybe in a thousand."

"That's pretty permanent to me," she said. "Defeating the demons now, even if they do come back later, will save the lives of *everyone* I know—everyone I ever will know. And as a normal person who can't call on aurym to disappear from this world whenever I want to and leave everybody behind, I. . . ."

The way Justin's face fell at those words told Leah instantly that she had gone too far.

Leah held one hand up. "I didn't mean it like that," she said.

Justin swallowed hard against a lump in his throat, then turned away, looking silently into the fireplace again.

Fool, she scolded herself. *You're not wrong, of course. He has left in the past. But he finally opens up to you, and this is how you honor his trust in you?*

A few silent moments went by. Enough for Leah to notice that several of the same species of flying insect, the firefly-moth, had found their way through the breaks in the temple roof to take shelter from the storm. They were flitting about in the corners, safely distant from the flames in the hearth, leaving trails of light as they flew.

"Do you remember the fireflies on the Greenspring River?" said Leah. "The ones in the woods while we were sailing?"

"Yeah," said Justin. "Back when we had just hired Gunnar to take us downriver on the *Gryphon*."

"We didn't even know who he was," said Leah. "Just some fisherman with a boat big enough for all of us."

"Remember when we were fishing?" said Justin. "And Pool tried to take Hook's bandana?"

"Hook made him pay for it—with his dignity," said Leah, remembering the sight of Pool, helpless in Hook's grasp, with an apple shoved into his mouth like a roasted pig.

Justin laughed. "That feels like a really long time ago."

Leah let the moment linger before she asked the question that had been on her mind for days.

"Justin," she said. "Are we friends?"

This *finally* got Justin to look her fully in the eyes, and he blinked at her in surprise.

"Friends?" he said. "Of course we are. But it's a little more than that, isn't it? I mean, I hope it is."

"I was so excited to see you back in that fortress," said Leah, remembering what it had been like to kiss him after all that time apart. "What we did in that moment felt right. But maybe it was just excitement. Maybe a moment is all it really was."

Justin's face went a little pale. The look he wore seemed to be a cross between disappointment and panic.

"The other day, when we were in those woods, I told you that you could tell me anything," said Leah. "And your response was, 'Thank you.' That was it. You didn't . . . reciprocate."

"Oh," said Justin. His voice sounded sticky and dry.

I thought I would have the same thing from you, Leah wanted to add. But she didn't.

High above, the moths flitted. In the distance, thunder rolled. Justin's hands were clasped tightly again. He barely seemed to be breathing.

"I built it up so much in my head, you coming back," said Leah, "but when I think about it rationally, all we ever really did was travel together for a while. We saw fireflies on the river. We got captured together. And after we escaped, we shared a kiss. One kiss. A long time ago. Maybe it was naïve to think we would have some sort of connection after all this time. Maybe it's just because you were gone so long, and I had so much time to think about it and idealize it. I mean, how well do we really know each other?"

Justin swallowed hard. He seemed incapable of looking away from the fire. Leah couldn't tell if what she was observing was heartbrokenness, introspection, or if he was just plain numb.

"It's just like he said," Justin mumbled.

"What?" said Leah.

"Nothing," said Justin. He turned to look at her, smiling sadly. "You're right. I didn't reciprocate, did I? I'm sorry."

"I wasn't looking for an apology," said Leah. "I wouldn't want you to do something insincerely. I only want you to reciprocate if that's who you really are. I just . . . thought it was."

Justin closed his eyes and hissed quietly between his teeth as if the words caused him true, physical pain. It was the look of a man whose world was falling down around him.

"You're still important to me," Leah said, trying to sound supportive. "I still care for you."

"I care for you, too," said Justin.

"And we're still in this together, no matter what," said Leah. "Okay?"

"Okay," breathed Justin.

Leah stood to leave.

Justin's hand caught her by the wrist, firmly but gently. Leah turned back to face him.

"Your mother's name was Helena," said Justin. "You had four brothers. The youngest of your brothers couldn't walk. One of the others—the oldest brother, I think you said—knew lots of bird calls.

"When you were little, you used to go adventuring in the palace gardens. On festival days, you used to like listening to bards recite poems and tell stories about faraway places. You were the youngest of the family, so you didn't think you would ever need to know all those lessons they taught you about politics, diplomacy, and leadership. You showed a gift for aurym-healing, so you enrolled in the Academy in . . . what's Nolia's capital city called again?"

Leah had to moisten her lips before she could speak. "Cervice," she said.

"Right," said Justin. "Cervice. I've never been, obviously, but I'd love to visit it someday. Anyway. The Academy of Cervice. You enrolled there for training, and you became a healer." He straightened his back and added, with intentionally overdramatic flair, "Your duty was to the infirm!"

Leah surprised herself by snorting a laugh.

Justin pointed at her. "And you do *that*."

"What?" she demanded.

"Snort when you laugh."

"I do not."

"You do! Not often, but you do." He was still holding her by the wrist. "Your eyes are green, but they have these tiny flecks of gold in them. You like things that are beautiful, like fireflies and glowing caverns, but you're also practical. You are brave, braver than me by a long shot. You are compassionate in the sense that you care about all people. But nothing matters to you more than *your* people—the people who depend on you. And I can only imagine how hard that must be right now.

"Leah. If I seem distant and cold, it's because I *feel* distant and cold. From everyone. I didn't want it to be the same way with you. It pains me that that's how it turned out. I haven't been a friend to you. And I'm not just saying this: I really am truly sorry for that. I'll try to do better. And. . . . And I agree that when I think about it rationally, it doesn't make sense. We really don't know all that much about each other. It's deeply irrational. But despite all that, you have to know, I don't just 'still care' about you. I care about you more than I care about anyone, in this world or any other."

Those final few sentences seemed to come tumbling out of Justin all at once, and in the aftermath, Leah found herself unable to speak. She could only stand there beside Justin, looking at him in the light of the flames, feeling the warmth of his hand on her wrist.

Finally, Justin let go of her.

Leah still hadn't thought of anything to say by the time she started walking away, intending to leave the room. Her legs felt weak. She wasn't used to feeling so weak. Or so uncertain. Or so irrational. It was less like acting on conscious choice and more like she was giving in to a deep, driving instinct as she stopped in the middle of the room, turned, and went back to the hearth.

"Can I just, maybe, sit with you a while?" said Leah.

Justin, wordlessly, repositioned himself so that he was seated on the floor with his back to the hearth. Leah sat down next to him, feeling the soothing warmth of the stones against her back. To her surprise, she felt a little scared as she tentatively edged closer to him, until their shoulders were touching.

She leaned against him, and he let her. She couldn't remember the last time she had leaned on someone or how long it had been since anybody, other than herself, had been able to make her feel safe.

CHAPTER 70

Not everyone had given up on Gunnar yet. But he almost wished they would, the way they kept interrupting and annoying him all the time.

Over the past week, he had done a very good job of preventing himself from slipping back into his right frame of mind for any longer than an hour or so. He had gone through phases like this before. His time as a young adult, causing trouble with other members of the royal court back in Eppex, came to mind. Or his earliest days back at the Brig, when he'd been doing his best to forget about his old life. Or his time in Cervice, before being recruited to go on a blasted treasure-hunting mission. And since he had been through such phases before, he did his best to try to tell himself that this time was just another one, nothing new for him.

And yet, the part of himself that remained capable of self-reflection regardless of chemical-induced impairment knew that this time was different.

This time, it wasn't for fun, or to forget, or to combat boredom. This time, it was because the voice in his head was getting louder.

This time, it was because his freeze-ups, the incidences when he lost control of his body and the world went sideways, were becoming more frequent. Drinking seemed to be the only way to silence the voice and prevent the sideways incidents.

It was when I learned about Ahlund, thought Gunnar. *That was when it got bad. It was never good. But I had it under some sort of control.*

But Ahlund.

Learning what had happened to his friend, trying to reconcile the terrible truth.

"It unraveled you," said the voice in his head.

Gunnar shook his head. He had gone too long without a drink. The voice was coming back.

And a *voice* was exactly what it was, now. Not intrusive thoughts. Not unwelcome self-talk. It was a voice. And it was growing louder. He could *hear* it all the time, unless he was blisteringly drunk. But even that was starting to lose its effectiveness.

For some reason, the people around him weren't content to leave him to his own devices. It would have been so much easier that way. But someone was always there. He would spot Lycon hovering around the edges of his awareness, probably trying to prevent others from seeing him like this. Or he would snap to full consciousness and realize that Adonica was leading him back to his tent, again. Olorus had tried to prevent him from finding any spirits to begin with by ordering the soldiers to hide the stores, throw them away, or burn them before they let Gunnar touch the stuff anymore. But there was always someone who could be talked into it giving him something. Sometimes, Sif did the same sorts of things, too. So far, no one else had punched him in the stomach, as far as he could remember.

But those who were most frequently around were Borris and Pool. He would wake up in his tent to find the two of them there, standing by the door flap, or sleeping close by.

At first, it'd seemed he had finally gotten his old drinking buddies back, that they had snapped to their senses and agreed to join him in his revelry once in a while, just like old times back at the Brig. But anytime he tried to get them to indulge alongside him, they turned him down, usually by shaking their heads sadly and saying something with dreadful finality, in a halfhearted, defeated sort of way like, "No, Cap'n."

He was used to being a source of irritation and annoyance. He wasn't used to causing people grief.

Gunnar stumbled out of the thick air of his tent, hoping to get a fresh breath of morning air to clear his head, before clouding it again of his own volition. But instead of the morning that he was expecting to find, it appeared to be the middle of the night. And instead of fresh, clean air, what he got was a steady downpour of rain that instantly doused him.

Gunnar grumbled in annoyance and kept walking, feeling the rainwater soak through his clothing. He didn't know how long it had been since he had bathed, so at least that was one less thing.

"It's all you do," said the voice in his head. "Cause grief wherever you go."

Gunnar squeezed his eyes shut and clenched his teeth.

"Things get worse around you," said the voice. "You carry bad luck around like a foul odor, and it spreads to all you touch."

"Shut up," whispered Gunnar through clenched teeth. "For the last time, *shut up*, and leave me alone."

"Oh, yes. Tell yourself *I'm* the problem. Because everything was going swimmingly before I showed up, right?"

Gunnar kept walking forward through the rain, no longer certain where he was going or why. He stumbled past the exteriors of the many tents of the Army of Light, looking for someone to ask, or order, to bring him a bottle of something, anything. There was no one to be seen, but there would be guards at the edge of camp keeping an eye on things. He would be able to convince one of them to get him something to drink. He always did.

"Do you know, Gunnar, that I could have killed you by now many times over?"

Gunnar stopped in his tracks, nearly falling over as the world spun a bit around him.

In all his encounters with the voice in his head, he couldn't remember a time when it had addressed him by name before. He found himself unsure of how to respond or even if he should.

I'm going crazy, he suddenly realized. *This is what it's like to lose your mind.*

"No, Gunnar. Your mind is the one thing you *won't* lose."

Gunnar took an involuntary step backward, though he wasn't sure what he was trying to step away from. After all, the adversary was inside him.

And that, he suddenly realized, was exactly what the voice was. An adversary.

An enemy. . . . *The* enemy.

"Such power," said the voice in his head. "*That*, Gunnar, is the only reason I *haven't* killed you yet. That magnificent power of yours. You have a way with aurym that's quite hard to come by, you see. It will be of great use to me."

Not sure why he was doing it but unable to do anything else, Gunnar started running. He ran toward the edge of camp, where he knew he would find those guards. He needed something to drink. Needed it bad. Failing that, he at least needed to see another human being. Needed to not be alone with this voice inside him.

"Running will no longer do you any good, Gunnar," said the voice. "Remember the way your tutors always used to tell you how much potential you had? An inborn potential for aurym power, one that your brother could never grasp. It's what first spurred the jealousy within him that led to his betrayal. A mind for intellectual pursuits. And a way with people that could have led you to become a great leader instead of the outcast and fool you chose to be instead. *Potential*, as your friends have called it, to *unite* people. Do you think that was all just hot air, Gunnar? Just empty words?"

Finally, Gunnar saw someone ahead, silhouetted in the light of a torch that was faltering in the rain but had not yet been doused.

"Hey!" Gunnar shouted as he ran. "Hey, over here!"

The guard on the edge of camp turned in Gunnar's direction at the sound of his voice.

Gunnar tripped and fell face-first into the muddy ground. He slipped, went sprawling, finally got unsteadily to his feet, and had to look around in confusion for a moment before he found the guard with the torch again. There were several others standing around him. All the more chance that they would be sharing a bottle, imbibing in something that Gunnar prayed would be strong enough to silence the voice. He resumed running toward them.

"You are more powerful than you know," said the voice as he ran, and as it spoke, it changed, taking on a deep, booming cadence. "It would be a shame for all that power to go to waste . . . WHEN IT COULD BE . . . *MINE*."

The guard turned toward Gunnar and held his torch aloft unsurely, startled by his approach. But Gunnar stopped in mid-stride, surprised by who he saw.

It was an adolescent boy. The arm that held the torch was disfigured, deformed.

"Oh, um, hello," the boy said, his voice faltering. "You must be Admiral Gunnar."

Gunnar squinted at him. "Who. . . ? Who are you?"

The boy cleared his throat. "My name is Justus, Sir."

"Justus," said Gunnar.

Gunnar had been out of the loop for some time, but not so far that he hadn't heard about the false ethoul. The spy. The prisoner who had been brought to their camp by that Guardian, Kallorn.

But this wasn't right. Why was he out here? The boy was being kept prisoner, under close watch.

"What are you doing—?" Gunnar started to ask.

The rest of the words in Gunnar's mouth died as Justus turned. The light from the torch held by his bad arm revealed a dagger in his good hand. And in his shadow, the motionless body of an Army of Light soldier lay on the ground before him.

"I'm sorry, sir," said Justus, a tear breaking from the corner of his eye. "I didn't want this."

Gunnar reached to his side. But his cutlass wasn't there. Of course it wasn't—until a minute ago, he'd been sleeping. Thank the seas he hadn't been in his right mind enough to take off his bandolier before passing out in his tent. He pulled one of the lobber-balls from it, filled with a payload of specially selected seeds.

Gunnar threw the dried, empty rind at Justus's feet. He called on aurym.

Nothing happened.

Gunnar blinked in shock. Aurym was there. He could feel it. But it wasn't working, because. . . .

Frantically, Gunnar reached up to his left side of his face, where his left eye had once been, to the empty socket where, for several years now, an aurstone had been set in its place. He did not take it out often. Why he would have taken it out this time, he couldn't venture to guess.

But it wasn't there. It was back in his tent somewhere.

"I'm sorry, Sir," said Justus again, now with tears rolling down both sides of his cheeks. "But you don't know what it's like. He tells me what to do, and I can't. . . . I can't help it, Sir."

But I do know what it's like, thought Gunnar.

It was too late for the guard on the ground, but there were others close by. Gunnar opened his mouth to shout for help and sound the alarm, just as the voice in his head commanded calmly, "NOW. FREEZE."

The world went sideways. Gunnar's body and mind seized up. And the words he was about to yell died in his throat.

It hit him as it always did: detachment from his body, terror, déjà vu, and the smell of burning wood. Gunnar was left standing still, unable to do anything but watch as Justus stepped forward. The boy slipped the dagger into a scabbard at his belt and pulled out a length of rope. And in the light of Justus's faltering torch, Gunnar could now see, scattered on the ground, the dead bodies of several guards from the Army of Light. The standing silhouettes surrounding Justus, whom Gunnar had at first mistaken for other guards, turned in his direction in unison, as if they were many puppets on the same strings.

Their heads were like skulls, desiccated with blackened flesh stretched taut over the faces in some places and hanging loosely as if partially ripped off in others.

Cythwraiths. Dozens of them. Perhaps fifty. Perhaps a hundred. Perhaps more.

A small part of Gunnar could still think, even if he could not act on his thoughts. That still-functioning part of him recognized their clothing. It was the missing Raeqlu infantry unit. And behind them, he recognized some of Megara's people. All of them had been transformed into cythwraiths.

No! thought Gunnar.

"YES," said the voice.

Some of the cythwraiths walked toward him, while others continued past him, into the encampment of the Army of Light.

PART X

SUPPER'S

READY

CHAPTER 71

Innocen picked at some flesh between his teeth with a knife as he walked. It had been stuck there since before his transformation into a cythwraith, a remnant of his last meal as a human being. In all that time, he hadn't been granted control of his body to perform the simple act of freeing it.

Finally, with a satisfying scrape against enamel, the rotten meat came free, and Innocen spat it out onto the dusty ground. He sighed with relief. There was no feeling like it.

It was night, Innocen thought, but such things were difficult to tell when one had no eyes and could only see the world through the sensations of aurym and daemyn. He was, however, quite sure that it was raining. He did not know how long this small degree of freedom would continue to be afforded to him by the Nameless One, but being in control of one's own body was a privilege that he would never again take for granted. People really didn't know how good they had it.

Still, the sensation of this new body could be quite annoying at times. Frequently, as he ran, the once soft but now dried out tissues would crack in places. Or the remnants of desiccated old skin would flake off and be left behind. Most of the flesh of his cheeks was already gone, leaving his teeth and gums exposed. His hessian tunic had been shredded to rags that hung from him like a cloak of spiderwebs, yet he couldn't bring himself to part with the remnants. It felt like one of the few things still tying him to the person he had once been. And anyway, he could feel places in his upper back where the fabric was stuck fast in the oozing, open sores where his skin had split to reveal the demonic, chitinous black bone beneath. If he were to peel the clothing off, he wasn't sure how much of his skin would come with it.

All this was far preferable to what it felt like when the Nameless One was in control—when Innocen's consciousness was sequestered to a tiny corner of his mind, and every part of him was locked in endless agony.

Considering the alternative, he had no choice but to do as the Nameless One told him. And so, as ordered, and after several days of running through the forests of the Mistlands of Erum, Innocen was almost to Rohghost.

Situated on an isthmus that jutted out into the sea, separating the Bay of Anemoi from the Ellenean Ocean, Rohghost had only one approach by land: a barren canyon between a set of ancient walls. It was known as the Thunder Corridor.

The floor of this place was a dusty causeway, beaten down by the passage of eons' worth of travel. The walls, meanwhile, might have been mistaken for a natural canyon if not for their straightness and uniformity. It seemed clear that these high walls were the remnants of some ancient civilization, though the passage of time had hidden most of the features.

Partway through the empty corridor, Innocen stopped, struck by how loudly his footsteps echoed in the silence of this empty canyon. . . . And how easy it was to hear the approach of the group of several giant creatures that he suddenly realized were crawling over the top of the walls.

With a cry of ambush, several great forms, larger than cythraul, twenty feet tall if they were an inch, vaulted down from the top of the walls on both sides. There were ten of them at least, and they came sliding down the sides of the manmade canyon at nearly free-fall speed before landing sure-footedly on the Corridor floor, some in front and some behind.

Innocen had always been small-statured, even by human standards, and each of these creatures was four times his height. Some of them wore rags. But others, he was surprised to see, were outfitted in giant sets of armor and carried huge weapons. Each one had a single great eye in the center of its head.

The foremost of the cyclopes, holding a sword twice as long as Innocen was tall, stepped forward to look down on him.

A'thri'ik weapons and armor, realized Innocen.

"CREATURES FROM ANOTHER TIME," rang the voice of the Nameless One inside Innocen's head. "NOT VERY INTELLIGENT. BUT STILL, THEY HAVE THEIR PURPOSES."

They're on our side? asked Innocen, mentally.

The head cyclops charged without warning, swinging its sword at Innocen. It moved remarkably quickly, considering its size. But the thing might as well have been moving underwater compared to Innocen's hyd-powered movements.

I'll take that as a no, thought Innocen.

He jumped straight up and over the horizontal swing of the massive sword. He heard the hiss of its passage behind him as the air was violently displaced by the attack.

The swing brought the creature's arm close enough that it was no great reach for Innocen to latch himself onto one of its a'thri'ik pauldrons and, in a few quick motions, climb hand-over-hand up the front of the monster's body.

Innocen had made many mistakes in his life. But if there was one lesson he'd learned, it was to do what you were going to do without any hesitation, before the other party could act—no putting yourself at unnecessary risk. If he'd always lived by such a policy, he might not have found himself in this body. But, as it was, all he could do was make the best of what he still had. So he did not hesitate as he lunged for the cyclops's head, drove the knife he'd been using to pick his teeth deep into the corner of the creature's eye socket, and pried outward.

CHAPTER 72

Gunnar's body was still locked up, his every muscle frozen in place, as the boy named Justus finished tightening the knot that bound his hands together. The rest of the rope extended in a length outward from Gunnar's hands. Behind Justus, dozens of shadowed forms of cythwraiths came forward, stepping over the dead bodies of guards.

Move, thought Gunnar, feeling the intensifying rain batter against his head. *Don't just stand here like this and let it happen. Do something. Defend yourself!*

"You will move," said the voice in his mind, "WHEN I TELL YOU TO MOVE."

Thunder rolled in the distance. Justus's shoulders twitched at the sound of it. He looked down at the body of the nearest Army of Light soldier on the ground before him and let out a shaky, nervous breath. Gunnar realized that he could see the shallow rise and fall of the soldier's chest.

"I—I didn't kill him, sir," said Justus. "Master Avagad lets me do things my own way, sometimes. I did it like I did with Justin. My father was a healer, so I know some of the powders and potions they use, how much to use to put a man to sleep, and what flavors to use to hide the taste of it in a drink. I don't want to hurt anybody, so I don't, when I can help it. But these others. . . . The turned ones did it. They killed them. I can't stop them. They don't belong to Avagad like I do. They belong to the Nameless One. I can't control what they do."

Justus tugged on the length of rope as if Gunnar were a dog on a leash.

"WALK," commanded the voice in Gunnar's head.

To his disgust, his legs began to move, and as the small army of cythwraiths lingered about the edge of the encampment, Justus led Gunnar the opposite way—out of camp, toward the darkness of the surrounding woods.

"It might not be so bad," said Justus. "Avagad first contacted me through dreams. Then, after a while, he could talk to me while I was awake. He tells me to do things, but when I do well, he rewards me sometimes. Like when I was in the fortress, with that Warlord. Being her prisoner, pretending to be Justin, was unpleasant. But Master Avagad gave me the most wonderful dreams."

They don't belong to Avagad like I do, thought Gunnar. *They belong to the Nameless One. . . .*

Gunnar tried to focus. What did that mean? He felt certain that if only he could clear his mind enough to collect his thoughts, he would have the willpower to fight this dark force that had taken control of his body. But when was the last time he'd had a clear mind? It was almost never clear anymore.

He'd been trying to silence the voice. But had he, instead, made it easier for the dark force to slip in?

Gunnar recognized the facial features and clothing of some of the cythwraiths passing him by. Some, he knew only as acquaintances he'd met in passing. Others, he remembered by name. People he had served with.

Was that his fate? Was that the Nameless One's plan for him?

"IT IS NOT FOR YOU TO KNOW *MY PLAN*," said the voice.

Get out of my head! Gunnar commanded inside his mind.

"NO," said the voice. "MY HEAD NOW, GUNNAR. MY HEAD. MY BODY. MY POWER."

Gunnar's legs continued to move as the leash tugged him forward, pulled by Justus.

Of course their presence in this part of the world had not gone unnoticed by the enemy. And of course demon attacks had been rare.

The Raeqlu infantry unit that had disappeared. Megara's missing people. The Army of Light's poor census-taking. Instead of attacking, the demons were picking off small groups and individuals one at a time, turning them into cythwraiths instead of killing them—snatching people right out from under their noses.

And now, it was happening to Gunnar.

The voice. The control over his mind. How many others, he wondered, had succumbed to this very sort of fate? How many, acting on dark thoughts from outside of themselves, or having their very bodies commandeered, had simply wandered off into the woods at night to never be seen or heard from again? Marched off to join, willingly or unwillingly, the cause of the enemy?

We didn't sneak in unnoticed, thought Gunnar. *The enemy knew we were here all along.*

"YES, I KNOW YOU ARE HERE," agreed the voice in response to Gunnar's thoughts. "AND I AM QUITE PREPARED FOR YOUR ARRIVAL."

But something about that statement rang false to Gunnar.

No, he thought. *You're not prepared.*

Otherwise, why would you need me? Or any of these others? Otherwise, why not just send your cythraul to attack our army whenever you pleased?

And there was something else.

It's Justin, isn't it? thought Gunnar. *You're not prepared for him.*

Gunnar felt something shudder painfully through him. Not a thought or spoken words, but something more like raw emotion. Anger. And perhaps, unless he was incorrect, something like unease.

And in that brief moment of anger and unease, Gunnar blinked his eye. His body was, for a split second, partially under his control again.

Quickly, Gunnar tried to move his hands. But, just as quickly as the darkness had lost control over him, it regained it.

"THE ANGEL'S POWERS HAVE BECOME FORMIDABLE," said the voice in Gunnar's head. "BUT I HAVE SERVANTS WHO CAN CONTEND WITH HIM. SERVANTS LIKE AVAGAD. . . . SERVANTS LIKE *YOU*, GUNNAR."

Servants like Avagad and Gunnar? Avagad served this thing? And Gunnar was on the same level?

Go to hell, thought Gunnar.

"INTERESTING CHOICE OF WORDS," said the voice. "LET US GO THERE TOGETHER."

CHAPTER 73

Innocen held tight to the hilt of the knife as the monster thrashed and roared in tones so deep that they shook him to the bone. His knife strike had found its mark at the corner of the creature's eye socket, but to Innocen's surprise, it hadn't punctured the eye. Instead of the soft ocular tissue he'd expected to find, the cyclops's eye was as tough as leather.

Innocen attempted to wedge his knife deeper, to pry outward, to gouge the eye from its socket. But even hyd-powered strength wasn't enough to keep his grip as the six-fingered hand of the cyclops swatted him and sent him flying.

Innocen landed on the dry floor of the Thunder Corridor, tumbled once, got his hands beneath him, and flipped himself up to land surely on his feet in a cloud of dust. Ahead of him, the leader of the cyclopes was remarkably unfazed by the knife still protruding from the corner of its eye socket. Its single eyelid twitched a bit. Nothing more. It glared at Innocen. And so did the other nine giants.

The strike of the massive hand had torn loose part of what remained of Innocen's scalp, which now hung from the side of his head like bark stripped from a tree. He reached up, peeled his scalp off in annoyance, leaving a string of flesh behind, and discarded it. It landed on the dusty corridor floor, looking like a pelt. The air felt surprisingly cold against his exposed skull.

"THESE ONES ARE NOT MY SERVANTS," said the Nameless One in Innocen's head. "BUT I HAVE A GROWING COLLECTION OF THEM."

I see, thought Innocen as the ten cyclopes started forward, converging on him.

One of them attacked. It moved more cautiously than the first one now that it had seen what Innocen was capable of. Still, Innocen was able to easily avoid the massive war hammer coming down at him in an overhand swing. The head of it sank a foot deep into the ground where he'd been standing a half-second before, throwing up an eruption of rubble.

"LEAD THESE ONES TO ROHGHOST, SO I CAN ADD THEM TO MY COLLECTION," said the Nameless One. "PROVE YOU CAN DO THIS WITHOUT LOSING ANY OF THEM, AND I MAY ALLOW YOU TO CONTINUE TO CONTROL THIS FORM."

Can I have just one? It has been so long, and I hunger for living aurym.

Another attack in Innocen's direction. Another easy evasion. But they were coming all at once now.

"I WILL CONSIDER IT," said the Nameless One.

Innocen grinned. He jumped, struck one of the cyclopes in the side of its head just to antagonize the creature, and then took off running down the Thunder Corridor toward Rohghost. Glancing over his shoulder, he was delighted to see all ten of the rage-fueled monsters were in pursuit.

CHAPTER 74

Gunnar's body continued to walk forward, led by the rope in the boy's hands. He could do nothing about it. Could say nothing. Could make no noise that might alert someone, anyone, to what was happening. All the while, the shadows of the cythwraiths lingered, barely visible in the darkness. He couldn't tell if they were there to attack or to cover Justus's escape, with him as a hostage.

"I really am sorry," Justus was mumbling as they walked, and the tone of his voice was so pitiful that Gunnar was almost inclined to believe him. "I have no ill will toward you personally, Sir, and I hate to do this."

"YOU SEE THE PATHETIC SLIME AVAGAD FINDS TO SERVE HIM?" said the voice in Gunnar's head. "HIS DAYS ARE NUMBERED. SOON, HE, LIKE YOU, WILL BE MINE, FULLY."

The implication hit Gunnar hard. This darkness that had ensnared him—*Avagad* served *it*. But there was conflict there. The darkness had contempt for him.

All this time, we thought Avagad was the master, thought Gunnar.

"MASTER?" said the voice. "AVAGAD IS NOTHING."

Gunnar silently cursed himself. Were *none* of his thoughts safe from this thing?

"This shouldn't have had to happen to you, Sir," Justus was saying. "It was the queen who Avagad was really after. That's why I had to pretend to be Justin. To set a trap for her. But then Justin himself showed up, and she got away, and so we had to take you instead, and. . . . And it shouldn't have come to this, is all. I promise you, I really don't wish any ill will—"

Justus's words were abruptly cut off. The young man gave a muffled cry and fell over sideways as something connected with the side of his head.

Another painful ripple of emotion shot through Gunnar's being. This time, the predominant feeling was shock—shock strong enough that Gunnar's legs stopped obeying the darkness's commands.

Justus's body hit the ground in a limp heap. The length of rope that bound Gunnar hung slack from its tether at his wrists.

"You see that?!" came a lisping voice from the shadows. "Got the little bugger first try!"

Borris!

Justus lay motionless on the ground before Gunnar. The rock Borris had hit him with rested in the mud nearby. The cythwraiths, which had been still as statues a moment before, all turned toward the source of the voice.

"I hope ye've got about fifty more rocks or it was fer nothin', ya braggart!"

Pool!

As one, the cythwraiths started moving.

In the lapse of the darkness's hold on Gunnar, he kneeled, grabbed the knife from the scabbard that hung from Justus's belt, and began to saw at the rope that bound his wrists.

"*STAY!*" boomed the voice in Gunnar's mind.

Gunnar dropped the knife and nearly fell to the ground, his entire body locking up. He was frozen again.

But at the same instant, there came a sound like a ship's hull slamming against a rocky shore. Gunnar felt the impact emanate up through his feet, and several of the cythwraiths ahead of him were suddenly thrown backward by a shockwave. Gunnar was free enough to move his head, and now that he knew where to look, he saw the source: an aurym-powered attack, from a massive battle hammer with a flat mallet surface on one side and a spike like a pickaxe on the other.

Ptolemec.

With a whooping war cry, another figure raced forward out of the shadows, leading with a long spear, driving it through cythwraiths that had been knocked to the ground.

Elzirda.

A cythwraith near Ptolemec raised a club, preparing to strike him. There came a loud *clack* from somewhere in the darkness, and the cythwraith went down, the gleam of a crossbow bolt's projectile point visible protruding from its head in the torchlight.

Estoq, too! Gunnar thought. *But that won't be enough.*

"Attackers!" shouted Gunnar. "To arms! To—!"

"*SILENCE!*"

Pain lanced through Gunnar's head. It dropped him to the ground, made him writhe in agony.

The feeling of shock emanating from the darkness within Gunnar was galvanizing into anger. While some of the cythwraiths started attacking the newcomers, others came lurching forward, toward Gunnar.

That was when a beam of green energy suddenly illuminated the night and came sweeping through several of the closest cythwraiths.

Two of them were sliced in half by solid aurym. A few more went reeling backward with screams of pain, smoking from contact with the energy.

Justin? thought Gunnar in surprise.

And then, following the beam with his eye, he spotted a small figure outfitted in full a'thri'ik armor, with a glowing green sword raised.

No, he realized. *Itz!*

Itzacoatl the Ecbatan, the old man Leah had befriended beneath the Shifting Mountains and a user of a'thri'ik like Justin, swung his sword again. Another beam of aurym power went sizzling through the night, cutting down cythwraiths one after another. It was followed shortly by another shockwave from Ptolemec's battle hammer. Elzirda, meanwhile, pressed the attack, dodging the swing of an ax from a cythwraith before her, then driving her spear through its throat and out the back of its neck. Another came at her from the side only to fall, clutching at a crossbow bolt protruding from its abdomen.

In the middle of the intensifying chaos, Gunnar heard what he had been waiting for: a loud blast from a horn, sounding the alarm to wake the encampment.

But Gunnar couldn't move, still couldn't do anything but stand stock still.

"*ENOUGH!*" commanded the voice in his head, brimming with rage. "TIME TO GO. *NOW!*"

To Gunnar's horror, his body started to run—away from camp. Toward the darkness of the surrounding forest. Toward the cythwraiths.

"Wait! Stop, Cap'n!" said someone from beside him.

Before he had gotten more than a few feet away from Justus's unconscious body, someone snagged the rope still attached to his tethered hands. He had hardly even managed to fray the fibers in the brief moment of lucidness when he'd had the knife, and his bonds held tight.

Gunnar's body was pulled back around by the counterweight only long enough to see who was holding the other end.

Pool, his old crewmate from the original *Gryphon*, his fishing buddy from the Greenspring River, and one of his only real, enduring friends in this world held the other end of the rope. He clutched it with a look that was part determination, part desperation, trying to keep Gunnar in place.

"Not that way!" said Pool.

Gunnar's body, of no fault of his own, wrenched hard against Pool's grip on the rope. With devilish strength beyond his own, he managed to turn back around and keep moving, making forward progress in spite of the rounder, heavier man's full weight anchoring him.

As Gunnar pulled himself along, a set of arms suddenly grabbed him around the chest and hugged him tightly, attempting to hold him back.

"Cap'n! Not that way, please!" said Borris, close to Gunnar's ear.

Even with Pool and Borris both trying to hold him back, Gunnar's body, independent of his mind, continued to surge forward with improbable force.

Borris resorted to sliding downward until his arms were squeezed tightly around Gunnar's knees. He made himself dead weight, his legs dragging along the ground behind him. And still, Gunnar kept moving.

"KILL THEM," said the voice in Gunnar's head.

No! Gunnar screamed inside his mind.

He could only watch as his own body stopped moving, turned, and brought both of his tethered fists down together onto the top of Borris's head.

Borris's body jolted with the impact, but his hands still gripped to Gunnar like grim death, his fingers clawing at his boots. Gunnar could see approaching torches, could hear shouting and clashing of weapons as the Army of Light rushed to face the cythwraiths, but they would get here too late. Gunnar's hands were already reaching down, wrapping the rope around Borris's neck and pulling it tight to strangle him.

"Sorry for this, Cap'n," said a voice from behind, "but ye'll thank me in the mornin'!"

Gunnar's head whipped around. He only had time to register Pool coming at him, rock in hand, before he felt the impact against the side of his skull, and everything went black.

CHAPTER 75

Olorus got to the tent before Hook, moving at a pace much closer to a run than Hook's more measured stride. It wasn't that he was unhurried; he was just too focused on keeping an eye on the shadows around him to risk being caught off-guard due to carelessness.

Given what had happened earlier this night, one couldn't be too cautious.

Hook checked both sides of the command tent before entering and found them clear, then threw back the flap and ducked in out of the rain. He found Zechariah standing in the center of the tent, the interior lit by a combination of lanternlight and the green glow of a'thri'ik armor pieces. Surrounding Zechariah were Olorus, Adonica, Kallorn, Itz, Lycon, Megara, and a woman with a crossbow strapped to her back whom Hook recognized as a frequent companion of Gunnar's recently: Estoq.

Olorus joined the others at the center of the tent. But Hook, for now, was content to linger in the corner. Only Adonica looked up, briefly, to acknowledge his presence.

"Is this a common occurrence in your camp?" Kallorn was asking. "To have demons attempt to abduct people in the night?"

"We have examined the fallen," Olorus said, ignoring Kallorn's question. "It appears that many of the cythwraiths are from that missing Raeqlu regiment we've been wondering about. Plus, some soldiers who had been serving under Megara until recently."

Megara hung her head in sorrow.

"The ones who disappeared," said Zechariah. "As if they had simply wandered off in the night."

"The very same," said Olorus.

"Kinda like how Gunnar was wandering off," said Adonica, "with that boy, Justus, leading the way."

"He almost got away from us," said Estoq. "Gunnar could have disappeared into the woods, and we might never have even known what happened to him if not for his two mates."

"Borris and Pool?" said Lycon.

"When they saw that Gunnar was missing from his tent, they went searching for him and spotted Justus tying him up," said Estoq. "They didn't want to raise an alarm straight away for fear that it would alert Justus and give him a chance to escape. So they ducked into the nearest tent to ask for help. It just so happened that I, and the rest of the crew from the vertical city, were there. Us and, thankfully, Itz."

Itz, who still had his a'thri'ik sword sheathed at his side with one hand draped over it, smiled and gave a little bow.

"Borris led us there," continued Estoq, "and to everyone's surprise, Borris himself attacked first. With all the aurstones around, he made do with an ordinary rock. A beauty of a shot, and down went the false ethoul."

Zechariah stroked his beard with his good hand, deep in thought, and in the ensuing silence, Hook found himself studying the interior of the tent.

Perhaps it was a strange time to take note of such a thing, but Hook had become aware that, over the course of the time that Leah had been gone, the command tent that had served as her base of operations, where she carried out duties related to leading the Army of Light, seemed to have become Zechariah's permanent abode. Leah's belongings had been relegated to a crate in the corner. Her maps were marked up with the old man's handwriting.

When they'd had their meeting of officers and leaders, who was it who had done all the talking, and from a position of assumed authority? And how long had it been since he had called on a meeting of Leah's advisors to discuss a matter of strategy? On the contrary, the old man seemed to be making a great deal of decisions unilaterally, without consulting anyone at all.

In short, it was becoming increasingly easy to forget that Zechariah was only leading the Army of Light in an interim capacity.

Or, he is only supposed to be, thought Hook.

"Estoq, was it?" said Zechariah. "Thank you. You are dismissed. I shall call on you if I have any further questions."

Estoq was visibly taken aback by the terseness of her sudden dismissal. But she took a deep breath and nodded.

"Yes, Sir," she said.

She brushed past Hook and exited the tent with a look of clear annoyance on her face. Judging by the troubled glances shared between Lycon and Adonica, and Megara and Olorus, at the exchange, Hook wasn't the only one perturbed by it all.

"The cythwraiths and the boy were eradicated, I take it?" said Zechariah, turning his attention to Itzacoatl.

"The cythwraiths, yes," said Itz. "Only a few escaped from us and retreated into the forest. But the boy lives. He has been healed of his head injury and is back in custody."

"How the hell did he get free in the first place?" demanded Olorus, wheeling on Kallorn.

Kallorn arched a yellow eyebrow. "He was left under the watch of several guards. Nolians, if my memory serves. I wonder, has anyone checked to see if those guards are accounted for? Or have they, too, *wandered off?*"

"I . . . don't know," admitted Olorus.

"I'll find out as soon as we're done here," said Lycon.

"A census," said Zechariah. "I've been telling Leah for months, we must take a bloody census, and we must keep it updated with all these *strays* she keeps taking in! And we must perform head counts every night to see that everyone is accounted for. I will instate the policy tomorrow, *myself.*"

Only now did Hook, frowning deeply, step forward to gain the attention of the room.

"The boy, Justus, described being contacted by Avagad in dreams," signed Hook. *"He said he was given instructions. Made to do things."*

Olorus growled in frustration. "There's always some new devilry with this enemy. . . ."

"That is twice now that the kid has caused problems," signed Megara.

"That's right," said Adonica. "At what point do we stop being such pushovers and put a stop to it permanently?"

"That was my vote for dealing with him the first time," said Kallorn. "But your commander—*and* Justin—both ordered that he be kept alive."

"The situation has changed," said Zechariah. "We may have to take matters into our own hands."

"Justin seemed to think that that boy might serve some greater purpose," said Kallorn. "Personally, I would prefer to do things my way. But I also find myself trusting those two. Their instructions may yet prove prudent in some way that I cannot foresee."

"You all miss my point," signed Hook, signing with large, sweeping gestures so as to quiet them all. *"If Avagad can communicate with a boy through dreams, and if our people can be tricked into leaving the safety of camp, then could other things be happening we do not yet know about?*

"And, instead of being instructed to wander off in the night, what else could they be made to do?"

For a few moments, everyone was silent.

Then Hook signed, *"Has anyone* here *been hearing voices?"*

Those present exchanged looks with one another. One by one, Olorus, Hook, Megara, Kallorn, Lycon, Adonica, and Itz all shook their heads to indicate the negative, but it was strange that nobody said a word. No one but Zechariah.

"I don't wish to even broach this subject," he said. "But, considering the circumstances and all that has happened, I'm afraid we can't keep waiting on Leah and Justin like this. Our enemy has clearly gained unprecedented power if he, or they, or whoever or whatever it is, can so thoroughly invade the mind and turn friend into foe. I fear that the longer we tarry, the more incidences like this will happen. It may be more prudent for us to take action."

"Take what action?" Olorus prodded.

Zechariah brought his hook-hand down on one of the maps unfurled before him—one of *Leah's* maps.

"March on the demons' lands," said Zechariah. "Use the island chain Lycon's research discovered to bypass the Bay of Anemoi and take the Army up the peninsula, into the heart of the demon lands. Proceed with the plan. Rely on our numbers. And topple Avagad from his seat of power, as we meant to do from the very start."

"Without the Commander's consent?" said Adonica, squinting a bit.

"And without the ethoul?" signed Megara. *"Even when we know he has returned?"*

"The boy is powerful," spoke up Olorus. "I saw it with my own eyes."

"He's close enough now that he could help us," said Itz.

"*If* we wait for him," added Kallorn.

"With all due respect, Advisor," said Lycon. He placed no special emphasis on Zechariah's title, but it could not have been a coincidence that he chose to use it. "I don't know how many of us would be willing to go along with a plan that goes against Commander Anavion's wishes."

Zechariah took this all in, then stepped forward, cleared his throat meaningfully, and crossed his arms in a slow, deliberate fashion. The display was dramatic enough that nobody paid Hook, who had stepped back in the corner, much mind.

Slowly, carefully, Hook slid his belt knife from its scabbard, and as Zechariah began to speak, he moved the knife to hold it hidden behind his back.

"You individuals represent the inner circle of this army," Zechariah said, lowering his voice to speak beneath his breath. "If we can all agree on that, then let us also agree that what I am about to say *shall not leave* this tent."

Slowly, Zechariah exchanged looks with every person assembled. Hook thumbed the edge of the knife behind his back as Zechariah watched him.

"Perhaps," Zechariah said, "this army should proceed, with Leah's consent . . . whether she has given it to us or not."

Hook could feel the change of atmosphere. Several of the members of Leah's inner circle were preparing to speak up at once, Olorus and Adonica not least of all. But Zechariah cut them all off before anyone could say a word.

"Now is not the time to decide," he said, speaking in a voice so much louder than his previous statement that he regained total and utter command of the room. "For the moment, I bid you think on my words. We will reconvene and discuss this matter at a more auspicious hour. But know, all of you, that this war is happening with or without Leah and Justin alongside us."

It was a testament to the old man's charisma that his word alone was enough for even *this* group to consider the matter closed.

One by one, they departed. Lycon, Adonica, Megara, Kallorn, Itz, everyone. No one noticed as Hook pushed the tip of the knife behind his back into the fabric of the tent, just behind his position in the corner, and silently cut a small slit.

Finally, it was only Zechariah, Olorus, and Hook who remained inside the command tent. Then, to Hook's surprise, even Olorus turned and left without a word.

Zechariah locked gazes with Hook. Hook stared back at him. He had already discretely replaced his belt knife in its scabbard. But it was hard to read the old man, hard to tell what he had or hadn't seen, or what he knew or didn't know.

It was Zechariah who finally stood down, bending over the maps at the table before him and rubbing at his eyes.

Hook turned and exited the tent.

But he did not go far.

CHAPTER 76

A louder-than-usual rumble of thunder woke Justin. Even after he opened his eyes, it took him a few moments to realize where he was: in the overgrown temple.

Or perhaps it hadn't been the thunder that had woken him. He had a terrible feeling deep in his heart. Or maybe in his gut. Somewhere, something had gone terribly wrong.

"*Daemyn is corrupted aurym,*" rang Avagad's words in his head. "*The Nameless One takes the life force of aurym, distorts it, taints it, and recycles it as his own.*"

Justin tried to shake off the sensation by taking stock of his surroundings. He had fallen asleep seated with his back to the hearth, and several hours must have passed because the fire within it had died down to nothing but softly glowing coals, providing minimal light or warmth.

Rainwater was leaking through the cracks and openings in the temple roof in a dozen places, enough that it had formed a puddle on the floor that had reached the leg of his trousers. He moved his leg away from the puddle and, in repositioning himself, realized that Leah was still beside him, still leaning against him, her head against his shoulder. She, too, had fallen asleep, but his movement caused her to stir awake.

As one, their faces turned toward one another. Their foreheads touched. Wordlessly, as if it had been decided upon long beforehand, they pressed their lips together.

Justin felt Leah's fingertips tracing lines down his back. He placed his hand on her hip to pull her closer. There was only the rain against the temple roof, the rumble of distant thunder, the moths silently tracing glowing lines in the air, and them.

CHAPTER 77

Hook took only a few steps from the command tent before stopping in his tracks, ducking low, and slipping into the shadows.

Hiding and fighting, thought Hook.

With the thunder rolling in the distance and the rain coming down all around him, Hook crept back to the corner where he had been standing in the interior of the tent a few moments before.

"Has anyone here been hearing voices?" Hook had asked, to which everyone assembled had shaken their heads to indicate the negative.

Everyone but Zechariah, who had not answered at all.

Carefully, Hook positioned himself at the spot of the cut he had made in the tent fabric with his belt knife, at about eye-level in a crouching position, and he peered through the tiny hole.

At first, all he saw was the interior of the command tent, precisely as he'd left it, with the old man in the same position, bent over Leah's maps, looking like his usual self.

But then, something happened.

Hook would have been hard-pressed to accurately describe what he saw, but it was as if something suddenly went out of Zechariah. Like he was exhaling a breath that he'd been holding for a long time. All at once, there was something different about the old man.

Hook's eyes narrowed. It was hard to place what exactly had changed. Something about Zechariah's body language. His posture. The way he carried himself.

It was as if, all at once, he was. . . .

A different person, thought Hook. *I'm seeing a different person entirely.*

It was as if Zechariah was gone. In his place was someone who simply looked like him.

The person who had been Zechariah stood completely still. Then, he casually stretched out his good hand in midair as if reaching for something.

From across the tent, a quill suddenly leaped, untouched, from its place in an inkwell. It shot across the room as if pulled upon by invisible strings. He didn't even bother looking up as the quill landed securely in his outstretched hand, and he bent over the map and started making notes.

As the old man wrote, Hook thought he saw his lips moving. He was mumbling something under his breath. Talking.

To himself, wondered Hook, *or to someone else?*

CHAPTER 78

"They don't belong to Avagad like I do," Justus had said. "They belong to the Nameless One."

Gunnar's eye snapped open.

Or at least, he thought it did. For a while, despite his eye being open, his surroundings remained black. Even when a bit of nearby lanternlight made it through, everything remained hazy and indistinct.

He blinked to try to clear his vision and was greeted with a pain in his head unlike anything he'd ever felt before, right behind his eyes. He reached up to his face and found his fingers shaking violently. Sweat coated his skin. His hair was soaked with it. His good eye stung. And the room around him silently spun.

His stomach heaved. Urgency spurred him to motion, but his body felt so hollow and his muscles so weak that despite his best effort, he hadn't even fully turned over before the vomit was squeezed out of his convulsing stomach and came racing out of his throat. Most of it ended up on his shoulder, some on the floor, and the rest on his face. A set of hands helped turn his head the rest of the way, preventing any of it from going back down his throat.

When Gunnar's hollow insides ceased squeezing like a set of bellows, he looked up to see that the hands holding him were Lycon's. He was in his quarters, in his own bed, in his tent.

Lycon sighed. "How do you feel?"

"Maybe the worst," said Gunnar, "that I've ever felt in my life."

"That makes sense," said Lycon.

Gunnar's whole body felt empty. Every part of him was quivering. He felt hot and cold at the same time. And his brain felt like it had been impaled on a spike.

"My head," said Gunnar, squeezing his eye shut. The pain pulsated between his temples, throbbing with every beat of his heart.

"You were so drunk that Pool had to crack you a good one to stop you from running into danger," said Lycon. "You even attacked Borris. Do you remember?"

Gunnar nodded. He remembered, all right. He decided to refrain from telling Lycon that it hadn't been drunkenness that had made him do those things.

"You owe the two of them your life," said Lycon.

"Where are they?" asked Gunnar.

"I came to give them a break so they could sleep a few hours," said Lycon. "You've been in and out of consciousness for the past two days. They've been tending to you all that time."

"Two days? That long?" said Gunnar. "I don't. . . ."

He trailed off, felt himself about to be sick again, and leaned over. Lycon had to help him again just so he could get clear of the bed. When it was all over, he collapsed back into the bed and lay there, shaking.

"What's happening?" he gasped. "Why . . . do I feel like this?"

"As I said," said Lycon, in the process of dipping a rag into a bowl of water and wiping down Gunnar's bedroll, "it has been almost two days."

Apparently, Lycon thought that this was explanation enough for what was happening. He did not seem particularly happy to be dealing with Gunnar's troublemaking again. How could Gunnar hope to try to explain that this time, it had been different?

The flap of the tent opened, spilling infernal, piercing daylight into his quarters. Gunnar groaned and shielded his eyes.

"He's up!" said Pool.

"Blimey, it's good to see him awake," said Borris.

"Yes, he's up," agreed Lycon. "I'll be back with more rags and some fresh water. He's going to need them."

With that, the big man took his leave.

As Borris and Pool took up positions beside Gunnar's bedroll, Gunnar looked up at them.

"I'd be in deep bilge right now if it weren't for you two," he said. "Thanks, boys. It's lucky you were watching."

"Well, it weren't luck, exactly," said Borris, looking embarrassed.

"We was keeping an eye on you, Cap'n," said Pool. "Been worried about you, the way you've been acting."

Gunnar managed a small, appreciative chuckle and was about to say something properly irreverent to lighten the mood when he noticed the fresh scar on Borris's head, just beneath the hairline.

"Did I do that?" he asked.

Borris shrugged. "With all the dumb scrapes I been in over the years, who can say where they all come from?"

A fresh tremor ran through Gunnar, shaking him from head to foot and causing his hollow-feeling insides to contract.

"Boys," said Gunnar. "Find me something to drink."

Borris licked his lips uncomfortably. Neither he nor Pool said a word.

"Come on, lads," said Gunnar. "We used to suck the Brig's barrels dry. When we went, we went large. Nothing's changed, has it?"

"Yes, it has," said Pool.

The sternness in the little man's voice seemed to surprise Borris just as much as it did Gunnar.

"Cap'n," said Pool. "We're gonna help you."

"If you want to help me," said Gunnar, "get me something to drink."

"This is the only way, Gunnar," said Borris.

Gunnar felt himself quivering again as he looked at Borris. He didn't think he could remember a time when Borris had called him by his first name. It was always Cap'n—or Admiral when he actually remembered Gunnar's correct title and rank.

"We'll help ye through this," said Borris. "We'll take care of ye."

Gunnar felt his teeth clenching in frustration. But no, it was not frustration. It was anger. Anger at the two of them for what they were doing to him. And somehow, at the very same time, love for them for what they were *trying* to do.

He closed his eye tight and fought against another wave of nausea and pain.

Are you still in here, you bastard? he thought. *Are you enjoying all this?*

No response. For the first time in a long time, no response from the voice in his head.

"Fine," said Gunnar. "All right, damn it, fine. It won't work anyway if it has to be done for me against my will. So if it makes you two happy, I'll do it."

Borris and Pool smiled at one another in astonished relief.

"Just, for now," said Gunnar, "let me rest. I feel tired. Sick and very, very tired."

"Aye-aye, Cap'n," said Pool.

Borris said nothing but gave a sloppy salute.

Then the two stood and exited the tent, leaving Gunnar alone on his bedroll, feeling sick and miserable and as if he wanted to die, but somehow, new.

You didn't get me, thought Gunnar, resting his head and closing his eye. *You tried, and you got close, but you failed. You can't get Gunnar Erix Nimbus so easily.*

No response again.

At least, not at first.

"FAILED?" said the voice in Gunnar's head, so loud and sudden that it made Gunnar gasp in spite of his resolve. "YOU ARE ALREADY MINE."

No, thought Gunnar. *No, damn it. Please, no—!*

The world went sideways.

Gunnar's every muscle locked up. Pain lanced through his head. A fresh outflow of vomit rose up from his stomach, and this time, he could not turn himself.

"*EVERY LAST ONE* OF YOU," said the voice of the Nameless One, "IS ALREADY MINE. YOU JUST DON'T KNOW IT YET."

Alone in the tent, Gunnar lay still and stiff on the bedroll, feeling the vomit bubble and gargle where it pooled in the back of his mouth. He couldn't clear it.

He was running out of air. He was choking. It was sliding down into his lungs.

"SWEET DREAMS, GUNNAR."

Gunnar's world faded to black.

CHAPTER 79

Innocen had flesh stuck between his teeth again. He greatly wished he still had his knife to pick it free with, but he hadn't thought to pull it from the eye socket of the cyclops. Instead, he had to settle for the sharp, bony tip of his own blackened, skeletal index finger, wiggling it back and forth between his teeth to try to pry the fresh piece of meat free.

The Thunder Corridor was behind him, as were the cyclopes. True to his word, the Nameless One had dealt with them, using an ambush not so different from the one Innocen had fallen victim to within the manmade canyon.

Nine of the cyclopes were now the Nameless One's thralls, new additions to a growing collection of cythwraith-cyclopes.

But the tenth and smallest of the cyclopes, the Nameless One had given to Innocen.

Finally, Innocen managed to pick the cyclops flesh free from between his teeth. Instead of spitting it out, he sucked it down his throat.

Innocen had heard that these lands fell within the borders of the Ecbatan Empire, but the closer he'd gotten to Rohghost, the clearer it had become that many years had passed since any human occupation had been attempted here. Either it was too dangerous to live in these lands, or the region's dark reputation preceded it.

To call Rohghost a city was a bit liberal. It had once been one, long ago. Now, it was only a maze of ruins. But demons were not known for being selective about their creature comforts.

Cythraul waited tirelessly atop the defenses of Rohghost—walls that had probably stood twenty or thirty feet tall long ago but had since been eroded so thoroughly by the strong ocean winds that what remained were only smoothed humps of stone. In places, it looked as if the demons had attempted to repair breaks in the wall, but mostly, they had been left to deteriorate. Little wonder. After all, what *wall* was stronger than a cythraul?

And yet, thought Innocen as he passed through the gates and into the city, *what are they defending?*

Demons had no need for cities. They didn't even need shelter. With the Nameless One's prescient hive mind, even a base of operations was unnecessary. And yet, here they were. But why?

Innocen had been given no further instructions yet, only to enter Rohghost. So he walked through the streets, examining the strange architecture. Many of the structures seemed to have once been pyramidal in shape, but the hands of time had turned them into irregular, misshapen domes, many with collapsed ceilings or parts missing. The dusty ground beneath his feet was beaten flat and marred with the tracks of coblyns and cythraul alike. The city's interior, however, had far fewer demons than he would have expected.

After a few minutes, he began to hear something. A loud banging and pinging. Following the noise, he found himself at a half-collapsed complex of buildings. The missing walls gave him a clear view of the interior: a great foundry with glowing furnaces and smoke pouring into the air. The forges and anvils were being worked not by cythraul or coblyns but by wraiths—half-demons that had once been human. Poor wretches like Innocen, in other words. Dozens of them worked to smelt and forge what appeared to be giant blades of varying designs. Others beat leathers of unknown origins into shape for enormous boots or stitched crude clothing of illogical sizes.

Of course, Innocen didn't see any of this. Not through physical vision, anyway. Mostly, he saw outlines. Shadows. Hints. In some cases, he saw more than his physical eyes could ever have seen. In others, the best he could do was draw inferences.

As Innocen watched, a twelve-foot-tall cythraul emerged from the foundry, hefting a six-foot-long bastard sword in its great hand, testing the weight of its new weapon. Then it marched past Innocen, out onto the street.

Forges for making demon arms and armor, thought Innocen. *Is that what they are guarding?*

It seemed unlikely. This was work that could have been done anywhere. No, there was something else going on in this city—

"Ah, my friend. Innocen."

Innocen wheeled toward the voice. With the extrasensory perceptions he had gained through daemyn, he was not used to being snuck up on. Yet, as he turned, even when he looked directly *at* Avagad, it was still difficult to see him.

He can shroud his presence, thought Innocen. *Like the ethoul did back at the fortress.*

A jolt of rage surged through Innocen. The man currently standing only a few yards away from him was the same man whom Innocen had attempted to treat with, only to be overcome by aurym powers that had proven far more formidable than he would have anticipated. Bested by Avagad's powers, he had been defenseless against the transforming touch of daemyn, administered by a cythraul.

In short, it was this man's fault that Innocen was the monster he was today. It was this man's scarred face that had been the very last sight taken in by Innocen's physical eyes before his vision was replaced by daemyn, before his consciousness became locked within himself.

"Look at you," said Avagad. "Hideous."

Innocen made the mistake of clenching his jaw in anger. The pressure caused two teeth to break from their roots and fall out the open sides of his cheeks.

"It is very rare that the Nameless One allows his thralls to resume control of their bodies," said Avagad. He spoke with great difficulty due to the injuries to his face, and he periodically raised a handkerchief to the side of his mouth to wipe away accumulated spittle. The words came out strange and halting. "With your hyd-powered speed, with me standing right here at your mercy. . . . Oh, wouldn't it feel so wonderful to plunge your hand into my stomach and pull out my intestines for a feast?"

"Yes," said Innocen in a deep, grating, monstrous voice. "It would."

Avagad made an appraising sort of noise in his throat. "I commend your restraint," he said. Then he turned his back to Innocen and added, "Follow me."

The temptation to attack Avagad had been high while standing face-to-face with him, but it was almost too great to resist while his back was turned.

He wouldn't give you a chance to try it if he didn't have some trick up his sleeve, thought Innocen. *Or perhaps he knows the Nameless One would retake control over me if I attempted anything.*

"I COULD OVERRIDE HIS TRICKS IF I SO CHOSE TO," the voice of the Nameless One echoed through Innocen's mind. "ALL THE SAME, RESTRAIN YOURSELF. THIS SERVANT'S PURPOSE IS NOT YET FULFILLED."

As you command, Master, thought Innocen, and he followed Avagad through the streets of Rohghost.

A few moments later, Avagad stopped.

Before them was a complex of three monumental pyramids. The central structure was the tallest, with a great, yawning doorway at its front. From it, lines of coblyns and cythraul were emerging, walking outward in ranks along a causeway that led out of the city.

"Here is where the Nameless One will unleash the true might of his armies upon the Oikoumene," said Avagad. "They are marching on Justin and the army of that princess even as we speak."

Innocen made no effort to hide his grin. Avagad was wrong, of course. That was not what was happening. But it seemed he didn't know that.

"You do know," Innocen said in his pained, monstrous voice, "what the Nameless One *really* plans to do, don't you?"

Avagad's aura, visible through the extrasensory perceptions of daemyn, flared with unexpected anger.

"You know," continued Innocen, "that he intends to come here bodily. And it frightens you. Doesn't it, Avagad?"

All at once, the ranks of cythraul emerging from the pyramid stopped in mid-stride. They stopped, and every last one of them turned to face Avagad. His aura seemed to shrink a little, to grow small and cold.

Yes, thought Innocen. *It frightens you even more than I thought.*

Every one of the cythraul's mouths opened.

"MY ARRIVAL DRAWS NEAR," came the Nameless One's voice, emitted from a hundred dagger-toothed mouths at once.

Avagad took an involuntary step back from Innocen and the ranks of the cythraul. There was such fear in him. Such weakness. It was just like a human to feel such things.

"SHUDDER AND REJOICE," said the legion of voices. "FOR I HUNGER FOR THIS WORLD. AND MY SUPPER IS READY."

The story comes to an end in
THE CYCLE OF AURYM

NOTE FROM THE AUTHOR

My name is Corey McCullough. I'm the author of the book you just read, and I just want to take a moment to say, from the bottom of my heart, thank you for checking it out.

I've had the privelege of meeting a lot of readers over the course of my author journey so far. As a group, readers are fascinatingly diverse, but I've found that they all share a few things in common: they tend to be passionate, empathetic, and altogether awesome. And, being the genuinely awesome people they are, they often want to know the best way they can support their favorite authors, so I've come up with **five easy ways** you can help your favorite author keep the dream alive. To make it simple, I've listed them in order of easiest-to-do to most difficult.

1. **Contact the author** to let them know you finished the book. (This is not a promotional thing. It's just encouraging for an author to learn that someone has read their story, and a simple reach-out can go a long way toward helping them stay motivated.) For me, you can do so by texting me at (814) 499-1311.
2. **Follow the author** on your favorite social media platform.
3. Share a **picture of the book** on social media.
4. Leave an **honest customer review**. Positive *or* negative, ratings and reviews help by providing legitimacy to products.
5. Subscribe to the author's mailing list so you don't miss their next book. For mine, go to **coreymccullough.com/signup** (I hope to see you there).

There are so many stories yet to be told, so many worlds yet unseen. Please take a minute to do one or two of the items listed above for your favorite author. You could change the fate of an entire universe.

Thanks again for reading,

Corey

ACKNOWLEDGMENTS

Thank you to my wife and kids. Your ceaseless support and patience make all these stories possible.

Thank you to my parents. You always believed in my dream of being an author.

Thank you to my proofreader, Roxana.

Massive thanks to my "street team" of beta readers, including Amanda McGinness, Stefanie Henne, and John McCullough, for their invaluable feedback.

A very special thanks to super-fans Amanda McGinness and Cheryl Shoup for their support.

But most of all, my gratitude goes to you, the reader. The book you just read was written and self-published by an independent author. The choice to self-publish my books was motivated by a desire to retain total ownership and complete creative control of my work. This choice, as you can imagine, comes at the cost of many of the resources available through major publishing houses. But, by reading this book, you have made it possible for me to continue to share stories that entertain and delight. Thank you.

You can be a champion of independent art by spreading the word about artwork, music, games, and books by indie creators.

About the Author

COREY MCCULLOUGH has worked as a ghostwriter, copy editor, proofreader, and archaeological field technician. He lives in western Pennsylvania with his wife Vanessa and their four children. His favorite pastimes are reading, writing, spending time with his best friend (Vanessa), and, most of all, being a dad.

www.coreymccullough.com
Instagram @core.author
Facebook.com/core.author
X (Twitter) @core_author
TikTok @core.author
Text (814) 499-1311

Visit **patreon.com/coreymccullough** to download full novels, read short stories available nowhere else, gain early access to Corey's new work, and receive other exclusive content.

Limited-time offer: Get 3 FREE audiobooks

For a limited time, you can download or stream these 3 full, unabridged audiobooks by Corey McCullough.

Go to **coreymccullough.com/audiodeal** to get yours.

www.ingramcontent.com/pod-product-compliance
Lightning Source LLC
Chambersburg PA
CBHW030628020726
47493CB00006B/1616